THE FELINE KIND OF MAGIC

is of a special and secret nature. It is a power upon which those magnificent, fur-covered beauties can draw to forever bewitch the humans they have decided to claim for their own. And in the all-original tales included here, these four-footed masters of all they survey will easily bespell cat lovers everywhere with such enchanting legends of cat and human partnerships as:

"Teddy Cat"—Her father gone, the teddy bear he'd given her destroyed, she needed a true friend and protector, and she was about to find a very unique playmate indeed. . . .

"Partners"—Each cat life holds its special responsibilities but only rarely does a new incarnation lead to the kind of life-and-death challenge that Firecat was about to face. . . .

"But A Glove"—Cursed or blessed from birth to become a werecat, he thought himself alone in a world of ordinary humans—until he found himself staring into the jaws of Death. . . .

These are just a few of the twenty winding trails to advent[ure] [these gu]ides will lead you along in—

CATFANTASTIC III

CATFANTASTIC III

EDITED BY

Andre Norton &
Martin H. Greenberg

DAW BOOKS, INC.
DONALD A. WOLLHEIM, FOUNDER
375 Hudson Street, New York, NY 10014

ELIZABETH R. WOLLHEIM
SHEILA E. GILBERT
PUBLISHERS

Introduction © 1994 by Andre Norton.
A Woman of Her Word © 1994 by Lee Barwood.
A Tangled Tahitian Tail © 1994 Clare Bell.
Saxophone Joe and the Woman in Black © 1994 by Charles de Lint.
Teddy Cat © 1994 Marylois Dunn.
Cat O' Nine Tales © 1994 by Charles L. Fontenay.
Partners © 1994 by P. M. Griffin.
. . . But a Glove © 1994 by John E. Johnston III.
Fear in Her Pocket © 1994 by Caralyn Inks.
A Tail of Two SKittys © 1994 by Mercedes Lackey.
Hermione as Spy © 1994 by Ardath Mayhar.
Moon Scent © 1994 by Lyn McConchie.
Cat's World © 1994 by Cynthia McQuillin.
Snake Eyes © 1994 by Ann Miller and Karen Rigley.
One Too Many Cats © 1994 by Sasha Miller.
Noble Warrior Meets with a Ghost © 1994 by Andre Norton.
ConnectiCat © 1994 by Raul Reyes and Elisabeth Waters.
The Cat-Quest of Mu Mao the Magnificent © 1994 by
Elisabeth Ann Scarborough.
The Cat, the Wizards, and the Bedpost © 1994 by Mary H. Schaub.
To Skein a Cat © 1994 by Lawrence Schimel.
Asking Mr. Bigelow © 1994 by Susan Shwartz.

First Printing, February 1994
1 2 3 4 5 6 7 8 9

CONTENTS

INTRODUCTION

Tails hither, tails yon, once again upheld in pride and satisfaction. The feline histories which appeared in CATFANTASTIC I and II have brought suggestions from a flood of readers asking for more, especially, in some cases, about favorites.

SKitty, that unflappable space traveler, makes a second appearance. Hermione gives another detailed report on the serious duties of a reputable familiar. Drop, the bespelled cat-man, has a narrow brush with runaway magic. And Ede's earrings alter lives in a most drastic fashion while Noble Warrior upholds the honor of his royal race.

There are also newcomers who will find their own advocates, or so we believe. The venturesome felines herein range afar, but always to a purpose, and with strong effects on life, history, mere humans, and their own surroundings.

—Andre Norton

A WOMAN
OF HER WORD

by Lee Barwood

This story is in memory of Jack, who loved all animals; Twee, who loved cats; and Butterscotch and Sweetie, who loved dogs.

Tarberry could smell the grief on Nessa's friend Nell the moment her car pulled into the driveway. He knew the scent well; Nessa, too, had smelled of grief when she picked him up and brought him home. Grief, and anger. Her grief had saved his life; her anger had saved others.

But Nessa had not smelled of the Bright Paths, as Nell did. Her grief had not led her to think of following her beloved one into the beyond-dreams he'd found. But Nell apparently thought of little else from what Tarberry could tell. He'd heard Nessa talking on the farspeaker to her friend, and in the way he had of understanding human thoughts he'd known that Nell longed to follow her lifemate no matter where he'd gone. Life had become an ordeal and a burden for her; she felt abandoned and alone.

The big black Persian stood by and watched as the two women fell into each others' arms and cried. He understood his Person as few animals, even cats, could; if he'd thought about it in such detail, he might have wondered why he knew what Nessa thought and said in ways that Doc, the big shepherd next door, didn't, or Tina, the delicate Siamese down the street, couldn't. But he merely closed his china-blue eyes and waited in the sunlight till the women were ready to pay attention to him.

Occasionally humans who cheat death are supposed to acquire an extra sense—prescience, telekinesis, clairvoyance. But humans are not the only creatures paid in uncommon coin for an extra brush with the Reaper; animals, too, may find that they know, or can do, things that were previously alien to them.

Tarberry, the product of a breeding mill, had been on the point of death when Nessa had bought him from his "breeder" and brought him home, literally, from a flea market nearly two years ago. He had understood her thoughts almost from the time she'd first held him, and so to him his ability was normal.

He understood them now; they were filled with worry for her friend Nell. Nell was considering taking the Bright Paths before she was ready, to look for her mate. She had admitted that to Nessa a few nights ago, and that was when Nessa had begged her to come and visit first.

Nessa did not want Nell to take the Bright Paths yet. That was a hazardous undertaking, to follow that road when one was not ready for it. He himself understood Nell's longing; he had felt it a hundred, a thousand times since he'd recovered. Every time he heard the cries of other animals suffering in breeding mills, he would see the shimmer of the Bright Paths as they beckoned to the living, offering solace and peace, freedom from pain and, above all, reunion with loved ones already on the Paths.

But even he knew that it was not yet time for Nell to go. Nessa had gotten her here, hoping to give her a reason to stay. But she would need help.

Tarberry sat patiently and groomed his already immaculate coat as the two women clung to each other. He would help Nessa. He wasn't quite sure how, but he would find a way. Nell wasn't ready yet to take the road so many others had taken. He, Tarberry, would have to help her prepare.

Nell cried a lot, he decided as he followed them inside at last. But there was nothing healing in her tears. Nessa had cried a lot in those first weeks, too; she had cried for her dead littermate and for Tarberry, although he was getting better, and for all the other animals she had not been able to save. Tarberry had groomed tears from her face many times in those weeks, as he grew stronger and healthier, and he could tell when they began to taste of healing grief instead of despair. Although he had not yet tasted

Nell's tears, he knew what he would find. He could tell by the smell. There was only despair.

He lay down nearby where he could watch them disposing of the luggage. Nell had had no one to groom and console her; she had no one to share her grief and pain. No wonder she was so unhappy.

When the two women at last headed for the kitchen, Tarberry followed. No sooner had Nell seated herself at the kitchen table than she found fifteen pounds of soot-black Persian in her lap, purring and kneading his claws gently against her chest.

"So this is Tarberry," Nell said wonderingly. "He doesn't look a bit like that malnourished waif you sent me pictures of."

"That 'breeder' is out of business now," Nessa told her. "Her and about a half dozen more like her. It's taken time and a lot of effort, but we're finally getting through to the authorities around here that just because there was no humane society it didn't make it right to torture animals." Nessa had become an animal rights activist since moving to the Ozarks; she'd seen enough casual cruelty toward animals to last her a lifetime, she'd told Nell more than once, and the way many farm animals were treated didn't even make good business sense. "And the cats and dogs—it would make you sick," she'd told Nell months ago. "Raised in wire cages, *living* in cages, their poor feet never touching anything softer than wire, their toes all crippled and deformed; bred too young and too often, and killed off when their litters don't live anymore. Neglected and underfed and never groomed, or cuddled, or let loose to run around on grass. That's no life for an animal, especially one that's supposed to produce pets for people to love and cherish." She'd gotten together with others who felt the same way and started a humane society in Blackburn County, which didn't have one, and she and the others had started going after the kitten and puppy mills.

Nell had thought about that a lot since Eddie died—about how she might feel if she had a cause, something that she was so dedicated to that it would give her a reason to go on now that Eddie was gone. She knew he'd be disappointed in the way she'd lost interest in things. Eddie had been interested in *everything*.

But there wasn't a single thing left, she'd thought again and again, that she cared enough about to hang around and see through. She was just so tired, so tired of living without Eddie, of making decisions without him, of the relentless solitude, that nothing seemed to make any impression on her.

In fact, when Nessa had called last week, Nell had scared her. She hadn't meant to; she'd been feeling particularly low and everything had just sort of spilled out before she knew it. Nessa, horrified, had made her swear to come down and visit before she "did anything irrevocable." And Nell, whatever else she was, was a woman of her word. She'd promised, and then she'd come. She didn't expect anything to change her mind.

Now she sat at Nessa's kitchen table stroking Nessa's cat. The cat was purring, and Nell felt a sudden stab of grief for the dog she and Eddie had had. Spice had been old when she'd finally died last year, and she and Eddie had decided that they wouldn't get another animal till they were home to spend time with it. They'd bought a place in the Ozarks, not too far from Nessa, where they'd planned to retire in a few more years. Then, they'd decided, they would raise all kinds of animals and garden.

But then had come Eddie's sudden illness, and Nell's widowhood.

And all the plans had gone out the window.

Tarberry looked up at her and gave a questioning "Mmrwrr?" He butted his face against her chin and reached up with a paw to stroke her cheek. The softness of his touch startled Nell.

"My goodness," she said through her tears. "I never saw a cat do that before." She sniffed again.

Nessa smiled as Tarberry nestled closer to Nell and curled up in her lap. "You've never had a cat, have you?" she asked.

"No," said Nell, running her fingers through Tarberry's long soft fur. His china-blue eyes, startling in his coal-black face, narrowed to slits and he began to purr, a deep and throbbing sound that vibrated through Nell's whole body. "We had Spice, of course."

"Your shepherd. I remember her."

Nell's tears started afresh. She hugged Tarberry, who put up with the indignity and indeed leaned into it. "We missed her terribly." She bent her head and cried into Tarberry's fur; his purring never stopped.

"Maybe you should get another pet," Nessa said. "It would be good for you. You know how many we find all the time, and there are never enough homes."

"I'm not sure I want to," Nell said slowly. "Responsibility scares me. I can't make decisions, and I can't even be responsible for myself anymore. I don't want to be responsible for a helpless animal."

"I think you need to," said Nessa softly, but she didn't press it.

I know what to do, thought Tarberry as he felt the tears seep through his fur to dampen his skin. *I can help her, and I can help them.*

Tarberry's special talent was understanding, *hearing* in a way few humans or animals could. He could *hear* Nell's thoughts, and something else—the voice of a man who had loved Nell very much. The voice told him things, and he listened.

After all, cries of distress were his specialty.

He could hear the less fortunate animals—those languishing in puppy and kitten mills in the isolated Ozark countryside. Every time he heard one, he would tell Nessa; he would go to her and demand attention, then lead her to those who had called him—again and again.

Nessa was more than his Person and his savior, she was his hero. She had not stopped at saving one sick, too-young kitten from certain death. She had gone back to find out the name of the woman who sold underaged, half-starved kittens at the flea market every few weeks. And she'd stopped her. Then she'd found others who felt the same way she did, and had gone on a crusade.

Tarberry had been half-starved, put on adult food long before his milk hunger had changed. He had been covered with fleas and infested with worms. And he had barely been able to stand when Nessa had taken him home with her and hand-fed him, wormed and de-flead him and nursed him to a health he had never known before.

Tarberry remembered all this very well. He remembered

the woman who had bred his mother, and then killed her. He knew the cries of those in similar situations. His own personal crusade had begun once he realized he could steer Nessa toward other breeding mills where animals suffered terribly.

Tarberry would tell her where they were—he could hear them when Nessa traveled around doing art shows—and the rest would be up to her. She would do whatever it was she did, and soon other humans would come and take away the hurt and the sick and the dying. Some cries would cease, some ease; and Tarberry would be content for a little while.

The two women sat up late talking, crying, reminiscing. Nell talked about her fears and grief to Nessa as she had not been able to do since Eddie died two months before. Nessa told her how she had fared after her brother Larry's death, and offered suggestions on how to cope. Through it all, Tarberry sat in Nell's lap or next to her in the chair, never leaving her side, and she held him, stroking his fur and holding him close. His very presence was a comfort.

Tarberry slept on Nell's bed that night. "Slept" was perhaps not the right word; Nell slept little, tossing and turning and crying from time to time. She and Eddie had been very close; they had spent all their time together, even working together as so many couples couldn't. Every phase of Nell's life was emptier, lonelier, desolate without him. And she found herself clinging to Tarberry as if he were her own. The cat accepted it, accepted her, reaching up periodically to bathe the tears from her face. The rough sandpaper of his tongue surprised her each time it happened; Tarberry distracted her from her grief, gave her warmth and uncritical affection that made the night a little less long and dark.

She needs, this woman, thought Tarberry. *She needs the way Nessa did when she found me. I hope she will let me do what must be done.* And when Nell at last settled into an uneasy sleep, Tarberry slept beside her, his warm softness easing her dreams just a bit.

A few days later the women loaded Nessa's artwork into her van and set out for a three-day outdoor craft show. They would camp at the site, sleeping in Nessa's van; she knew many of the other sellers at the show, an annual event, and that night when they went back to their camp-sites it was like a party around the campfire. Nessa introduced Nell to those she hadn't yet met in the course of the day's business, and they had a group cookout; several had even brought guitars and keyboards. Tarberry was there, of course, close by Nell's side; if Nessa thought it strange that her cat spent so much time so close to her friend, she said nothing.

Nell enjoyed listening to the music, but she felt very alone in the midst of strangers. She missed Eddie so much that the ache seemed stronger, not weaker, every day. She found without thinking about it that her hand reached out for the cat, who stayed close and offered his own form of comfort.

When it was so late that Nessa at last caught Nell nodding off, the two went back to Nessa's van, Tarberry weaving in and out between their ankles as they went. Nessa folded the rear seat down and set Nell to fetch the bedding from the back of the van. When they had the bed made and were comfortable, Tarberry leapt up and settled himself firmly next to Nell.

But his settling in didn't last long.

The voice came, high and thin, and woke Tarberry out of a sound sleep. He lifted his head, ears alert, and stayed motionless for several minutes. The women sleeping next to him had heard nothing; the wail was inaudible to all but the just-awakened cat. It was not sound but a voiceless cry that pierced his heart. The cry came from a female cat, and she was dying. If he could not help her, her young litter would die, too.

They were close to this campsite; so close that after a moment, Tarberry moved cautiously and jumped down without waking the women. He slipped through the open window and made his way cautiously through the grass in the moonlight.

The place was horrible. Tarberry quivered with fury and pity as he stalked around this latest breeding mill. This one was worse than anything he had ever seen.

Cats and dogs in wire cages chewed at deformed feet whose long-untrimmed claws had grown into the pads.

Long-hairs, dogs and cats both, suffered from hair so badly matted and felted that in places it had peeled away to reveal raw, red, ulcerated skin. Fleas jumped in clouds; kittens and puppies, weak from too-soon switches to adult food, lay listlessly and whimpered for their mothers. Tarberry moved from cage to cage on toes whose claws ached to slice open the humans responsible for what he saw.

He paused at one cage, in which lay a tangle of puppies and kittens. The puppies were no bigger than the kittens, some toy breed in favor and thus more subject to abuse than the larger ones. The cries of some of those kittens held something too familiar. In the way he knew things, he knew that these kittens were kin. Somewhere they had shared an ancestor—and not too long ago. Perhaps they might even be kin to one of his littermates.

He decided that this time he would have to do something different, something radical. He pawed and batted at the door of the cage until it came open; then he slipped inside, inspected the tiny frail forms lying on the dirty wire, and selected one as his target.

He reached down and seized the nape of the tiny kitten's neck in his mouth; he would take it back to Nessa, and then to Nell. But to his surprise, when he lifted the little animal, there came a growl, so soft it was almost inaudible, from the puppy next to it. With an effort the puppy struggled to its feet, baring its teeth in an effort to defend its companion against the intruder.

Peace, little brother, thought Tarberry. *I'm taking him to safety, and soon someone will come for you, too.* He left the cage, the kitten firmly held in his jaws, and headed back for Nessa.

Tarberry's return through the moonlight with the kitten was swift and angry, haunted by thoughts of the animals he had left behind—and by the puppy who had tried to defend a kitten. That one, he resolved, must come, too—to the same home as the kitten he carried. Tarberry was an uncharacteristic cat; he liked dogs. And he knew that Nell liked them, too.

He managed to get back in to the van, and laid the kitten on Nell's chest. Then he went to Nessa, who stirred drowsily and came awake when she realized that Tarberry was sitting on her chest.

When she saw Tarberry's eyes glowing redly in the darkness, she knew that the time had come for her to contact her friends again. Tarberry had found another breeding mill.

And then she saw the kitten.

She woke Nell gently. "Don't move," she said. "There's a kitten on your chest."

"A kitten? What—what are you talking about?" Nell was groggy.

"Tarberry found another breeding mill. I have to go call some people and get help. Will you be all right? I didn't want you to wake up and find me gone."

Nell nodded. "I'll be fine," she said. "Is there anything I can do to help?"

"Yes," Nessa said. "This time he's brought back this kitten, and the poor thing's in terrible shape. I can't stay and take care of it; I have to get things moving. I don't know what to do with it." She hesitated. "Actually," she said slowly, "Tarberry brought it to you." She gently lifted it from Nell's chest so her friend could sit up. Once Nell could take the little animal from her, Nessa handed it back and put on a light in the van.

Nell was shocked at the lightness of the kitten, but when she saw its condition in the light she was horrified.

"It's—it's barely alive," she whispered.

"I know," Nessa said in a tight voice. "That's why I have to go. Will you stay with it?"

"Sure," she said. Nessa dressed quickly, grabbed her camera, and was gone.

Tarberry, drawn by the cries of the other animals, could barely wait for Nessa to follow him. He paced as she placed calls from the campground's pay phone and she could see his lips crinkling as he hissed, apparently at the memory. She finished as quickly as she could and let him lead her through the night to the place of misery he had found.

As she moved from cage to cage, snapping pictures for evidence, he slipped back into the cage and found the puppy who had growled at him. Lifting it by the scruff of its neck, he jumped out of the cage and was about to start back for the van when suddenly there was a sharp sound and a bright light.

"Stop right there or I'll call the sheriff," came a man's voice. Tarberry shrank into the shadows with his little burden and waited.

"You go right ahead," Nessa replied. "I bet he'd be real interested in seeing the condition of these animals. You go call him. In fact, I'll come with you."

"You don't come a step closer," warned the man. "And you give me that camera."

"No, I won't," Nessa said.

"You're trespassing, and I can just shoot you where you stand."

"I'm unarmed and I haven't done anything," Nessa returned. "But if anybody should be shot, you should—for what you've done to these poor animals."

"I've read about you," the man said suddenly. "You're one of them people who take pleasure in stealing other folks' livelihoods."

"No, I just hate to see animals abused," Nessa returned.

"What abuse? These animals're fed. They've got shelter, water. What more do you want?" His voice was harsh and frightened.

"You call this fed? When their ribs are showing and their hair is falling out? And when's the last time they had shots?" she snapped back. "Or their toenails cut? Or their coats brushed? Or a bath, for God's sake? Don't you people ever see what you're doing to these animals?"

Suddenly Tarberry *heard,* in the way he heard the cries of the animals, what the man would do to Nessa. He dropped the puppy and flew at the man, claws flashing in the moonlight, landing with unerring accuracy where he could do the most damage. There was an explosive noise that Tarberry didn't understand, and the man shrieked. Nessa screamed; Tarberry hit the ground and retrieved the puppy, then butted against Nessa's ankles. She was only too glad to follow him as they raced through the moonlight back toward the campground.

Nessa's friends were there to meet her when she got back. She left Tarberry and the puppy with Nell, and led her friends through the night to the breeding mill.

Nell was again shocked at the condition of the puppy. But Tarberry was impatient with her slowness. He jumped into her lap and began to groom the two babies, his rough tongue cleaning their coats with a determination that made her cry. This time Tarberry ignored the tears, tending his two new charges; Nell wiped her eyes and gently set the two little ones on the bed. Then she rooted through the ice chest and pulled out milk and eggs and butter. She put more lights on and set up the camp stove, then cooked an egg for the babies to eat.

By the time—nearly dawn—that Nessa came back, red-eyed and grim from her second expedition, the two little ones were sleeping in the bed and Nell was curled up protectively around them, also asleep. Tarberry had been dozing on Nessa's pillow, but looked up at her entrance.

Nessa said nothing but watched her friend for a moment. The memories of the night's work churned in her mind; most of the confiscated animals would live, but several had had to be destroyed. These two little ones hadn't even been seen by a vet yet, but somehow it appeared that Nell had gotten them cleaned up and fed. Nessa could see the wreckage of their meal in the trash.

Just then Nell moaned in her sleep. The puppy stirred and half woke, then began to lick her face. Tears began to leak from Nell's closed eyelids; as Nessa watched, Tarberry moved over and began to wash them away.

He could hear the man's voice again. This time he spoke to the woman, and though she cried she listened. At last she seemed calmer. Her face relaxed; the puppy stopped licking and went back to sleep.

Nessa sighed wearily and stretched out on the bed next to Nell as gently as she could. Morning, she thought sadly, would be brighter for some of the animals, at least. She tried not to think about the others as she dozed off. Tarberry contentedly curled up next to his Person and purred himself to sleep, as pleased with his own night's work as he could be.

After a morning trip to the vet, the two returned to the campsite. As Nessa opened her booth a little late, Nell sat on the grass and cuddled her two tiny charges. Tarberry sat nearby and supervised.

"A Shih Tzu puppy and a Persian kitten," Nell said for the fourth time. "How can people do things like this?" She stroked the little ones' fur—thin and rough, but the vet had assured her that with care it would grow in and they'd both be beautiful. To her they already *were* beautiful, Tarberry knew. The babies were sleeping on full stomachs, and had had all the medicines and inoculations they were old enough to have.

Nell shook her head. "You know, I had the strangest dream before I woke up this morning," she said at last to Nessa. "It was about Eddie." She watched the two sleeping babies, carefully not looking at her friend. "We were all together—Eddie and me, and Spice, and these two. But they were grown, and Eddie was telling me what a special pair they were. 'They make their own magic, Nell,' he said. 'You have to take care of them till it's time for us to be together again. Promise me.' " She sighed, a tear rolling down her cheek. "So I promised him." She traced the tail of the smoke-gray kitten; it ended in a tuft of snowy white. "Then he talked to them. 'Firefly, you and Shadow have work to do. You stay with Nell till I call you.' " She sighed at her dream-memory of the little Shih Tzu panting happily, sun bright on his shadow-gray coat, and the little Persian's tail twitching, its white tuft indeed like a firefly in the dusk. "How long do you think it'll take to find homes for the others?"

"Maybe a month, maybe more," Nessa said. "There were so many—and a lot of them will have to be rehabilitated before they can be adopted. The older ones were really in sad shape." She held her breath.

"Then it wouldn't hurt if I—if I kept these two?" Nell asked hesitantly.

"It would be a big help," said Nessa, the lump in her throat easing. Nell would be all right now, she thought. She was, after all, a woman of her word. If she took on the care of Firefly and Shadow, she would take care of them.

Tarberry sat and groomed himself in the sunlight. The smell of the Bright Paths was fading. Two little voices, at least, no longer cried in misery. And other cries had ceased. He was content.

A TANGLED
TAHITIAN TAIL

by Clare Bell

I really didn't intend to be the first European on Tahiti,
but my paws touched the black sand beach on June 23,
1767, days before that grubby lot from the frigate *Dolphin*
got ashore. I should give some credit to Cap'n Sam Wallis
since he got the ship from Spithead all the way here. But
by the time we made Tahiti, he was down with the colic
and about as much use as a sick . . . well, anyway.

The history books don't mention my landing, much less
the fact that I got involved in a Tahitian war.

This, of course, while the *Dolphin* was still mucking
about off the coast. Even if Cap'n Sam had mentioned me
in his journal, the passage would have probably been edited
out by that meddlesome lubber Hawkesworth who was hired
to "polish" Wallis' style. As for the war, only the Tahitians
and I ever knew about it.

If truth be told, it was the ship's helmsman who banged
the *Dolphin* into the rocks. Never could steer worth a tin
farthing, me mum said. That single time that salt-soaked
old queen was right. The rest of the time she was wrong,
especially about me.

I suppose I should back up a bit, since I seem to be
telling this all tail-first.

Me mum got herself in the family way by a ragged old
tom from an East fens coal-hauling ship. We kittens were
born in the captain's stocking drawer during the passage
round the Horn. I think that's what got me started all
wrong in life. You'd think that a kitten born in the Roaring
Forties would be able to shrug off heavy weather, but to
this day I get the collywobbles whenever the wind rises.

Somehow I inherited none of the talents that make a

ship's cat. Perhaps it was because I turned out to be a marmalade ginger while all my brothers and sisters were the more usual black and white. They could all caper nicely when the boatswain's mate played a hornpipe on his tin whistle, but I couldn't seem to get the hang of it. They caught rats down in the storage rooms, but whenever I tried, I seemed to pick the biggest, nastiest customers and got the tar whaled out of me.

The one talent I did have went unappreciated by family and crew alike. The single thing ships have in abundance besides rats, weevils, and scurvy is cordage. There's rope, whipping, lashing, and sail-maker's twine. The day the old cook dangled a frayed end between my paws was the day I found my calling.

Me mum put it very well when she grabbed me by the scruff that morning and hauled me to the forecastle. "I don't know how you managed it, Jeremy, but you have managed to snarl, tangle, fray, chew, bedevil, or otherwise make unusable every spare piece of cordage on this ship. If the boatswain catches sight of you, he'll toss you in the drink, so make yourself scarce."

With that, she left me sitting on the forecastle rail, thoughtfully licking my ginger coat. I had begun to wonder if there was more to my talent than kittenish energy. Just diving into a coil of spare line and thrashing around in it could not possibly have produced such a wealth of snarls, tangles, and Gordian knots as I managed to achieve.

No. My gift was definitely magic. Not the showy white-light sort of magic, but a quirky, disorderly magic that finds its best expression in cats like me.

And express itself my magic did, until the crew probably thought the ship was being haunted by a ghost who hated order. I swear that I would only have to walk by a neat roll or coil of cordage for the stuff to get *itself* into a mess.

Looking back on it, I imagine that such happenings must have been worrying for the *Dolphin*'s crew. I suppose the ship's helmsman might have been a bit distracted. He certainly didn't look where he was steering. Not that day.

One instant I was sitting, brooding, on the forecastle rail. The next thing I knew, there was this horrid bang-crunch that threw me clean over the bowsprit.

We had fetched up on that heap of coral later immortal-

ized as Dolphin Bank. It stopped the ship dead, but I kept
on going, spinning arse over teakettle over the reef and
into the lagoon.

I landed with a yowl and a splash, went under, and struggled up again. One look behind convinced me that there
was no way back through the heavy surf breaking about
the ship. And no one would be out to rescue me. They were
all trying to keep the ship from being beaten to kindling by
the sea.

I pointed my nose toward land and set my four paws to
paddling. I might not last two rounds with a galley-rat, but
I can swim, which is more than I can say for those sailors.
The beach didn't look all that far away across the pretty
blue lagoon, but I was definitely starting to lose the wind
from my sails long before I scraped bottom.

And that was when a son of a sea serpent grabbed my
tail. I let out a yell fit to wake the dead, but it turned into
a gurgle when my mouth filled with water. That hook-jawed
old moray eel must have figured he'd have a quick nosh of
ship's cat.

I'd never seen anything like that eel before. He looked
as though some fish had a roll in the hammock with a
snake. He was long and winding with a rippling fin all
around, and big nasty jaws. He was tough, too. I got some
good rips and bites into his slimy skin, but he kept jerking
me under. It was getting harder and harder to snatch a
breath. I began to think I'd end up as dogfish's dinner when
there was this tremendous splash and old Hook-jaw was
yanked right out of the water.

I quit tussling and stared up. My nemesis was curling,
flapping, and wriggling around like mad, trying to bite the
small brown hand that had two fingers hooked through his
gills. One good whack on the head with a wood club sent
Hook-jaw to finny heaven, and he was tossed in the bottom
of the strange-looking little skiff that had come up beside
us.

I wasn't about to stick around to congratulate my rescuer; for all I knew, the folk here might fancy cat even
more than eel. I was plowing a wake toward the beach
when something seized my scruff and hauled me out of the
lagoon. I was too weary and soggy to put up much of a

struggle. After a few wriggles and claw-swipes, I just hung there with my eyes closed and my whiskers down.

When I finally did open my eyes, I stared into the largest, deepest, brownest eyes I have ever seen in a human face. They were surrounded by thick black lashes and held a look of utter amazement. My whiskers were nearly touching a very flat, widespread child's nose as the little Tahitian girl held me up in front of her with both hands.

She seemed as fascinated with my eyes as I was with hers, but after a while she put me down in the bottom of her funny narrow-hulled skiff. My first instinct was to abandon ship a second time, but going several rounds with old Hook-jaw had worn me out. I certainly didn't want to chance running into another like him.

The child seemed to know how to handle that odd little skiff of hers. No sooner had she picked up a paddle then we were skimming over the lagoon. As I shook the brine out of my coat, I wondered what kept the skiff from capsizing, since the narrow vee-shape of the hull gave it no stability whatsoever. Then I saw the outrigger float attached to the skiff by two poles lashed crosswise to the hull. It was an odd way to build a boat, but it seemed to work quite well.

I imagine my little Tahitian was baffled as to where I had sprung from, but that didn't keep her from accepting me as a passenger aboard. My rescuer could only have been about eight or nine, yet here she was all by herself on the lagoon. Not only that; she had made quick work of a moray eel twice as long as me. In some ways she was more than a match for the toughest London street urchin, yet I have never seen a child with a gentler face or such deep, expressive eyes.

She had nice coloring for a human; a ruddy golden-brown skin. After living all my life with Englishmen who were pink as pigs or as pale as bed linen, I found the sight of her refreshing. Her hair was coarse and straight, giving off a blue sheen as it flowed down her back. She had a huge flower stuck behind one ear and a short faded skirt made from tough papery stuff.

The muffled sound of sails flapping made me look back across the lagoon to the stranded ship. The *Dolphin* was not only stuck on the coral reef, but had become the object of attention of many brown-skinned men in sailing skiffs. I felt a surge of alarm, not only for my mother and siblings, but for the *Dolphin*'s crew as well. They might have been an ill-mannered, unappreciative lot, but their ship was the only home I'd ever known.

As I watched, I felt the wind shift. The ship's foresails were laid back and then her bow swung off the reef. In a few moments she was floating free. She swung about, the mainsails bellied, and she bore away from the reef. No one aboard gave any sign of realizing that someone, namely me, had been left behind.

I squashed a wild urge to swim after her. I would only drown in the heavy surf. But I could not help putting my paws on the skiff's gunwale, staring out to sea, and giving a plaintive wail as the *Dolphin* grew smaller and smaller against the sky.

Even though the Tahitian lass had no idea what sort of an animal I was, she heard the mournfulness in my voice. Putting her paddle aside, she gathered me, damp and bedraggled, to her breast and held me against her soft, sun-warmed skin. She spoke to me quietly. It didn't matter that I knew not one word of her language. I felt as though she understood my loss. Her comfort touched me deeply, for never had a human being showed me so much affection.

When she set me on her lap, I licked a paw and began to scrub one ear. Me mum always said that things look more cheerful after a good wash. The way the little Tahitian gaped at me said that she had never seen an animal do anything of the kind before. Her reaction brought home to me that there were probably no other cats on this island.

Well, buck up, lad, said I to myself. *You have a new friend and a good one. You may miss the ship and your family, but you didn't really fit in. You came from an exploration ship and here's a whole new land to explore.* True, I hadn't exactly chosen to be born in the captain's stocking drawer, or to be chucked off the forecastle rail by a bad steersman, or to become eel-fodder, but I would make the best of it.

The swift glide of the little skiff over the lagoon also helped to lift my spirits. For one thing, it didn't have the lumbering rocking motion that made me seasick, and for another, the lagoon was incredibly beautiful. As we paddled into shallower water, the deep sapphire color lightened to turquoise, then translucent green-yellow. Millions of brightly-striped fish flicked about just beneath the surface, making my tail twitch.

The skiff and its outrigger grounded on fine black sand. The girl hopped out and waded in the shallows, guiding the little craft to shore and pulling it up on the beach so I could disembark without wetting my paws.

Then she grabbed old Hook-jaw (now thoroughly dead) by the gills. Slinging him across her shoulder and with me trotting at her heels, she tramped merrily across the beach into the groves of waving coconut palms.

All sorts of luscious, strong-scented flowers nodded on bushes along the trail, looking saucy, as if they were sticking out their tongues at me. Their perfumes made my nose tingle.

The girl came at last to an open-air house consisting of four support poles and a thatched roof woven from palm fronds. The walls were mats that were rolled up to let the breeze through, quite a practical arrangement for the warm, humid island weather.

Out of the house came a pleasantly plump middle-aged woman wearing a longer version of the papery skirt and a cloaklike garment of the same stuff over her shoulders. She looked too old to be the girl's mum and too young to be her grandmother, so I decided that she must be an auntie.

My little companion displayed old Hook-jaw and Auntie gave cries of admiration. Auntie was less enthusiastic about me. She peered down at me in puzzlement, frowning and asking questions. The girl could only shrug.

I followed the pair as they took the eel to a deep pit near the house. I thought at first that the pit was a rubbish dump, but when I felt the heat coming in waves off the big stones in the bottom, I realized that it was a cooking hearth. Auntie deftly gutted old Hook-jaw, parceled him up nicely in some huge leaves, and laid him on the hot stones along with a lot of strange vegetables. I was startled when they covered the food with leaves and mats and then heaped dirt on it, but I figured that was the Tahitian version of an oven.

While the food was cooking in the pit-oven, a middle-aged man came out of the house. He was dressed in nothing except a scrap of paper-cloth wound about his ample waist.

From the way he spoke to Auntie, I decided that he must be Uncle.

After a mystified glance at me, Uncle pottered about gathering fallen coconuts, still in their dry, fibrous husks. He took them all to a sharpened stake set into the ground, lifted the first and brought it down hard, impaling it on the point of the stake. At first I thought he was knocking holes in the nuts to get at the meat. Then I realized that he was using the stake in a rather ingenious manner to pry off the outer husk.

I had assumed that it was the coconuts he was after, but to my surprise, he seemed to value the brown matted stuff he stripped off more than the nuts themselves. I later learned that coconuts that had already fallen were considered too old and dry for eating. To get good fresh ones, you had to climb a tree and pull them off.

When Uncle had a good pile of coconut husks, he crammed it all in a big shell full of salt water and let it sit. He then took out another batch of the stuff that had soaked a while and went to work on that.

Letting the husk seep in brine freed the long fibers from all the other bits and pieces. Shaking the wet out of a handful of fibers, Uncle began rolling them down his thigh with his palm.

I had no idea what this production was all about until I saw the length of twisted cord emerging from beneath the callused edge of his hand. He was surprisingly quick at making it and soon the length was sufficient to be wound into a coil. I watched, overjoyed. I had thought that my one true happiness in life had sailed off with the *Dolphin*.

Uncle was so busy twisting coconut husk fibers into sennit cord that he paid me no attention. I was so fascinated by the twine snaking out from beneath his fingers that it was all I could do not to bound right into his lap and snatch at it. As it was, I did manage to control myself for a while. Uncle had made enough of his coconut twine to roll into a ball before I sidled up and tapped it with a paw. At the sight of the ball unwinding I went wild.

The coconut sennit was beautiful stuff—even better than sail-maker's twine. I was in heaven, batting the ball around and wriggling in the stuff as it unwound. My peculiar magic soon asserted itself, transforming the cord into an impossibly snarled mess around my paws. But I didn't care, for I was deep in bliss.

Uncle jumped up and started yelling, dancing around as if he had sat on a wasps' nest. At the commotion, Auntie ran up with a gourd full of salt water and dumped it on me as if I was a cur in a fight. Then they both hopped around, gesticulating and shouting like mad folk. My instincts took over, telling me to head for high ground. Brine, snarls and all, I scrambled up a corner-pole of the house onto the roof.

I crouched on top of the coconut thatch, feeling completely at sea. I had expected some minor irritation, and perhaps even a kick in my direction, but such rage and panic? What had I done?

Thank heavens my Tahitian lass appeared, or I would probably still be sitting on the roof. She politely told Aunt and Uncle to back off, shinnied up the corner-pole herself and coaxed me down. Once she had me, she slid down and spirited me off into the bushes.

I got some clue to the nature of my crime when my little Tahitian, having gotten me far enough away, put me down on a vine-covered log and began taking the twine off me. She had a sharp-edged shell, but she didn't cut the stuff. Patiently she undid the worst of the knots, even my prize tangles. Not only did she take care not to damage the coconut cord, she handled it very carefully, almost reverently. When she had it all straightened out and rolled up again, she muttered what sounded like a prayer.

Then she sat me on her lap and scolded me thoroughly, pouting and wagging a finger in front of my whiskers. (I didn't understand what she said then, but I picked it up later.) "Little-dog-who-climbs-the-house," she said seriously, "you must not play with my uncle's sennit."

Her annoyance with me didn't last long. Her sunny friendliness soon asserted itself. She dried me as best she could with her paper-cloth skirt. She stroked and cuddled me, giggling with delight when I purred. After playing with me for a while, she gestured at me to stay put while she returned to the house.

To my regret, she took the rolled-up sennit string with her, but she evidently traded it back to Uncle for some grub. When she returned, she had two filled coconut shells.

Obviously she had never fed a cat before. The stuff in the first shell looked like thick, sour, purple milk. She called it "poi." It was the stickiest, gooiest muck I have ever had the misfortune to put my tongue into. Even worse than the ship's burgoo porridge. I've learned to tolerate poi since, but I thought then that I would gag to death before I got that first mouthful down.

To make matters worse, the shell of liquid she put down for me was seawater! I learned later that her people liked to dip food in ocean brine, relished it straight, and even fed handfuls of it to babies! I didn't want to be ungrateful, but I simply could not drink it.

I was half-wondering whether this was intended as punishment for messing up Uncle's string when we heard Auntie calling. With a hasty pat, the girl ran away, leaving me to cope with the native provisions.

An odd snuffling sort of laughter made me whirl around, claws ready, tail and temper flaring. Being twice doused with brine and then being expected to drink it had not aided my disposition. And I hated being laughed at. Especially by a pig.

I wasn't completely sure he was a pig, although he had a snout, trotters, and little piggy eyes. He was black, bristly and wild-looking, unlike the sedate porkers kept in cages on the ship. His ears stuck straight up, like mine. One had a hole in it to hold a tag that had been plaited from a coconut leaf. He had a funny straight tail with a tassel at the end and he kept flipping it about. With his long legs, he looked quite fit and trim (for a pig, that is).

Luckily I had gained a smattering of Hoggish from the shipboard swine. Since beast-languages around the world seem to be pretty much the same (unlike the myriad chatterings of humans), I was able to make myself understood, despite my feline accent.

"It is not worth losing your temper, Dog-who-climbs-the house," the boar said easily, but I noticed that he tipped his head to give me a clear view of his tusks.

"Perhaps you can tell me who you are and why you decided to poke your snout into my business," I growled back. "And I am not a dog!"

"You must be new to this part of the island if you do not know me," said the Tahitian pig. "I am Mahui Pua'a, sacred boar of the great god Oro. My littermates were sacrificed in the *marae*, but I was set free with Oro's sign in my ear."

I smoothed my fur. I didn't give two rotten fish heads about any great god Oro, but I respected those tusks. I noticed that Mahui was eyeing the shell full of purplish goo with great appetite. I was very thirsty and my skin was starting to itch from all the salt in my fur.

"You can have that muck," I said. "Just show me the nearest stream."

With a few snuffles and slurps, the purple-white goo was gone down the boar's throat. He kept his part of the bargain, leading me to a brook where I could get a decent drink and rinse off.

While I perched on a flat rock and fluffed my fur in the sun, Mahui told me what sort of country I'd tumbled into. I was also curious about the little Tahitian lass and her family.

"The little *vahine* is called Rori," he told me and then explained the family setup. The couple I called Auntie and Uncle were really more distant relatives of the girl's parents, who had died. They were fostering her, raising her as their own child.

Swapping children around between families was evidently common here. If someone didn't have a child, they asked their relatives for one. If a family had an overabundance of youngsters, they'd gladly give one away, for they knew that the child would be as well-loved and cared for as if it had been raised in the birth-household. Essentially the child had two families that it could fall back on instead of just one.

I'd heard from my mother that queens often shared their kittens in such an arrangement. It seemed so beneficial for all involved that I wondered why human beings didn't adopt something similar. Now I had finally found people who seemed to do things the sensible way.

When the conversation turned to the girl's uncle, I remembered the fuss that was made over my playful indulgence with his coconut cord. Apparently Mahui was first alerted to my presence by the noise of that fracas. He had hidden in the bushes and watched, evidently with great amusement.

"I have never seen a dog who wanted to play with *aha,*
he said, giving the island name for the coconut sennit.
"Fetching sticks, yes. They do that endlessly. But this urge
to undo windings of cord and roll around in it—that I do
not understand."

The way he put it made me feel pretty silly, but I felt I
had to defend myself.

"I am not a dog," I reminded him. "I am a cat. Cats like
string. You are a hog. Hogs like rooting things up. You
never ask why you like it. You just do."

He was pretty bright, I'll give him that. He seemed to
understand even though there was a terrific cross-species
gulf between us. "Your sennit-play doesn't bother me," he
said thoughtfully, "but the islanders put great value on
cordage. It holds together their houses, their weapons, and
other things. They also use it to wrap the images of their
gods. If I were you, I'd control myself."

I heard Rori's voice in the distance, calling me. I thanked
Mahui for his advice and said I hoped I would meet him
again.

"You will," he said. "I make rounds of the district and
stop here every few days. Enjoy Tahiti, friend. *Ia ora na.*
May you live well."

And with that he trotted off, his little tasseled tail flicking merrily.

I wish I could say that I had taken Mahui's advice. He
seemed to be a sensible soul, for a hog. But the truth is
that my craving got the better of me. Every time I saw that
coconut string, I was into it. And the islanders used a lot
of the stuff. Everywhere I went, people were lashing poles
together with sennit to make house-frames, wrapping
wicker god-images, making fishnets, and a hundred other
tasks.

The long and short of it was that I got into trouble. A
lot of trouble. I must have annoyed every man, woman,
and child in the district. I simply could not restrain myself
from diving joyously at coils and reels of it.

My mother would probably have called it an example of
my perverse temperament. I suppose the truth is that a gift
such as mine just has to be used.

Only natural feline agility saved me from getting clubbed,
speared, stabbed, or stamped on. I ended up perched on

so many roofs that Rori's original name for me stuck. To my intense annoyance, my Tahitian name became Uripi Fare, (spoken "ureepee faree") which means dog-who-climbs-the-house. The "uri" part, which meant "dog," got dropped. I became Pifare.

My little Tahitian lass, Rori, was so busy extricating me from various tangled encounters that she scarcely had time to do much else. Yet her affection for me never faltered. Even when she was subjected to a torrent of abuse from another outraged house-builder or fisherman who had found his precious cordage reduced to a hopelessly snarled mess, she defended me stoutly.

I could see that soon she as well as I would become *persona non grata* in paradise. Had it not been for the little girl's grandmother, I would have been shark-bait after only a few days.

She was an extraordinary woman, that grandmother. She, out of all the adults in the district, seemed to understand me as well as Rori did, even though the old woman never could have seen a cat before. Her full name was Te Vahine Vaoatua, but she went by the shorter version of Vao. Old Vao was a *tahutahu,* a medicine-woman or healer, with a bit of the priestess thrown in as well.

Vao kept to herself in her little hut. I didn't meet her until the day that Rori brought me there. The poor girl was nearly in tears. Everyone wanted her to get rid of me. Even Uncle and Auntie joined in the clamor when Uncle found me one day blissfully chewing his fishline. I was an evil spirit, a goblin, a shade from the *Po,* the Room of Night.

I could tell that even Rori had begun to think so, although a part of her desperately wished otherwise.

"How can my Pifare be a goblin from the Room of Night?" Rori asked, holding me on her lap and stroking me. "He feels and sounds so nice."

"Pifare may have come from the far horizon, but he is not from the Room of Night," said old Vao. She peered at me with filmed brown eyes and touched me with withered, bony fingers, yet I felt no urge to withdraw from her. There was a certain intense light in Vao's eyes that seemed to come from deep inside. It illuminated her lined face and gave it an ancient beauty.

"What other explanation can there be?" asked Rori, discouraged. "I am fond of Pifare, but he gets into so much trouble!"

"Perhaps what you and others see as "trouble" can be seen in another way," said the old *tahutahu*. "Every animal has a reason for being what it is or for doing what it does."

Vao had a short roll of sennit in her hand and she dangled the end in front of me. My ears and whiskers came up and I reached out with a paw for the dangling string.

The *tahutahu* gazed into my eyes, murmuring questions to herself. "What draws you to the *aha*, Pifare? Do you sense the sacredness of it, the need our people have for it? You look so intently at the cord and reach out for it, so you must know."

Rori looked up at old Vao, her despair starting to fade. "Then I can keep Pifare?"

"Yes, keep Pifare. To those who criticize, ask, how can an animal who is drawn by the power of the *aha* be evil? Here, Pifare," she said to me as she laid the roll of sennit on the ground. "This is what you seek."

I needed no further encouragement. I jumped down from Rori's lap and was soon happily covered with loops of coconut string.

"He has blessed the *aha*," Rori's grandmother said with a laugh as she gathered me up into her lap. Patiently, she undid the snarls and rolled her twine back up into a ball.

I can't say that Vao's insight about me made life much different for Rori. I was still a mischief and people still scolded her about it. Having heard Vao's words, she could shrug it off and regain her cheerfulness.

Soon, however, Rori and her folk had more to worry about than my antics. I had been on Tahiti for several days when bad tidings came to the district where Rori lived. It seemed that the chief of the neighboring principality had gotten his nose out of joint about something and was preparing to make war on us.

I must say I was a bit disillusioned when I heard that. These people had seemed so gentle, peaceful (except when I was messing up their cord), and different from the truculent Europeans. I thought they might not indulge in the barbaric exercise of ripping each other to bloody bits.

My dismay was nothing compared to Auntie and Uncle's. The news threw them into a paroxysm of fright. They began gathering up food and other things in bundles, preparing to abandon their house and lands to the enemy. When they were not scurrying around, Auntie and Uncle sat and lamented, wailing and screaming in a way that made my fur stand on end.

Rori seemed to drift off into a pale and silent world of her own. I could rouse her out of it, but only briefly. Even old Vao huddled in her hut, staring at the fire and muttering under her breath.

I was completely baffled. I could understand their fear, but not this overwhelming helplessness. It was almost as if they were just going to lie down and let this high-ranking bully take whatever he pleased, which didn't sit particularly well with me. My scraps with the galley-rats had shown I wasn't much of a fighter, but surely there was something I could do.

Tasks went undone, food was left uncooked, the yam and taro gardens went untended. I thought I had managed to understand and adapt pretty well to Rori's world, but I could not fathom this. It was out of character with the islanders' usual self-sufficiency and resourcefulness. Nearly at my wit's end, I sought out Mahui. Surely a sacred boar with the mark of a god in his ear could tell me what was going on.

As soon as I found Mahui and told him about the impending war, he gave me a very strange stare. "Pifare, you must leave the girl and her family. Go to another district. Find another house."

I was dumbfounded. "Why?" I demanded, my ginger fur starting to bristle. I was no fair-weather sailor. Rori and Vao had become my friends. I would stick by them, come hell or high water.

I knew nothing of Tahitian wars, but I'd somehow gotten the impression that they were more like tomcat fights; mostly bluff and bluster, with one party backing down before any blows were struck.

According to Mahui, however, this chief took his wars pretty seriously. "Soon everyone in Rori's family will be dead," the boar said. "And you will as well, if you don't leave."

I listened in dismay as Mahui told me how a determined invader could lay waste to the land. "Once enemy warriors are through killing everyone they can find, they destroy everything. They cut down coconut palms, pull up taro plants, ring-bark breadfruit trees. Anyone left alive soon starves to death. It is a pretty wretched business, Pifare. I don't intend to stay around for it, and I'd advise you to do the same."

"Is there no way to put a stop to it?" I asked.

"I suppose that a band of warriors from this district will try to fight off the invaders, but they will either be killed or have to flee to the mountains with everyone else. We haven't had much success against this chief in the past," Mahui added. "I don't think this time will be any different. You'd better get used to the idea."

Mahui might accept such a thing, but I could not. I don't know if it was the cat in me or the European, but I refused to abandon my bright and sunny Rori to such a fate. Maybe Mahui was right and there was nothing anyone could do. Maybe that was true for pigs or humans, but I, after all, was a cat!

"I am going to stop this war," I said.

Mahui gave his piggy laugh again. I'm sure he didn't mean to be cruel, since he genuinely seemed to like me. Perhaps he was just startled at my audacity.

"Pifare, my friend, I have seen this many times and the outcome never changes. Everyone believes there is nothing to be done."

"Not everyone," I growled.

The boar looked at me tolerantly. "Bang your skull against a coconut tree if you wish," he said. "But do not complain if a coconut falls on you."

"Mahui," I asked, "if I find a way, will you help me?"

He didn't hesitate. "Yes. You may be foolish, but there is something noble in your spirit. If you need me, ask any pig in the district. I will hear."

I walked thoughtfully back to Uncle's house, my tail in the air. At least I had enlisted Mahui's support. Exactly what he and I would do together, I had no idea. And that was bad, because we had to act soon. The warring sides had to go through some prefight ceremonies, but Mahui said that the rituals would only last three days.

Three days to stop a devastating invasion! The task

seemed hopeless, even for a cat. I curled up to sleep that evening feeling a bit low.

The following day I was more cheerful. Perhaps if I went and did some scouting in enemy territory, I might happen upon a way to stop the impending invasion.

I wanted Rori to come with me, but that would be hard, since I had no way to tell her why. The only thing I could do was to pluck at her skirt with my claws, then trot a short way in the direction that I wanted her to go, hoping she would follow.

It didn't work. She was too sunk in the fatalistic mood that had descended on Auntie and Uncle. She did rouse enough to notice my frantic behavior, but instead of following after, she scooped me up and took me to old Vao's hut.

The grandmother was busy pounding cooked breadfruit in a trough. I suppose she decided that someone ought to prepare some food even if everything was about to fall apart.

Rori told her grandmother why she had come. She was worried about me, she said. I was doing things I had not done before; running back and forth like mad and tugging on her clothing. When she put me on the ground, I went through my routine while Vao watched. I tugged at her skirt as well.

"Pifare wants us to go with him," Vao said.

"I know." Rori answered. "But where and why?"

The old woman crouched, staring into my eyes. "Little beast, you are drawn to *aha*. Is this where you go now?"

I gave a loud meow. If only they would follow me and stop wasting time!

"I have heard that the enemy's priests will soon finish the war ceremonies," Rori whispered, frightened tears glimmering in her eyes.

"Perhaps that is why Pifare is trying to make us come with him."

Rori stared up at her grandmother. For the first time in days, I saw a spark of hope in her eyes. "Do you think the great gods have sent him to help us?"

"I do not know," replied old Vao. "I know only that he has magic, and the magic is intertwined with the sacred sennit. I will go with you both."

Vao quickly wrapped the mashed breadfruit she'd been

pounding in hibiscus leaves and stowed it in a coconut-frond basket. Then we were off.

I won't dwell on the journey, except to say that it was quite a tramp through steamy island jungle. Mahui soon joined me, since I managed to send a message to him by one of the free-roaming district pigs. Mahui was a godsend, since he knew the way and was a good trailbreaker, shoving the heavy foliage aside so that Rori and Vao could pass easily along overgrown paths.

I also think the boar's presence helped convince both the old woman and the girl that the Tahitian gods favored our mission, even though both Rori and Vao were a little afraid of him. It also raised my status in their eyes. Anyone who could pal around with a pig who was consecrated to Oro was not any ordinary animal!

No one challenged us as we crossed the jungly ridge of hills that separated our district from the rival one. I wasn't surprised. Had Mahui and I been leading a group of men, we probably would not have gotten two steps across the boundary, but an old woman and a little girl—what harm could they do? Mahui and I might have attracted attention, but we kept ourselves well-hidden in the bushes whenever our two travelers encountered other people.

Mahui also knew a lot about how the Tahitians made war on each other. The island was not set up very well for fighting on land, the boar explained. Most of the districts were in river valleys, separated from each other by steep ridges that spread out like the spokes of a ship's wheel from the center of the island. Once a war party had climbed over, they were too tired to do much serious scrapping.

But, like most humans, the Tahitians had apparently figured out ways to have their wars without too much difficulty. One way was to load everybody in huge double-hulled war canoes and paddle around to the next district. If the other chief had boats waiting, there was a fight on the lagoon. If not, the invading party started at the beach and worked inland.

Watercraft were the key to the whole operation, said Mahui. The chief who could command the largest war fleet was usually the winner. Sometimes if a chief was feeling particularly nasty, he and his henchmen sneaked over to the opposing side's beach and hacked up or burned their war canoes. That, according to Mahui, was considered pretty dirty fighting and was generally frowned upon.

Dirty fighting or not, it sounded like one way to halt this invasion before it got started. Although how a cat, a sacred pig, a child, and an old woman would manage to put a beach full of canoes out of commission still wasn't exactly clear.

With this vague idea in mind, I had Mahui lead us to a place near the big sheds where the war canoes were kept and repaired. There was also a large yard nearby where craft were built, repaired, and consecrated to the gods.

It was dusk by the time we found a place to hole up. Vao parceled out the food and we all had a quick meal. Even I managed to eat some mashed breadfruit, although I would have much preferred one of the fat coconut rats I heard scampering about. Mahui and I shared watches that night, since Vao and the girl needed a full night's sleep.

The following morning I decided to do a little scouting. Leaving Mahui to look after the others, I crept through the underbrush until I found a hideaway close to the boat-building area. From there I spied on the canoe builders as they worked.

I saw craft in all stages of construction and repair. Having seen only the smaller outrigger skiffs like Rori's, I had no idea how huge and long these war canoes were. Some were as long as the *Dolphin*, though not nearly as high or wide. They were made to seat hundreds of warriors and I could see what Mahui meant when he said that they were crucial to any attack.

The sight of the war canoes disheartened me. How could I and my companions disable those monstrous things in less than two days? They seemed to dwarf even my seemingly unlimited destructive abilities.

I was about to retreat and pursue some other angle of attack, but I figured I'd stick around and watch for a while. I just might pick up something I could use.

The first thing I noticed was that no single tree was long or thick enough to shape into a war canoe. The things had to be pieced together from parts cut to fit. Their method made sense, since that was the way the ship's carpenter aboard the *Dolphin* repaired the ship's boats.

I could see that the woodworkers were very skilled at

shaping planks with hand adzes. They also used fire to hollow out the center of huge logs to make a dugout and added planking to build up the sides. The wood was often elaborately carved.

One thing, however, baffled me. I had seen no nails, screws, spikes, or any of the metalware used to fasten together the *Dolphin* and her small boats. Nor had I seen any use of glue strong enough to bind wood and not wash away in the sea. How did these folk put their craft together?

And then I looked even more closely and I had my answer. *Aha*. Sennit.

Every single plank, thwart, runner, and keel section was bound together with coconut cord. The Tahitian shipwrights bored matching holes in adjoining planks. The hole-drilling was a long laborious process, since they used shell and stone augers. Once it was completed, the planks were literally sewn together by stringing wet coconut cord through the holes and yanking it hard. The boat-builders used a little tool that resembled a y-shaped crowbar to pry under the binding and make it as tight as possible. Once the cord dried, it shrank, making the binding even firmer and tighter.

The men repaired their old canoes by taking them apart plank by plank and lashing the parts with new sennit. I realized that most of the work going on was this kind of refitting. New craft took a long time to build. The time was better spent fixing and strengthening the ones they already had.

There must have been hundreds of fathoms of that tough coconut twine in use in the canoe-building area. And more coiled in hanks in a cane-walled storehouse nearby. Miles and miles of the stuff. My paws tingled to get at it.

Instead I crept back to tell Mahui of my discovery. He suggested that we wait until cover of dark before mounting an assault on the boatyard. While I stayed with Vao and Rori, the boar went out to do some scouting of his own. When he returned to us, he had some news. He'd managed to get into the sacred courtyard or *marae* of the warring chief and poke about a bit without being chased out. Sometimes being a sacred pig is useful.

"The chief is gathering his warriors and the priests are

finishing the battle rituals," the boar told me. "As soon as those war canoes are launched and loaded, the invasion will start."

As darkness fell, Rori, Mahui, and I began our stalk up to the low wall that surrounded the boat-building area. We left Vao behind, for she said that her old bones were not up to creeping through the jungle. Besides, she could make a distraction to draw attention away from us, if needed.

Rori, however, was determined to go with us. This was doubly brave of her, since women and girls were forbidden to enter a place where war canoes were being made or repaired. If I was caught, I'd probably just be chased out, but if the men found Rori, they'd kill her.

Keeping hidden wasn't easy, since there was quite a crowd of people in and around the boatyard. Work was going on by torchlight, and priests were there as well, dressed in fringed and feathered cloaks and tall, feather-covered wicker headdresses. They were drumming, chanting and blessing the war boats and everything used to make them. Luckily their racket would cover any noise we might make. We slipped from shadow to shadow in places unlit by any torchlight, until we were at last crouching beneath a shrub that grew against the low stone wall. With our heads hidden by leaves, we peeked in.

I heard Rori gasp in despair and I couldn't blame her, for the war canoes stood like great threatening gods, their gleaming black carved prows and sterns rearing fiercely up into the darkness. Many had elevated decks, like fighting platforms, built over the two hulls. Some were on rollers, ready to be pushed to the beach. Others still had bits missing, but most appeared to be almost complete. I gave a soft wail of dismay. Had we come too late?

Mahui pushed his way past me and put his snout on top of the wall for a quick look. "The chief is impatient. He wants those war canoes ready by morning. You have to stop that."

"How?" I asked.

The pig made a sideways motion with his head that expressed the same feeling as a human shrug. Clearly I was supposed to be the brains of this team. He would help as much as he could, but it was up to me to give direction.

I narrowed my eyes at the ominous shapes of the war

canoes. The polished and carved hardwood of their stern-posts gleamed in the torchlight. They had been made with devotion and care. They were beautiful in a fierce alien way, but they would bring death and ruin to those I cared most about.

I studied the nearest hull, all aswarm with men binding its planks together.

"How much cord do the workmen have?" I asked the pig, who was a bit longer-sighted than I was.

"Not enough to finish," he answered.

My mind began to sketch out a possible plan. "Good," I said. "They will have to get more."

Mahui told me that the sennit the shipwrights used had been specially consecrated. It was kept in a small cane-walled storehouse. "Is that the only place?" I asked. Mahui grunted. "Yes."

"Good." Rori and I would creep along outside the marae wall until we were as close to the storehouse as possible. Then we'd go over and I'd try to get in.

"There's a hole that the rats have made," said Mahui. "It is hard to find. I'll have to show you."

Mahui was athletic enough to climb over the wall, but too big not to attract notice. He said he would sneak in the main entrance and meet us at the storehouse.

I was a little skeptical about his aptitude for stealth, since, after all, he was a pig. But he had been roaming these island jungles for years. We said a few final words before separating. I got Rori to follow me by a light tug on her skirt and we began sidling along the marae wall.

By the time we got to a place opposite the storehouse, the priests were conducting a blessing ritual around one of the canoes. The drums boomed and the chanting droned. I saw, with alarm, that men were starting to roll some of the craft from the yard to the beach.

Rori watched tearfully, but she made not one sound, not even a sniffle. We huddled between the inside of the stone wall and the canes of the storehouse. My fur prickled at the smell of all the sennit inside.

I made a brief attempt to find the hole that Mahui had spoken of, but he was right—it was too well hidden. I decided to wait until he appeared. If he did. I still doubted he could get through that crowd unnoticed. His ear tag might protect him if he was seen, but he was still taking a risk. If any of the chief's minions got upset, even a sacred pig of Oro might wind up as pork cutlets.

A cold chill crept over me at the thought. I never imagined I'd ever have much regard for a pig, but Mahui was unlike any European pig I'd run into. He might not be a cat, but he was a strong, dependable friend. Rori liked him, too.

"Here I am, Pifare," came a porcine whisper from what looked like just another shadow. In another instant Mahui was beside us.

The hole was high up, just under the eaves of the storehouse. That's why I couldn't find it—I'd been expecting something more on my level. I could have climbed, but my claws would have made a racket on the cane walls. Instead I got Rori's attention and got her to boost me up. She had to go up on her tippy-toes to do it.

I scrambled through and jumped down to the packed-earth floor as quietly as I could. The storehouse was packed with coconut-fiber twine; enough to put together a fleet of war canoes. I felt suddenly overwhelmed. There were massive amounts of the stuff. And I had to make every bit unusable.

"Pifare," said Mahui softly through a slight crack in the cane walls, "one of the workmen has left the canoes. He appears to be fetching more sennit. Whatever you plan, do it quickly."

I thought about dousing as much of the cord as I could with a good spray of urine, but would that be discouragement enough? These people seemed to tolerate some sorts of strong smells. With my bad luck, cat-piss might be one.

No. I would have to rely on my magic. If I didn't get the job done in time, maybe I could faze the sennit-fetcher with an unexpected attack and delay completion of the boats. On the other hand, he might just whack me on the skull with a club and that would be that.

The faint sound of footfalls was starting to get louder. Saying a quick cat-prayer to the forces of disorder, I dived into the nearest coil.

I knocked hanks of cord off low shelves, clawed it out of wooden boxes, unwound reels, scattering their contents all over the floor. I writhed, rolled and wriggled in the sennit as if I was possessed. My gift woke and the loops of cord started to dance like a basketful of demented snakes.

But it was not enough. Though I had snarled a good portion of the stuff, the shipwright would still find enough undamaged to complete the war canoe.

I redoubled my efforts, bounding all over that storehouse like a rubber ball thrown into a box, throwing cord into the air. Not good enough. Where was that unbounded gift of disorder that had so bedeviled the *Dolphin*?

Perhaps it was that crack of torchlight, or the grating of the cane door as the workman began to pull it aside. Something in my mind seemed to pop loose like a stopper out of a gin bottle. Every length of cord in the storehouse spun itself free and rose up in wild rebellion. Loops and ends flailed about, wound around each other, ducked and dived, knotted and re-knotted until everything was one gigantic, unholy, impossibly tangled mess.

And there I was, in the middle of it, so completely wrapped up that I couldn't move a muscle, but I didn't need to. That coconut string knew who was its master and it gleefully obeyed the demands I gave it.

What the canoe-builder must have thought when all that string literally exploded out of the storehouse at him, I have no idea. He only shrieked and fell in a dead faint while the unruly twine coiled all over him.

His brethren made one or two attempts to recover enough sennit to finish the job, but every time they tried, I made the cord yank itself from their hands so fast it that burned their fingers.

The nearby workmen had fallen flat on their faces—those who hadn't leaped the boatyard wall and fled. The priests tried some counter-magic of their own, with chants and hand-flourishes, but what is human sorcery to cat-magic!

Perhaps my gift relished a challenge, for all at once the twine's rebellion spread from the storehouse to the sennit on the nearest war canoe. The neatly made bindings undid themselves, whipping their ends back through the holes in the boat planks.

Loosened, the planks sagged and fell, while the gleeful lengths of coconut cord wound around each other in mischievous embraces. The yard resounded with the noise of wooden planks falling from hulls and clattering on the ground. One war canoe after another fell victim to the spreading plague.

Nothing the men did could stop it. More priests were summoned to pray and chant and even the chief himself came running, but all they could do was gape and fall on their faces as their war boats fell to pieces. The sennit from the canoes and the sennit from the storehouse writhed together in one monstrous, irretrievably snarled up monument to the infinite feline capacity for disorder.

And I was at the heart of it, savoring every moment.

Old Vao, who must have been chuckling to herself at the frantic efforts of the canoe-builders, came to the boatyard entrance and stepped boldly inside. No one lifted a hand against her; not even the chief. They were all too paralyzed by fright.

The priests appealed to her to stop the wild antics of the sennit, which she did, of course, since I obeyed her request.

In a creaky but firm voice, Vao scolded the priests and the chief. "The gods did not agree to this war. If the chief began it, disaster would fall upon his people." Pifare would see to that.

Rori, who had been huddling behind the storage house, came out to join her grandmother. Mahui also came to Vao, his black bristly presence adding to her air of authority.

Once I made the sennit quiet down, Rori waded into the mess to try and extricate me. It was quite a job, but at last she got me loose.

Well, the long and short of it is that the chief gave up on his war. His district made peace with ours and everything settled down again.

The boat-builders tried to salvage their sennit, but it was in such a hopeless snarl that they could only burn it. They did eventually make more and put the canoes back together, but the war boats went back into the sheds and stayed there.

I decided to stay with Rori's folks on Tahiti. I could have gone home, since the *Dolphin* actually turned up again a few days later, but I was getting far too fond of Vao and Rori. Mahui, too.

When the tale of my exploits made the rounds of the island, I became quite a celebrity and was treated to a banquet of freshly caught fish. Obviously, the Tahitians had the right attitude.

When Captain Cook's crew showed up a few years later, they gave some cats to the local gentry. One was a sprightly ginger lass who became my *vahine*. I had everything I could want, including several litters of Pifares. Only a few of the kittens have my talent. The Tahitians are probably grateful for that!

I forgot to mention that these folks also play games with loops of cord. They don't know the proper name for their string figures, so they call them *"fai."*

What do I mean by the "proper name"? I'm surprised that you have to ask.

Why "cat's cradle," of course!

SAXOPHONE JOE AND THE WOMAN IN BLACK

by Charles de Lint

A cat has nine lives. For three he plays, for three he strays, and for the last three he stays.
—American folklore

I love this city.

Even now, with things getting worse the way they do: Too many people hungry, or cold, or got nowhere to sleep, and here's winter creeping up on us, earlier each year, and staying later. The warm grate doesn't do much when the sleet's coming down, giving everything the picture-perfect prettiness of a fairy tale—just saying you've got the where-withal to admire a thing like that, instead of always worrying how the ends are going to meet.

But you've got to take the time, once in a while, or what've you got? Don't be waiting for the lotto to come in when you can't even afford the price of a ticket.

It's like all those stories that quilt the streets, untidy little threads of yarn that get pulled together into gossiping skeins, one from here, one from there, until what you've got in your hand isn't a book, maybe, doesn't have a real beginning or end, but it tells you something. You can read the big splashes that make their way onto the front page, headlines standing out one inch tall, just screaming for your attention. Sure, they're interesting, but what interests me more is the little stories. Nothing so exciting, maybe, about losing a job, or looking for one. Falling in or out of love. New baby coming. Old grandad passed away. Unless the story belongs to you. Then it fills your world and you don't have time to even glance at those headlines.

What gets me is how everybody's looking to make sense of things. Sometimes you don't want sense. Sometimes, the last thing in the world you need is sense. Work a thing through till it makes sense and you lose all the possibilities.

That's what runs this city. All those possibilities. It's like the heart of the city is this old coal furnace, just smoking away under the streets, stoked with all those might-yet-bes and who'd-a-thoughts. The rich man waking up broke and he never saw it coming. The girl who figures she's so ugly she won't look in a mirror and she finds she's got two boys fighting over her. The father who surprises himself when he finds he likes his son better, now that he knows the boy's gay.

And the thing is, the account doesn't end there. One possibility just leads straight up to the next, with handfuls of story lying in between. Stoking the furnace. Keeping the city interesting.

You just got to know where to look. You just got to know *how* to look.

Got no time?

Maybe the measurement's different from me to you to that girl who gives you your ticket at the bus depot, but the one thing we've all got is time. You can use it or lose it, your choice. That's how come we've got that old saying about how it's not having a thing that's important, but how we went about getting it. Our time's the most precious thing we've got to offer folks, and the worst thing a body can do is to take it away from us.

So don't you go wasting it.

But I was talking about possibilities and little stories, things that maybe don't even make it into the paper. Like what happened to Saxophone Joe.

I guess everybody knows how a cat's got nine lives and I'm thinking a few more of you know how those lives are divided up: three to play, three to stray, and the last three to stay. Maybe that's a likeness for our own lives, a what do you call it, metaphor. I don't know.

But grannies used to tell their children's children how if a cat came to live with you of its own accord during one of its straying lives, why you couldn't ask for better luck in that household. And that cat'd stay, too, unless you called it by name. Not the name you gave it, or maybe the one it gave you—it comes wandering in off the fire escape with its little white paws, so you call it Boots, or maybe it's that deep orange like you'd spread on your toast, so you call it Marmalade.

I'm talking about its secret name, the one only it knows.

Anyway, Joe's playing six nights a week with a combo in the Rhatigan, a little jazz club over on Palm Street; him on sax, Tommy Morrison on skins, Rex Small bellied up to that big double bass, and Johnny Fingers tickling the ivories. The Rhatigan doesn't look like much, but it's the kind of place you never know who's going to be sitting in with the band, playing that long cool music.

Used to be people said jazz was the soul of the city, the rhythm that made it tick. A music made up of slick streets and neon lights, smoky clubs and lips that taste like whiskey. Now we've got hip hop and rap and thrash and I hear people saying it's not music at all, but they're plain wrong. All these sounds are still true to the soul of the city; it's just changed to suit the times is all.

One night Joe's up there on the Rhatigan's stage, half-sitting on his stool, one long leg bent up, foot supported on a rung, the other pointing straight out across the stage to where Johnny's hunched over his piano, fingers dancing on the keyboard as they trade off riffs. There's something in the air that night and they're seriously connected to it.

Joe takes a breath, head cocked as he listens to what Johnny's playing. Then, just as he tightens his lips around the reeds, he sees the woman sitting there off in a dark corner, alone at her table, black hair, black dress, skin the same midnight tone as Joe's own so that she's almost invisible except for the whites of her eyes and her teeth, because she's looking right at him and she's smiling.

Dark eyes, she's got, like there's no pupils, watching him and not blinking, and Joe watches her back. He's got one eye that's blue and one eye that's brown, and the gaze of the two of them just about swallows her whole.

But Joe doesn't lose the music, doesn't hesitate a moment; his sax wails, coming in right when it should, only he's watching the woman now, Johnny's forgotten, and the music changes, turns slinky, like an old tomcat on the prowl. The woman smiles and lifts her glass to him.

She comes home with him that night, just moves in like she's always been there. She doesn't talk, she doesn't ever say a word, but things must be working out between them because she's there, isn't she, sharing that tiny room Joe's had in the Walker Hotel for sixteen years. Live together in a small space like that and you soon find out if you can get along or not.

After a while, Joe starts calling her Mona because that's the name of the tune they were playing when he first saw her in the Rhatigan and musicians being the way they are, nobody thinks it strange that she doesn't talk, that she's got no ID, that she answers to that name. It's like she's always been there, always been called Mona, always lived with Saxophone Joe and been his woman.

But if he doesn't talk to anyone else about it, Joe's still thinking about her, always thinking about her, if he's on stage or walking down a street or back in their room, who she is and where she came from, and he finds himself trying out names on her, to see which one she might've worn before he called her Mona, which one her Mama and Papa called her by when she was just a little girl.

Then one day he gets it right, and the next morning she's gone, walked out of his life like the straying cat in the story the grannies tell, once someone's called her by her true, secret name. What was her name, this woman Joe started out calling Mona? I never learned. But Joe knows the story, too, cats and names, and he gets to thinking some more, he can't *stop* thinking about Mona and cats and then he gets this crazy idea that maybe she really *was* a cat, that she could change, cat to woman, woman to cat, slipped into his life during her straying years and now she's gone.

And then he gets an even crazier idea: the only way to get her back is if he gets himself his own cat skin.

So he goes to see the priest—not the man with the white collar, but the hoodoo man—except Papa Jo-el's dead, got himself mixed up with some kind of juju that even he couldn't handle, so when Joe goes knocking soft on Papa Jo-el's door, it's the *gris-gris* woman Ti Beau that answers and lets him in.

Friday night, Joe's back in the club, and he's playing a dark music now, the tone of his sax's got an undercurrent in it, like skin-headed drums played with the palm of your hand and a tap-tap of a drumstick on a bar of iron, like midnight at a crossroads and the mist's coming in from the swamp, like seven-day candles burning in the wind, but those candles don't flicker because the gateways are open and *les invisibles* are there, holding the flames still.

Saturday night, he's back again, and he's still playing music like no one's heard before—not displeasing, just unfamiliar. Tommy and Rex, they're having trouble keeping the rhythm, but Johnny's following, note for note. After the last set that Saturday night, he walks up to where Joe's putting his sax away in its case.

"You been to see the *mambo*?" Johnny asks, "playing music like that?"

Joe doesn't answer except to put his sax case in Johnny's hands.

"Hold on to this for me, would you?" he asks.

When he leaves the club that night, it's the last time anybody sees him. Sees the man. But Heber Brown, he's been working at the Walker Hotel for thirty years. When he's cleaning out Joe's room because the rent's two months due and nobody's seen him for most of that time, Heber sees an old tomcat on the fire escape, scratching at the window, trying to get in. Heber says this cat's so dark a brown it's almost black, like midnight settled in the corner of an alleyway, and it's got one blue eye, so you tell me.

You think Ti Beau's got the kind of *gris-gris* potion to turn a man into a cat, or maybe just an old cat skin lying about that'll work the same magic, someone says the right words over it? Or was it maybe that Joe just up and left town, nursing a broken heart?

Somebody taped that last set Joe played at the Rhatigan and I'll tell you, when Johnny plays it for me, I hear hurting in it, but I hear something else, too, something that doesn't quite belong to this world, or maybe belonged here first, but we kind of eased it out of the way once we got ourselves civilized enough. It's like one of the *loa* stepped into Joe that night, maybe freed him up, loosened his skin enough so that he could make the change, but first that spirit talked to us through Joe's sax, reminding us that we weren't here first, and maybe we won't be here the last either.

It's all part and parcel of the mystery that sits there, right under all the things we know for sure. And the thing I like about that mystery is that it doesn't show us more than a little piece at a time; but you touch it and you've just got to pass it on. So if Joe's not with Mona now, you can bet he's slipped into someone else's life and he's making them think. Sitting there on a windowsill, maybe looking lazy, but maybe looking like he knows something we don't, something important, and that person he's with, who took him in, well she stops the tumbling rush of her life for a moment to take the time to think about what lies under the stories that make up this city.

Things may be getting worse in some ways, but you can't deny that they're interesting, too, if you just stop to look at them a little closer.

Like that old man playing the clarinet in the subway station that you pass by every day. He's bent and old and his clothes are shabby and you can't figure out how he makes a living from the few coins that get tossed into the hat sitting on the pavement in front of him. So maybe he's just an old man, down on his luck, making do. Or maybe he's got a piece of magic he wants to pass on with that music he's playing.

Next time you go by, stop and give him a listen. But don't go looking for a tag to put on what you hear or, like that cat that runs off when you name her, it'll all just fade away.

TEDDY CAT

by Marylois Dunn

Cory Johnson was allergic. Not to everything. Just to everything her mama and papa didn't want her to have.

When they went into town on a Saturday, Cory remembered her other papa, her real papa, buying her an ice cream cone at the drugstore. Now, when she begged for a cone, Mama would say, "You can't have one. You're allergic."

Cory wondered how Mama knew she was allergic. Other kids who were allergic broke out in rashes or breathed funny. Cory didn't do either of those things. She had to trust Mama and give up the things she was allergic to.

Papa died and was buried on the hill behind the house. He was barely in the ground when Boone came to live with them. He was the one who noticed. She was sitting in the wicker rocker in the parlor rocking Teddy Bear and listening to Jack Benny on the radio. Wrapped in a clean white towel as always, Cory didn't want him to get dirty as her other bears had and Teddy Bear never did. He was as clean as the day Papa gave him to her. His gray fur was rubbed off in places and one button eye had come loose and chinked as she rocked, but that didn't matter. He was clean and he was hers.

"Ain't that child got no better toys to play with?" Boone asked her mama. "That bear's a disgrace."

"Teddy's her favorite," Mama said. "Jack gave him to her."

"I think she's allergic to the fur. Listen to how she's breathing."

Cory sniffed big and tried to breathe more quietly but her nose was stuffy from the cold she caught from Jimmy Garner at school. Jimmy always had a runny nose and he was generous with his germs.

Nothing more was said about the bear but Cory was uncomfortably aware of Boone's narrow-eyed gaze. Watching.

The bus deposited her at the end of the lane on Monday afternoon, and Cory walked up the dusty road, books in one hand, shoes in the other. She liked the warm, satiny feel of sand between her toes. She made long drag marks in the sand as she walked.

Mockingbirds sang spring songs in the snowy grancy graybeard trees. Redbuds were feathery pink and dogwoods hinted white in the deep woods. She sang the song Dennis Day sang on the Benny show "To-ra-lu-ra-lu-ra, To-ra-lu-ra-li" all the way up the lane and into the house.

Cory sighed with relief when nobody was at home. Mama worked at the hospital and Boone was off in the woods loggin'.

Cory stomped the sand off her feet before she entered the house. Her books went onto the table beside her bed, the shoes under the curtained rack which held her clothes. She hung her school dress to be ready for tomorrow and put on the worn jeans she played in before she looked for her friend, Teddy Bear.

Teddy Bear wasn't there. The cradle Papa had made for her when she was born was in the corner. The white towel she wrapped around Teddy Bear was folded loosely in the cradle. The towel was empty. The cradle was empty. Teddy Bear was gone.

Cory felt a moment of blind panic before she began to hunt. First, she went through her room, then the entire house, looking quickly. When she didn't find Teddy Bear, she began in one corner of her room, searching methodically on top of, in, and under everything. Not in her room, the kitchen, the parlor, the dining room, the bedrooms, did she find him.

Teddy Bear was gone.

She went outside and looked over both porches, on the roof, under the house. Teddy Bear wasn't there either.

At the woodpile where she sometimes played, Cory found a strand of gray fur clinging to the ax handle, and one brown-button eye lay almost hidden in the chips below the chopping block. In the cold ashes of the fire pit, she found the other eye, blackened by flame.

Cory didn't cry. She had learned not to cry around

Boone, and now she never cried. She held the strand of fur and the buttons for a while, thinking where to hide them in a private place. There was only one.

Papa's cross stood inside a small wire encased space. She went inside and dug down into Papa's grave burying the last of Teddy Bear where Papa could protect him. Perhaps they would comfort each other.

From the woods, she brought woodbine and wild azalea to sweeten the air for Papa and Teddy Bear before she returned to the house.

Cory rerolled the towel until she could almost feel Teddy Bear inside. With the roll under one arm, she made a peanut butter sandwich and went onto the back porch to sit on the steps where she could see Papa's grave. As she watched, something jumped atop the gate to Papa's plot, hovered there a moment, and then flew to the ground in an easy leap.

The cat approached her, tail stiffly erect, as if he knew he would be welcomed. "Merow?" he inquired.

Cory looked around. She didn't see anyone and she had not heard the rattle of Boone's old truck.

"Meerow?" the cat asked again.

"Hello," she said.

The gray and white tom sat down in the sand. "Mero," he replied.

"Are you hungry?" Cory asked.

The cat stood and put his front paws on the lowest step looking into her eyes as he said, "Merr."

She shared the soft parts of the sandwich and he ate daintily though he made her laugh when a gob of peanut butter stuck to the roof of his mouth. He stretched his mouth wide, making comical faces while his rough tongue searched out the sticky stuff.

Until the sandwich was gone and he sat down against her thigh to wash, she didn't attempt to touch him. She watched him wash for a while before she began to stroke his rough fur.

The cat did not seem to mind. He went on washing, pausing now and again to give her fingers a swipe with his sandy tongue when they came within his reach.

The cattle guard at the head of the lane rattled. Boone's truck clattered toward the house. In two bounds, the cat disappeared under the house and Cory ran to her room to leave the rolled towel before she started supper. She was peeling red potatoes as Boone came into the kitchen.

" 'Ja have a good day at school." Boone put the coffee-pot over a gas burner to warm the leftover coffee. " 'd you pass that spelling test?"

"Missed one word. 'Itinerary.' Don't know what use that dumb word is anyhow. Itinerary ain't a usin' word. Just a spellin' word."

"I-T-I-N-E-R-A-R-Y. Even I can spell that. Learned in the Service. You never know what words you're gonna need. Learn 'em all."

Cory didn't answer, keeping her face impassive as she concentrated on the potatoes.

Boone sat at the table, hands cupped around the warm coffee mug. "You been playin'?"

Cory shook her head. "No time. Fixed a sandwich to eat on the back porch. Then I come in to do the potatoes like Mama told me."

She did not mention Teddy Bear, smiling to herself at Boone's increasing frustration. He wanted her to say something. He wanted to say something but didn't quite dare.

Mama came in, dropping her jacket on the hall tree and taking up her apron as she entered the kitchen. "Thanks for helping Mama, Cory. How was school today?"

"All right. Jimmy Garner's out again. I guess that cold got worse."

Mama kissed the top of her head and gave Boone a different kind of kiss. "How was your day, Honey?"

"Not much. Woods are too wet to do much loggin'."

They gave each other a significant look but neither mentioned Teddy Bear.

The subject was closed all evening. Cory went off to bed, not having mentioned Teddy Bear or the cat she was already beginning to call Teddy Cat in her mind.

Mama did not usually come in to say "goodnight." To-night, she sat on the side of Cory's bed. "I see Teddy is gone." She pointed toward the cradle with her chin.

"No, Mama. I sleep with Teddy Bear every night." Cory lifted her covers enough for Mama to see the rolled towel she clutched against her body.

"That's not Teddy. That's just a towel."

"Teddy Bear isn't a person, Mama. Not like Daddy was. Teddy Bear is anything I want him to be. Boone can burn this old towel, too, if he wants, but there'll be something else tomorrow. He done took you, but he ain't never goin' to take Teddy Bear away from me."

"Hush, child. You want Boone to hear you?" Mamma didn't touch the towel and after a while went back to her bedroom.

Cory heard Boone's angry voice, but he didn't come into her room that night.

Sometime after midnight, Cory was awakened by a noise at her window. Cory looked outside. There, in the bright moonlight, was Teddy Cat looking up at her.

"Mero." His soft voice greeted her. Cory slipped the latch, pushing the screen out. Teddy Cat leapt onto the windowsill and entered, rubbing against the window frame, walls, Cory, and anything else solid enough to be rubbed.

Cory picked him up and put him on the bed while she spread the towel. Teddy Cat seemed to understand that the towel was for him. He lay down, shoving hard with first one shoulder, then the other. He rolled onto his back, paws in the air. Using his tail as a rudder, he hunched himself closer to Cory without putting paw to bed.

Over and over, she whispered how clever he was. How beautiful.

Of course, Cory knew with his battered ears and scarred face, he was not a beautiful cat. He was a wild woods tom, come to make her pain a little less. Teddy Bear and Papa had sent him to do what Teddy Bear couldn't. He could talk cat talk, purr like a truck with a missing cylinder, and when she was in school, he could hide himself from Boone.

Teddy Cat understood about Boone. He hissed and keened angrily when he heard Boone's voice or his approach on those nights Boone came into her room. Cory did not know where Teddy Cat hid. Out the unlocked screen, she supposed. As soon as Boone left, Teddy Cat returned to snuggle and rub her chin with his head, wiping her tears with a prickly, tickly tongue. In only moments he had tickled her to silent laughter with his whiskers.

Teddy Cat endured being rolled into the towel like a baby doll and snuggled close. She never saw him leave. In the mornings she would wake with the empty rolled towel in her arms. As much she could be, Cory was happy.

If she had not tried to feed Teddy Cat, Boone might never have known about him. While school was on, she brought home bits from her lunch and what other scraps she gleaned from the lunches around her. Her friends, learning her secret, saved choice bits for her cat.

Summer changed everything. She hated being alone with Boone all day. Cory discovered the first day that he rarely went loggin', but rather, laid around the house waiting until almost time for Mama to come. He got into his truck and drove off to come home after Mama, pretending he'd worked hard all day.

Cory waited for those few moments that he was gone to get bits and pieces from the refrigerator for the cat.

Boone left the pattern one day. "Got a job to do today, girl. Sure hate to leave you here by your lonesome, but a man's gotta work."

Cory watched him drive out of sight before she got out her fishing pole. Two hours of peace on the bank of the creek told her the fish were not going to bite, not even the voracious sun perch. While she fished, Teddy Cat lay in the small patches of sunlight he found on the forest floor, watching. He liked to eat the small fish she crisp fried for him, but when she stood to go home, he followed uncomplaining.

Cory came from the woods to the back porch by way of her Daddy's gravesite. The bright yellow Black-eyed Susans she had picked in the woods made a splash of color in the sunlight. Teddy Cat rubbed her legs, seeming to approve her choice of flowers.

Going directly into the kitchen, Cory cooked bacon scraps and dipped a piece of bread in the bacon fat for Teddy Cat.

She was not listening to anything but the wren's song as she broke the bread into small pieces and put Boone's plate onto the porch for Teddy Cat.

Boone's footsteps were light as he slipped through the house to stand in the kitchen door. "Throwing good food to stray cats, are you? Can't you find something useful to do around this house instead of lollygagging on the back porch? I come back to get my ax. Looks like I got me a cat to chop." Boone picked up the sharpened, double-bitted ax and gave a tentative swing toward the cat.

Teddy Cat made no move to disappear this time. Instead, he stretched to his full height, arching his back, every hair on end. He opened his mouth but did not hiss. Instead, the sound that came from his throat was more that of the wild woods panther they sometimes heard in the night.

Cory was not afraid. For the first time, in Boone's presence, she felt no twinge of fear. Instead she looked around from where she sat on the steps to the kitchen door. "This ain't no teddy bear you can chop to pieces. This here's a real live cat and a tough one, too. You better leave us alone. Just go to work and leave us alone."

"I'll teach you to smart mouth me, Missy," Boone swung the handle of the ax in her direction, stepping backward as the cat leapt for his face.

Ripping at the eyes with his claws, clinging to Boone's nose with his teeth, driving his long back legs like two chain saws into Boone's throat, Teddy Cat attacked like a wild thing.

Boone screamed as he dropped the ax and tried to pull the cat away from his head. Several moments passed before he succeeded in pulling Teddy Cat loose. If his intention was to toss the cat into the yard, he did not succeed. Instead, he dropped the fighting cat as he fell to his knees. The furiously raking hind legs had done their work. Blood spurted from Boone's throat and he made strange gurgling sounds as he tried to stop the pulsing flow with his hands.

Teddy Cat crouched, ready to leap again, until Boone folded down onto the porch with his knees drawn up close to his chest, muscles jerking in spasms which stopped after a while.

Cory watched with openmouthed astonishment from the steps. She had never seen a cat attack a person before and would not have believed in the possibility. She did not know what to do at first and then there was nothing to be done.

Teddy Cat stretched and came over to rub against Cory. His paws left bloody tracks on the porch and she rubbed his head for a few moments until he sat down to give himself a thorough wash.

Cory sat watching. She saw Teddy Cat twist around to

clean all the way down to the tip of his tail. She saw a golden beam of sunlight shimmering on Papa's grave. The yellow Susans she had put on the grave that morning shone brightly, almost with a light of their own.

Heat from the sand rose in colorless waves adding to the illusion of movement. The whole plot inside the fence seemed to be wavering with the heat.

Teddy Cat came over and thrust his head under her arm. "Merrow," his softest voice whispered.

A strange word like "tulip," no, more like "tulipa" sprang into her mind. The thought faded and she knew Teddy Cat had to leave. She didn't try to keep him.

Cory stroked him, taking him into her lap for a last hug. When she was done, Cory put the cat down onto the steps.

He trotted toward the fenced grave site, stopping only once to look back. His tail switched back and forth before he leapt to the top of the post and disappeared into the shimmering light.

Cory stood up, shading her eyes with her hand, but she could not see Teddy Cat anywhere. A cloud shadow took away the sunbeam that caused the strange light, and Papa's grave ceased to waver, looking again like a grave decorated with fresh flowers from the woods.

Before she called to tell Mama about Boone, she took the half-gallon box of ice cream from the refrigerator and filled a cup with Strawberry Swirl to eat while she waited for everyone to come. Now she could eat ice cream. Cory knew she wasn't allergic anymore.

CAT O' NINE TALES

by Charles L. Fontenay

*"If man could be crossed with the cat
it would improve man
but deteriorate the cat."*
                                        —Mark Twain

Adrian Glenn turned the battered Volkswagon bug into the estate of Nine Tales and was struck by the size of the trees, massive oaks and sweetgums. The graveled drive curved among boles framing parklike alleyways.

He came in sight of a big brownstone manse, undoubtedly Nine Tales itself ... and a cat bounded into the roadway ahead of him and stopped abruptly. Adrian jammed hard on the brake. A Blue Point Siamese it was, far more aristocratic than his own good-natured Thomas, snoozing in his room back at the Cedar Rock Inn. The cat leveled an insolent blue gaze on him and strolled casually into a clump of privet bordering the house.

Braking for the cat had stalled his engine. Adrian started the Volkswagon again and parked it near a luxurious Mercedes and a brilliantly red sports car whose brand he could not identify, went up broad steps and across a terrace to double front doors, and wielded the knocker. He was admitted by a butler.

"There's a cat out there," said Adrian. "A Siamese. I almost ran it down when I drove up."

"That'll be Margravine, sir," said the butler. "Miss Colfax's cat. She ran away a few weeks ago and we haven't been able to lure her back yet."

Without further comment the butler escorted him into a large drawing room. Adrian's knowledge of furniture was such that if he specified something like Hepplewhite or Empire in one of his novels he had to make a trip to the library to find out what he was writing about, but whatever the appointments of this room were they were elegant, probably very expensive, and reasonably comfortable.

A couple entered the room together: a stocky, dark young man with smoldering eyes and a beautiful woman of pale face and pensive mien, both in their thirties.

"I'm Clifton Niger, Mr. Glenn," the man introduced himself, "and this is my cousin, Donna Colfax."

Adrian blinked. He had expected Miss Colfax to be older, at least middle-aged, probably very prim and haughty, and he hadn't expected the young man at all.

"Are you the Miss Colfax I'm supposed to contact about the book?" he asked doubtfully of the woman as she seated herself a little apart from them. It was Niger who answered.

"I hope you'll accept our apologies," said Niger, "but we were completely surprised by Mr. Westerbrook's announcement you were coming here under the impression you had some agreement to write about Nine Tales. No such agreement was made, with Mr. Westerbrook or anyone else."

Adrian was stunned. Berman had said he had a commitment. . . .

Adrian Glenn was a rueful refutation of the romantic notion of all authors as wealthy men (or women) working only when inspiration strikes. He had come far for an orphan whose parents were killed when he was ten, but his fifteen published novels, along with many short stories and uncounted articles, provided a meager and occasional supplement to the interest from a trust fund his father had left him. By careful management, he lived and worked in a small house in a small town, enjoying himself more than most people in more lucrative trades but a stranger to million-dollar advances and vacations in foreign climes.

Thus when his agent, whom he had never met but who was prompt at claiming his 15%, suggested Adrian might be interested in researching and writing the family history of a rich lady who lived about fifty miles from his home, Adrian definitely was.

"What you'll have to do, old boy, is live in and work on the scene, so you'll have constant access to Miss Colfax's records and her reminiscences," said Berman Westerbrook over the long distance wire. Berman liked to affect an English accent. "It shouldn't be an unpleasant stint, as she lives in a sort of castle, with gardens and servants all over the place."

"Do you have a publisher interested this time or is this purely speculative?" Adrian asked cautiously. Berman chuckled.

"This one's gold-plated, old boy," he said. "Old Miss Colfax *owns* a publisher. Or she might as well. We're guaranteed an advance, from *her,* a lot better'n anything you've gotten on a novel. Besides royalties, if any."

At the figure he mentioned, Adrian decided on the spot he could put off finishing the novel he was struggling with.

"But that kind of research and writing will take a while," Adrian objected. "If I'm going to live in for the project, I don't mind closing up the house, but I can't leave Thomas here and I'm damned if I'm going to farm him out that long."

The object of Adrian's concern was perched on his shoulder, green eyes half-closed. As they talked he lifted a hand to stroke the thick fur. Thomas, easygoing and self-satisfied, was a tabby-coated alley cat, companion and sometimes inspiration to long-divorced Adrian.

"Thomas? Your cat?" Berman laughed. "I say, old boy, I wouldn't want you to do without your familiar! You'll have no problem taking the beastie along. Miss Colfax, I'm told, is a cat-lover herself."

Now it looked as though he wasn't going to move in after all.

Berman *had* said "old Miss Colfax." Adrian looked helplessly at Donna Colfax. The young woman's eyes seemed ... well, the only word Adrian could think of at the moment was "agonized." She opened her mouth, but before she could speak Niger called sharply, "Imhotep!"

At his call a large golden-brown cat of Abyssinian breed strolled into the room from somewhere, leapt upon Niger's lap and turned yellow eyes, not on the newcomer but on Miss Colfax. Miss Colfax closed her mouth and remained silent.

"But my agent ... Westerbrook ... was positive he'd arranged for me to come here and research the family history," protested Adrian. "Is there another Miss Colfax?"

"There was. The old lady. Donna's mother, also named Donna Colfax," said Niger smoothly. "She died recently.

But ...." He chuckled. "... Miss Donna Colfax would be the last person to want anyone to air the history of the Colfax family. No, Mr. Glenn, you've been victimized by some local busybody trying to stir up trouble."

He's lying, Mr. Glenn!

Adrian almost started out of his chair. That had been ... sounded like ... a feminine voice crying out desperately, here, in this room. But Niger gave no sign of having heard anything and Miss Colfax's eyes were downcast, her mouth still closed and silent. Confused, Adrian decided it must have been imagination, his own inner (intuitive?) reaction.

"Look, Mr. Niger," he said angrily, getting to his feet, "I accepted this job in good faith, even closing up my house to devote all my time to the project here. And Westerbrook's an honest agent, who wouldn't make such an agreement unless he'd made sure it was a legitimate offer. I...."

Niger held up his hand, interrupting.

"I understand you may have been put to some inconvenience, Mr. Glenn," he said. "But it *is* a mistake. We'll be glad to reimburse you for your expense in coming here. I'll contact Mr. Westerbrook about it if that's satisfactory to you."

Before Adrian could reply that nothing really would satisfy him but to proceed with the project to which he had agreed, the cat on Niger's lap said loudly, "Miau!" And Donna Colfax arose abruptly and hurried from the room.

Adrian sat down again. He was still angry. He didn't like Niger and he didn't like what had happened.

"Talk to Berman about 'expenses' if you want to," he said brusquely, leaning toward the man, "but *I'm* the one who's had my thought processes on a complex plot interrupted to come up here and take on this assignment. Mr. Niger, there's nothing I can do but accept your dictum for now, but I promise you I, personally, am going to follow this up and find out how such a 'mistake' was made."

"As you wish, Mr. Glenn," replied Niger coolly, stroking the cat on his lap. Imhotep bent a yellow gaze unwinkingly on Adrian. "But you may be getting into something beyond your depth."

*   *   *

The mansion and its surrounding estate of huge trees were on one side of a valley, the slope behind them steep, rocky, and cedar-clothed. The village of Whiplash, a bit farther down, straddled a wide creek. Adrian drove back to the Cedar Rock Inn, determined not to let this business go by default. Remembering that odd ... voice or his own intuition? ... *He's lying, Mr. Glenn*, he was convinced Niger was out to cheat him, for some reason, out of the advance for which Westerbrook had contracted.

Westerbrook had made the deal with a *Miss Colfax*—and why had young Donna Colfax never said a word during the entire interview? Deaf and dumb? No, maybe Donna Colfax had some impediment preventing her from speaking, but there was nothing wrong with her hearing. Adrian had seen in those anxious eyes that she understood every word spoken between him and Niger.

"There's something wrong here, Thomas," he said to his cat, and telephoned Berman Westerbrook.

"What the hell? *I* don't know what it's all about," said Berman, too distressed to adopt his English accent, when Adrian related his conversation to the agent. "It was Miss Donna Colfax herself who got in touch with *me* about doing the family history—or she said that was who she was. I don't know anything at all about this Niger guy. He wasn't mentioned."

"Did you meet Miss Colfax?" asked Adrian. "I mean, from the way you talked I thought of her as an elderly lady, but the woman Niger introduced as Donna Colfax is no older than I am."

"I sure got the impression from her voice she was an older woman," said Berman. "But, as I say, I just talked to her on the phone and accepted the whole business on good faith. I do have a signed contract and the advance or I wouldn't have told you to go ahead with it. If her signature's forged, though, there's no way we can hold the Colfax family accountable."

"Maybe you did make the deal with the older Miss Colfax," suggested Adrian. "Niger said there was an older lady, also named Donna Colfax, but she died recently."

"She'd have had to die damn recently to have agreed to this venture before she did," said Berman. "I worked it out with her no more than a week ago, right after I cleared it with you, and got the contract back in the mail two days later. The only thing I can recommend, Adrian, is that you pack up and go home, get to work on your novel, and I'll do what I can to find out what happened."

As disappointing as it was, that sounded like reasonable advice to Adrian. It was already afternoon, he'd had no lunch, and he decided to pack this evening, stay in the village overnight, and head for home in the morning.

However, about four in the afternoon he was notified by the desk at the Cedar Rock Inn that a messenger was there with a package for him. Curious, Adrian went downstairs.

The "package" was a large bouquet of lavender dahlias. A note, in an envelope, was attached to it.

"Mr. Glenn, I am an admirer of your writing," the note read. "Please consider these flowers a token of my appreciation of your book, *John's Case*."

It was signed "Donna Colfax."

Puzzled, Adrian questioned the messenger, a youth with long, unruly hair. The boy explained he was one of the gardening staff at Nine Tales, Miss Colfax had been in the garden that afternoon as she often was, and she had picked the bouquet, scribbled the accompanying note, and sent him into town to find Mr. Glenn.

Well. Adrian took the flowers back upstairs to his room, acquiring a vase for them from the desk clerk. What the heck? A bouquet, when she hadn't spoken a word to him? And dahlias? Who ever heard of sending a bouquet of *dahlias* to somebody?

Adrian's writer's brain began to manufacture theories. Maybe, unable to speak for some reason, she chose this means of communicating. Communicating what? But if she wanted to express admiration for his writing (a rare enough tribute, for him) why hadn't she brought out one of his books for an autograph while he was out there, or something like that?

But wait. *John's Case*? She mentioned that particular novel. Why that one, specifically?

Oh! *John's Case*, a book of his published about three years earlier, was a murder mystery and the solution had revolved around the detective understanding, as others did not, a message in the traditional *language of flowers*. Dahlias! In that language dahlias meant "treachery, deception!"

Maybe, as in the case of his character in *John's Case,* Donna Colfax would be in danger if she sent him an open message, so she chose this code which would not be suspected by the one she feared. Treachery ... deception. She must be telling him that fellow Clifton Niger was trying to pull something up there at Nine Tales.

Adrian made up his mind on the moment. He was *not* going to give up and go home.

"Hotshot," he said to the somnolent Thomas, "there's something funny going on out at that place and I'm going to find out what it is. I'm not letting that jerk Niger cheat me out of the best advance I've ever been offered."

Thomas expressed total disinterest in the matter. He was aroused enough by his master's attention to yawn and stretch, then he collapsed comfortably against Adrian's leg and gave himself up to purring.

"You're no help, you damn cat," said Adrian disgustedly, and phoned Westerbrook again.

"What is it now?" demanded Berman somewhat crossly. "Look, I haven't had time to check into the situation, Adrian."

"I've got a question for you, Berman," said Adrian. "Do you suppose that publisher would still be interested in the Colfax family history if I do it on my own, without the coöperation of the family?"

"Probably not," replied Berman promptly. "I think the publisher was interested only because Miss Colfax was going to underwrite it. Hell, Adrian, you know there's no market for stuff like family histories! They're basically vanity publications, and *you* sure aren't in any position to finance a publishing project that doesn't have anything to do with you."

"Well, okay. I was afraid of that. But I've decided to stick around here in Whiplash for a while and look into this Colfax family history on my own, anyhow. You never know, I may come up with something spectacular—and salable."

"You're more likely to come up with a total waste of time. What about that novel?" demanded Berman with a touch of anguish in his tone. "At least it has some possibilities and I was hoping to get it from you in a couple of months."

"The damn novel can wait, for a while anyhow," replied Adrian firmly.

"Oh, for Christ's sake! What makes you so determined to follow up on this thing, Adrian?"

Adrian looked over at Thomas, whose lazy self-indulgence had been disturbed by his resort to the telephone. The big gray cat had jumped up on the table and was sniffing at the lavender dahlias in the vase. He turned a green gaze on Adrian and in it Adrian detected a spark of something . . . something strange.

"Dahlias," Adrian replied. "And my cat."

Adrian awoke in the middle of the night to the conviction of a presence in his room. It took him a moment to come fully awake but then he was overwhelmed by a sense of evil pervading the dark hotel room. Evil . . . and danger.

He sat up in bed and reached for the bedside lamp. He pressed the switch. Nothing happened. The room remained dark.

"Damn!" he muttered. "The damn bulb's out."

He looked around the room, straining his eyes in the faint light coming through the window from the street. He did not see Thomas, who had been curled up near his shoulder when he went to sleep. But a faint movement atop the counterpane at the foot of the bed caught his eye.

Electric prickles racing through him, Adrian pulled up his feet in fright. There was a little dark spot down there on the counterpane, moving. A mouse? But whatever it was it exuded a frightening aura of menace—and it began moving upward toward him, crawling, scrabbling.

All at once a shadowy streak arced through the air and out of the dimness. Thomas landed on the little dark spot like the predator he was. There was a flare of sparks, Thomas yowled and recoiled straight up, landing again with a plump. But the little dark spot had vanished and the atmosphere of the room was suddenly clear again.

The bedside lamp came on abruptly and Adrian was staring down at Thomas, his fur fluffed, his claws dug into the bedclothes where the little dark spot had been. Thomas returned his stare with green eyes in which the excitement of the hunt still flickered.

"What the hell?" Adrian demanded.

Thomas relaxed, his fur smoothing, and padded up to Adrian, beginning to purr. Adrian cautiously stretched out under the covers again and Thomas curled again near his shoulder. After a while, Adrian went back to sleep.

His last thought before he drifted into slumber was of Niger and Imhotep's yellow eyes.

Researching local history in a strange place was no problem for Adrian. He had written enough articles on local legends to know exactly how to go about finding his sources of information. Whiplash was much too small to have a library, but it had a tavern, there were some elderly residents still running their own shops, and there were churches, the minister of one of them a lifelong fixture in the place.

Thus it took him no more than a day of poking around to determine that the person he should talk to was old Mrs. Belinda Jimison. She lived in a small white house across Potter's Creek from the inn.

"Of course there's something wrong about the whole thing!" said Mrs. Jimison positively as soon as Adrian told her of the nature of his mission to Nine Tales and the blank wall he'd run into. "I've known Donna Colfax all my life—casually, you understand, because we're not of the same social level—and if she died *I* never heard anything about it. Besides, she is and always has been *Miss* Colfax. So how could she have a daughter, young man?"

"I don't *think* I misunderstood Niger," said Adrian. "But maybe he meant she's Miss Colfax's niece, as he's her nephew."

"Well, I never heard of him, either." Mrs. Jimison was a spare, energetic, gray-haired lady with remarkably unwrinkled features and faded blue eyes. The parlor of her little house was simple but neat as a pin. "I wonder ... could we be having a return of the conditions of the late 1930s?"

Adrian blinked.

"I don't understand what you mean," he admitted.

"Of course you don't. But I've lived here in the Valley of Nine Tales all my life and I remember. Mr. Glenn, dark clouds veiled that old house on the hill in 1914 and again in the late 1930s. It was as though a storm were coming up, there and there alone, but in reality storm clouds were gathering all over the world. And now look what's happening again in that place over there where the Great War began, Sarajevo. Will you join me at tea?"

"I beg your pardon?" Adrian was thrown off balance by the sudden change of direction.

"My family, like Donna Colfax's, was English and I was reared to the institution of afternoon tea," she explained with a faint chuckle. "The water's hot and I have some very nice cakes today. We can talk so much more informally over tea."

Adrian accepted, and when Mrs. Jimison had brought in the service and poured the tea she settled herself comfortably in a wicker-backed chair and asked, "Has anyone told you yet why Nine Tales has its name?"

"No, ma'am. You're the first person here I've had an opportunity to talk to about the family."

"Good. It's better not to go to inferior sources first. The name is a pun, of course—the cat-o'-nine-tails was a whip used for discipline on the old sailing vessels—but it refers to the numerous stories the villagers have always liked to spread about the Colfax house and estate. And all of these stories coalesce around one long-standing legend."

"And what legend is that?" asked Adrian. The tea was fragrant, of a flavor unfamiliar to him, and the cakes were crisp and tasty.

Mrs. Jimison's smile at him was a strange one.

"Now you're going to have to suspend your disbelief for a time if you're going to deal with rural tradition, Mr. Glenn," she warned. "You may have noticed that the house, Nine Tales, and the village are in a valley. From Indian times this valley has been reputed to be a gateway for ... well, 'forces,' and a medicine lodge once stood where the mansion is now. The Colfax family has served as guardian of this gateway, assuring that only benevolent forces come through and keeping out the forces of evil that also exist beyond it."

"Oh?" Adrian obeyed her admonition, suspending disbelief for the sake of discussion. "And how has that been done? By ritual or something?"

"Never you mind," said Mrs. Jimison. "The important point is that Miss Colfax contacted you about writing a 'family history,' meaning, I assume, making public some of the legend of the gateway. But this man Niger was telling you the truth when he said Miss Colfax would never reveal the secret history of the Colfax family ... *unless* she was confronted by an emergency, the balance of the gateway was endangered, and she needed to put out a call for help."

Adrian's mind went back to the bouquet of dahlias he had received.

"I can't see how getting her family history published would help her in that," he said. "Or why she'd pick me, particularly, for the job of writing it. I'm basically a novelist and fiction writer."

"You asked something earlier about 'ritual,' which means you have some common misconceptions," said Mrs. Jimison. "Things like the affairs of Nine Tales aren't dealt with so directly. I do know from one of the longtime servants at Nine Tales that some time ago Miss Colfax is supposed to have sent out a call for a long-lost nephew. Not by letter, or advertisement—or ritual, either."

"Niger implied he's her nephew," said Adrian. "That is, he said this young woman Donna Colfax is his cousin and he identified her as Miss Colfax's daughter."

"I told you, Donna Colfax couldn't possibly have a daughter. I don't know if this Niger fellow is a nephew or not, but if he is he's the wrong one and she was fooled by ... didn't you say he has a cat?"

"Yes, ma'am. Abyssinian. Purebred, I suppose."

"That should have told her something," said Mrs. Jimison with some asperity. "The Abyssinian is a gentle, lovable cat, but it goes back to ancient Egypt, when all kinds of wicked creatures were aboard. Pyramids! Humbug!"

Adrian finished his tea and, without asking, Mrs. Jimison replenished his cup.

"Well," he said dubiously, "my agent's right that if I go ahead with researching and writing this Colfax family history it's pretty sure to be a bust financially. But I wonder if you've been telling me going ahead with it on my own would help Miss Colfax in ... in whatever she's trying to do."

She shook her head.

"I told you, these things are done indirectly," she said. "If you had seen Miss Colfax herself—and I wonder if these two wicked young people are holding her incommunicado somewhere in her own home—she might not have wanted you to write and publish the family history at all. Something else entirely, I'd guess. In any event, since you can't contact her, there's nothing you can do to block Niger in whatever scheme he has in mind. If he's working through that Abyssinian, you'd have to work through an alliance with a cat for that."

"Well, I don't know about an 'alliance,'" said Adrian, "but I do own a cat. A common, ordinary tomcat."

Mrs. Jimison's face brightened.

"Ah," she murmured, "Donna knew what she was doing after all. Let me correct you, Mr. Glenn. You don't own a cat. Nobody does. If you have a cat in your household, it's the cat who owns you."

Adrian laughed.

"So I've heard, often," he said. "But, since it seems I qualify on that ground, I have to plead total ignorance of any magic, or whatever it is you're saying one does with cats. I do have Thomas and he's here with me, back at the hotel, probably cussing me thoroughly for leaving him there alone all day. But I don't have the slightest idea what I should do to 'use' him."

"I'm not the one to consult about the nature of your cat, Mr. Glenn. For that you need to talk to Homer Ruben. He's an old man who lives in a little house on the other side of Favian's Drug Store. Tell him I sent you to him."

Homer Ruben showed no interest whatsoever in Adrian's theory that Niger and possibly the young Donna Colfax had moved in on the "real" Miss Colfax and blocked Adrian from writing her family history, nor yet in Mrs. Jimison's legend about Nine Tales being some kind of magical gateway that might even influence the course of world affairs. A wrinkled old man with sparse gray hair, bad teeth, and a wart on his forehead, he appeared concerned only with some abstract theory of his own about cats. He reminded Adrian of one of those atomic scientists who ignores the likelihood his researches will result in destructive weapons, caring only that they bear out his hypotheses as to the nature of the atom.

"So Belinda Jimison thought you ought to talk to me,

did she?" he asked, leaning on his hoe. Adrian had caught him weeding his garden. "Dunno why if you don't write books about cats, just them story things. Say you got a cat? How do you and your cat get along?"

"Why, he's my buddy," replied Adrian, surprised. "Independent-minded like all cats, of course. Now and then I catch him looking at me like he thinks I don't have good sense. But he likes to sleep with me and sits on my shoulder when I'm writing sometimes. My agent calls him my 'familiar.'"

"Witch-type, is that what you're sayin'? I've heard that kind of talk. Folk have the wrong idea on cats as 'familiars.' They think the witch uses the cat for doing magic. It's pretty much the other way around, I'd say."

"I don't get your meaning."

Whereupon the most remarkable change came over Homer, his vocabulary, the way he came across. From the moment he used the word "analogy" he seemed more akin to that atomic scientist to whom Adrian had compared him than an elderly villager tilling his garden.

"I'll give you an analogy, young fellow," said Homer. "Let's say a bunch of people travels to one of these here space planets they want to settle on, but when they get there they find there's already some of them alien critters living there who're just as smart as the folks. What's more, they've got limbs and abilities to do things on that planet, the way it's set up, like human folks can't. But the people that went there from this Earth have a couple of advantages: the alien critters don't know how smart we really are, for one thing, and for the other we know how to control the way they think and act without them realizing it. You see what happens? We sidle our way into their thinking and manage them to doing things *we* want done, while they're thinking all the time we're just their pets."

As though he'd said the last word on it, he went back to his hoeing.

"Oh," said Adrian thoughtfully. Then he chuckled. "You mean those critters who've been disembarking from flying saucers weren't little green men at all, they were cats?"

"I don't mean any such of a fool thing," replied Homer severely. "I mean things ain't always what they look to be."

"Well, look," said Adrian, crestfallen, "the reason I came

over to talk to you was that Mrs. Jimison seemed to think I might be in a position to help correct whatever she implies has gone wrong up at Nine Tales. Since I do own a cat—or, as both of you put it in different ways, I'm owned by a cat—she suggested I talk to you. What you've been telling me is an interesting theory, if that's what it is, but it doesn't tell me a thing about how to do *that*."

"You going to stick your nose into that, are you?" asked Homer. "You goin' up there?"

"Like I said, if you've been paying attention, I've already been up there once," said Adrian impatiently. "That's how I got the idea something's wrong. I hadn't thought about it but, yes, I suppose I will go back up there if I can do any good by it."

"That young fellow who moved in on Miss Donna's got a cat," said Homer positively. "Hasn't he?" Adrian hadn't told him about Niger and Imhotep.

"Yes, an Abyssinian."

"You do know something about cats, anyhow," said Homer approvingly. He attacked a weed with the hoe as though it were a personal enemy. "Tell you something, young fellow. He's got a cat and he's settled in there. If you go back up, you ain't going to do no good without you have your cat with you."

"Well," said Adrian, "Thomas isn't some fancy purebred. He's just what folks call an alley cat."

"He's a cat, ain't he? And if he's been with you a while, you got to figure the way you think and act about things fits in with the way he'd want them."

Adrian chose to leave the Volkswagon at the Cedar Rock Inn and walk up the hill on his return to Nine Tales. It wasn't a long walk and he preferred to approach the place undetected, in case he wanted to prowl around a bit. He considered taking Thomas on a leash, as he did sometimes when he took the cat into town with him, but decided instead to carry Thomas in his arms. Thomas didn't mind.

He wasn't sure what he was going to do when they reached Nine Tales. Slip into the house and spy around? He didn't know. He entertained some vague idea the elder Miss Colfax might be confined somewhere within its walls and perhaps he could find her and talk to her.

They were making their way carefully through the towering trees toward the brownstone house when a heavy weight landed on Adrian's shoulders from behind, staggering him. He dropped Thomas who, roused from a doze, twisted and landed on his feet.

Adrian tried frantically to dislodge the animal from his back but it clung, its claws sinking in. It was the Siamese! He knew that. The slender cats were traditionally "guard dogs" for the kings of Siam, notorious for leaping on intruders' backs from high places. Adrian cringed, expecting at any moment to feel the cat's teeth clamping into the back of his neck, but the bite did not come.

Thomas, dislodged, trotted busily around to investigate the attacker clinging to his master's back. Thomas growled, rearing up to place his own forepaws on the back of Adrian's leg . . . and the Siamese let go and dropped lightly to the ground behind him.

With a muttered oath Adrian turned to find the two cats standing face-to-face, their noses together. His shoulders still stinging from the claws of the Siamese (what had the butler said its name was? Margravine?) he braced himself to intervene in a cat fight.

Then he realized: Margravine was a female. She evidently wasn't in heat but was at a stage where Thomas was not in the mood to attack, as he would with another male. The cats sniffed at each other for a moment, then Margravine turned and raced into the woods.

Thomas started after her at a fast lope, but at Adrian's sharp command the cat stopped and returned to him—somewhat to Adrian's surprise, for Thomas had a mind of his own.

He picked the gray tomcat up in his arms and proceeded cautiously in the direction of the house. As he came out of the woods in sight of it he saw Margravine again, perched on a stone wall some distance from the house itself. Donna Colfax arose from behind the wall, looking across it in his direction.

He had been spotted despite all his care. With a shrug, he went up to the young woman on the other side of the wall. She was in a flower garden, in which she apparently had been working, and behind her was a summer house, with a path leading away to the mansion of Nine Tales.

"Mr. Glenn," she greeted him. "You have a cat! I chose right after all!"

She *could* talk! Why had she said nothing before? She put her hand on Margravine to stroke the Siamese gently, then stooped and came up to hand him a pink geranium she had plucked.

Geranium . . . *John's Case*. In the language of flowers an oak-leaved geranium meant friendship. Adrian decided to take the bull by the horns.

"Miss Colfax, I hope I'm not speaking out of turn, but I'm not satisfied with what I've found here at Nine Tales," he said. "And I don't like your cousin, Mr. Niger. Did or didn't you—or your aunt or whoever the other Miss Colfax is—contract with my agent for me to write a Colfax family history?"

"Clifton Niger is not my cousin, Mr. Glenn," she said. "And there is no other Miss Colfax."

"Niger told the truth about that, then? She did die?"

"No," said Donna Colfax. The one word. Adrian studied her face quizzically. The light was not dim, it was full sunlight, but her features seemed to flicker, uncertain in form, as in a vague twilight. Adrian blinked.

"The book," he said. "Miss Colfax, *somebody* contracted with my agent for me to research and write a history of the Colfax family and Nine Tales. Was it you?"

"I'm still under restraint," she replied obscurely. "But writing something like that's not important, Mr. Glenn. What's important is that I asked for a nephew I wasn't even sure existed—a nephew with a cat."

That twist of the conversation baffled Adrian.

"Berman didn't say anything about a nephew," he said. "I remember Mrs. Jimison did. But I could hardly be your nephew, though I don't know much about my parents' families—you and I are about the same age, I'd say. What was your nephew supposed to do if you found him?"

"Not write a family history," said Donna Colfax. "Your cat, Mr. Glenn. Margravine's not strong enough alone. When you came here today, were you planning to talk with Clifton?"

"To tell you the truth, I don't really know what I planned when I decided to come back here. Just look around and see what I could find out, I suppose. Do you think I *ought* to talk with Niger?''

"That has to be your decision," she said. "If you do, take your cat."

With a pleasant smile of farewell she turned and went into the summer house. Margravine leapt off the wall and followed her.

Well, had he had it in mind to go into the house and confront Niger, or not? He hadn't really thought about it one way or another, but the idea had its appeal. He certainly wasn't afraid of the dark young man and he could think of some choice things to say to Niger about this business of intervening in his legitimate contract to write the Colfax family history.

Where did Niger come in on this, anyhow? Donna said he wasn't her cousin, as he claimed to be. And he couldn't be her mysterious "nephew," any more than Adrian could be. He must be some interloper who had moved in on this young woman and taken over control of Nine Tales—and somehow of her, too, and of her behavior.

And what did cats have to do with it? Her Siamese, his Abyssinian? And, the way she talked, Thomas?

He did take her advice and carried Thomas under his arm when he went around to the front door and was admitted by the butler. There was hardly any alternative—he couldn't just leave Thomas outside to wander around the grounds.

He was escorted to the same drawing room and sat down on a settee, holding Thomas on his lap. Presently Niger entered. He stood for a moment in the doorway, looking at Adrian without speaking, and Adrian thought a look of concern crossed his face as he caught sight of Thomas. Then he came on in and took a seat in a chair facing Adrian.

"Well, Mr. Glenn," he said. "Back again? I've been in touch with your agent, Mr. Westerbrook, but we haven't reached an agreement yet on restitution for your trouble. He seems to think there should be some kind of default payment in addition to expenses."

"After all, fifteen percent of the advance agreed on would be a substantial fee for him," Adrian pointed out, feeling his way. "I'm less interested in that than I am in knowing what the hell's going on here, Mr. Niger."

Niger hadn't called in any way Adrian could determine, but the Abyssinian cat, Imhotep, stalked into the room and jumped into Niger's lap. Thomas, on Adrian's lap, raised his head and turned green eyes on the newcomer.

Right behind Imhotep came Donna Colfax with Margravine in her arms. Quietly, she took a seat on the other side of the room.

Niger put both hands on Imhotep, not stroking him but clutching him firmly.

"I think we've had quite enough of this, Mr. Glenn," said Niger sharply. "I explained to you that a mistake was made about your writing a book about Nine Tales and I've offered compensation. But you've lingered around here, obviously in a mood to cause trouble. The affairs of the Colfax family are none of your business, and I'd advise you to write it off, go back home, and resume whatever it is you do for a living."

As though to punctuate his words, Imhotep fixed a yellow stare on Adrian's face and said loudly, "Miau!"

That did it. With a growl, Thomas leapt from Adrian's lap and started across the floor toward Niger and Imhotep, his belly close to the floor, his fur fluffed out, and his tail held straight behind him, its tip twitching ominously. Imhotep was another tomcat! And Thomas' intent was obvious.

For a moment his chosen adversary held firm, mouth wide, hissing. But when Thomas stopped no more than two feet from him and his master, crouching as though to spring, Imhotep broke. He vaulted from Niger's lap, raced across the room, and vanished through the open window.

At that Margravine took a hand. She came across the floor to Thomas' side, to stand with him glaring at Niger, both of them growling. Niger cringed.

"Mr. Niger," spoke up Donna Colfax, "your cat has abandoned you. I believe it would be wise of you to leave Nine Tales and go back where you came from. Now."

Niger did not answer. He arose from his chair and left the room, glancing apprehensively back over his shoulder at the two cats.

"Thank you, Mr. Glenn," said Donna. She approached to take the chair vacated by Niger and Adrian was astounded to see she was no longer the beautiful young woman he had met here first and with whom he had talked across the stone fence. She was elderly, at least sixty, her pleasant face framed in gray hair.

"Uh . . . Miss Colfax?" he asked doubtfully.

"Yes," she said, "I am Donna Colfax—the real Donna Colfax. The change in me was Clifton Niger's doing—for what purpose I don't know. I did contract with Mr. Westerbrook for you to write a family history, in desperation when it seemed my call for my nephew had failed. But it seems my call didn't fail. I think when we look into the records of both our families, Mr. Glenn, we'll find you really are my nephew."

"Well, if we're kinfolks," said the bemused Adrian, "maybe you don't mind telling me what this whole thing has been about."

"We'll have plenty of time for that," said Miss Colfax. "I'd like for you to be my guest for lunch here tomorrow. But if you talked with Mrs. Jimison, I think you've already guessed most of it."

She leaned forward to pet Thomas. He purred under her hand.

"Thank you, too, Thomas," she said. "I think you and Margravine are going to be very good friends as time goes on."

At her invitation Adrian had tea with her, then went back to the Cedar Rock Inn with Thomas. As soon as he reached his room he turned on the television set. He was curious to see what developments were occurring in Bosnia-Herzegovina.

PARTNERS
by P. M. Griffin

The change felt odd, as it always did, not painful but rather uncomfortable, psychologically more so than physically. It was a pushing and pulling all at the same time and then a tremendous squeezing sensation as his soul was once more inserted into a mortal shell.

His eyes opened. He found that he was now a much bigger cat with long legs and tail and muscles tempered by the demands of the hunt. He was also leaner than he could ideally be, and he was conscious of being very hungry. His gray coat, short as it was, did indeed have the potential for great beauty, but it was in a shocking state. More disturbing than the alteration in his appearance was the strangeness of his smell between the smoke and the lack of reproductive hormones. He had been permitted to enter this ninth and final incarnation as a fully grown young tom, but Bastet had insisted on sending him into it neutered, as if he were a strayed or abandoned pet.

That had been a blow, though he knew his prowess would be restored when he again returned to the Wide Realms at the close of this last mortal life. His name—his former name—was prominent in the best pedigrees. . . .

Well, he was no Persian now, just an ordinary cat of the city streets with an empty belly and fur not only filthy but badly scorched. His costume, the goddess had called it, was necessary to the realism of his role and to arouse immediate sympathy in the human whose life he was supposed to share. He was fortunate, he supposed, that she had not decided his hide should display some of the same damage, or he would have a deal more to endure than disgruntlement over lost powers and place.

The site to which they had come was decidedly unpromising, the yard of a three-story burned-out building. The fire that had done it was not long over. Everything was covered with ash and soot. Debris and dirty puddles littered the ground, and the reek of old smoke and burning filled the air.

His nose wrinkled in disgust as he looked around. *Where is my Partner?* There was no smell of a human in the immediate vicinity, or of any other living thing apart from some rank greenery that had survived the heat and trampling and a variety of insect types.

She will be here soon.

The exquisite platinum-furred divinity who ruled over all felinekind looked closely at her charge. *Firecat,* she said softly, *the decision is still yours. This human queen's soul is a match for yours, as close a match as I have ever seen between cat and one of her species. If you go with her, you will be happy for all your life, happy as you have never yet experienced and cannot begin to comprehend until you do, but there are uncertainties regarding this particular incarnation. It may pass as I wish and will for ye both, a long, thrice-blessed life together, but the moonbeams of the possibilities surrounding ye are complex and close set, and they shimmer about one another so rapidly that I cannot discern the pattern into which they will probably fall. It could too easily prove that this final life will be tragically short with an agonizing death at its close. I want to do well by you, little Firecat, and I cannot find it in my heart to order you into what might well prove a painful doom.*

No, he thought sourly, but she had pricked his curiosity and desire, and then she had laid it all before him to decide, thereby absolving herself of guilt, whatever happened as a result.

Reason demanded that he reject the whole ridiculous idea outright, of course. Suffering was definitely not his specialty, and he had no interest whatsoever in acquiring any expertise in the art, but Bastet had promised him Partnership.

His eyes closed. Partnership. How often had he wondered why no one would take so to him as he had sat in his stud cage or show cage and watched the bonding begin between mere pet-quality kittens and the humans coming to adopt them, when he had seen it in nearly every household pet and their inordinately proud companions sharing the show hall with him? He had enjoyed the finest care and won boundless admiration, but no one had ever loved him like that. In all his eight previous lives, not one being had ever needed him or his love.

I have chosen, Lady Bastet, he said firmly, serenely. *I agreed to accept what this life would hand me before you placed me in my new body.*

Well said, brave cat.... Your Partner has come. Go to her now with all my love and blessing, and may ye both follow the Plan to its ultimate end and joy.

Eva leaned against one of the remaining fence posts and craned her neck to study the gutted structure.

Fortunately, the building had been deserted, so no family was left desolate by its loss. More important still, no one had been seriously injured, not even the drifter whose carelessness had started the fire. He had been treated for smoke inhalation and released after Frank had dragged him out.

It had been quite a night, she thought wearily. This was her block, and she had turned out with the rest of the neighborhood to watch the blaze. It had been an exciting experience but also a terrifying one. It was the first time she had seen Frank and his comrades, all of whom she knew either in person or by repute, in action. The whole thing might have been routine for them, but her heart had not stopped hammering until she had done a nose count at the end of it all and assured herself that the entire fire company had come out of the inferno apparently intact. That had not left much of the night for sleeping.

The touch of soft fur against her ankle and a simultaneous demanding yowl brought her out of her reverie.

The woman looked down to meet a pair of bright green eyes in a pretty gray face. The cat twined himself around her legs, and she automatically knelt to stroke him. "Why, hello, little one. I haven't seen you around before."

The gray would have been a fine-looking animal had he been receiving proper care, but he showed all too clearly the lack of that. He was thin and dirty beyond his own ability to remedy, and the thick coat was horribly matted.

More than matted, she realized with an ugly jolt. Fire had done some of that damage. Even a couple of the long whiskers were curled and shortened.

"You poor baby! Are you hurt?" He did not act as if anything were wrong, but, according to Frank, cats are not malingerers. By the time they acted hurt or ill, the situation could already be desperate.

The gray suddenly climbed onto her lap, planting four grimy paws on her tan skirt. He rested his head on her arm, then, to her complete astonishment, he rose on his hind legs, put his front paws about her neck, and rubbed his cheek against hers, purring loudly all the while.

Eva's arms came around the incredibly friendly foundling. "All right, baby," she whispered. "Everything's going to be all right."

He let her pick him up and carry him to her car, which was, fortunately, close by. He trembled a little, and his eyes looked both huge and very round, but he did not otherwise display fear despite the terror he must have known and the strangeness of this experience. Eva talked softly to him, hoping to reassure him and keep him quiet. She did not need to have to manage feline hysterics while she was driving.

What next? The cat looked well enough, but a veterinarian should confirm that. No telling what damage the smoke and heat might have done to him, especially with this long delay before getting him to treatment.

The who and where were no problem. This was home territory, after all, and Frank's vet was close. It was late enough now that he would be open, and she could claim the case was at least a minor emergency to explain her lack of an appointment. She could arrange for a proper examination and shots once she was sure there was no immediate medical crisis.

Firecat—he was not surprised when his rescuer had given him the name Bastet had already put on him—found life in Eva's small apartment both pleasant and peaceful. The woman herself was a delightful attendant for a cat, and their relationship was the proving of everything he had ever heard said in praise of Partnership. He thrived on the love he received and returned it in full measure.

He was quick in recognizing Bastet's wisdom and consideration in sending him into this life already an adult. His Eva needed a cat companion, and a mature, stable being such as himself was far more suitable for the position than would be a fluff-brained kitten. The young of catkind were charming, but their high energy level could be trying to one seeking peace after a day's labor, be it what humans called work or a good, long hunt.

His Partner appreciated what she had in him. He was aware of her affection in their every interaction, from the kiss she planted on his head in the morning with the accompanying injunction to "be good and mind everything for her" to the eagerness with which she swept up his purring body into her arms upon her return and sat down to hold and stroke him with hands that seemed to have been created with the knowledge of how to please a cat. He did not find it demeaning or, Bastet forfend, canine to wait at the door for her. Love such as this deserved acknowledgment and its full reward.

When alone, he slept or made himself useful after the manner of his species. When Eva was present, he tried to remain near her while she was busy with various, mostly incomprehensible human tasks. They often played together as well, wrestling, chasing one another, or using the balls and other toys with which she showered him.

Firecat was grateful for her attention and the care she invariably exhibited to assure his welfare and contentment. In truth, he began to feel almost guilty. According to the Plan, cats and humans were to walk together through this realm they both shared, individuals of each species bonding together in a Partnership in which each member actively supported and helped the other. He had until now believed that his company, his presence alone, was a sufficient blessing to fulfill his part in any relationship with a human, but he had always been a fair-minded, honest feline, and he more and more frequently worried that he was simply not carrying his complete share. He wanted to be of real help to his human.

The apartment offered little scope for his talents, unfortunately. There were no mice or larger pests to hunt. Bugs, flying or crawling, were hardly more numerous, even now, at the height of the summer. Only the dust balls gave him any scope to display something of his hunting skills.

In truth, they did keep him moderately busy, and Firecat thought it was a good thing for Eva that he had come when he did. His arrival appeared to have coincided with an invasion of the pesky things. There had been very few at first, but soon, they were present in great profusion. The fluffy gray masses kept appearing, no matter what his Partner did to sweep or pick them up. He was forever chasing after one or another of them. Eva appreciated his efforts, too, and she actually called the fluffs "Firecat Tumbleweeds," doubtless to honor his diligence and skill in the chase.

All the same, they were no danger to person, stores, or nest, only annoying to the human and rather fun for him. He could not count his management of them as his proper share in the Plan as it devolved upon him. Had he not been able to render his Partner one really significant service, a service all the more gratifying because his success was in part the result of Eva's trust in him, he would have been seriously concerned about his performance of his duty.

As early as his first incarnation, Firecat had come to realize that humans have execrably poor judgment when it came to reading their own kind, particularly those of the opposite gender. Eva was better than most in that respect. Nearly all her friends were nice, mostly other queens like herself who spoke in pleasant, soft voices and made a great deal of fuss over him. Of the toms, his favorite was Frank-tom. This male visited often, usually asked for Firecat before anything else, and frequently brought the gentle little long hair whom he had called Sparkplug after finding her as a skinny kitten on top of a crate of the things when he had been fire inspecting a warehouse.

One night, however, Eva had put on some clothes much brighter than those she usually wore and left him alone in the apartment. When she returned, it was very late, or very early, rather, and she was in the company of a strange male. Firecat's ears did not go back, because he did not feel the newcomer was physically dangerous, but, though Justin-tom was far too big to be deposited in a litter box, that was clearly where he belonged. When he had sat down—in Frank-tom's chair—Firecat had stood by his feet and mimed his opinion of the newcomer.

Justin-tom apparently had no contact with cats and did not understand at all, but he could see by the shock and then the laughter in Eva's eyes that she fully comprehended his meaning. She had said nothing beyond the untruthful

statement that he expected a treat when she came in and
picked him up and carried him into the kitchen, where she
did, indeed, present him with a handful of his favorite
dry food.

She had whispered to him as well. "All right, Double
Trouble. You've made your point. Quite a few of my
friends claim they heartily regret not heeding their cats'
initial judgment of potential mates. I think I'll listen to you
before I wind up playing the fool. Justin's charming, but
he does come on awfully strong. I doubt either of us'll be
the better for seeing him again."

True to her word, Justin-tom faded into history, and the
summer continued its idyllic course. It was fiercely hot, but
there seemed to be no moisture in the air, and so the high
temperatures remained bearable. Firecat was fully accustomed to life in his apartment by then and would not have
elected to change it even to return to the joys of Bastet's
justly famed domain.

He was not given a choice about that. One evening, Eva
literally bounced into the room and swept him up for their
nightly cuddle.

"Tomorrow is August 1," she cooed, "and that, my rich-
est and rarest, my sweetest and fairest, means that we have
two glorious weeks to spend as we will!"

The cat squirmed, excited by her excitement, and she put
him down. "We're going to pass them all by ourselves in a
rustic cabin out in the woods by a lovely little river."

Even as she was speaking, Eva was pulling things from
her single clothes closet and the wardrobe that augmented
it. The cabin was her Uncle John's, and "rustic" was a
rather kindly description of it. A full bathroom containing
a washing machine did fill one corner of what was otherwise a single room, for John did not like the idea of pollut-
ing the surrounding woods or waterway with soap residue
or human waste, and there was a large gas-powered refrigerator, but he had put in no heat, no telephone, and no
electricity. There was also no stove; cooking had to be done
on the open fire or on portable facilities brought for the
purpose. Some of the family claimed he had arranged it
like that to keep everyone away, an accusation she privately
could not entirely discount. John was a somewhat eccentric,

quiet-living bachelor who disliked crowds and fuss. She had always enjoyed a good rapport with him, however, perhaps because she herself had been quiet and reserved even as a child and because she was willing to accept both the cottage and the neighboring wildlands on the same terms as he did. She did not mind enduring the inconveniences of the place for the privilege of enjoying the lovely site and for the pleasure of being able to use it to slip away for a time from the bustle of work and city life in general.

Initially, Eva had planned to have Frank cat-sit for her, a service she had provided for him often enough, but she'd soon changed her mind. Her misery over the idea of leaving Firecat behind had overshadowed her pleasure in the upcoming holiday. She loved that little gray ball of constantly shedding hair. He was fun to be with. He was beautiful as no creature of any other species could be. He was just plain nice. The cat welcomed her home each day, he loved her, and he gave her the priceless opportunity to love him in return and to care for him. She was not about to go off without him.

Firecat watched the ordered turmoil curiously, occasionally trying the softness of a pile of clothes or sizing the two half-packed carry-on bags by leaping into them, but, chiefly, he remained aloof. He did not care for all this confusion, temporary though it might be.

It did explain at last the craziness to which his affection for Eva had forced him to submit during these past several weeks. First, she had purchased a flea collar with a name tag attached to it and put it on him, then she had strapped him into a harness and accustomed him to walking with a leash—actually it was not too bad once one got used to it—despite his initial strong reservations. From the start, he had enjoyed riding around in his new car seat, which allowed him the option of napping or sightseeing as the humor moved him. They were apparently leaving the apartment for a while, going into the wide, not-always-friendly world beyond, and his Eva was doing what she could to keep him with her and safe. That realization sent a warm glow through him, and he felt glad now that he had not made a greater fuss about the leash. The least he could do was try to cooperate with her care.

*　　*　　*

It was officially morning but certainly not day when the pair set out in the car Eva had rented for the holiday. Four-wheel drive was a necessity to cover the last ten miles to the cabin and to function anywhere around it. Firecat was not at all certain that he liked being ousted from his comfortable bed and his domain at so unholy an hour, but the ever-changing sweep of scents and sights and sounds were intriguing, and he had to admit his Partner had provided comfortable traveling accomodations for him. Curiosity won out over annoyance before a battle even had time to develop between the two emotions.

It was a long drive. The city gave way to the more open and attractive suburbs and those to genuine farmlands, great, open fields punctuated by lone houses and outbuildings and by the small communities servicing them.

Gradually, patches of trees began to appear, growing larger and handsomer the farther north they sped until at last, in late afternoon, only trees and the road on which they traveled remained.

Eva was frowning slightly. Something had seemed wrong to her for quite a while, and she suddenly realized what it was. She pulled to the side and got out as she had often done during the drive, either to get something to eat or to stretch her legs, but now she merely went a few feet into the treelands and knelt on the ground. She worked her fingers into the leaf litter and the soil below.

Moments later, she returned to the car. She sat there a while, stroking the purring gray. "Everything's as dry as old newspaper," she told him thoughtfully, with some concern. "That's why the leaves don't look as fresh as they should." The exceptionally dry weather and almost nonexistent humidity that had been such a delight in the city was something else here.

She had observed the signs of drought in the more open country to the south as well, she realized now, but grass burned brown was a familiar sight this time of year, and she had paid no heed to that, especially since irrigation was keeping the crops reassuringly green. With the trees, it was different. She had been coming here for enough years now that she was sensitive to what should be. The loss of briskness had touched off an alarm in her.

Firecat merely gave her a superior look and continued

purring. Humans! Here, he could smell growing things.
Every sniff told of birds and squirrels and other good, hunt-
able creatures instead of hordes of humanity, machine
stink, the rest of the foul reeks associated with the city. It
was just like these sometimes ridiculous beings to fret over
nothing and fail to enjoy or even notice the glory of the
present until it slipped by and was lost. Then they mourned
over it.

Minutes after she resumed driving, Eva pulled off the
well-maintained state road and entered upon the sorry
track leading to her uncle's place. Ten bone-jarring miles
later, she came to a stop in the little natural clearing where
it stood.

It was pretty. Every time she saw it, she thought that.
The small meadow was just enough above the river, stream
really, flowing beside it to be reasonably secure from the
occasional seasonal overflows. The forest swept around it,
sheltering and framing it. The trees marched down to the
very bank of the river opposite the clearing. The stream
itself was still more dramatic. A miniature cliff some thirty
feet high lying right athwart it, creating a waterfall that was
a never-ending delight.

The shingled building fit perfectly with its surroundings.
It was small and square with a high-pitched roof, a propor-
tionally tall chimney, and two windows balancing the single
door. Windows pierced the rear wall as well.

It took her another hour to get properly settled, for Eva
never let necessary tasks wait while she indulged in
pleasures.

The unpacking and storing turned out to be an adventure
in itself on this occasion. Firecat seemed to have cloned
himself into a dozen cats, and there was nothing she did, no
cubbyhole she opened, that did not receive his fascinated
attention. The woman dared not shut any chest or cabinet
again without first confirming his whereabouts, and it
seemed for a while that she could not turn around without
exposing a new potential hazard which had to be countered.

Despite all her care, a few incidents did occur. Eva was
just stowing the last of the canned goods she had brought
to sustain them when a metallic clattering issued from what
she had believed was the safely closed storage closet.

Hopping off the chair she had been using in lieu of a ladder, she ran to the place. It had no lock, and Firecat had apparently worked the door open with his supple claws. He was now busily engaged in hauling out a long, snakelike gray tube.

Her eyes widened. "Let that go, you tarred rogue! That's Uncle John's oxygen! He won't thank either of us if his emphysema kicks up and he finds the tubing full of little holes."

Hastily rescuing and testing the canister, she restored it to its place beside another like it and firmly shut the closet door once more. "Keep out of there, Double Trouble," she warned, "and keep away from that radio," she added, seeing where the cat's attention had shifted. "I'd feel like a failed citizen if I didn't hear the news once a day, small comfort though it is."

She swept him into her arms, then reached for the leash and cat carrier. "Come on, my Laddy-O. Let's go for a walk and see if we can't work some of that energy off before you get us both in extremely deep and uncomfortably warm water."

Once outside, she put Firecat down. He stretched in pure pleasure. This was glorious! The grass was high, a veritable jungle to him, like those his ancestors had once trodden. There were things to chase, intriguing, moving things, or there would be if his Partner did not insist on their keeping walking. As it was, serious hunting, any sort of hunting, would have to be postponed. He just might be able to slip outside later . . .

Eva, for her part, examined the area carefully. The vegetation was lusher and heavier here than it was farther in thanks to the nearby river, but even so, the choking grasp of the drought was apparent. The meadow probably seemed like a forest to Firecat, but it was nothing in either height or thickness of growth to the tangle she usually found upon her arrival, and everywhere, the trees told the same tale.

She sighed. "It's a cold meal for both of us tonight," she told her furred companion. "Tomorrow, we get a gas cooker from the general store. I may love cooking over the fire, but these woods're like tinder. One spark could send them up in smoke."

She scooped up the cat, who was making a far too determined examination of a particularly large and loud bumblebee, and dropped him into his carrier, which consisted of a pouch of heavy material tied around the woman's shoulders and carried against the front of her body.

Eva walked down to the river. The waterway, too, was feeling the lack of rain. It was low in its banks, probably no more than waist to chest deep in most places.

"Oh, look!" Her eyes had automatically traveled along the stream to the falls. There, the lessened flow revealed a dark opening behind the shimmering cascade. "A cave!"

She trotted over to it and found that she could just peer inside at a dark space about ten feet high and maybe about twice that in depth. Large stones, boulders, littered the pool flooring it, the tops of several of them projecting well above the surface of the water.

"They're like purposely laid stepping stones. See, cat, if I hop on this one and then that flat rock beyond it, we could go inside without so much as getting very damp. You wouldn't take a splash at all." Her eyes sparkled. "I'm going to give it a try, anyway, love.

"Get set!"

So saying, the woman hugged the carrier to her and jumped, first to one stone, then to the next. Yet another leap brought her into the erstwhile hidden cave behind the falls.

Firecat shook his head disapprovingly. Eva had miscalculated the amount of water that would reach him, and there was far too much of the element about for him to have a very high opinion of the place, but his Partner seemed quite delighted with it. She perched upon the nearly flat-topped boulder and laughed. "I could be a mermaid sitting here and combing my long, yellow hair. Except, of course, that I don't have long, yellow hair. I don't even have long hair."

To the cat's disgust, she spent several more minutes looking around, then she regretfully made the unpleasant return—though she apparently enjoyed even that part of it.

"Well, how was that, little friend?" she asked when they were on real ground once more. "I'll have to write Uncle John about this." She glanced at the sky. "It's starting to get dark. I don't know about you, but I'm beat. What say we bed down early tonight and continue our explorations bright and early tomorrow?''

Eva rapidly fell into the sleep of the tired and the just. So did Firecat at first, but the night is a cat's time, and he had things to do. This interesting new realm had to be explored, and, unlike the apartment, there were small intruders to be removed before his Partner could be troubled by them.

For a good two hours, he enjoyed himself thoroughly, living as a cat on holiday should, but then, he began to grow uneasy.

Firecat leapt to one of the screened windows. He was not alone in that feeling. There seemed to be a lot of movement outside, unhappy, hasty movement, all of it in one direction.

There was noise, too, quite audible to his sensitive ears, and a smell.

He knew, then, and he whimpered. Of course, he recognized it. All wild things did, and cats are essentially wild in their souls. This was older than humans and their houses, older and stronger and very terrible for a small animal to have to face.

Eva would have to be warned. The frail senses of her species would never wake her in time. He would have to rouse her so she could run, or maybe drive away. She would probably forget him in her fear. He knew he must resign himself to that and tried to do so. If only she would at least leave the cabin door open so he would be able to flee himself . . .

He leapt up on the bed, crying the call the most subtly vocal of his kind had used from time immemorial when faced with this dire threat. He caught Eva's hair in his mouth and pulled hard.

The woman awoke. At first, she lay where she was, feeling as if her mind was stuffed with wool, but then she sat bolt upright. Firecat! Was he ill? Hurt? She had never heard a sound like this in her whole life. It was more like the wailing of a child than an animal . . .

In the darkness of that cabin, the color drained from Eva's face. No, she had not heard its like, but Frank had, and he had shown her printed testimony of other firemen who had as well, from cats trapped and threatened by a major fire.

She made herself draw a deep breath and think clearly. Everything was quiet, at peace. She had time, some time, at least. She pulled on her boots, then slipped the cat carrier over her arms and shoulders and stuffed the nearly rigid gray into it. "Sorry, old fellow, but we might have to move fast later. I don't want to have to hunt you up if we do."

The woman went to the window. Everything seemed dark and still.

Dark, but not quiet, not entirely. There was almost no wind at the moment here at ground level, but she could hear it whistling far above. Not whistling. Screaming. Her eyes closed. There were probably a number of possible causes for the phenomenon, but the one filling her thoughts now chilled her heart.

She ran to each of the rear windows, but the wall of trees blocked most of the sky save that patch directly above. No matter. She had her answer. They did not block the air, and she did not believe the smoky taint in it stemmed entirely from her imagination.

Almost in slow motion, she switched on the radio. Within seconds, her fears were confirmed. A crown fire, big, hot, and moving fast over a broad front, was racing almost right for her cabin. It had begun suddenly and had gotten a good start before its discovery. Fed by tinder-dry fuel and fanned by a high breeze, it had soon swept completely out of control, transforming in less than two hours from a savage fire into the awesome and too rightly dreaded fury of a full fire storm.

Eva's head snapped toward the back windows. She could hear it already, she thought, a distant howling roar like the scream of the damned issuing from some impossibly distant hell.

She made herself concentrate, plan. If she did not, they were both dead. Perhaps they were dead anyway, but if there was a chance, she wanted to find and at least try to take hold of it.

The car was out. It could not cross the river, and the fire was sweeping up along the road. She could not plough through it, and to think of trying to outflank it by fleeing

parallel to it was equally ludicrous at this stage. It was
much too late for that. An escape on foot, even following
the river, was not worth considering. There was not a sufficient volume of water to shield her from what she feared
was approaching when it finally, inevitably overtook her,
even should she be able to remain beneath its surface in-
definitely. That she could not do in any event, and one
could not come up to breathe superheated air and survive.

They still had a hope, or the ghost of a hope. Eva took
her backpack and began sweeping things into it, cans of
food that they both would be able to use, a couple of can-
teens of water, her medical kit. The obligatory compass,
knife, hatchet, and even maps were already inside. She also
looped the light blanket from the foot of her bed into the
carrying straps. Lastly, she put on her jacket, a cap of
John's, and her work gloves. The additional clothing would
guard her from scrapes and from small flying debris and
sparks. It might be a while before they connected with rescuers once this was all over. They would be in no danger
of becoming lost and perishing of want, certainly, not with
both the river and the road to guide them out, but it was
not a bad idea to plan for their comfort and well-being in
the interim.

There was nothing more she could think to do, apart
from disconnecting the gas tank, which she quickly did. The
woman stood still in the middle of the cabin, hugging Firecat to her. He looked up into her face with enormous,
round eyes. He was controlled, praise heaven, perhaps reassured a bit by her relative calm, but she could feel the
trembling of his little body, the racing of his heart. "I'll do
the best I can, baby," she whispered. "You gave us the
chance. Now, I'll try to carry my part." Maybe she could
shield him, even if she did not make it herself. . . .

Eva swallowed hard and forced her mind onto a more
useful track.

What next? The fire was still not in sight. It might bypass
the cabin altogether.

The human shook her head. Such saves did happen now
and then, she supposed, but only a fool would depend on
one of them. There also might be precious little time in
which to act once the conflagration did make itself apparent. Such blazes could move fast, she knew, almost incon-

ceivably fast at times. It would be best to go now. Better spend an uncomfortable night than die.

She looked around to see if there was anything she might have forgotten. A new thought, a new terror, struck her, and she took the oxygen tanks from the closet, hefting one under each arm. There was danger in bringing them but maybe a lot more in letting them stay behind.

She left the cabin, locking the door after herself, although she knew that to be a totally superfluous precaution.

Firecat meowed sharply. She looked at him, then around her. "You're right, little friend. We don't have all that much more time after all." The open sky showed what the tiny views of it visible through the windows could not. An orange-red tinge tainted all of it, seeming to grow stronger with every second. There was sound, too, the soughing of high wind well above her, and behind, maybe far, though she could not judge that with any degree of certainty, an infernal crackling roar.

Eva did not run—the ground looked strange in the night, and she did not dare risk a fall—but she hurried as rapidly as she dared to the riverbank and then to the falls. Moments later, she was inside the cave.

Firecat whimpered, aloud and more painfully still in heart. What was she doing? They should be fleeing, as the wild things of the place had already done. Even now, with all this delaying, it might be too late. It might have been too late from the start. This was probably the fate, the death, Bastet had predicted for him. . . .

The woman lowered herself onto the flat rock on which she had sat during their first visit and set the cylinders down beside her, near at hand whether she wanted to use them or toss them and their violently flammable contents into the water. She held her cat close and waited, trying for his sake to keep her fear in check.

She could see a little through the place where they had entered.

Something bright hit the water, sizzled. Another. Firebrands! The main conflagration was sending outriders before it.

Her grasp tightened. A scarlet tongue leaped up in the grass of the meadow. Within moments, it doubled in size as it battened on the dry vegetation.

The minutes went by, fearful minutes. The cabin, everything in the clearing, was ablaze, but they were safe. Even the smoke was not too unbearable.

It was then that horror closed Eva's throat. What she had seen thus far was not terrible. It was a big and dangerous fire. The nightmare was now upon them.

She heard it first, fire whose scream was the fury of hell itself and the screech of the wind driving before it, a near-hurricane born of the vast energy of the blazing storm, then the forest behind the burning clearing literally exploded into light and flame.

Fire storm. She had read about this force, horrifying descriptions of its effects recorded well after the fact. Few who encountered its raw rage firsthand survived to recount their adventure.

Almost nothing in its path could withstand its passing.

The force, the utter power, of this thing was almost beyond comprehension, although its genesis was understood well enough. Given the right combination of strong winds and ample fuel, a huge, violent wildfire could with dreadful suddenness transform into the fury bearing down on the clearing, tearing through forests as readily as a smaller blaze would through dry hay, sucking up ever more fuel and ever more air, feeding upon itself and driving itself until it was a vortex of flame and superheated air that paled the fury of either hurricane or volcano.

It was a twin horror, for the gale engendered in that raging furnace was a lash capable of shattering nearly anything attempting to resist its wrath, an invisible battering ram that snapped trees, entire stands of them, as if they were twigs.

The heat of the megastorm was intense. Trees incinerated almost upon contact. Bridges, modern, well-built bridges, collapsed, not merely because timbers burned but because the steel beams and plates covering and supporting them softened and twisted; it required temperatures in excess of 1,200 degrees to affect the metal so.

Tears filled her eyes. What cruel insanity had made her imagine a woman and a cat could come through all that?

Firecat looked up at her. His tongue rasped against her cheek. Eva had done well. He wanted to tell her that. Coming to the cave had been a smart idea after all. The fire

was staying outside, away from them, though it remained
a dire peril.

Love for his Partner swelled inside him. She had not
forgotten him. More than that, more than just bringing him
with her, she was protecting him and would go on trying
to protect him even if the fire came and she could do nothing to defend herself. He could feel that determination in
her. This final incarnation had been privileged, he thought,
whether he perished here or went on to remember this
night with pride and joy. Few cats indeed had companioned
with such a one as this.

Eva gazed into the frightened, trusting little face, and her
control almost shattered. She could not bear the thought
that so much innocence and so much love should be seared
out of existence.

There was nothing more she could do for him, for either
of them, except to physically shield him, fold herself as
much as possible around him, that and pray.

The human used her will to get a grip on herself. They
were not dead yet, and if her reasoning was in any way
accurate, they should come through this testing sound.
Trees died because they were fire's natural fuel. Bridges
died because they were high and received the full brunt of
the conflagration's ever-rising heat and rage. She and Firecat, on the other hand, were below, not above, it all,
screened by many feet of solid rock and good earth. The
water around them was moving fast, too, its coolness constantly replenished by fresh upstream sources. It should not
boil, and even if it did, they were not actually in it.

She turned her back to the waterfall and the slit of a
clear entrance and crouched as low as she could go to present as small a target as possible for any force sweeping in
from the hostile world beyond.

Firecat nestled against her. The danger was still out
there, growing stronger and more terrible with each fast-
flying moment. He knew that, but so did his Partner, and
Eva's fear was not that of panic, nor did she seem resigned
to death. As she had trusted him earlier, believed in the
truth of his warnings, so would he try to believe in her
now. Making the supreme effort, he forced himself to purr.

His human stroked his head, and her lips touched him
lightly between the ears. "We should be all right. You're a

survivor, my little friend, and you bought us the time we needed. I don't think we've wasted it."

His purring increased in strength. It was a fine thing to have Eva for a Partner. He hoped she was right, that they would live and be well and be allowed to continue walking together in the glory and happiness of the Plan for many good years to come.

It was a possibility, but the outcome still remained in question. The forest fire was upon the area in full force. Both sides of the small river were involved, and all beyond the cave was a chaos of noise and hideous light.

It did not breach their defense. The air was distinctly hot, but not dangerously so. The real heat, and with it the bulk of the smoke, was being swept up, sucked into the great swirling maw consuming the treetops far above.

The gray trembled then. There was no fire in their cave, but something was dreadfully wrong. He began to really panic, to struggle, for the first time. He could not breathe properly. He could not breathe at all! The air was being pulled away from him. Not only that, his throat and chest were starting to hurt, as if even the air inside his body was being taken away . . .

Eva flattened out on the rock and pulled the carrier up so that his head lay beside hers. She held a black, ugly, rubbery thing over their noses and mouths. There was a disturbing hiss and an unpleasant blowing that caused him to try to jerk away, but the carrier and her free hand restrained him. Then he found that he could breathe easily again.

They remained thus together, human and cat, face against face, sharing the life-giving stream of oxygen while horror and madness reigned around them.

A seeming eternity went by before a measure of quiet returned to the universe beyond. It held, and Eva at last felt that she could try removing the mask. The air was good again, and she left it off.

More time went by, a lot of it, but finally the last glow, the last roar, of the fire vanished from her senses' perception, and the pair ventured forth from their refuge, Eva carefully stepping from stone to stone to avoid soaking the clothing she might have to keep on for several days to come.

It was a blackened and dreadful land that met their eyes. Nothing lived and nothing stood, apart from charred, wind-shattered stumps. Only the river flowed as it formerly had, and even that was dark with a load of ash and debris.

"We'll stick to the water, I think, for a while, at any rate," the woman told her friend. "The ground's probably still hot, at least in some spots, and there may be a lot of live embers buried in the general rubble." Besides, the road might either be impassible or undiscoverable or both in this mess. She was no woodswoman and would do best to stick to this sure route to safety. Follow it far enough going with its flow, and she would reach help.

First, though, they would eat. . . .

Firecat meowed. His head darted sharply back and forth as he stared into the sky. It took several seconds longer before the human's weaker hearing detected the sound that had alerted him. A helicopter.

Eva quickly hopped to another rock to bring them more nearly into the center of the stream. Even as she whipped off her jacket, the machine appeared.

She waved the garment frantically, praising the good Lord and Lady Luck that it was a light, bright color.

At first, she thought the pilot had missed her—he certainly had no call to expect any sign of life in this place—but then the chopper turned and prepared to land.

The woman gave her companion a great hug and a kiss between the ears. "You're well-named, Laddy-O, and you'll be a properly acknowledged hero after this. If it hadn't been for your waking me, we'd both have been crisped in the cabin, and if you hadn't been so brave and quiet, I would've had a much harder time doing anything at all."

Firecat purred happily. If he was a hero, so was his Eva. She had saved them both, too. His waking them would have accomplished nothing had she not turned her human knowledge and strength to the task of winning their safety. It had taken both of them to beat the fire.

His purring rose in volume until it seemed to rival the less pleasant clatter of the helicopter. Yes, they had done it together, won the future his goddess had wanted and wished for them, but that was only right, only natural. By Bastet's paws, was that not what Partnership and the Plan were all about?

. . . BUT A GLOVE

by John E. Johnston III

To Tyrell, Linda, and Beau

"Tom, this is our anniversary! What do you mean we can't be together tonight?"

Anniversary? How can people have an anniversary when they're not married? "Excuse me, Lori?"

"You don't even remember that we met a year ago today, do you, Tom Mackintosh?"

Uh-oh. Tom suddenly had a sinking feeling in the pit of his stomach. "We did?"

"Yes, we did. And you've been gone for two whole weeks, and now you're trying to tell me that you're just too busy tonight to spend any time with me." Lori put one hand on her hip and started tapping a foot on the sidewalk.

Tom sighed. "That's not how it is, Lori. I just have something that I have to do the next few nights. I don't have any choice in the matter, so I thought I'd ask you to an early dinner this afternoon because I was going to be so busy for a while."

"Early dinner! Hah! I get a quick meal and then get sent home before sundown, while you spend the night with someone else!"

"Lori, there isn't anyone else."

"Oh, yeah? Well, let's see: every once in a while you're just not available for a few nights. You don't answer your phone or your door, and your car sits there in back of your house." *Uh-oh. She's been checking on me.* "Do you think that I'm stupid? There's another woman."

"No, there isn't."

"Then give me another explanation."

Tom thought for a few seconds. "I can't, Lori."

"Ah-hah! I knew it!"

Tom hated scenes like this, but they just seemed to happen to him over and over again. *Well, I can't very well tell her the truth.*

Lori glared at Tom. "I knew that you wouldn't have an explanation!" She spun on her heel and stormed off across the street, throwing a parting message over her shoulder. "Good-bye forever, Tom. Don't call me, don't write me, and don't even think about me!"

Tom sighed again. He would miss Lori. She was more than a little temperamental, but for all her faults she was bright, well-read, well-educated, stylish, and pretty. She also loved animals.

Even more than she ever knew, as a matter of fact.

Tom watched her walk out of sight and then spoke to the empty street. "Want the explanation, Lori? It's real simple: every time there's a full moon I become a cat. A big, fluffy, yellow tomcat, in fact." Frustrated, Tom kicked a mailbox so hard that it hurt his foot, and then walked the long block to his car. *I hate this. I'm never going to be able to have any kind of long-term relationship with a woman.*

Tom drove home, angry at himself the entire way. Tom's house, in the expensive Kentwood subdivision, was one that his real estate friends called "a classic two-story." Kentwood was one of the older neighborhoods in town, and it was known for expensive homes that were spaced fairly close together on well-landscaped lots. Tom couldn't have afforded the house himself; his father had left it to him. *Along with a few other things. Thanks again, Dad.*

Tom parked his car in the driveway off the alley behind his house and heard a familiar friendly canine whine as he got out. His next-door-neighbor, Bob Hammond, had a big red Doberman pinscher named Beauregard who only liked three people in the world: Bob, Bob's wife, and Tom. "Hello, Beau," said Tom, walking over to Bob's back gate. "How are you? Better than me, I'd bet." Tom reached his hand over the gate, and Beau raised up on his hind legs and put his front paws up against the gate so that Tom could scratch his ears. "Catch any squirrels today, Beau? Guard the yard well?" Beau, a dog of good heart but very simple mind, didn't mind anything that went on outside his yard but tolerated nothing within it with the exception of the three people he approved of. *Heck, Beau probably only puts up with me in the yard because I feed him when the Hammonds are out of town.*

"Bye, Beau. Have a good day." The sun was setting as Tom went in his back door. He checked his watch. *Got a few hours left until the full moon.* He walked upstairs and into his bedroom and stared at part of his legacy: an elaborate family coat of arms, mounted on the wall over the head of the bed. It showed a cat, raised up on its hind legs to strike, and bore the motto: "Touch not the cat, but a glove." At the bottom was the clan name: Mackintosh, part of a confederation of Scots clans known as Clan Chattan. *Why couldn't I have been a Campbell? They have no strange hereditary problems and have a great tartan to boot.*

Tom propped open his bedroom window with an odd-looking H-shaped metal device, and then bolted and locked the device into the window frame. *I won't ever make same mistake Dad did. I'll always get back here in time.*

Becoming a cat every full moon was bad enough, but the complications that went with it made it even worse. First off, Tom just didn't turn into a cat; when the moon became full, his consciousness was mysteriously transferred into a large, yellow cat that suddenly materialized from who-knows-where and appeared on his abdomen. *Wasn't that fun the first time that happened? Well, at least I learned right off not to wear clothes that my cat form might get trapped in. And I also learned not to use claws on my human form when I was a cat.* Second, to return to human form, Tom had to have his cat body in physical contact with his temporarily-unused human body when the full moon set, or suffer some major—but still unknown—consequences. Tom had been able to figure that last one out by himself from what had happened to his father.

Once Tom had begun making the transition and understood a little about it, it was easy to look back and see that his father showed all of the signs of a man who went through the same changes himself. His father was noted for sleeping alone next to an open window, regardless of the weather, and had been known as a very private, reclusive, and secretive man. His father had ended up paying a steep price for having the condition; his mother-in-law, who stayed with Tom's family after her own husband died, had unexpectedly strolled into this very room one night, seen

Tom's father calmly asleep on the bed with the window propped open and, as an enemy of fresh air, had closed the window. Early the next morning, a large cat had awakened every member of the household—except Tom's father—by screeching and throwing itself over and over again at that very window from the tree limb right outside. Tom and his mother and grandmother had watched the cat trying desperately to get through the window, and tried fruitlessly to wake Tom's father up to ask his advice. After about an hour of this, the cat had given up and vanished, shortly after which Tom's father had stopped breathing.

Tom knew now that the cat had been his father, trying to get back to his body before the moon went down. *I wonder if he lived on as a cat.* He hadn't understood the incident at the time; Tom was only thirteen when it occurred and hadn't begun going through the changes himself until he was eighteen, when the meaning of what Tom had seen became clear to him. *What happened to Dad will never happen to me. Never.* Tom had added the bolts and locks to his father's old metal window prop after he had begun making the transition himself. *It'd take Harry Houdini to get this prop out of the window now.* Tom now left the house every night secure in the knowledge that the window would be open when he returned, and he was also smart enough to make sure that he knew how long each full moon would last and when he had to be home. The memory of his father made Tom play things very safely.

Tom read a book and tried to relax until it was time to get ready, at which point he took off his clothes and lay down on his bed. *This is ridiculous.* Tom was, as far as he knew, the only living person in the world who went through this. Among the things left to Tom by his father was a note that read "Things to tell Tom" with two cryptic entries: "Not all are" and "Others." Tom thought he'd figured out the first part of the note. Through espionage in feline form on other people who were descended from the families of Clan Chattan, starting with his own cousins, Tom established to his own satisfaction that his relatives—or at least all of the ones that he could find—did not turn into any type of animal under the influence of the full moon. The latter part of the note was even more cryptic than the former. "Others?" Could "Others" and "Not all are" mean that there were, indeed, others like Tom out there somewhere? Tom desperately wanted there to be others like him, but outside of that cryptic note, Tom had never seen or heard even a hint of such a thing, and Tom had made a point of studying everything that he had been able to find out about the subject in great detail.

It was easy for Tom to be angry at his father. Not only had his father's genes placed him in this situation, his father had vanished without leaving Tom any kind of decent written explanation or any help whatsoever. On top of that, he'd given Tom a joke name: Thomas Catlett Mackintosh. The whole name said "tomcat" in big letters. *Great joke, Dad. Thanks a bunch.* Tom suddenly got a wry smile on his face. *Well, at least you didn't name me Felix.*

Tom's emotions vanished as he felt the familiar tingles of the transition begin. They started off faintly, gradually grew in intensity, and finally peaked ... and Tom found himself once again to be a large, yellow cat, one that had suddenly materialized on the abdomen of the human body Tom had been occupying a few seconds earlier. *Off we go.* Tom took control of his cat body, gently stepped off his now-unused human body, and hopped from the bed to the window sill. With a quick jump he was in the orange tree outside and headed off.

Being a cat was always a pleasure for Tom; he enjoyed the smells his cat senses could detect and he really liked the lithe feel of his cat body. Tom jumped from the tree to the top of the fence separating his property from Bob Hammond's and watched Beauregard raise his head up and track him. While Beau would go after any cat that actually dared to enter his yard, cats on the fences were something that Beau never really cared about. *See you later, Beau.* Tom hopped down to the alley and took off south toward Third Street at a lope.

He made it the entire long block to Third Street before he realized what was missing tonight: Tom hadn't seen or smelled another cat the entire way. That was unusual; normally the alley had at least two or three other cats in it. *Oh, well, maybe they're all across Third Street.* Tom looked both ways across Third Street, found a traffic-free moment, and trotted across. *Well, there'll be cats here.*

Only there weren't.

Tom started looking and smelling for cats, but there was nothing to be seen and little to be smelled. Finally, Tom found a track that he recognized in an alley: that of a female he called Rose, who'd had a fresh litter of kittens the last time Tom had seen her. Tom tracked her to where she normally stayed, and found a scent track that indicated she and the kittens had left there and gone elsewhere in a hurry. Overlaying the scent of Rose and the kittens was a strong and obnoxious scent that Tom couldn't identify. Whatever it was, it made Tom's fur want to stand on end.

Tom followed Rose's and the kittens' scent around a corner, to a quiet cul-de-sac off of Third Street near the Third Street Veterinary Clinic. There, at a storm drain, he smelled something the smell of which he had grown to hate: death. *Oh, no, Rose. Not you.* The kitten smell went into the storm drain. The obnoxious smell didn't. Tom was too big a cat to fit into the storm drain entrance to see where the kitten smell went. *Maybe the kittens got away.* Rose hadn't. *Good-bye, Rose.*

Very upset now, Tom started checking for cats. He went to an area off of Third Street that was almost always patrolled at night by an angry yellow tomcat that Tom called Jeremiah, who was probably one of Tom's own offspring. There was no Jeremiah to be found. Tom went to the one place he knew he could always find a cat, the backyard that was the regular court of the languid Persian female that Tom called Lady Kay. There was no sign of Lady Kay either.

There was, however, a lot of the strong and obnoxious smell all over, and here and there was the horrible odor of death. Something was very, very wrong. There was something hunting cats . . . and, unless Tom's nose was mistaken, some dogs, too. *It's not a dog, it's not a big cat, and it's not human. Smells closer to a dog than anything else, though.*

The rest of Tom's evening was spent in cautious patrol work. He skulked, he scouted, and he slithered, but he turned up no more clues about what was going on, and didn't see another cat the entire time. The sky finally told Tom that it was time to head home. *Don't have much longer. These short full moons in the late summer sure don't leave you with much time to prowl.* Tom trotted over to where the alley that went by his house continued on past

Third Street and turned north toward Third Street and home. He was almost to Third Street when he stopped cold. That obnoxious smell was suddenly very, very strong.

Tom froze. Turning to his left, he looked into the corridor between two garages where there was a small stand of shrub. Tom looked closely into the shrub, and he could see that there was something large and blurry in there. Suddenly, whatever it was raised up, and Tom was looking into what he knew instinctively were the yellow eyes of Death. The human part of his mind stopped and said, "Coyote," but his feline reactions had him in full flight toward Third Street and home before the coyote had time to react any further. Tom was a very fast cat and he took full advantage of that speed as he headed for Third Street at a pace few cats could match. He heard the coyote chasing after him and Tom ran as he had never run before. *Coyotes are faster than cats, aren't they? Or are they?* Tom reached Third Street, hearing the sounds of the coyote behind him as he ran. As Tom closed on Third Street, he looked at the cars on the street, timed their speeds in his mind, and adjusted his direction slightly: he hit Third Street at full speed and virtually flew straight across it into the alley on the other side without having even to slow down a step. Shrieking brakes and honking horns told him that the coyote had not been able to do the same thing. *Hah. Got you there.*

Tom had reached very familiar territory now. There should be an orange tree just down the alley—right there— that was not only on the same side of the alley as Tom's house, but was also one that he should have enough lead time to climb. Tom heard the coyote coming up behind him, smelled the orange tree, got within jumping range of it, jumped as high as he could up its trunk, and scrabbled up the trunk of the tree by his claws for his life. He heard and felt the coyote behind him leap and hit the tree underneath him. *Hah. Too late.*

Tom reached a horizontal limb and flattened on top of it, swiveling his head down to look at his pursuer. What he saw was frightening: the largest coyote that Tom had ever seen or heard of was sitting patiently at the base of the tree, looking up at Tom with an evil malevolence that Tom found chilling. *So you're the killer. Whatever are you doing*

*in my neighborhood? Why aren't you chasing rabbits up in
the hills where you belong?*

*Well, there's nothing more that I can do here. Good-bye,
Killer. I'll see you again.* Tom went higher up the tree,
crossed to a long limb, jumped from it onto the roof of the
corner home's garage, and began roof-, fence-, and tree-
walking home. The coyote paralleled him on the ground,
obviously waiting for Tom to have to take to the ground
again. Tom, however, knew something the coyote didn't:
the combination of the number of large trees in the neighborhood and the proximity of the neighborhood houses to
one another gave Tom a convoluted but safe high road
home to his own window via limbs, fences, and roofs once
he had made it back to his own block.

Tom made it back to his window with some time to spare
before the change and looked back to see the coyote sitting
in the alley behind his house, calmly staring at him. *Good
night, Killer.* Tom jumped through his window. *Until we
meet again.*

Tom didn't feel all that well the next morning. His arms
and legs hurt, and he was even more tired than he usually
was after one of his cat nights. A shower and breakfast
made him feel somewhat better, but he still wanted to go
back to bed. He didn't, though; instead, he called the city's
Animal Control office to see what he could find out about
the coyote running loose in his neighborhood.

"Animal Control. Jordan speaking."

"Yes, ma'am, my name is Mackintosh. I live in Kentwood, and last night I saw a coyote in the alley behind my
house. Do you know anything about that?"

"Mr. Mackintosh, I'm going to let you talk to Mr. Gage.
Hold on."

A pause of a few seconds, and then, "Gage here. Jordan
says that you saw a coyote over in Kentwood last night."

"Yes, I did. A very large coyote, in fact. Can you explain
that to me?"

"Sure. Remember the brush fires in the hills the last couple of weeks?"

Tom didn't. He'd been out of town. "No, I was gone.
What happened?"

"Well, about half of the natural coyote habitat around

here was destroyed. The survivors are hungry, and a lot of them have moved into town to try and find food."

"This one's after the cats in my neighborhood."

"That's not news, they're after cats all over town. Want to know what else they've done? They've eaten all of the ducks in Monroe Park and some of the smaller animals at the zoo. Heck, one of them even got the mayor's wife's poodle the night before last. Boy, is she upset."

Uh-oh. "Mr. Gage, that's all bad news, but can you do anything about the coyote in my neighborhood?"

"Sure, we'll get him for you. Give me your address." Tom gave it to him. "It's going to be a while before we can get to him, though."

"What exactly does 'a while' mean, Mr. Gage?"

"Well, the mayor, the City Zoo, the Parks Commission, and a couple of other neighborhoods are in line ahead of you, and we only have so many traps and so many officers. We'll get all the coyotes, though, and we'll get to yours when we can."

"And just how long might that be?"

"Well, Mr. Mackintosh, that depends on how fast we take care of the other problems."

"But just how long could that be? Give me the worst case, would you?"

There was a pause. "Don't quote me on this, Mr. Mackintosh, but it'll probably be weeks. Maybe a month. Maybe longer. If you have a cat, I'd advise you to keep it indoors."

Tom's shoulders sagged. "Thank you, Mr. Gage. Can I get you to call me so I know when you're going to be in this neighborhood?"

"Sure. Leave your number with Ms. Jordan."

Tom did, and then hung up the phone and sat lost in thought. *Well, there's no help coming any time soon, the odds on me finding that coyote while I'm in human form are minuscule, and I can't do anything much to him but provide him with a meal if I do find him again while I'm in cat form. And every day—or night—that I do nothing about him will probably cost lives.* Tom walked to the window and looked out into Bob Hammond's yard. Beauregard sat under the big tree in the middle of the yard, calmly scratching himself. *Hmm, I wonder just what you'd make of that coyote, Beau?*

And then the idea hit him.

The setup work in human form that night was easy; Tom slipped over to Hammond's alley gate just after sunset, reached over the fence and unlatched the gate so that it was just slightly open: open enough that it could it be forced open from the outside, but not enough for Beau to get out. Beau walked over to the gate while Tom was there and made friendly noises. "Good Beau. Down, boy. Don't lean on the gate, okay? Good Beau." Beau sat down with his head cocked at an angle and looked at Tom. "Get some sleep, Beau. Big night tonight." Tom went back up to his room, propped and locked the window open, checked the time, and got ready for the change.

When it came, Tom was out the window and headed for the alley in a flash. *Third Street, here I come.* He made it across easily, and worked up and down the streets and alleys around Third Street, concentrating on the area around the Third Street Veterinary Clinic, carefully checking for the coyote, and carefully avoiding positions where he might be jumped or ambushed. There wasn't a sign of the coyote—not a scent since last night, not a sign of a struggle, not a track. After a long and hard search, with time starting to become an issue, Tom gave up. *Another night.* Tom headed back to Third Street, figuring to lope across it and make his way home quickly and to try again tomorrow night.

Tom waited until there were no cars coming, and made it across Third Street at a brisk walk. He was just starting down the alley leading home when he smelled it: coyote. Suddenly, out of the cluster of trash cans in the back of the house on the left corner, a gray streak flashed, leaping straight and true for right where Tom was. Tom ducked underneath the leaping coyote and, doing the unexpected, ran for his life straight toward the trash cans. He could hear the coyote hit the ground hard and try desperately to reverse direction. *Hah. Too late. You overcommitted.* Tom leapt over the now-scattered trash cans his foe had concealed himself in and headed straight for the low storage shed he knew was at the back of the house. *This is the Maguire place. Storage shed, plum trees, three-story house. Fairly safe.* Tom jumped, caught the wooden edge of the shed in his claws, clawed and swung up to the top of it, and then leapt from the shed to a large horizontal branch of the Maguire's prize plum tree. From fifteen feet up, Tom looked directly down onto the coyote, who had followed him on the ground as soon as he had been able to. *Well, you missed again. You ought to bathe more often, your smell gives you away. I got away from you again. You're not that good.*

Then it dawned on Tom: he was on the other side of the alley from his house.

There was no safe way home from this side of the alley.

And if Tom didn't get home within about twenty minutes he'd be a cat forever . . . or maybe worse.

And sitting down below him was a large, deadly, probably very hungry coyote patiently waiting for his chance to make Tom into a late dinner.

Well, Killer, you didn't miss after all. You got me, even if you'll never understand how.

Tom calmed his initial panic. *I have to think. There has to be a way out. There is always a way out.* Tom turned ideas over in his mind and finally concluded that his only real hope was to head for home and make a break when his best chance came. *Maybe a car will come down the alley and create an opportunity for me to get across. Maybe the coyote will get bored and leave. Maybe he'll fall asleep.* The coyote carefully paced Tom as he headed from tree to roof and back to tree again on his way up the alley toward his house. *And, then again, maybe he won't.*

It took Tom about ten minutes of roof and tree work to make it to the house directly across the alley from his own. He sat on the flat roof of his neighbor's garage, staring across the alley at his own house, fence, and trees. *Thirty feet. I could make it in a flash. I could jump to the top of my fence, or I could go through Hammond's gate and get Beau. It would just take a few seconds.* Then pessimism set in. *Thirty feet? It might as well be thirty miles. I'd never make four of those feet before that coyote would be on me.*

The coyote sat patiently in the alley, watching Tom and waiting. *You've done a lot of damage, you lousy coyote. One day you'll pay for that.*

Tom checked the sky. He was running out of time. *Well, maybe I can make a break for Hammond's gate, and maybe I can hit it hard enough to attract Beau's attention, and maybe, even if I can't get through it, just maybe I can knock it open far enough for Beau to work his way out, and maybe Beau will get this killer after he gets me. Looks like my best shot.* Tom raised up and stretched, trying to look bored. The coyote snapped to attention. *Crap.*

And then, unexpectedly, sauntering toward the two of them from the Third Street side of the alley was the last thing Tom expected to see—another cat. It was a young reddish-orange female, and she looked as though she was paying no attention at all to her surroundings. *Cats don't normally act like that. If she doesn't see that coyote and she gets any closer....*

She did get closer. The coyote patiently looked at her, checked Tom, weighed his choices and chances, spun, and then everything seemed to happen at once. The coyote turned and ran full speed at the reddish-orange cat, and the reddish-orange cat did the fastest pivot Tom had ever seen—*she's faster than I am*—and headed full speed for the nearest tree. Tom immediately jumped off of the garage roof and broke for Bob Hammond's alley gate as fast as he could run. Tom glanced back—*I shouldn't be turning my head to look like this*—as he ran and saw the female reach the tree and leap upward to try to escape the coyote's fangs. The female cat wasn't as big as Tom and couldn't jump as high, though, and the coyote was blindingly fast; he jumped and was able to catch her in his jaws by her lower right leg. Tom thought she was done for, but she planted her left rear claws in the coyote's nose, twisted them, pulled free of the coyote's jaws when they popped open in shock, and scrambled up the tree to safety. Without a second's pause or thought, the coyote did an immediate full pivot and made straight for Tom.

Too late, Killer. I'm too close to the gate. Tom straightened himself up, jumped for the gate, balled and buttoned himself up in midair as best he could, and then hit Hammond's back gate with all the force that a large cat at a dead run could bring to bear. The gate popped open just far enough for Tom to scramble through. Right behind him Tom heard the coyote hit the gate hard, bounce back, and then start forcing the gate open far enough to admit his larger body. Tom didn't turn around but raced full speed for the Hammond's orange tree. He leapt, hit the tree, dug his claws in, and was ready to climb to safety when he suddenly felt an excruciating pain: the coyote had him by the tail. *Well, this is it. I didn't make it after all.*

Only it wasn't it. Suddenly, there was a noise.

A growl.

A very deep growl.

Beau's growl.

The coyote obviously had heard it, too; he let go of Tom's tail, and Tom scrambled straight up to the nearest safe branch and looked down. What he saw made him a very happy cat: Beauregard was standing between the coyote and the gate with a look of pure territoriality in his eyes. *Here it comes. Get him, Beau!*

And then Tom looked up at the sky. *Uh, oh. The moon is almost gone!* Tom wanted to stay and watch what happened, but he had no time: he streaked along the branches, jumped to the roof of his house, dove through the window, and barely made it back to his human body just as he felt the change starting. *Never cut it this close before. Never will again.* And then he was gone.

Tom awakened in human form. It was early morning, and Tom didn't want to get out of bed; he was a little groggy and more than a little sore. Then Tom remembered the night before and tried to get up all at once. He had a problem doing that, though; there was an excruciating pain in his behind. Tom did a half roll in the bed, looked at his backside and made a face: it was obvious that any sitting down that he was going to do for the next few days was going to be extremely painful. Tom carefully swung his legs over the side of the bed and headed gingerly for the window. *Beauregard, how did you make out?*

Looking out the window, Tom could see the aftermath of what must have been the canine battle to end all canine battles in Hammond's yard below. It was a battle that the coyote had obviously lost: the yard was torn up, there were patches of fur everywhere, and there was what was obviously a dead coyote over by the gate. Lying next to the coyote's supine form, though, was Beauregard, and from where Tom was he didn't look all that much better off.

Damn. Tom threw clothes on as quickly as he could, given his painful posterior, grabbed a blanket, and ran downstairs and over to Bob Hammond's front door as fast as he could, trying to ignore the pain in his rear the whole time. *A shame that I can't use the tree route in this form.* Hammond answered Tom's repeated loud knocking on his front door wearing a bathrobe and a puzzled look. "Tom, what are you doing over here at this hour of the morning?"

"Bob, Beau's been badly hurt! I saw him from my window!"

"What? How?"

"Looks like a dogfight of some kind. Come on!" Tom, still uninvited, slipped past Bob Hammond and ran through his house into Bob's backyard. Beau looked even worse up close than he had at a distance; when he saw Tom coming, though, he lifted his head up a little and tried to wag his tail. *Stay alive, Beau. Stay with me.*

Tom started slipping the blanket under Beau. "Bob, we need to get Beau to the vet right now. Get your car, and I'll get Beau." Tom was grunting as he picked Beau and the blanket up gently—*Beau, you are one heavy dog*—even before Bob answered him.

"Can't, Tom," said Bob. "My wife took the car about a half hour ago. Can we take yours? I'll be dressed in a minute." He looked around. "That's a dead coyote! What in the dickens happened here? How did a coyote get in my yard?"

Tom didn't answer Bob's last two questions. "Bob, we can take my car. And I can wait for you to get dressed, but I'm not sure Beau can." Tom staggered under his load toward Hammond's partially open alley gate, beyond which Tom's own car sat parked in his own alley driveway just a few feet away.

"You go on without me, then," said Hammond. "You know where the Third Street Veterinary Clinic is? Take him there. There's a new vet there, but they still know him and me there. Leave Beau there, tell them to put it on my bill, and come back and get me."

Well, I ought to know where the Third Street Clinic is, given that I patrolled around it half of last night. Tom didn't know who the vet was, though. *Funny, I'm a part-time cat, and I don't know any veterinarians . . . heck, I've never even been to a veterinarian.* Tom gently maneuvered the blanket and a softly moaning Beau over the dead coyote—*got you, you killer*—through the gate, and into the passenger seat of his car. Tom got in the car, backed it out, and then drove far faster than he normally would have toward the clinic, all the while trying very hard not to sit down. *Here I am, driving like a teenager and sitting on half of my rear end. What a life.* Then the real absurdity of the situation hit Tom, and he started laughing out loud. *This is great. This is probably the only time in the history of the world that a dog has ever been driven to a veterinarian by a cat.*

Tom was still laughing when he reached the clinic. Disregarding the signs, he parked the car in the red zone right out in front, got out painfully, and limped around to the passenger side. Tom reached in and picked Beau and the blanket up as gently as he could and staggered under the load—*what do you weigh, Beau? Feels like a hundred pounds*—toward the clinic door. A young woman wearing surgical scrubs and a startled expression opened the door for him, and he found himself in a reception area. "Emergency," he said. "Badly injured dog. Where do I take him?"

"Straight to the vet. Follow me," said the girl. Tom did, and carried Beau down a hallway and around a corner into what was obviously an examination room. The room wasn't empty; there was a redheaded woman in surgical scrubs in there lecturing a seated woman who was clutching a lapdog. *Sheesh, lady, that's one ugly little dog.* Tom ignored them, walked right past the woman in scrubs, and set Beau and his blanket down as gently as he could on the large metal examination table in the middle of the room.

The redheaded woman suddenly stopped her lecture, went right to the table, and began looking Beau over quickly. *Are you the veterinarian?* She looked at Tom suspiciously. "This is Beau, Mr. Hammond's dog. Who are you? I've met Mr. Hammond, and you're not him. Where's Mr. Hammond? Just what happened to Beau?"

And hello to you, too, lady. "I'm the next-door neighbor. Bob told me to bring Beau to you. Beau got into a fight with a coyote. By the way, are you the veterinarian?"

The redheaded woman started, and turned way from Beau and looked Tom square in the eyes. *Green eyes. A redhead with green eyes. Freckles, too. Lovely, but bad news, I bet.* "A coyote?" she asked, in a softer voice. "What happened to the coyote?"

"Dead as a post," said Tom.

"Good," said the woman. "Make sure that you bring the body in later. I'll need it." She turned her back on Tom and started working on Beau. Over her shoulder she said, "And, yes, I am the veterinarian. Would you mind waiting in the reception area? I have a lot of work to do here." The fat woman with the lapdog had vanished. *Ran her off for good, I'll bet.*

Tom walked into the hallway while the veterinarian began yelling at her assistants to bring her various things. Tom was tired and his rear end hurt. *Well, I'm not going to go sit in the reception area in this condition. I'll walk around a while instead and wait and see if Beau's okay. Then I'll go get Bob once I know for sure what's going to happen. Don't want to drive any more than I have to in this condition.* Tom turned in the opposite direction from the reception area. The clinic was oddly shaped; it was built in a sort of a deformed U shape, and when Tom walked toward the other arm of the U, the sounds of barking dogs and angry cats made it clear that there must be kennels in the back. *Wonder if any of the missing cats might be injured and in the kennels here? Can't hurt to look.*

Tom passed a series of what looked like empty examination rooms and the veterinarian's private office on the back way to the kennels but didn't stop to look in. When he walked past the dog kennels to the cat area, he smiled. Sitting in the second row of kennels, his muzzle and side stitched up and with one leg in a cast but still looking like a defiant yellow feline pirate for all that, was Jeremiah. Two cages over and one up was Lady Kay, stitched here and there, a little the worse for wear but still looking smug. On the bottom row, in a cage with a bottle feed attachment, was Rose's litter of kittens. *Looks like Rose held that coyote off long enough to see you kittens safely into the storm drain where he couldn't get you. I'll bet somebody heard you crying in there later and got you out and brought you here.* Tom smiled again. *Things are looking up. I wonder how many more made it?*

Better go check on Beau. Tom walked back down the hallway and looked into the veterinarian's office as he walked by. There were a lot of framed diplomas and certificates mounted on her office wall. *Wonder where she went*

to school? Ah, there's the vet school diploma. UC Davis,
eh? Not a bad school.* And then Tom saw what was also
mounted on the wall besides the diplomas and certificates
and froze on the spot.

Mounted on the wall, behind the veterinarian's desk, was
a familiar coat of arms—a Clan Chattan coat of arms, angry
cat and all. The cat was a little different in this coat of
arms, and Tom didn't recognize which branch of the clan
it was from, but Clan Chattan was Clan Chattan. *Well, well,
well. Hello, cousin.* And then Tom had a thought that almost staggered him.

Tom was still standing in the hallway facing the office
door some time later when the veterinarian finally appeared in the hallway.

"There you are! What are you doing here? Why aren't
you in the reception area? Where's Mr. Hammond?"

Hello again to you, too, ma'am. Smiling, Tom motioned
to her. "You need to come here to find out. How's Beau?"

He wasn't surprised to see the redheaded vet limping
slightly as she walked up the hallway. The bandage on her
lower right leg, even though pretty well hidden by the surgical scrubs, was visible when you knew to look for it. Her
anger, on the other hand, was far easier to see. "Beau's
badly hurt, but he's going to be okay. What are you doing
back here? What do you think gives you the right to . . ."

"That does," said Tom, pointing into her office at the
coat of arms. "And full moons. And that doesn't even mention the fact that I'd bet everything that I own that you
were the one who distracted that big coyote last night long
enough for me to get through that gate!"

The woman was looking at him with those same green
eyes, but this time they looked as large as saucers. She
didn't say anything, and her face remained impassive.

*Uh-oh. Maybe she's afraid to admit what she is. Maybe I
just stepped in it. Well, here I go down the drain again.* "I
think that you and I kind of belong together, and you probably know as well as I do that there's a full moon tonight.
Would you like to meet somewhere tonight and do a little,
well, shall we say, howling at the moon together?"

The woman just looked at him for a moment. Finally,
she spoke. "What's your name?" she asked in a very
quiet voice.

"Tom. Thomas Catlett Mackintosh." Tom saw the corners of her mouth turn up in a slight grin when she heard the name.

"Doctor Melanie Farquharson."

"Charmed."

"About tonight?"

"Yes?" *Here it comes.*

"I'd like you to know that I have never once in my life agreed to go out with a man that I just met, but I wouldn't miss being with you tonight for the world."

"You wouldn't?"

"No, I wouldn't. You see," she said, smiling and reaching forward to take Tom's arm gently, "I've been waiting for a man like you all of my life."

FEAR IN HER POCKET
by Caralyn Inks

His mate leaned against him. He could feel the tremors of pain and exhaustion coursing through her. "Not much farther and you can lie down," he reassured her, adding a mental caress at the end of his mindspeech. "Soon your birth cycle will start and you'll begin your path to completion as you die your first death." He tried not to flinch when her mind's voice, filled with suffering and disgruntlement, whipped across his.

"Why am I not as the rest of our Pride? Why is it necessary for me to seek an alien's help to die?"

"In this circumstance the answer to WHY offers only emptiness, confusion, and unnecessary pain. Seek only the NOW of each moment. That is the path to peace, the renewal of death." He bent his head and licked her ear, audibly purring. "We chose to follow the One. His path directs our paws onto strange byways. Great is the gift the One laid upon us by giving us nine lives. Do not question, accept. Each life we live, each death we survive compresses us as we come nearer to the fulfillment we are driven to seek. That is our burden, our joy."

"Must it hurt so?" she half-groaned. "The pain feels like a live creature is inside me gnawing its way out."

He wanted to ease her, but he had nothing but the truth to give her for comfort. "Without pain we would not understand joy nor appreciate our multiple lives. Suffering is a testing ground, a refining fire, a battle. If we cannot win through to the other side, all nine lives are lost and there is no rebirth; we die completely." The edge of the forest lay before them. He braced himself so his mate could slide down his body to the earth. He ached to be at her side as she gave birth. Not to be with her as she died twisted his heart, but his presence was forbidden by Pride Law. He must stand

116

*watch so that the alien and her cubs would come to no harm
while the human served the Pride.*

*To the best of his ability he hid his fear from her. Rare
were the times that one such as she was born. Her lives lay
so close to one another that only the Wee Brothers and Sisters could help her. If she survived, she would become one
of the most powerful magis in the world.*

*"Remember, though our help comes from an alien, she
guards and preserves the power of some of our dead.
Through Pact with her Pride and ours this has been done
for seasons upon seasons. This human family is not like
those who hunted us to near extinction for the power resid-
ing in our bodies. Now, rest cradled in my mind. I will block
your pain until it is time to leave."*

Jayle looked up on hearing Mar's shout of laughter and
Little Oran's infectious giggle. She grinned at the sight of
her two sons. Mar held a paintbrush in one hand, his carving knife safely above his head in the other as Little O
grabbed him about the knees and tried to climb the high
stool Mar sat on. Mar shoved one of his feet between his
brother's legs, half lifting him in the air, then abruptly lowered it. Little O slid to the plank floor. Down but not defeated, Little O grabbed Mar's foot, pulled off his shoe,
and began to tickle him.

"It is too a g–good cat. It'll see just fine!" he shouted.

Mar pretended to struggle to free his foot. "Since when
does a cat have nine eyes? You squirrel bait. It's nine *lives*
they have, not eyes!" Mar retorted, his deep voice escalat-
ing into a squeak as it had been tending to do the past
few months.

"I'm no squirrel food, Stupid. They eat nuts, not little
boys."

Jayle felt a sharp dig at her ankle. She looked down and
met the gaze of Skunk. The battered tomcat tolerated all
of them except Little O, and him Skunk loved. They didn't
need a guard dog; with him around nothing could step into
his territory that he didn't know about it. She'd seen him
run off a bear. Jayle respected Skunk. They were partners,
remaining so until her husband, Inji, returned from selling
their hearthcrafts at the Merchant's Fair. Together they
held a deep responsibility. Skunk curled his lip to reveal

his fangs. He snarled deep in his chest. He lashed his tail until its white stripe moved like an aroused snake.

"What is it, Wee Brother?" she asked. Jayle watched him walk through the open workshop door to join the farm cats waiting for him in the warm spring sunlight. All had an aura of excitement. She met Skunk's piercing gaze. Jayle nodded. At her signal he stalked off, the other cats following him. She let her potter's wheel slow to a stop. Dropping a damp cloth over the plate she was working on, she fought back a shiver of fear. In the forest behind the house a camilicat waited.

For generations the family she'd married into kept a secret Pact with the wild, intelligent cats; in return the Pride warned them when danger threatened. If that were the case now, they would be here. No, one of them must be near its dying time.

Before her husband, Inji, left he promised that she would not have to face this. He'd told her the camilicats' cycle came upon them only at year's end and it was rare for the family to be called to assist the forest cats more than once a generation. Two years ago Inji, Skunk, and the Wee Brothers and Sisters helped a camilicat through its birth-death cycle. She had remained in the house with the children. On Mar's twelfth birthday they told him about the camilicats; Little O at three years of age was too young to be trusted with the truth. If it became known that camilicats were more than fireside tales, the cats' forest sanctuary would become their graveyard. Jayle knew what to do, but the thought of doing it without Inji frightened her. She had some time to prepare; the camilicat and its mate would not venture out of the forest until darkness lay secure upon the land and she and the Wee Brothers and Sisters reassured them of their safety. Taking one of her mother's homilies to heart, Jayle put her fear in her pocket to look at later.

"What's this about nine eyes?" she asked the boys.

Mar glanced at her, laughter dancing in his dark eyes. He wiggled his foot back in his shoe. "We shouldn't let Oran paint. See what he's done to the cat-shaped platter I carved." He handed her the wooden tray. Bright patches of primary color covered the surface.

Jayle looked down at her youngest child. Brushing tawny hair off his paint-smeared face, she said, "It's beautiful.

I never saw a cat with nine eyes. Why did you paint it that way?"

"He'z a brave cat," Little O said earnestly. "Tha'z why he'z bright an' has shiny colors."

"Oran, you didn't answer me." Jayle tried not to smile when he lowered his head, scuffed his feet. He peeked through his hair at her. "Hmmm?" she said, raising one eyebrow.

" 'Cuz he said I could since I didn't know how to paint nine lives."

Jayle asked, "Who?"

"Skunk. He tol' me if'n I wanted to paint nine eyes I could. So I did. Skunk's always right!"

Mar grinned, "Why do you keep telling us Skunk talks to you?"

" 'Cuz he does, all the time in my head and," he paused for a moment, then said in a rush, "so do chickens."

"Chickens!" Mar picked Little O up. He held him above his head, dodging Oran's dangling arms and legs. "What do they talk about?"

Oran giggled. "Worms and the rooster and eggs,"

"I just don't know where you get your ideas."

"Oh, I finds 'em all over the place. They tries to hide, but I'm a good hunter, jus' like Skunk taught me."

"Well," Jayle said, "speaking of chickens, it's time for you boys to do your evening chores. I'll take Mr. Nine Eyes Cat to keep me company while I fix supper."

Oran squealed as Mar slung him over his shoulder. Little O laughed in delight. Bracing his hands on Mar's back he raised himself up to look at her. He shouted, "Thanks, Mama. Mr. Cat will like that!"

Jayle moved about their home, making sure all the curtains were pulled so no light could seep out. Skunk came along behind her, leaping onto each window ledge to sniff at the pegs latching the shutters.

"Mom," Mar said. "Let me do this. No one will come out here after dark. Everyone knows Dad's gone to Ox Tail Inn for the annual Merchant's Fair. The camilicats will be safe. We live more than a league from the village. If someone needs something, they'll come during daylight. Can't you trust me to make the house secure?"

"I'm sorry, Mar, of course I trust you. I'm nervous about the camilicats. What if one of them dies in truth?"

"Well, it hasn't happened yet. Even if it did, no harm would come to us by Pride Law. Dad told me the things to remember were: to make their likeness as accurate as humanly possible, stay out of striking distance of their paws as they often thrash about because of the pain they're in, and always speak honestly. I sure wouldn't lie to someone as big as a pony, that has claws longer than my fingers, and knows exactly what I am thinking. Mom, as you keep telling me, put your fear in your pocket. Pay attention to what's in front of you. If you do that, everything else will come about as it's supposed to." He paused, tried to lift only one eyebrow the way she could. He failed, shrugged his shoulders, saying, "Right?"

Jayle laughed as she crouched down beside Skunk, "That's giving my own words back to me with a vengeance." She lightly touched the big tom's scarred head. "Skunk, will you check to see if Little O's asleep?" Skunk climbed the ladder to the boy's sleeping loft. Oran couldn't fool Skunk as he had the rest of them on many occasions. The big tom soon leapt back down to the floor, the white stripe down his back and tail luminous in the candlelight, excitement all but bursting from his tattered ears. He headed for the back door in the kitchen. Impatient, he snarled at her.

"I'm coming, Skunk."

"Mom, wait. I need to ask you something."

"Yes?"

"It's about Oran. Do you think he really hears chickens or Skunk talking to him?"

The concerned look on Mar's face stopped her from putting him off. Her sons were more important to her than a dying camilicat. "I thought he was just playing make believe. Now, I'm not sure. Chickens don't have much of a brain, but worms, eggs, and roosters would be what they think about."

"Could he be developing a Gift, like speaking mind to mind or mage powers?"

"I don't know. The Gift rises seldom in humans, but when it does, one can count on it to reveal itself in unusual ways. Your brother's very young to manifest such signs.

We'll just have to wait and see. Now, I must leave." Jayle gripped his forearm. "Take care. I'll return at dawn."

Jayle followed Skunk out the back door wishing the night finished and Inji home to share the responsibility before her. She missed him intensely. When he got home, she promised herself she'd stake him out in the yard, cover him with cracked corn and turn the chickens loose. He deserved no less for being wrong about the camilicats, though the fool man would only lie there making jokes about which hen had the fattest thighs. She smiled at that thought. Heart lighter she picked up the pitchfork she'd left leaning against the house earlier, trusting Skunk's instincts over her own to discover anything out of the ordinary around the farm. As they circled the outbuildings, all the farm cats joined them. When they reached the kitchen door again, Skunk turned to face the forest, half-crouching, belly low to the ground. He slowly stretched out one paw, then another; as if stalking prey he led them toward the forest. Jayle followed. Knees bent, she held the pitchfork low. Silent as moonlight the farm cats fanned out behind them. A few feet from the forest's edge Skunk arched his back. He took a few sideways hopping steps until he reached her side. At that moment two camilicats stepped out from under the shrouded trees onto the moon-glazed verge edging the forest. A voice spoke directly into her mind,

"Mistress, we greet you and the Wee Brothers and Sisters who guard you. Is everything ready for my mate?"

Jayle never admired Skunk more than when he approached the large camilicats and boldly touched noses with the male. Somehow, she knew it was the male who had spoken to her. Awe, fear, and excitement tumbled for supremacy in her mind as she wondered how to project the words, "all is prepared," from her mind to his.

"It is not necessary to wrestle with your thoughts. Simply speak aloud. We understand human speech. Please, we must hurry. My mate's dying must be ended between the death of this day and the dawn of the next.

With his words came a wave of pain that nearly dropped Jayle to her knees. The farm cats must have felt it, too, as all of them rushed to the large female. They circled her, brushing up against her and murmuring soft mews of concern.

"Forgive my mate, but her time is nearly upon her. She is young, so cannot fully shield others from her suffering. This is her first birthing and death. Shame and heartache I carry that my claws cut too deep to aid her in this battle. We must seek your help and the Wee Brothers' and Sisters'. If she does not escape whole from the sloughing of her old life, she will lose her soul and die the final death."

"Follow me," Jayle answered. Now that the female's pain touched her, Jayle found she could not fully block it out, nor did she desire to. No one should suffer like that. She opened the side door to the workshop, closing it when all were inside. Shelves covered the rear wall. In the winter they held the hearthcrafts her family made to sell in the spring. Now they were nearly empty. The wall backed up against what looked like a high mound of boulders on the outside, but when she pushed two shelf supports the wall slid back and to one side revealing a deep cave. To illuminate the chamber she lit three lanterns and hung them from iron hooks driven into the stone.

"Come," she said when the mated pair hesitated. "This place has sheltered many of your kind. We have brought only ease and healing to all who've sought it. Look." Jayle pointed to the large receptacles lining the deeper curve of the cave. Some were made of wood, some of stone, others of clay. Upon them all were carved or painted cats. Jayle didn't need to count to know that each bore eight portraits, no more. What happened when the big cats experienced the ninth death, none but they knew.

"You can see that not one death urn has been desecrated. Down the long years we've faithfully guarded what lies here." Jayle saw the tension ease in the male. The female leaned against him while he supported her to a pallet carved from stone. She sighed as she lay down.

"I must leave now. To stay would only increase her pain. I will guard your land, your loved ones, so no harm will come to them while you help my mate."

"Before you leave," Jayle said, "could you give me names to call you by. Not your true names!" With a rush she added, "'I know not to ask for that, but it would help me to have something by which to call you." Jayle saw the camilicats look at each other, then the male walked through the cave entrance.

"You may call her River, me Wind."

"Thank you, Wind." Jayle opened the door to the outside for him. She latched it behind her. When she returned to the cave she found the cats swarming over River: purring, nuzzling, licking her. Skunk sat on a stone ledge just above River.

Jayle went to the back of the cave and picked up the tall, gracefully curved jar she'd made. The blue-white slip she'd used on the jar made a perfect background for River's portrait. If the cat survived, seven more portraits of her would adorn the jar. Jayle regretted she could not do them all. Camilicats lived an amazing length of time. She'd be worm-bait long before the jar was completed. Family records did not say who discovered that carving or painting the likeness of the camilicat eased the death/birth cycle, only that it did.

Jayle looked up at Skunk's impatient snarl. He was right. She must begin. Jayle sat down within arm's length of River. The bond that had formed between them when they first met at the forest's edge remained. Through it she felt River's apprehension. With swift strokes she brushed the camilicat's outline onto the jar. Then she concentrated on the face. Silver fur, dappled here and there in rosettes of light and dark gray, was streaked with creamy lines. The glow from the lanterns reflected off the long guard hairs in pinpoints of red-gold to form a nimbus about River. Dark charcoal outlined the forest cat's open lips. Between them hung her tongue, dry from River's heavy panting. The face complete, Jayle looked up at Skunk.

"You can begin," she said.

Skunk raked his claws down River's face. He slashed the flesh over River's cheeks. Jayle gagged, swallowed. She expected a gush of blood. None came. Instead, two of the barn cats began to lick the furrows and tug at the wounds with their teeth. The fur and skin peeled cleanly away, revealing damp, newborn fur. Inji had told her of the process, but mere words could not convey the reality.

The camilicat's breathing quickened. River grunted as more of her skin parted. Skunk hissed, startling Jayle out of her appalled fascination. She and the Wee Brothers and Sisters were a team. If any of them lagged, it would prolong River's ordeal. Jayle painted swiftly. As she finished each part, Skunk and the farm cats split and peeled another section of River's old life away.

Death warred with the camilicat's emerging new life. River's agony increased. Her eyes took on a dry hot look. Exhaustion slowed her movements. River's breath grew shallow and labored, then ceased for several heartbeats. Jayle found herself leaning over River, begging,

"Breathe! Please, by the One, breathe." Not knowing what else to do, Jayle put her paint-stained hands on River's chest and pushed. Again and again. A foul rush of air spewed from River's lungs. Jayle drew up her leg, wedged her knee high underneath River's leg where it joined at the shoulder. With the whole weight of her body she pushed. She felt bony ribs bend. River coughed. Then sucked in a ragged breath. That welcome sound echoed off the stone walls, breaking the tense silence. Jayle wept as River's breathing steadied. She touched the camilicat's face, looked into River's amber eyes, and said, "You're going to be just fine."

Jayle sat down, legs too weak to hold her up. She noticed for the first time that about the stone platform many of the Wee Sisters and Brothers lay in a stupor of exhaustion. At that moment, Jayle realized the farm cats were bearing part of River's suffering. Jayle didn't understand how they did it; she didn't care as long as River survived. She, too, yearned for River's death and rebirth to be finished.

Jayle found herself painting almost mindlessly in the effort to be free of the echo of River's dual battle not to succumb to death and to emerge into her second life. At times it seemed to Jayle her own flesh parted beneath Skunk's claws. Her eyes stung from salt-seasoned sweat. It dripped off the end of her nose. She nearly wept in relief when she saw only the rear paws remained unpainted. Rapidly she brushed on dark brown. In a fine line Jayle stroked yellow-cream highlights on ivory claw tips. She was done. With a cry of joy building in her throat Jayle turned to River....

Skunk screamed! Jayle jerked, paintbrush flying from her fingers. She rose to her knees. Skunk was trying to claw his way out through the door. Only once before had she seen Skunk so wild, when Little O had been cornered by a bear. Oran! She scrambled to her feet, stumbled to the door, all thoughts of River erased by sudden terror for her son,

"Is it Little O?" she yelled. Skunk turned, slashed her leg with his claws. No longer questioning, she flung open the door. Jayle ran into the yard. The kitchen door banged against the outside wall. Mar stood on the back step, yelling,

"Mom! Mom! Where are you?"

"Here!"

"Hurry," he sobbed. "Little O's hurt."

Jayle shoved by him, following Skunk. She skidded to a halt. Oran lay at the foot of the loft ladder.

Jayle gently slid her arm beneath Little O's neck, supporting his head in her other hand. She fought the nausea that threatened to overwhelm her when she felt the bones in the back of his skull move. Carefully, she eased his head onto the crook of her arm, then slid her other arm under his knees, drawing him close to her breast. Jayle stood.

"Mar!" she commanded, "stop crying. I need you."

"But, Mom!" he wailed.

Compassion warred within her, but she shoved it aside. There wasn't time for it. "By the One!" she shouted. "Enough! Get out of my way." She passed him, stopped before the kitchen table. "Mar, take a deep breath. Another. Good. Now get me two blankets." She looked down at Little O. Blood ran from his nose in a thin stream and his limbs flopped. From beneath his nightgown his feet stuck out. His toes must be cold. Hysterical laughter threatened to burst from her. She worried that his feet were cold when death sat on his heart. Wild with need, she prayed,

"Anything. By the One, I'll give anything so he lives. Oh, please." She opened her eyes when Mar stumbled into the room.

"Here, Mom."

"Unfold a blanket. That's right. Spread it on the table. Good. Now fold one edge down a couple of times to form a pillow. That's right." She eased Oran down, covered him.

"What do we do now, Mom?"

"I don't know."

"Is Little O going to die?"

Jayle pulled Mar into her arms. She held him with all her strength. She sobbed once, then fought back the tears that threatened to strangle her. "He's hurt real bad, son, and fixing him is beyond my power."

"Healer Lirdon?"

"Even his." She pushed Mar back, but kept him within the circle of her arms as an insistent wail pierced her chaotic thoughts. It came from Skunk. Irritated, she said, "Not now, Skunk."

The tom ignored her. Skunk continued to half-snarl, half-yowl. He leapt upon the table. Skunk wove his way carefully around Little O. His gaze intent on her, he jumped off the table and went to the back door. Somehow, one of them must have shut it. With a yowl, he looked from it to her.

"I said not now!"

With an impatient snort Skunk leapt back upon the table, stalked up to Little O, and paced back and forth beside him.

"Mom, I think he's trying to tell you that there's something outside that might help Little O."

"Wind!" Jayle ran to the door. Hope rising within her, she flung it open. She nearly fell when the door banged against her as the male camilicat padded into the kitchen.

"How was your cub hurt? I guarded the ways. Nothing threatened this place."

"Mar, answer Wind's question."

"Little O woke," Mar answered, "because he dreamed camilicats were dancing in the moonlight. He wanted to dance, too. When he tried to climb out of the loft, his feet tangled in his nightgown. He fell, hitting his head on the table by the ladder."

The male looked from Jayle to Oran. *"The little one who is hurt has the Gift? If we'd known, we would have sought other means of help for my mate."*

Without waiting for her to speak, Mar said, "We were just wondering about that today, but we really don't know. None of our family has ever been Gifted."

"Some humans with the Gift sense us, are drawn to us. We hide from most. A few we welcome, those who choose to walk our ways and leave the human path. They are never as young as Little O. How long has he been manifesting the Gift?"

"You mean," Mar said, "that Little O really hears what Skunk and chickens think?"

Skunk hissed. When he was sure he had her attention, he turned and gently laid his head on Oran's chest. Stunned, Jayle looked at Wind. "I thought he was just playing 'make believe.'"

Not so. Wee Brother says they could always hear one another. Come, bring your son to my mate. There is no time to question or argue. By the Pact we have with you we swore no harm would come to any who dwelt here in return for your aid. There's a chance River can help. Hurry. There is little time left before the dawn."

Jayle picked up Oran. She followed Wind, with Skunk and Mar at her heels. At the open way to the inner chamber, Wind halted. "*I can go no farther. My mate knows what happened and is willing to try to save your cub's life. Paint as you've never painted before. You must beat the sun. The power to battle life and death is strongest at the moment the night ends and the birth of a new day begins.*"

River lay on the stone pallet, glorious in the beauty of her resurrection. Beneath her rear paws her discarded life lay in a crumpled pile. A single charcoal ring circled the tip of her tail, revealing to all who understood she'd completed one of her life cycles. River's voice brushed urgently across Jayle's mind.

"*Place your child against my side. Lay his head between my forepaws.*"

Trembling violently Jayle did as River asked. "What are you going to do to my child?"

"*If possible, save his life.*"

"How?"

"*By giving him one of my lives. Are you willing to sacrifice anything so your son may live?*"

"Of course!" Apprehension shot through her veins. She reached out and grabbed Mar's hand. "I won't give up Mar." Jayle shivered at the sound of pity she heard in River's voice.

"*No. He is safe. It's Little O you must yield.*"

"What do you mean. I thought you said you could save him."

"*I can completely strip from myself one of my remaining lives and give it to Oran. This is dangerous even with one*

of my people. To my knowledge we've not done this with a
human. To give him this chance I must wrap him in th
essence of myself. I believe it is worth the risk. Oran's bu
ding Gift and his youth are in his favor. And deep insid
himself he's fighting to survive, otherwise his injuries woul
have overcome him." River paused, looked at her search-
ingly, then added,

"Jayle, you don't have to go through with this. It might
be better for you if you just let him die, because if this
works Little O will become a camilicat. He may not retain
any memory of you or his human life."

"What? Become a CAT! Not remember I'm his
mother?" Jayle wanted to sweep Oran from between River's legs; only the fear of causing him further harm stopped
her. Harshly Jayle said,

"I hate this! I hate you. None of this would have happened except for you."

"Mom. Please, Mom. She's only trying to help."

Grief, fear, and crazy thoughts scrambled about in Jayle's
skull like a flock of starlings frightened by Skunk. The forest cat's words began to sound in her brain. 'It might be
better for you if you let him die. Better for you.' By the
One, she now understood what River said and felt shame.
Could she be so selfish as to let her son die rather than
give him to someone who might save his life? Her shoulders slumped. For a moment Jayle rested her head on
Mar's chest. The sweet throb of his heart sang in her ear.
Whatever the price she must pay, Jayle wanted life for both
her sons.

Jayle looked up at Mar. The naked grief in his eyes
echoed hers. He was shivering. She pulled him close to her
side. Jayle licked her dry lips. She asked him, "Mar, this is
your decision, too."

"It's his only chance, Mom." Unable to sustain eye contact with Mar, Jayle bowed her head. In her line of sight
were Little O's bare feet. It was an effort, but Jayle forced
herself to ask, "River, will Little O be completely lost?"

"I don't know."

"You said it's dangerous. Could you die, too?"

*"Yes. But more important than my life is the Pride and
the Pact we have with you. It must be healed. We failed in*

*our task. You did not. If we hadn't come, your son would
still live."*

Mar clung to Jayle. His body shook with the force of his
sobbing. She felt as if she were being torn in two. She
touched Little O's toes. They were cold. Jayle recoiled,
then forced herself to remain still, when River reached out
and laid her paw upon her hand. The camilicat was only
offering comfort. River's forepaw felt warm, soft, vibrant
with life. Little O would feel like this.

"How can I help?" Jayle whispered at last.

*"Bundle Oran in the skin of my old life. Leave an opening
over his breast and belly."*

Jayle wrapped Little O in the skin, tucking it over his
feet. Reluctantly, she relinquished him to River's embrace.
"Should I call the Wee Brothers and Sisters to help you?"

*"No. Only I can give away a living life. Now, on my
funeral urn you must add to my portrait a young cub. Give
him Oran's eyes. Paint, if you can, the heart of his essence.
Can you do this? If you cannot, I must know. I'm not willing
to give one of my lives away if you are not going to do
your best."*

- "You'll get it," Jayle promised. "Come, Mar. Sit beside
me and lend me your strength." She noted that River did
not object when Skunk curled up against Little O's feet.

Jayle tried to picture Little O as a camilicat. It was impossible. With relief she thought of Wind; male, strong,
gentle with his mate, radiating a wild beauty. Gradually, a
picture formed in her mind. Jayle sought among her paints
the exact hew of Little O's tawny-colored hair. Then she
added a dab of rose-madder and began to paint.

River's gentle voice came to her, *"Do not be frightened
by what I must do."* With that Jayle glanced up. Appalled,
she saw River rake her claws down Oran's chest and belly.
But only tiny beads of blood welled up against his gray-
white skin. River then scored her own flesh so deeply Jayle
could see pearly globules of fat, the sweep of muscle; both
were obscured by a wash of blood. River smeared her
blood on Little O's exposed skin, then over the fur covering
him. Jayle couldn't bear to watch. Forcing her attention
back to the urn, she brushed onto the cub's face Little O's
bright, summer blue eyes. She strove with all her being to
put as much of Oran into the portrait as she could.

"Mom?"

"What, Mar?"

"Could you paint in Skunk?" His voice broke. Like a small child he wiped his runny nose on the back of his hand. "It'd make me feel better. They ... they were always together."

For the first time in what seemed like hours, Jayle smiled. "That's a good idea. Little O'll be the only camilicat that has a battered tomcat for a familiar." Using a fine brush she etched in Skunk, his ragged ear and all his battle scars. Jayle leaned back to check her work. She was finished. Jayle looked up to tell River, then scrambled over to them. They lay tangled together. She could not see Oran, but a surge of hope set her heart to racing. River breathed. Jayle half-jumped when something moved under them. Frightened to see her child transformed, Jayle tried to look away but couldn't. She jerked, dropping her paintbrush, when Mar spoke.

"You fool cat," Mar said, laughing nervously as Skunk heaved himself from under River. He grabbed Jayle when River opened her eyes. The camilicat stood. Beneath her lay a young honey-gray camilicat. The cub opened his eyes. They were hot summer blue.

Jayle gasped, "Little O!" She took a step toward him, holding out her arms, but the cub backed up and hid behind River. From that safe place he looked curiously about.

"He is no longer Little O. He is my child. I promise I will tell him of you, the sacrifice you made for him. He will know two mothers gave birth to him."

All reason fled Jayle. Rage blinded her when the full import of what River said sunk in. Jayle felt as if River had gutted her. She lunged. Then screamed when Mar grabbed her,

"Let me go!"

"Mom, wait. Look at the cub."

Jayle shook her head; then, against her will, she looked. The cub stood nose to nose with Skunk.

Mar put his arms around her, saying, "Little O always wanted to be like Skunk."

Mar's words rang with a truth that shocked some sanity into her. She nodded and stepped back from River. "Mar's right. I think if Little O could have chosen for himself he'd have said yes to becoming a camilicat and laughed with joy during the process. Little O loved to laugh." She glanced at the cub, then quickly away. "River, I should apologize for reacting to your words. I agreed to this, but there was no way I could understand the reality of my loss until it happened." Futilely, Jayle scrubbed tears from her face. The tears simply would not stop flowing. Jayle saw compassion in River's eyes and part of her wanted none of it. Torn between gratitude and hatred for the big cat, Jayle said, "I don't like this, but it's better than death. Please, this is tearing me apart. Take him and go. I can bear no more."

Little O lived but, oh, the pain of the choice she'd made burned. She felt something tug at her leg. Skunk. For once he didn't look at her with a snarl on his scarred face. Instead he stretched up, bracing his paws on her thigh. He purred, and licked her hand.

"Why, thank you, Skunk." For a moment he gazed at her, then ran after Little O, grabbed his tail between his teeth, and sat down. She almost laughed at the surprised look on the cub's face when he turned to see what clung to his tail.

"River," asked Mar. "Isn't the cub small for a three-year-old?"

"*No,*" she answered. "*We age at a slower rate than you humans do.*"

Jayle and Mar followed them outside. The birds were sleepily muttering time-to-wake-up sounds. Skunk dashed between and around Little O's legs as he used to do when his friend had two legs. Jayle could see the cub thoroughly enjoyed the game. He missed his step, tumbled over Skunk, and fell in a heap. She saw the oddest expression in the cub's summer blue eyes as he looked at the black tom cat. Jayle shivered when she heard a young voice say,

"*You—you'z Skunk.*"

Jayle clutched Mar. Hope flooded her, lending her the courage to turn her back on the camilicats, the cub, and Skunk as they walked away.

A TAIL
OF TWO SKITTYS

by Mercedes Lackey

The howls coming from inside the special animal shipping crate sounded impatient, and had been enough to seriously alarm the cargo handlers. Dick White, Spaceman First Class, Supercargo on the CatsEye Company ship *Brightwing*, put his hand on the outside of the plastile crate, just above the word "Property." From within the crate the muffled voice continued to yowl general unhappiness with the world.

Tell her that it's all right, SKitty, he thought at the black form that lay over his shoulders like a living fur collar. *Tell her I'll have her out in a minute. I don't want her to come bolting out of there and hide the minute I crack the crate.*

SKitty raised her head. Yellow eyes blinked once, sleepily. Abruptly, the yowling stopped.

:She fine,: SKitty said, and yawned, showing a full mouth of needle-pointed teeth. *:Only young, scared. I think she make good mate for Furball.:*

Dick shook his head; the kittens were not even a year old, and already their mother was matchmaking. Then, again, that *was* the tendency of mothers the universe over.

At least now he'd be able to uncrate this would-be "mate" with a minimum of fuss.

The full legend imprinted on the crate read "Female Shipscat Astra Stardancer of Englewood, Property of Bio-Tech Interstellar, leased to CatsEye Company. Do not open under penalty of law." Theoretically, Astra was, like SKitty, a bio-engineered shipscat, fully capable of handling free-fall, alien vermin, conditions that would poison, paralyze, or terrify her remote Terran ancestors, and all without turning a hair. In actuality, Astra, like the nineteen other ships-

132

cats Dick had uncrated, was a failure. The genetic engineering of her middle-ear and other balancing organs had failed. She could not tolerate free-fall, and while most ships operated under grav-generators, there were always equipment malfunctions and accidents.

That made her and her fellows failures by BioTech standards. A shipscat that could not handle free-fall was not a shipscat.

Normally, kittens that washed out in training were adopted out to carefully selected planet- or station-bound families of BioTech employees. However, this was not a "normal" circumstance by any stretch of the imagination.

The world of the Lacu'un, graceful, bipedal humanoids with a remarkably sophisticated, if planet-bound, civilization, was infested with a pest called a "kreshta." Erica Makumba, the Legal Advisor and Security Chief of Dick's ship, described them as "six-legged crosses between cockroaches and mice." SKitty described them only as "nasty," but she hunted them gleefully anyway. The Lacu'un had opened their world to trade just over a year ago, and some of their artifacts and technologies made them a desirable trade-ally indeed. The *Brightwing* had been one of the three ships invited to negotiate, in part because of SKitty, for the Lacu'un valued totemic animals highly.

And that was what had led to Captain Singh of the *Brightwing* conducting the entire trade negotiations with the Lacu'un—and had kept *Brightwing* ground-bound for the past year. SKitty had done the—to the Lacu'un—impossible. She had killed kreshta. She had already been assumed to be *Brightwing*'s totemic animal; that act elevated her to the status of "god-touched miracle," and had given the captain and crew of her ship unprecedented control and access to the rulers here.

SKitty had been newly-pregnant at the time; part of the price for the power Captain Singh now wielded had been her kittens. But Dick had gotten another idea, and had used his own share of the profits *Brightwing* was taking in to purchase the leases of twenty more "failed" cats to supplement SKitty's four kittens. BioTech cats released for leases were generally sterile, SKitty being a rare exception. If these twenty worked out, the Lacu'un would be very grateful, and more importantly, so would Vena Ferducci, the attractive, petite Terran Consul assigned to the new embassy here. In the past few months, Dick had gotten to know Vena very well—and he hoped to get to know her better. Vena had originally been a Survey Scout, and she was getting rather restless in her ground-based position as Consul. And in truth, the Lacu'un's lawyer, Lan Ventris, was much better suited to such a job than Vena. She had hinted that as soon as the Lacu'un felt they could trust Ventris, she would like to resign and go back to space. Dick rather hoped she might be persuaded to take a position with the *Brightwing*. It was too soon to call this little dance a "romance," but he had hopes. . . .

Hopes which could be solidified by this experiment. If the twenty young cats he had imported worked out as well as SKitty's four half-grown kittens, the Lacu'un would be able to import their intelligent pest-killers at a fraction of what the lease on a shipscat would be. This would make Vena happy; anything that benefited her Lacu'un made her happy. And if Dick was the cause of that happiness. . . .

:Dick go courting?: SKitty asked innocently, salting her query with decidedly *not*-innocent images of her own "courting."

Dick blushed. *No courting,* he thought firmly. *Not yet, anyway.*

:Silly,: SKitty replied scornfully. The overtones of her thoughts were—why waste such a golden opportunity? Dick did not answer her.

Instead, he thumbed the lock on the crate, a lock keyed to his DNA only. A tiny prickle was the only indication that the lock had taken a sample of his skin for comparison, but a moment later a hairline-thin crack appeared around the front end of the crate, and Dick carefully opened the door and looked inside.

A pair of big green eyes in a pointed gray face looked out at him from the shadows. "Meowrrrr?" said a tentative voice.

Tell her it's all right, SKitty, he thought, extending a hand for Astra to sniff. It was too bad that his telepathic connection with SKitty did not extend to these other cats, but she seemed to be able to relay everything he needed to tell them.

Astra sniffed his fingers daintily, and oozed out of the

crate, belly to the floor. After a moment, though, a moment during which SKitty stared at her so hard that Dick was fairly certain his little friend was communicating any number of things to the newcomer, Astra stood up and looked around, her ears coming up and her muscles relaxing. Finally, she looked up at Dick and blinked.

"Prrow," she said. He didn't need SKitty's translation to read that. He held out his arms and the young cat leapt into them, to be carried in regal dignity out of the Quarantine area.

As he turned away from the crate, he thought he caught a hint of movement in the shadows at the back. But when he turned to look, there was nothing there, and he dismissed it as nothing more than his imagination. If there *had* been anything else in Astra's crate, the manifest would have listed it—and Astra was definitely sterile, so it could not have been an unlicensed kitten.

Erica Makumba and Vena were waiting for him in the corridor outside. Vena offered her fingers to the newcomer; much more secure now, Astra sniffed them and purred. "She's lovely," Vena said in admiration. Dick had to agree; Astra was a velvety blue-gray from head to tail, and her slim, clean lines clearly showed her descent from Russian Blue ancestors.

:She for Furball,: SKitty insisted, gently nipping at his neck.

Is this your idea or hers? Dick retorted.

:Sees Furball in head; likes Furball.: That seemed to finish it as far as SKitty was concerned. *:Good hunter, too.:* Dick gave in to the inevitable.

"Didn't we promise one of these new cats to the Lacu'-teveras?" Dick asked. "This one seems very gentle; she'd probably do very well as a companion for Furball." SKitty's kittens all had names as fancy as Astra's—or as SKitty's official name, for that matter. Furball was "Andreas Widefarer of Lacu'un," Nuisance was "Misty Snowspirit of Lacu'un," Rags was "Lady Flamebringer of Lacu'un" and Scat was "Garrison Starshadow of Lacu'un." But they had, as cats always do, acquired their own nicknames that had nothing to do with the registered names. Astra would, without a doubt, do the same.

Each of the most prominent families of the Lacu'un had

been granted one cat, but the Royal Family had three. Two of SKitty's original kittens, and one of the newcomers. Astra would bring that number up to four, a sacred number to the Lacu'un and very propitious.

"We did," Vena replied absently, scratching a pleased Astra beneath her chin, "and I agree with you; I think this one would please the Lacu'teveras very much." She laughed a little. "I'm beginning to think you're psychic or something, Dick; you haven't been wrong with your selections yet."

"Me?" he said ingenuously. "Psychic? Spirits of Space, Vena, the way these people are treating the cats, it doesn't matter anyway. Any 'match' I made would be a good one, so far as the cat is concerned. They couldn't be pampered more if they were Lacu'un girl-babies!"

"True," she agreed, and reluctantly took her hand away. "Well, four cats should be just about right to keep the Palace vermin-free. It's really kind of funny how they've divided the place up among them with no bickering. They almost act as if they were humans dividing up patrols!" Erica shot him an unreadable glance; did she remember how he had sat down with the original three and SKitty— and a floor-plan of the place—when he first brought them all to the Palace?

"They are bred for high intelligence," he reminded both of them hastily. "No one really knows how bright they are. They're bright enough to use their life-support pods in an emergency, and bright enough to learn how to use the human facilities in the ships. They seem to have ways of communicating with each other, or so the people at Bio-Tech tell me, so maybe they did establish patrols."

"Well, maybe they did," Erica said after a long moment. He heaved a mental sigh of relief. The last thing he needed was to have someone suspect SKitty's telepathic link with him. BioTech was not breeding for telepathy, but if such a useful trait ever showed up in a *fertile* female, they would surely cancel *Brightwing*'s lease and haul SKitty back to their nearest cattery to become a breeding queen. SKitty was his best friend; to lose her like that would be terrible.

:*No breeding,*: SKitty said firmly. :*Love Dick, love ship. No breeding; breeding dull, kittens a pain. Not leave ship ever.*:

Well, at least SKitty agreed.

For now, anyway, now that her kittens were weaned. Whenever she came into season, she seemed to change her mind, at least about the part that resulted in breeding, if not the breeding itself.

The Lacu'teveras, the Ruling Consort of her people, accepted Astra into the household with soft cries of welcome and gladness. Erica was right, the Lacu'un could not possibly have pampered their cats more. Whenever a cat wanted a lap or a scratch, one was immediately provided, whether or not the object of feline affection was in the middle of negotiations or a session of Council or not. Whenever one wished to play—although with the number of kreshta about, there was very little energy left over for playing— everything else was set aside for that moment. And when one brought in a trophy kreshta, tail and ears held high with pride, the entire court applauded. Astra was introduced to Furball at SKitty's insistence. Noses were sniffed, and the two rubbed cheeks. It appeared that Mama's matchmaking was going to work.

The three humans and the pleased feline headed back across the city to the spaceport and the Fence around it. The city of the Lacu'un was incredibly attractive, much more so than any other similar city Dick had ever visited. Because of the rapidity with which the kreshta multiplied given any food and shelter, the streets were kept absolutely spotless, and the buildings clean and in repair. Most had walls about them, giving the inhabitants little islands of privacy. The walls of the wealthy were of carved stone; those of the poor of cast concrete. In all cases, ornamentation was the rule, not the exception.

The Lacu'un themselves walked the streets of their city garbed in delicate, flowing robes, or shorter, more practical versions of the same garments. Graceful and handsome, they resembled avians rather than reptiles; their skin varied in shade from a dark brown to a golden tan, and their heads bore a kind of frill like an iguana's, running from the base of the neck to a point just above and between the eyes.

Their faces were capable of something like a smile, and the expression meant the same for them as it did for humans. Most of them smiled when they saw Dick and SKitty; although the kreshta-destroying abilities of the cat were not something any of them would personally feel the impact of for many years, perhaps generations, they still appreciated what the cats Dick had introduced could do. The kreshta had been a plague upon them for as long as their history recorded, even being so bold as to steal the food from plates and injure unguarded infants. For as long as that history, it had seemed that there would never be a solution to the depredations of the little beasts. But now—the most pious claimed the advent of the cats was a sign of the gods' direct intervention and blessing, and even the skeptics were thrilled at the thought that an end to the plague was in sight. It was unlikely that, even with a cat in every household, the kreshta would ever be destroyed—but such things as setting a guard on sleeping babies and locking meals in metal containers set into the tables could probably be eliminated.

When they crossed the Fence into Terran territory, however, the surroundings dropped in quality by a magnitude or two. Dick felt obscurely ashamed of his world whenever he looked at the shabby, garish spaceport "facilities" that comprised most of the Terran spaceport area. At least the headquarters that Captain Singh and CatsEye had established were handsome; adaptations of the natives' own architecture, in cast concrete with walls decorated with stylized stars, spaceships, and suggestions of slit-pupiled eyes. SolarQuest and UVN, the other two Companies that had been given Trade permits, were following CatsEye's lead, and had hired the same local architects and contractors to build their own headquarters. It looked from the half-finished buildings as if SolarQuest was going with a motif taken from their own logo of a stylized sunburst; UVN was going for geometrics in their wall-decor.

There were four ships here at the moment rather than the authorized three; for some reason, the independent freighter that had brought in the twenty shipscats was still here on the landing field. Dick wondered about that for a moment, then shrugged mentally. Independents often ran on shoestring budgets; probably they had only loaded enough fuel to get them here, and refueling was taking more time than they had thought it would.

Suddenly, just as they passed through the doors of the building, SKitty howled, hissed, and leapt from Dick's shoulders, vanishing through the rapidly-closing door.

He uttered a muffled curse and turned to run after her. What had gotten into her, anyway?

He found himself looking into the muzzle of a weapon held by a large man in the nondescript coveralls favored by the crew of that independent freighter. The man was as nondescript as his clothing, with ash-blond hair cut short and his very ordinary face—with the exception of that weapon, and the cold, calculating look in his iron-gray eyes. Dick put up his hands, slowly. He had the feeling this was a very bad time to play hero.

"Where's the damn cat?" snapped the one Dick was coming to think of as "the Gray Man." One of his underlings shrugged.

"Gone," the man replied shortly. "She got away when we rounded up these three, and she just vanished somewhere. Forget the cat. How much damage could a cat do?"

The Gray Man shrugged. "The natives might get suspicious if they don't see her with our man."

"She probably wouldn't have cooperated with our man," the underling pointed out. "Not like she did with this one. It doesn't matter—White got the new cats installed, and we don't need an animal that was likely to be a handful anyway."

The Gray Man nodded after a while and went back to securing the latest of his prisoners. The offices in the new CatsEye building had been turned into impromptu cells; Dick had gotten a glimpse of Captain Singh in one of them as he had been frog-marched past. He didn't know what these people had done with the rest of the crew or with Vena and Erica, since Vena had been taken off somewhere separately and Erica had been stunned and dragged away without waiting for her surrender.

The Gray Man watched him with his weapon trained on him as two more underlings installed a tangle-field generator across the doorway. With no windows, these little offices made perfect holding-pens. Most of them didn't have furniture yet; those that did didn't really contain anything that could be used as a weapon. The desks were simple slabs of native wood on metal supports, the chairs molded plastile, and both were bolted to the floor. There was nothing in Dick's little cubicle that could even be thrown.

Dick was still trying to figure out who and what these people were, when something finally clicked. He looked up at the Gray Man. "You're from TriStar, aren't you?" he asked.

If the Gray Man was startled by this, he didn't show it. "Yes," the man replied, gun-muzzle never wavering. "How did you figure that out?"

"BioTech never ships with anyone other than TriStar if they can help it," Dick said flatly. "I wondered why they had hired a tramp-freighter to bring out their cats; it didn't seem like them, but then I thought maybe that was all they could get."

"You're clever, White," the Gray Man replied, expressionlessly. "Too clever for your own good, maybe. We might just have to make you disappear. You and the Makumba woman; she'll probably know some of us as soon as she wakes up, and we don't have the time or the equipment to brain-wipe you."

Dick felt a chill going down his back, as the men at the door finished installing the field and left quickly. "BioTech is going to wonder if one of their designated handlers just vanishes. And without me, you're never going to get SKitty back; BioTech isn't going to care for that, either. They might start asking questions that you can't answer."

The Gray Man stared at him for a long moment; his expression did not vary in the least, but at least he didn't make any move to shoot. "I'll think about it," he said finally. He might have said more, but there was a shout from the corridor outside.

"The cat!" someone yelled, and the Gray Man was out of the door before Dick could blink. Unfortunately, he paused long enough to trigger the tangle-field before he ran off in pursuit of what could only have been SKitty.

Dick slumped down into the chair, and buried his face in his hands, but not in despair. He was thinking furiously.

TriStar didn't like getting cut out of the negotiations; what they can't get legally, they'll get any way they can. Probably they intend to use us as hostages against Vena's good behavior, getting her to put them up as the new negotiators. I solved the problem of getting the cats for them; now there's no reason they couldn't just step in. But that can't go on forever, sooner or later Vena is going to get to a com unit or send some kind of message offworld. So what would these people do then?

TriStar had a reputation as being ruthless, and he'd heard from Erica that it was justified. So how do you get rid of an entire crew of a spaceship *and* the Terran Consul? And maybe the crews of the other two ships into the bargain?

Well, there was always one answer to that, especially on a newly-opened world. Plague.

The chill threaded his backbone again as he realized just what a good answer that was. These TriStar goons could use sickness as the excuse for why the CatsEye people weren't in evidence. A rumor of plague might well drive the other two ships off-world before *they* came down with it. The TriStar people could even claim to be taking care of the *Brightwing*'s crew.

Then, after a couple of weeks, they all succumb to the disease, the Terran Consul with them. . . .

It was a story that would work, not only with the Terran authorities, but with the Lacu'un. The Fence was a very effective barrier to help from the natives; the Lacu'un would not cross it to find out the truth, even if they were suspicious.

I have to get to a com set, he thought desperately. His own usefulness would last only so long as it took them to trap SKitty and find some way of caging her. No one else, so far as he knew, could hear her thoughts. All they needed to do would be to catch her and ship her back to BioTech, with the message that the designated handler was dead of plague and the cat had become unmanageable. It wouldn't have been the first time.

A soft hiss made him look up, and he strangled a cry of mingled joy and apprehension. It was SKitty! She was right outside the door, and she seemed to be trying to do something with the tangle-field generator.

SKitty! he thought at her as hard as he could. *SKitty, you have to get away from here, they're trying to catch you—* There was no way SKitty was going to be able to deal with those controls; they were deliberately made difficult to handle, precisely because shipscats were known to be

curious. And how could she know what complicated series
of things to do to take down the field anyway?

But SKitty ignored him, using her stubby raccoonlike
hands on the controls of the generator and hissing in frustration when the controls would not cooperate.

Finally, with a muffled yowl of triumph, she managed to
twist the dial into the "off" position and the field went
down. Dick was out the door in a moment, but SKitty was
uncharacteristically running off ahead of him instead of
waiting for him. Not that he minded! She was safer on the
ground in case someone spotted him and stunned him; she
was small and quick, and if they caught him again, she
would still have a chance to hide and get away. But there
was something odd about her bounding run; as if her body
was a little longer than usual. And her tail seemed to be a
lot longer than he remembered—

Never mind that, get moving! he scolded himself, trying
to recall where they'd set up all the coms and if any of
them were translight. SKitty whisked ahead of him, around
a corner; when he caught up with her, she was already at
work on the tangle-field generator in front of another door.

Practice must have made perfect; she got the field down
just before he reached the doorway, and shot down the hall
like a streak of black lightning. Dick stopped; inside was
someone lying down on a cot, arm over her dark mahogany
head. Erica!

"Erica!" he hissed at her. She sat bolt upright, wincing
as she did so, and he felt a twinge of sympathy. A stun-
migraine was no picnic.

She saw who was at the door, saw at the same moment
that there was no tangle-field shimmer between them, and
was on her feet and out in a fraction of a second. "How?"
she demanded, scanning the corridor and finding it as curiously empty as Dick had.

"SKitty took the generator offline," he said. "She got
yours, too, and she headed off that way." He pointed toward the heart of the building. "Do you remember where
the translight coms are?"

"Eyeah," she said. "In the basement, if we can get there.
That's the emergency unit and I don't think they know
we've got it."

She cocked her head to one side, as if she had suddenly

heard something. He strained his ears—and there was a clamor, off in the distance beyond the walls of the building. It sounded as if several people were chasing something. But it couldn't have been SKitty; she was still in the building.

"It sounds like they're busy," Erica said, and grinned. "Let's go while we have the chance!"

But before they reached the basement com room, they were joined by most of the crew of the *Brightstar,* some of whom had armed themselves with whatever might serve as a weapon. All of them told the same story, about how the shipscat had taken down their tangle-fields and fled. Once in the basement of the building—after scattering the multiple nests of kreshta that had moved right in—the Com Officer took over while the rest of them found whatever they could to make a barricade and Dick related what he had learned and what his surmises were. Power controls were all down here; there would be no way short of blowing the building up for the TriStar goons to cut power to the com. Now all they needed was time—time to get their message out, and wait for the Patrol to answer.

But time just might be in very short supply, Dick told himself as he grabbed a sheet of reflective insulation to use as a crude stun-shield. And as if in answer to that, just as the Com Officer got the link warmed up and began to send, Erica called out from the staircase.

"Front and center—here they come!"

Dick slumped down so that the tiny medic could reach his head to bandage it. He knew he looked like he'd been through a war, but either the feeling of elated triumph or the medic's drugs or both prevented him from really feeling any of his injuries. In the end, it had come down to the crudest of hand-to-hand combat on the staircase, as the Com Officer resent the message as many times as he could and the rest of them held off the TriStar bullies. He could only thank the Spirits of Space that they had no weapons stronger than stunners—or at least, they hadn't wanted to use them down in the basement where so many circuits lay bare. Eventually, of course, they had been overwhelmed, but by then it was too late. The Com Officer had gotten a reply from the Patrol. Help was on the way. Faced with the collapse of their plan, the TriStar people had done the only wise thing. They had retreated.

With them, they had taken all evidence that they *were* from TriStar; there was no way of proving who and what they were, unless the Patrol corvette now on the way in could intercept them and capture them. Contrary to what the Gray Man had thought, Erica had recognized none of her captors.

But right now, none of that mattered. What did matter was that *they* had come through this—and that SKitty had finally reappeared as soon as the TriStar ship blasted out, to take her accustomed place on Dick's shoulders, purring for all she was worth and interfering with the medic's work.

"Dick—" Vena called from the door to the medic's office, "I found your—"

Dick looked up. Vena was cradling SKitty in her arms.

But SKitty was already on his shoulders.

She must have looked just as stunned as he did, but he recovered first, doing a double-take. *His* SKitty was the one on her usual perch. Vena's SKitty was a little thinner, a little taller.

And most *definitely* had a lot longer tail!

:Is Prrreet,: SKitty said with satisfaction. *:Handsome, no? Is bred for being Patrol-cat, war-cat.:*

"Vena, what's the tattoo inside that cat's ear?" he asked urgently. She checked.

"FX-003," she said, "and a serial number. But the X designation is for experimental, isn't it?"

"Uh—yeah." He got up, ignoring the medic, and came to look at the new cat. Vena's stranger also had much more humanlike hands then his SKitty; suddenly the mystery of how the cat had managed to manipulate the tangle-field controls was solved.

Shoot, he might even have been trained *to do that!*

:Yes,: SKitty said simply. *:I go play catch-me-stupid, he open human-cages. He hear of me on station, come to see me, be mate. I think I keep him.:*

Dick closed his eyes for a moment. Somewhere, there was a frantic BioTech station trying to figure out where one of their experimentals had gone. He *should* turn the cat over to them!

:*No,*: SKitty said positively. :*No look. Is deaf one ear; is pet. Run away, find me.*:

"He uh—must have come in as an extra with that shipment," Dick improvised quickly. "I found an extra invoice, I just thought they'd made a mistake. He's deaf in one ear, that's why they washed him out. I uh—I suppose *Brightstar* could keep him."

"I was kind of hoping I could—" Vena began, and flushed, lowering her eyes. "I suppose I still could . . . after this, the embassy is going to have to have a full staff with Patrol guards and a real Consul. They won't need me anymore."

Dick began to grin, as he realized what Vena was saying. "Well, he will need a handler. And I have all I can do to take care of *this* SKitty."

:*Courting?*: SKitty asked slyly, reaching out to lick one of Prrreet's ears.

This time Dick did not bother to deny it.

HERMIONE AS SPY

by Ardath Mayhar

Upon perusing the Journal that contains the record of my long and, I hope, useful Life as Familiar to numerous prominent Practitioners of the arcane Arts, it is with some Hesitation that I reread this strange Account. Never had I (or, indeed my Instructors at the illustrious School at which I was trained) considered that at any point a respectable Feline of my Profession might become what the commoner Sort call a Spy.

Yet, when dealing with Wizards, one constantly finds one's Path beset with Strange and Unexpected Hazards and Duties. Such a Task befell me when I was a very young Familiar, as yet immature in my Profession. I had not yet Fathomed the Depths of Perfidy to which my Human Associates could stoop, and, being very young and ignorant, I considered the Assignment given me by my first Master, Aldonious Fury, to be a matter of Interest and excitement.

Fury was my very first Commission, assigned to me by the Dean of the School which was my Alma Mater. He was an irascible Gentleman, much given to Drink; later in life I considered him an inspired Example to set before a Novice, for in dealing with him I encountered my first Taste of Human Follies.

I was assigned somewhat Hastily, for the previous holder of my new Position had met with an untimely End while exploring the Rooftops of the Crescent in which Fury's House was located. A frantic Request from the Wizard implied some Emergency, and Tabitha, the Dean, instructed me and sent me packing to my new Task with less than dignified Speed.

It was the Habit of my dear School to send a new Graduate to her first position in a Hansom Cab, which was a

146

most civil Gesture. When the Driver, a rather surly and uncommunicative Person, deposited me at the curbstone before Number Six Camberly Crescent, I tipped him grudgingly before taking down my small Satchel and moving up the steps to the handsome carved Door.

A very young Maidservant opened at my Ring, and something about her Manner aroused my Interest. As yet, I was too young to understand the complex Attitudes of Humanity toward the simple fact of Reproduction, but I sensed a bit of Jealousy as she bent to take my Belongings (which were less than a handful to one of Human Stature) and led me down a spacious Hallway to the door of a Library. This puzzled me, for what could a Woman have to fear, as a Rival for Affection, from a Cat?

Of course, now that I am old in the Service of Humanity, I understand that Logic is no Element of Human Emotion, and I know, as I did not know then, that the Girl was jealous of Fury's Obsession with things magical and of Anyone or anything who might be Helpful to him in those Pursuits.

I was not thinking of such Matters, however, as I stepped softly through the wide Doors and looked up at my first Associate in the Arcane Arts. To my Surprise, I did not have to look *far* up, for Fury was a veritable Dwarf of a Man, and my Head (for I have always been uncommonly large for my Species) came almost to the Watch-chain that stretched across his Waistcoat.

He did not make the usual polite Remarks expected when meeting a new Acquaintance but plunged instantly into an incoherent Account of his Needs. My Teachers had trained their Students to deal with such Human Impatience, however. I removed my Novice's Collar, which was no longer an Indication of my Status, and put it into his Hand.

Understand, dear Reader, that when I speak now of Words between Familiar and Sorcerer, I do not mean verbal Speech. The Communication between those in my Profession and their Associates is far more Delicate and Silent. Yet I said to him, in a Manner that he understood instantly, "My dear Aldonious Fury, do sit down and send that impertinent Girl after Tea. Then we shall speak of your Problems in civilized Conversation. I cannot understand what you need, if you rant and ramble."

He had the grace to Blush. Sorcerers are, I have learned from long Experience, an impatient and arrogant Lot. Only a Cat, of all living Creatures including nonsorcerous Humanity, has the Confidence and Control needed to deal Rationally with them. Knowing that he had met his Match, Fury sank into a deep Chair and rang the Bell with unnecessary Emphasis.

"Tea, Amelia," he said. "And take Hermione's things to her quarters, afterward. Be respectful, mind you. I've noticed that sidelong glance you're giving my new helper. Don't think you can hide anything from me!"

The Admonition did not, I suspected at once, do anything at all to help my Position. The Glance Amelia sent in my Direction was filled with Malice that had only been Intensified by Fury's Words. But she left without Comment, and I turned my Attention to this, my very first Wizard, except for those Few who visited the Institution in which I was trained, in order to add their own input to our Education.

Although Fury seemed unwilling to indulge in conversational Niceties, I was able to convey the Greetings of his old Acquaintances among my Instructors, as well as to give him some Notion of my own Qualifications. All the While, I studied this Man with whom my professional Life would begin.

He was not a prepossessing Person. Short, square, and red-faced, he glared at Objects as well as at living Beings. In addition, he fidgeted with the tassels of his peaked Cap, the dangling chain at his Waistcoat, and the *objets d'art* on the small Taboret beside his Chair.

His Tea, when it came, smelled strongly of Spirituous Liquor, but the Dose seemed to cheer him and to quiet his Nerves to some Extent. When I had calmly lapped my Saucer of Milk, I returned to my own low Chair and waited for him to begin whatever Tale of Woe had brought me here so precipitously.

Amelia removed the tea things at last. When she was well out of Earshot, he drew together his bushy white Brows and his intensely blue Eyes shone out like small Creatures hiding in Undergrowth. My Paws twitched, feeling the need to Pounce, but I managed to control them as he began to speak.

"Ah . . . hmmm . . . Hermione," he said, his fingers madly engaged with his Watch-chain, "you must realize that a man in my position has a great deal of stress to deal with. A great deal. And calls upon my time—why hardly a day goes by that someone, great or humble, old or young, does not come to my door with life-or-death problems that only my arts can solve."

To an extent that was True, and I took his Words with some Seriousness. The World of Men is not conducted rationally, as that of my Kind seems to be. What their Laws and their Rituals confuse and disrupt must often be unraveled by the Magic of such Practitioners as Fury. I nodded solemnly.

"This means that I am frequently—almost constantly—exhausted, both physically and mentally. You can see that, I am certain," he continued. "Such weariness must be eased in some manner, and I personally prefer brandy to other methods. This *can,* though it seldom does, lead to a certain lack of alertness on my part."

Again I nodded. We had been given in-depth training in dealing with drunken Wizards.

"A week past, I found myself in need of such relaxation," Fury said, "and I made the major error of indulging in such unguarded behavior in the company of a—I will not term him friend. In the company of one whose perfidy I did not, at that time, suspect. To my consternation, I find that while I was incapacitated this *person* filched from me a certain personal item that has given him unacceptable *influence* over my actions at unexpected times, unless I am totally on guard. I must have a . . . something like *a secret spy* who will infiltrate his home and steal back the . . . matter that he took from me."

I felt a strange Excitement fill my heart. No Familiar that we had ever studied was assigned such an esoteric Task, and it was clear that my new Associate was in DIRE NEED of such help. The use of personal Items by the less meticulous of the sorcerous Breed is well known among my Kind.

Assuming an impersonal and professional Tone, I asked, "And exactly, what did this Person take from you? A lock of Hair? A Clipping from your Nails? I must know, if I am to Find and Return it to you."

At that Moment, Fury began to shiver as if taken with a Chill. His Mouth opened, shut, opened, shut, and it was obvious to me that he was unable to Speak. Instantly, I was at his side, rubbing my Fur against his right Hand, licking his Fingers, lending him my Strength to overcome this Attack from outside. My Efforts were not without Effect, for soon Fury closed his Mouth firmly, sighed with relief, and relaxed his convulsed Body.

"Thank you." His voice was weak, but the Words seemed Heartfelt. He cleared his Throat, coughed several times, and straightened in his Chair. "Yes, you must know. It is embarrassing to admit, but this man—this Damien—removed a *birthmark* from my hip while I was ... incapacitated. This *seizure* that you have seen is a result of his use of my own skin against me. How he knew of its existence I cannot imagine, but in some manner he had learned that I had such a mark."

"I understand what must be done," I told him. "I will study any Sketch that you might prepare for me, in order to give me some Notion of his House. Then I will go to my Rooms and prepare myself. Tonight I shall enter his Domain and find the thing that you must have returned to you." I studied his Face as I spoke, seeing his Look of great Pleasure and Relief.

"Then I will entrust to you a talisman that will safeguard you from his spells," the Wizard said. He took from his Waistcoat Pocket a thin length of Chain that glinted in the Light. "Slip this about your Neck," he said. "Until this misfortune, it has protected me well from the workings of my peers. Only the use of my own skin has overcome its potency, I am certain."

Nighfall found me in the Gardens of a modest House some Blocks from that of Aldonious Fury. The Shrubbery was untrimmed, the flowerbeds untended. The back of the House itself was shabby, the paint peeling, the brickwork crumbling.

The scullery Window was open a hand's width, and I set my claws firmly into the thick Vine of ivy that climbed the Wall. Once I was on the Sill, I slipped into that narrow Crack, blessing the flexible Muscle and Bone of my Breed.

Inside it was dark, as was Proper at such an hour. The

Kitchen beyond the musty scullery stank of Garbage, and I knew that Damien, whatever else he might be, was a poorly served Master. But I made my way through the noisome Darkness into the back corridor that I had noted on the Map provided by Fury. There I found the back Staircase, used by servants, and my quick Paws fled silently up the steep Flights.

I did not seek out the Sleeping Chamber of this rival Wizard. No, he would, we had agreed, keep his ugly Experiment in his Laboratory, shut away from the Eyes of Servants. The Law was very strict in dealing with the use of the Black Arts against the Life or the Peace of its Citizens. Damien, whatever his Skill, would not want to have his Neck stretched on a Gibbet or his Body chained in a dark Prison. Wizards, I was taught, value their Skins and their Comfort more than Most.

The Door was, of course, locked securely. But a Familiar has many ways of entering locked Rooms, and I sniffed about for a Rathole in the wainscoting of the corridor until I found one of suitable Size and great Age. Creeping through it, which was not easy even for one trained to slip through tiny Openings, I found myself amid the dust of generations inside the Wall. Luckily, this was a Wall added after the original Construction of the Pile, and it consisted only of two thick Layers of Paneling fastened to heavy Uprights. I followed my Nose until I found another Rathole that emerged behind the Tapestries of the Wizard's Inner Sanctum.

There was a dim Light burning, but that did not disturb me. Fury had said that he himself left Illumination in his secret Workrooms at Night. I squeezed through the hole and flattened myself along the Wall without even causing the Tapestry to ripple. This was, I congratulated myself, going to be a very easy Assignment.

Then I froze, every Whisker stiff with caution. Footsteps moved over the Parquet beyond the fabric, and the Motion of a large Body caused the Air to swirl against my Paws. The Wizard was, I realized with Horror, still up and working at his arcane Tasks.

I paused, thinking deeply. I had come so far. It was a Pity to waste the Effort already expended in this Venture.

I would wait until Damien completed his Work, lying silently in place until he saw Fit to remove himself to Bed.

Unfortunately, the Man seemed set to work the Night through. He puttered and pottered about, clinking Vessels, raising Stenches, amid the hissing of Steams and the muttering of boiling Retorts. My back cramped and my Legs stiffened, but still he would not finish his Work and go.

It seemed that Hours passed, though possibly it was less Time than I thought. At last I heard a Chuckle beyond the Tapestry. With a hiss of Dismay, I realized that a pair of Toes had intruded into my space beneath the wall Covering.

"Kitty-kitty-kitty!" shrilled a hateful Voice. "I have known you were there for hours, Kitty. You had best come out and let me look at you. If you are a mere mouser, I shall only use you to test my poisons. But if you should be a Familiar, sent by one of my victims to spy upon my endeavors, yours will be an interesting death!"

I thought with great Rapidity. The Chain would betray me instantly, I knew. Yet I must not lose its Protection. In one long gulp, I swallowed the gleaming Length. Then I said, "Mew?" in my most innocent and affecting Tone and batted at the Tapestry with one playful Paw.

A long, chemical-stained Hand reached for me, and I let myself go limp and began to Purr. The appearance of stupid Complacency can, my Instructors said, be more useful than an arsenal of Weapons, when used Correctly. As the Wizard held me aloft and Observed me, I could see the Doubt in his Gaze.

I purred more loudly, arching my back against his Arm and rubbing my Head against the front of his terribly dirty Robe. He dropped me instantly, and I landed Softly and looked up. "Mew?" I inquired in a melting Tone.

"I thought him intelligent enough at least to find another familiar," Damien grumbled. "The old fool just sits in his house and trembles and foams whenever I send the fit upon him, I suppose. Damme! And what shall I try on you, Cat? The undetectable potion for removing wealthy great-aunts or the agonizing dose that avenges wrongs and insults offered by unthinking idiots?"

I felt the chill of the chain in my Stomach, and in some Manner it comforted me. We of the Familiar profession have, as well, secret arts of our own, and I felt myself at least the Equal of this arrogant Man. But I only mewed again and rubbed against his Ankles, managing to leave a trail of loose Hairs that encircled his Legs.

He was muttering again, and his Words confirmed my own Conviction that he was one of those pitiful Beings who is contemptuous of the Powers lent to their Peers by Familiars. It was no wonder that this Man was, according to his own Words, conducting some sort of Campaign against others of his own kind because of real or imagined Slights.

He paused, as if suddenly comprehending the Spell that I was, with the help of that ingested Chain, weaving about him. His Lips curled, and he raised his Hands, gesturing as he began a Chant. It was one that I was taught to counteract when I was a mere Kit, and I diverted its Impact without pausing in my own Efforts.

Damien glared down at me, but now his hands were frozen in place, and his Feet were immobile. I continued the Purr of Enchantment while weaving my Pattern about his Legs, knowing that he would be confined to stillness for many Minutes, once the Spell was in place.

When Damien was completely helpless, I conducted my Search of the Laboratory. I found the pitiful patch of Skin, with its dark red blotch, stretched about a crude figure carved from Soap. Beside it were several Instruments, obviously intended for Use against my poor Master. Skewers and Candles and Rasps told me much about the ugly Imagination of this curious Wizard.

After detaching the bit of Skin, I thought for a moment. Then I took up a Scalpel, probably the very One with which Damien had detached that Birthmark from Aldonious Fury, and sliced a bit from the Calf of his right Leg. It hardly bled, so Neat was my touch, but I knew that this, in the Hands of one who had reason to distrust him, would quite possibly keep him Honest for a Time.

I regurgitated the Chain beside his Feet, gathered it up, and gave a last triumphant Purr before slipping again behind the Tapestry and leaving the House of Damien.

My return to the Fury Household was triumphant. Not only did I return the stolen Part to my Associate, I also brought a most interesting Speculation as to the way in which Damien had learned of the existence of that Birthmark, which was in a place not accessible to any except Fury's Intimates.

When called upon the carpet, Amelia wept. She confessed, after many Tears, that she had betrayed her Master to the wizard, in the belief that the skin would be used in the making of a Love Potion that would make him hers forever. When Fury began having Seizures, she was Terrified, yet she did not know what to do to Restore what she had caused to be Stolen.

"With all your faults, Aldonious, I love you," she sniffled. "I take great care of you, you must admit that. And I even help with your little nasties up in the workroom."

To my surprise, his eyes filled with Tears. "I know, Amelia. You're a good girl, in your way. I don't know how I'd get along without you, even after this."

As I said before, Humanity has most unrealistic Attitudes toward Reproduction. The answer was obvious to me.

"Marry her, you Fool," I told Fury. "Then you will never have to try to do without her. That's all she wanted, in the Beginning."

His small blue eyes filled with Amazement. Then he began to Smile.

I attended their Wedding, which was held quietly at a Registry Office. I wore a new Collar made from that magical Chain that Fury had given me. Afterward, I gave them my Blessings, and my Resignation.

Amelia would take excellent Care of the Wizard, I understood. I was not certain that she would be as careful of Me, however, for I now understood that two Females sometimes make awkward Tenants of the same House.

So that is the tale of Hermione as a Spy. Only once in my long Career has that happened, and it is with mixed Emotions that I recall that perilous Expedition. Now I know that it might well have had Results far other than those that occurred, and I am glad that it happened when I was young and ignorant of the many Pitfalls of the World as well as the endless Inventiveness of Wizards.

MOON SCENT

by Lyn McConchie

In memory of Rasti,
a good companion.

Amongst the cats of the hills I am known as Many Kills. The name was given in laughter because as a cub I landed upon a nest of hoppers and called for my kin to see how many enemies I had slain. These days none laugh, for when the Dark came prowling it was I who turned it back. But that is another tale and unfit for the evening. No, this is a tale of the Light I will tell now.

We are an old people; long have we dwelt in the high hills, beloved of the Moon and its Goddess who is our Bright Lady. The two-legged ones named us Dravencats for our ferocity and they leave us well alone. We know not whence we first birthed intelligence amongst us, but our natures are little changed from the beasts. Still, one who has cleverness to match cunning may learn, and learn we did. My line had ever been known for its far ranging and we watched when these new kind came to the hills. This was in the days of my many times mother's mother. Young was she but already beautiful, a wanderer and unwilling as yet to mate. She roved deep into the high hills until she came upon a settlement of these two-legs. There she watched with amusement their foolish comings and goings.

The great cat crouched in long grass at the edge of a clearing. Below her men labored to raise walls against the coming winter. The dogs might have warned them of the watcher, but they were away with the Huntsmen and besides, few would do more than whimper if they caught HER scent. She sniffed in disgust. These ones and their stinks. Their females reeked of sickly fumes used to disguise their own natural aroma. Their men stank of sweat gone rancid. Did they never wash? She groomed her own fur sensuously.

Below, a man leaned over the framework of the main hall and shouted.

"Where are you going, Nelda?"

"I'm taking the children to pick berries."

"Then be wary."

"I have my bow, and crippled Daniol comes also, to guard."

I watched as she trailed across the meadow toward me. A female, a male who halted along behind her, and half a dozen of their cubs. I had no cubs, but one day I would choose a mate and I, too, would have those who followed me thus. Something in the group interested me and I rose. They walked briskly, but the cubs darted here and there in the way of all young ones. Their scents came to my nostrils. The cubs smelled of summer, the smells of dried grasses and a faint flowery smell I did not know. I picked a patch of longer grass and drifted into the heart of it, where I could watch and satisfy my curiosity.

"Nelda?"

"Yes, sweetheart."

"Are there really bad things in the hills?"

"Well—we know that there are places here that are not friendly to our kind. Then there are the great cats. Where there are some dangers, there may be others we still don't know. So we must be wary."

The cub nodded solomnly, and hidden in the grass, I nodded agreement also. Not that I had understood her words. But the emotions behind them had touched me sufficiently for me to guess the meaning.

The berrypickers moved around the huge clump of scrub. The female and the larger cubs had become engrossed in their task. It was the smaller one who became bored. First she sat and ate some of her gleanings, then she moved to explore near where I lay. I watched in amusement. She would be near three as they judged age. No danger to me.

The cub pushed through the long grass. Peering between the thick stalks, she suddenly saw me and gave a small squeak of surprise. Still amused, I waited to see what she would do. I had little time to wonder. With another squeak,

this time of delight, she hurled her small body at my loung-
ing form and embraced me with all her tiny strength. Startled, I would have struck her down, but the warmth of her
emotions flowed over me, and I was loath to end my watching. I relaxed back again. Content, she nestled into my fur
and, as small cubs will, fell swiftly into sleep.

I lay there, cradled on warm earth in sweet sunshine, and
considered. A wicked feline thought made me remain.
What of the others, those two-legs who picked close by?
How would they react when they saw her? I could withhold
my claws until the last minute, then slay her before them
and be away. I was Swiftclaw. No two-legs could kill faster
than I. It would amuse me to see their fear, to play with
them as I often played with the little grass runners I caught.
This was a new game. I settled to wait. The cub awoke
before they found her gone, so I endured her bedecking of
me in a garland of grass flowers made into a necklace.

All the while, she stroked my fur, babbling in her cub
tongue, hugging me with her slender arms. As soon as they
came, I would— The cub was making that strange two-leg
sound. A sort of burbling noise that denotes happiness in
their kind. Somehow it made me feel strange, too. A sort
of warmth that ran through my body. Without thinking, I
licked her face gently and listened to the sound. I found I
was purring to match it. She snuggled into my chest, head
tucked under my throat. My powerfully muscled forearms
encircled her. She would be a good kill. Another lick and
to my surprise, I was licked back. Again the strange feeling
held me.

Was this how it would be with cubs of my own? Her
head thrust against me in affection. A gesture very similar
to our own. I considered. After all, a cub. No threat. No
danger. I could enjoy the adult's reactions without blood-
shed. I relaxed again, content as the cub stroked my fur. I
was Swiftclaw. What need had I to kill cubs! I could hear
voices now; they were closer and more strident. It seemed
likely they had missed the cub. A gust of fear scent smote
my nostrils. Yes—they were afraid for her. Now was the
time I could play my game. I lifted my nose to test the
breeze. We live much by scent, my kin and kind. Far away
I could taste the woodsmoke from their fires. Closer was
the scent of the grass they had bruised as they passed to

the bushes. Nearby, the sun-warmed scent of berries and the tang of spilled juice. Below my nose, the aroma of warm skin and healthy young animal. I breathed in. There! Another wave of fear mingled with anger. The sound of a two-legs as it pushed through the long grass toward where I lay. The wind shifted and I knew it was the female. Now for my game!

Nelda thrust through the thick-stemmed grass, her eyes searching. Tracks here? Yes. She followed, lifting her voice in a frantic cry.

"Nanda, Nanda? Child, where are you?"

An answer caught at the fringe of her hearing. "Here!"

"Where? Call again, dearling."

"Over here, Nelda, with Tarin."

Tarin? Tarin had been Nanda's beloved stuffed toy lost in the shift to new territory. The child still grieved for it after many months. How could the toy be here? Nelda thrust into a small sun-warmed clearing and froze in utter terror for her foster daughter.

"Nanda, stand up very slowly."

She shuddered as the child bounced up, hugging the huge cat that eyed Nelda so wickedly.

"I have to go now, Tarin. I'll see you again."

The cub hugged me and I allowed her the intimacy as I watched the female through slitted lids. The terror she felt amused me greatly. It was well that she should fear Swift-claw. Then her scent changed to fear streaked with the red smell of fury. I laughed silently and paced forward. As her curved stick came up, I pushed my head against the child and she at once dropped to hug me to her, uttering the burbling sounds. I knew about those two-leg weapons. Had I not seen them kill the deer from many paces away? I knew that even I could die—but not while the child was within my claws.

"Nanda, it's time to go now. Say good-bye to Tarin."

I could hear how the female fought to keep her voice steady. The fear scent mixed with rage was almost overwhelming, but underneath it I breathed in the scent of the cub—no fear, only happiness.

"Nanda, come now!"

The cub left me and I moved carefully so that she was ever between the female and me. I lifted my eyes to meet the female's then and in that look something passed between us. She knew the game I played, so her fear was wholly swallowed up in fury's scent. I yawned in her face and leapt lightly into the grass. As I vanished, I could hear the cub wailing the word she had used to me, but I had no more time for two-leg cubs. I left them behind as I traveled higher. I chuckled silently as I loped. A fair day and a fine game, and all without blood. Truly, I was Swiftclaw the clever.

It was several years before I stopped mourning the second loss of my Tarin. It was several more before Nelda told me the truth. That it was no toy come to life that I had held in love that day, but one of the great cats from the far hills beyond our land. They were very rare and reports had it that they had intelligence. Certainly more than that of the usual beast. Nelda was sure of it.

"Didn't I see the brute with my own two eyes?" she said. "And didn't she know the fear I was feeling? Then she yawned in my face and was gone. It was a fine game she played with me and well I knew it. But still, she spared the little one when she could have killed and for that the Blessing on her."

Often as I walked in the foothills near our hold, I watched out to see if Tarin would return. Never was there any sign, but as the years passed it became a habit and always my eyes scanned, hoping for a sight of her. I knew, of course I knew, that the beasts were deadly. But somehow I believed that Tarin would know me again. I mocked myself even as I believed, knowing that animals in the wilds knew no mercy. No friendship. But still—the thought was there and I watched.

Soon I would wed. The son of a landholder had come asking for me and the wedding would be held in high Summer when all could travel to it. Not that I would be going far myself. Their lands adjoined ours and besides, Nelda had promised to come with me. Nurse to my children as she had been nurse to me. It was well into spring now and I was restless. I would walk the hills and pick berries. It might even be that I would walk farther, to where the stream deepened in pools and tasty fish lurked under the banks. They were rare and hard to catch, but I'd learned the way of it. They would do well on the table tonight if I could catch enough to share.

I tossed my woolen cape about my shoulders and slipped out. Now that we had land again, my grandfather sometimes remembered that I should behave as a Lady. Fortunate was I that mine was a love match. Enlann loved me as I was and there would be no delicate confinement for me inside the woman's bower. Instead, we hunted afoot and ahorse together, with bow and hawk in freedom. He'd told me privately that it was the opinion of his sire also, that a proud strong woman birthed better children. His mother had been one of that kind. She'd died holding raiders from the throats of Enlann and his younger kin. His father revered her memory and took no other lady to wife so that Enlann was his only child.

The land was beautiful in this spring. On one side it fell away towards the Lhandes so many miles away. To the other it rose slowly, first into foothills, then into the High Hills and beyond into mountains that seemed to touch the sky. We never went farther than the edge of the High Hills, but I often wondered what lay beyond, where the mountains became blue in the distance. A bare mile away lay the patches of berry bushes where we picked each year, straggling over another mile in length, so that Nelda often said they were planted originally as a line. It could be true. There were signs when we came that others could have been here before us. But if so, they were very long gone. I had heard there were even ruins on other Holds, but there were none on ours. The air was delightfully crisp as I walked so that I was seduced into making for the stream. I smiled to myself when I reached its babble and sat to remove my shoes. Grandfather would scold when he knew how far I had come, but not for long once he tasted my fish.

I padded along, nose low as I searched. Swiftclaw am I in truth, but let none name me lucky. Once I had a mate I loved, but the horns of the prey are as sharp as Death. I would take no other mate to my heart, but when my season came upon me I chose from those who battled for my favor. And so I held no territory but wandered far. At last I found myself here in the lands where I had roamed before I mated. Our people are long lived. I had seen almost twenty winters and by the Lady's Grace, would see more yet. I had reared many cubs but of all, none had been more precious to me than the one I had raised this spring. A demon, a raiser of rage and love. One who would do little he was told, or stay where I placed him. And now, I hunted for him again. I had returned from my prey to share with my son. Now I tracked him slowly, his sweet cub scent in my nostrils. From ahead I heard him call so that I raced to find him. Barely did I halt in time as a great hole opened in the ground before me. Far below my cub wailed for aid.

The sun was warm and the fish willing, for once. I donned my shoes again and lay back with a full kit of the delectable silver morsels. A nap would be pleasant and I could start back as the afternoon cooled in the shade of the hills. Far in the distance I could see the scavenger birds circling. Something must be dead or dying. Not that they were particular about that. If anything was merely trapped, it could be sufficient for them. Once I had found a trapped fawn with half its face eaten away. I still remembered that and shuddered at their sight. I wondered idly what it was they'd found? But today I intended to look for no horrors. I lay back and slid into a light doze.

Below me my cub called pitifully again. I fought back panic and studied his situation. As I had raced through the brush, so must have he. But still a baby, his reflexes slower, he'd failed to stop when the hole opened before him. Now he sat on his haunches, looking up trustfully for me to aid him. Panic grew. I could see no way to reach him and still be able to climb out again. If I pushed the log into the pit, it might land on one end, but even then it would be too short for him to climb it and reach the pit rim. I could stave off his death for a while. Food would be easily dropped down. But water? There was no way I could bring water to him. The blood of the beasts I offered, the dew on the ground, all would help—to give him a terrible lingering death as the insufficient moisture and a coming summer drained him of life.

A swishing sound alerted me and I leapt. A scavenger

bird died in my claws, its foul scent assaulting my nose. I sneezed and considered again. Time was even shorter than I had realized. Those things could fly down into this wide-mouthed pit. Once my cub was weak, they would eat him alive! In utter agonizing despair, I threw back my head and screamed a plea to the Moon Lady. "Aid me, my mother!" True, our kin no longer revere her as once we did; now that we are more than beasts she is not so much our Lady. But in extremity we remember. We no longer scream to the full moon, but yet—I cried again and again. Begging as a cub begs.

I'd slept for a couple of hours when something woke me. I sat up to listen. A sort of screaming howl, the anguish in it terrible to hear. If anything was so distressed, the least I could do was see what was wrong. My grandfather has spoken of this habit of leaping in where even a warrior would not dare. Today was not to be a cure.

I sneaked cautiously through the trees. Ahead of me the sound rose and fell in an agony of misery, and there was no way I could have kept myself from continuing forward. At the edge of the trees, I ran lightly across a width of grass and then into an area of brush with one lone tree, rising, vine-crowned from the center of the bushes. The sound came from near the tree and I slunk closer. My eyes focused to see—"Tarin!"

The two-legs' voice jerked me out of my anguish. My panic and grief broke into a terrible rage as I bared my teeth. Killing might not save my cub, but it would ease my mind. My head sank and my legs slowly began to fold into the killing crouch. Then the scent struck me like a blow. Not fear—joy! Why would a stupid, noseless two-legs stink of pleasure at seeing me? Through my grief and fury I smelled another scent. I searched my mind for the memory. Well did my dam teach me of the many scents. Time and again she spoke of them. I had learned. WE are intelligent and can learn from descriptions. Not for US alone the scent we know. We can teach another of it who is not there to taste the wind. Somewhere I had known this one. Then I recalled and nodded. The two-legs cub in a day very long ago. She, too, must recall. But how? All our kin knew that

the two-legs were noseblind—deaf as well. Perhaps there
was something they had that we did not. She did truly seem
to remember me. I rose from my crouch and moved back
above the pit to comfort my cub.

I saw the crouch and waited for her attack. Somehow I
was certain that this was the dravencat I had once known
and I could not fear her. She rose and I felt a flame of joy
that she recalled me. I followed slowly as she moved back
to the log. I could hear a tiny pitiful whimpering. I kept
my movements slow and smooth. In her state I must not
let her fear cause her to attack. A foot, a pause, then another step. Finally, I reached the log to stare where her
eyes fixed. There came a swish of wings, a throat-raw
scream of fury as she launched herself into the air. She
landed with a scavenger bird dead in her forepaws. There
came another small cry and I looked down—and down. In
a wide deep hole a dravencat cub sat miserably. In one
glance I knew Tarin's grief. Unable to reach him, unable
to leave him for the birds, yet unable to depart and allow
him to die. I remembered the fawn I had once found and
shivered. My eyes flew to the log again and then the tangle
of nearby vines. If I was strong enough, the cub might be
saved. But would she—could I show I intended no harm
to the cub? My mind ranged again until I recalled my package of fish. I turned smoothly and drifted back to the
stream.

The two-legs who had been the child was beside me as
the bird stooped. There was a gust of scent I did not know,
then another of disgust. I was faster yet and the thing died
within my claws. Well did they name me! Then she was
moving away and again came the strange scent. Was she
leaving us? No. She returned and I smelled fish. Fresh and
rich from the water. She offered them to me. I saw that
she understood courtesy as she averted her eyes that I
might eat in privacy.

It is not well to stare into the eyes of our kind. With us
that is an invitation to fight. At the very least it is an insult
to stare while we eat. I reached forward slowly to accept
her gift. The first I dropped to my cub, the second I took
for my own hunger. Below, my son flung himself·upon the

food and ate ravenously while he whined his pleasure. I took a third for myself and watched as the two-legs female sat to share quiet with me. As she did so, she made the burbling sound her kind use to indicate contentment. I half lay to eat and shortly she rose to walk about my cub's prison. Her kind are useless in many ways. They are less than we, yet those clever paws of theirs can do many things. Perhaps . . . I watched and waited. My nose full of the scent she exuded as she studied my cub and his prison.

I wandered around the hole, peering down as the cub fed eagerly. I was light of bone but strong. I should be able to climb down with little difficulty. The question was, could I climb back up bearing a heavy and doubtless squirming cub, and how happy would he be to allow me to even handle him? Absently, I dug another fish from the kit and realized that its strong fibers could be used to carry him. If I unraveled the handle, I could rework it longer to strap across my back. If I could persuade the cub to sit still in it, then I could use all my strength to climb. I reached for a vine. There was no use standing here thinking; I had to move. At least there would be a full moon tonight. Grandfather would be frantic very soon. When I did not return by dark, he would have every man in the hold scouring the area for me. It was to be hoped that they did not find us before I had rescued the cub. Tarin might remember and accept me. Somehow I had the feeling that she would not accept the arrival of a dozen armed males. Hastily, I began to weave.

There was another powerful wave of the scent as she peered downward. Then she was gathering vines. I was puzzled. Somehow she intended to aid us, but how? I watched as with those cunning paws she wove, making a long rope from many. Finally they stretched for several lengths and she carried them to the pit. Now she pushed at the log, rolling it toward the gap. The thing was heavy and she strained. Our kind never worked in such ways, but to save my cub I would do anything. I moved to the other end and thrust with my chest against the weight. Her scent showed her pleasure. I was right to do this. Slowly the thing moved until it spanned the opening.

*   *   *

It was so difficult to shift the log that I almost despaired. Then Tarin pushed, too, and slowly the weight shifted. Tarin thrust on one end while on the other I heaved and sweated. Finally, the log lay across the center of that dark gap in the earth. Then I reached for the vines I had woven into a form of ladder. The moon had risen by now and I prayed to Her whose symbol it is. Let her look favorably on my endeavors. Let me save the cub for Tarin!

Now at last the two-legs female moves, climbing down to my cub. He whimpers as she places him gently in that thing she carries over one shoulder. I hiss him to silence; she will bring him out to safety. He squirms and again I hiss a command as her hands slip. He must be still for his life! He freezes obediently, his small head peering up at me over her shoulder. She climbs slowly and I can tell his weight is almost too great for her strength. He is a fine cub and I am proud of him, but for this time I could wish him less well-grown.

The climb down was easy. Tarin appeared to have understood my intent, and the cub did not fight me when I picked him up. Fortunate it was that I had brought my carrysack with me to the stream. I set him inside and slung it over my shoulders. As I began to climb, he wriggled; a hiss from Tarin quieted him at once. For a moment I almost lost my grip and I felt the skin of my palms tear as my fingers clung with all my strength. Thanks to be Her that Tarin understood and commanded him.

I dragged myself higher thinking that the gifted ones were right. The great cats were more than beasts. Another handhold—another. My grip was failing—if only the cub were not so heavy! In my mind I saw a picture, I was falling. I could leave him below and climb out to live. Then came the picture of the fawn. I could not—I would not, leave him to THAT! I dragged myself up another length and then another, gritting my teeth savagely. Why was I doing this? They were not human, not my kind. I owed them no kinswoman's duty. But the fawn was in my mind, and I forced my hands to rise and grip again.

*   *   *

I could smell the blood on the two-legs now. Blood on the vines from her paws. We were not of her kind. Why would she share blood to buy a cub's life? She was almost to the log when her strength finally failed. I could smell the bitter nose-wrinkling scent of her despair as she hung there. I waited for her to drop my son as she managed to loose her hand and undo the thing she carried him within. Imploring, her eyes met mine and I understood. Cautiously, I crept along the log and crouched carefully. Keeping my balance with difficulty, I was able to reach past her shoulder, grip my cub's scruff, and raise his weight.

I moved back steadily along the log then. One swift leap and my cub was mine again and safe. Then I turned. Freed of his weight the two-legs had climbed the final distance and was dragging herself along the log to the pit side. She slumped beside me and put out a tentative hand to my son. I permitted it. Her hands stank of the blood she had paid for his life and I am Swiftclaw. None of my kind have ever said I gave less than her due to the Bright Lady. Surely this one must have been sent from Her. As she stroked my cub the strange scent welled up and thrust itself to my attention yet again. What was this smell? I knew it not and yet—I lifted my head to the risen moon and gave the cry of my kin and kind. A greeting, then a plea.

"Bright One, Lady who lights my hunting. Share wisdom with your daughter. Give knowledge to your Child?"

I saw that the female, too, gave thanks to the Bright Lady. It pleased me well, that she should keep my customs.

I sat at the edge of the pit and panted. My hands hurt, my fish were gone, and my grandfather would be furious. But the cub was safe and I could not resist putting out a hand to stroke the soft fur. Suddenly all my weariness slid over me and I slumped. Lifting my eyes, I could see that it must be nearing midnight. I gave fervent thanks to Her in whose hands rest all fools, and then without thought for my position, I rolled onto my side and slept as if I were stunned. Tarin must have cared for her cub and done the same, for when I woke at dawn she was stretched beside me. I stroked the cub again and then spoke as I would have done to any other fine Lady were they of a different kind.

"I must go now, my kind will be searching. May your

son grow straight and strong. May the Goddess protect you all your days. And may your death be quick and clean and all you might wish. May your years be very long upon this land and health yours through them all."

Tarin touched my arm with a huge paw. I was certain she understood the goodwill behind the blessing even if the words were not in her tongue. I stroked the cub one final time and then rose, gathering the ruins of my carrysack. Grandfather's men would find me soon. I must be away from Tarin before then. I looked back one last time as I crossed the clearing, to find them staring after me before also turning to leave, to return to the high hills.

I slept that night with my son beside me and the two-legs female beside us both. When she awoke, it was clear she would leave for her own den and that was as it should be. I watched as she smoothed the coat of my son with her hands. Those clever two-leg hands. Then she was gone. Still strong in my nostrils as we, too, departed, was her last scent. But now I, Swiftclaw, hunter of the hills, runner of the Mountains, I knew what it was. Bright Lady I thank you for the gift of knowing. This scent shall I keep in my mind and this story shall I tell to my son. To him and to his shall I teach it in turn. This is a new thing and precious. For now I know a new scent. A scent unknown to us before. Now indeed do I know it—the scent of Mercy. And my children and kin shall remember it down all our generations forever.

CAT'S WORLD
by Cynthia McQuillin

Cat awoke with a start, his whiskers twitching with agitation. He'd gotten little rest, though he'd slept overly long by his reckoning of the sun's position in the perpetually clouded sky. Stiffly he stretched, extending and retracting the claws in his fingertips. He closed his eyes and drew a slow, deep breath to quell the alarm that still resonated through his nervous system; it was unseemly for the Guardian of the Old Knowledge to betray such lack of control.

In keeping with his talent and training, he often wandered in the ghost-world when he slept. This time, though, while stalking the shadows of that strange energy double of his own reality he'd met with the old-one who was Guardian before him. But how could that be? His mentor was long dead. Seven cycles had passed since Cat had assumed the guardianship of the Cave of Rebirth with the old-one's blessing. Two months later they had laid that estimable elder's bones in the Cave of Ancestors, as they did with all of the feline remains they reclaimed. There was no doubt that it was he, for the carcass still bore his pouch of tools and the necklet of boar's teeth the elder had strung from his first kill.

Cat stood for a moment looking about the cave's entrance where he'd taken time from his reading to nap. All seemed as it should be, and he realized, when he'd finished his brief reconnaissance, that he was hungry. He reached into the hide pouch that hung from a braided cord around his waist and absentmindedly extracted a piece of the dried meat that his mate had packed for him. He began to chew, savoring the smoky taste and leathery texture. The old-one's last daughter was a good provider, he purred to himself as he pictured her face in his mind. Cat was proud to have such a partner; they were well suited to each other,

168

and it pleased him that she'd chosen to remain in his cave even though she was past bearing young. Many of the older females withdrew from the community to live out their days in solitude, growing resentful and ill-tempered.

The males, who were more guardians than hunters, stayed with the clan until they were too old to fight, then they would go off to die alone with dignity. Life was hard and food couldn't be spared for nonproductive members in any of the small, independent communities that had sprung up around the Big Lake territory. The one exception seemed to be the Guardian of the Ancient Knowledge. His only real duty as caretaker of the Cave of Rebirth was to preserve the records left by the creator.

Why, Cat wondered for the hundredth time, was *he* allowed to be a burden on the whole clan when he provided no real service? The machinery in the cave had shut down long ago and would never run again, nor would they have known what to do with it if it had still been functional. Of course there were printouts, notebooks and logs which were full of information. He dutifully spent at least part of every day reading and trying to understand these papers, but no one ever asked him to use the knowledge he'd so painstakingly gleaned. What was the use of knowledge that no one desired? After he'd gotten past his surprise at meeting the old-guardian in the ghost-world, he had posed that very question to him. Now that he'd finished his light meal and calmed himself sufficiently, he settled down in the waning sunlight of the clearing to ponder his mentor's reply.

"When first we woke from the long cold-sleep, it was in the mind of the first designated Guardian of Knowledge." The older cat sang the memory, like a mother with a kitten to suck. "The old knowledge must be kept for the time when the dream-walker would come. She whose vision will assure our birth, she whose memory will create our truth. While the circle of destiny remains open, our world remains unborn. Heed my song, Guardian of Knowledge, for there is a strange scent in the wind between the worlds which has stirred me from the long-dream to seek you here." His message delivered, he rubbed his nose against Cat's cheek in the farewell gesture, saying, "Warmth and full belly to you and yours. You shall see me no more." Then he was gone.

Having considered these words, Cat rose to reenter the cavern. Pressing the special pattern of buttons that opened the heavy metal panel, he slipped inside to touch the switch that brought the lights up. (These were the only electrical things that still functioned.) He glanced nervously around the outer chamber as though he expected another ghost to appear. When nothing untoward occurred, he entered the main section where the machines and records were kept. Yes, he decided after he'd checked each of the books and printouts, everything was in order just as it had been when he left. The old-one had taught him to read the strange characters that were the man-sounds made silent, and encouraged him to read the books, but he'd also maintained rigorously that they must always be replaced exactly as he had found them.

Cat thought this stupid at first, and protested what he considered a pointless waste of time; but when the elder feline had insisted, he'd done as he was instructed. The young Guardian had enjoyed unraveling the meaning of the words, but found the handwritten entries in Dr. Nelson's logbooks and Dr. Robertson's journal to be more difficult to decipher than the printouts or the text books. Most of these dealt with biology, and had pictures which he spent hours poring over. He was particularly fond of the one entitled *Modern Zoology*. Still, no matter how often he read them or how much he thought about the material they contained, most of what was here made no sense. What he *was* able to understand was mostly the same things he'd learned at his mother's belly.

Having prepared as best he could for the impending occurrence his dream-meeting portended, he pressed the button that lowered the lighting and departed. He'd walked barely to the edge of the glade and was about to enter the forest when he felt a strange tingling at the base of his spine. He lashed his tail instinctively and his nose twitched as he tasted the air for an unfamiliar scent, but there was nothing out of the ordinary. Again he started forward, but stopped suddenly as he caught sight of something moving within the dense growth. He noted uneasily that there was not the slightest sound to accompany that movement. Silently, he retraced his steps and dropped down behind the undergrowth near the cave entrance where he crouched, waiting to see what might approach.

Cat was dismayed by the appearance of the strange figure that emerged from the shadows of the twilight wood. The creature had the appearance of a young human female. (He'd seen several pictures in the comparative anatomy texts.) Though she looked quite substantial, his keen sense of smell told him she wasn't really there. He'd hunted the ethereal entities that sometimes troubled the ghost-world near the cave often enough to recognize the aura of psychic energy that surrounded her with a diffuse glow. But it disturbed him to see such a thing manifested in the physical world, especially so near to the Cave of Rebirth. As far as anyone knew, this was the last remnant of the old world within the territory they defended, perhaps in the entire world.

Cat continued watching and wondered if this apparition could be the dream-walker the prophecy spoke of, or if she was just a restless spirit, like the old-one, which had somehow managed to manifest itself in the waking world. She didn't have the look of a spirit about her, but his feline nature distrusted any occurrence out of the ordinary. Cautiously he rose, whiskers twitching with agitation as she drew nearer. She seemed not to notice him ... yet. He schooled his curiosity to patience and settled back again on his haunches. Cat recalled from the learning croons that all the human-ones had been gone from the world for more time than he could comprehend; that they had been destroyed in the war of forbidden weapons. The notebooks in the cavern agreed with this, stating that there was no hope of survival for any of the world's people if the weapons were unleashed. In fact, their creator had believed that no life form *could* survive the dead-time except for the few simple organisms that might mutate successfully or the specially created ones like himself. "Bio-engineered" was the word the log books used.

Though Cat was proud that he could read the books and papers left by those who had engineered their breed, the more recent generations saw little use in the records of the before-world beyond curiosity. They felt that there could be no wisdom in the words of a long dead race; and they grumbled during the lean months when his share of food was portioned out, often speaking of abandoning the cave. After all, they argued, hadn't the human-ones destroyed the world? The young ones preferred to spend their time stalking the shadows of the forest or gamboling in the glades, but he couldn't blame them for that. With a suppressed purr, he recalled the joys of tussling with his littermates in the diffuse daylight that warmed them through the cloud layer.

Perhaps they were right, though it seemed unfair to blame an entire species for the actions of a few. Cat furrowed his brow. If he could believe what was written in the books, then some of the humans had been good—many, in fact. Unfortunately, they had allowed a few demented aggressive ones to gain enough economic power and political support to take control of the weapons and use them. Cat wasn't quite sure what economic and political were, but he understood enough of Dr. Robertson's and Dr. Nelson's papers to know that some kind of battle had been fought and lost to trickery.

He shuddered, as he always did, thinking of the horror and devastation that had rained down on that long ago world, obliterating life and civilization. Yes, that was what the Cat-mothers sang in their sad, crooning memories. Clan wisdom insisted that the memory of the violence that had been unleashed, and the transformation of cats, must never be forgotten lest some group again try to gain domination over others through aggression. But they also sang older songs that spoke of trust and affection between cats and mankind. His ancestors had cherished human companionship, and he thought it a sad thing that they had all died so terribly.

The woman was closer now, walking with an easy strolling gait, her gaze distracted as though she were questing for something or testing a strange scent. Then she stopped and glanced anxiously around. "Here, Kitty, Kitty," she called, and Cat experienced a funny feeling in his throat. She sat down on a large stone and sighed. "Dammit, Shadow, why must you disappear right now?" Though the sounds she made were foreign to him, her agitation was so strongly projected that an image formed in his mind. It was that of a small furred animal with a catlike face, but this creature ran on four legs rather than standing erect, and its forelimbs had only stubby little fingers much like those in the illustrations that showed how his predecessors had been altered with each genetic operation. *How strange,* he thought, *what could this mean?*

* * *

Maria Santee moaned softly in dreaming. She hadn't slept well for several nights; but then, who could sleep with the stories of growing unrest on every telescreen, each nation decrying the weapons policies of the next? That was bad enough, but with the food shortages becoming critical and reclaimable water soon to follow, there were too many special interest groups crying for wholesale genocide. Rather than dying out, racism and nationalism had flourished under the new governmental regime. Those few psychics who'd survived the religious pogroms at the turn of the century were wracked with apprehension and despair as they sensed the impending death of their world.

Vainly, Dr. Peter Ingram's group at the Governmental Research Institute were seeking alternatives; at very least, they wanted to buy time. Since individual sensitives seemed unable to find answers or break past the barrier time had erected, it was decided that they would work in groups. Dr. Ingram had tested everyone who was willing, and had selected those with the highest psi potential and best control. Then he'd assembled three teams whose members were chosen for compatibility as well as balance of skills.

Each night one of the teams would meet. Joining the network of their wills into a lifeline, they would send one member of the group into the astral world to seek some information or turning point they might use to their advantage. So far they'd lost three people, two hopelessly catatonic and one dead from heart failure. After six months of negative results, Peter decided that the risk was too great, and had released the group members back to their previous research teams.

Maria was stunned, and argued passionately against abandoning the project. It had been her turn to carry the focus the previous night and, though she had no proof but her conviction, she was certain they were near a breakthrough. She all but pleaded for one more chance, but everyone was too tired and discouraged to pay any heed to her vehemence.

The young psychic had been in quite a temper by the time she got home, slamming about the kitchen as she prepared dinner for herself and her Siamese cat. Shadow sat patiently waiting by his bowl. He'd seen this sort of display often enough and knew she'd settle down and see to his wants in good time. As he expected, she noticed him within a few minutes and opened a can of his favorite catfood. Spooning it into his bowl, she petted him apologetically as he butted his head under her hand. When he finished eating, he leapt into her lap for his nightly dose of affection, purring and kneading enthusiastically.

"Yes, I know, Shadow," she sighed. "You love me, even if no one else cares a fig for what I think. It's just that we're so desperate, and I'm sure we were on to something last night. If only they hadn't pulled me back so soon!" She finished her meal in sullen silence, feeding him scraps as she ate. Then she went to take a shower.

As she stepped out of the bathtub, she suddenly realized how exhausted she was. With a sigh she shook her long dark hair out of the shower cap. "I just hope I can sleep tonight," she said. The cat was already on the bed waiting for her when she came in. He watched her fondly as she brushed her hair and plaited it into a loose braid.

Maria stretched, then came over to the bed and sat down, picking up Shadow to pet him so he couldn't knead the satin spread. Finally she released him and slid beneath the covers, turning on the televid screen to watch the news before she drifted off. He settled down next to her so she could continue to caress him absently while she watched. Shadow rewarded her attention with a deep, rumbling purr, almost louder than the droning voices on the televid.

There has to be something we can do! Maria's mind cast restlessly about for answers, but found none; and at last she sank into an uneasy doze. Shadow's purr softened as her hand grew lax across the coarser fur of his back. In the gentle luminescence of the night light, his Siamese cat's eyes glowed red; and he smiled knowingly for a moment. Then, with a sigh, he laid down his head and joined his mistress in dreaming.

It seemed to Maria that she'd been wandering for a long

while when she realized that she wasn't alone in the stark gray and white landscape of the astral world. She started as she felt something rub up against her leg, then looked down and saw with relief that it was only Shadow. It wasn't often that he followed her into the dream-space, but she was always happy to have his company. Normally he stayed behind to guard her sleep, waking her if something should threaten her while she lay dreaming. Cats had long been known for their psychic gifts; certainly that faculty contributed to their reputation as witches' familiars during the middle ages. Shadow had proven to be particularly gifted among his kind. She'd discovered this on one of those rare occasions when she found herself in a waking dream, stalking the night with him as her astral-self temporarily shared his small form. She enjoyed those experiences, for in the cat's form and life-force she found a sense of freedom and assurance she never felt in her own.

With an unusually sharp twinge of prescience, Cindy realized that Shadow had followed her to the dream world tonight for a specific reason. "What is it, old 'Mese' cat?" she asked, stooping to stroke his astral form. He rubbed up against her outstretched hand and then, with a demanding "meowr," he stalked deliberately forward. She wished, as she often did, that he could talk to her; but even in deep rapport his mind was too primitive, his imperatives too different. On the other hand, he did have ways of making himself understood. When she didn't follow immediately, he stopped a few feet away to look back over her shoulder; fixing her with an impatient look, he yowled as only a Siamese can yowl. It was obvious that he wanted her to follow him; and when he started off again, she was right behind him.

After what seemed like hours of following her cat through the ever-changing levels of the astral world, Maria was hopelessly disoriented. She was relieved when Shadow finally marched into a clearing, sniffed the wind, sat down with finality, and began to wash. Wearily she looked up at the looming, treelike forms that surrounded her in what appeared to be some sort of forest. The vegetation looked almost primeval, yet it was unlike the plants that she'd seen in any paleontology textbook. A sudden chill rippled through her, and Maria realized with alarm that all her mundane trappings had been stripped away on her journey. She stood now clothed only in her astral flesh, her long hair flowing like a luminous cloud behind her. A sense of urgency gripped her and she began walking again. There was something she must do and there was a limit to how much time she could spend here. Past experience told her that she moved through this world like a shadow, influencing nothing and leaving no impression; but if that were true, what could she possibly do here?

She had never come such a distance, even with the help of her circle; but suddenly she realized that her fatigue had faded away. In fact, now that she thought about it, a kind of exhilaration was running through her like an electric current. She supposed it was something like the phenomenon that long distance runners experience, where they hit the wall of their exhaustion only to gain a second burst of speed and endurance. But her exultation was cut short by the sudden knowledge that Shadow was no longer with her.

"Here, kitty, kitty," she called. She missed the cat's company, and was half afraid she might not be able to return without him. Reluctant to go on till he returned, she sat down on a stone at the edge of a clearing to wait. He'd been so purposeful in bringing her here that it seemed downright peculiar for him to disappear at this particular moment.

"Dammit, Shadow, why must you disappear right now?" Maria's hair crackled with the energy of her irritation, moving as if it contained a life of its own. She sat fretting for a few minutes before noticing, with a start, the odd manlike figure hunched down in the low vegetation across the clearing. Its head had a vaguely catlike outline and its eyes gleamed softly in the twilight as the creature watched her with a grave countenance. *Could this be Shadow*, she wondered, *transformed to a higher self on the astral plane?* She rose and approached him, her outstretched hand palmdown in the supplicant greeting most acceptable to felines. He was almost as tall as she was as he rose to meet her and she saw that he bore only superficial similarity to her Siamese companion. She sensed that another spirit inhabited this form, more intelligent and far older.

Cat was still wary when the woman approached him, but he detected no hint of threat in her gesture, only a weary hopefulness, so he allowed her to draw near. His whiskers itched with static excitement at the touch of the tremendous energy flow she embodied. "Welcome, Dream-walker," he said in his own mewling tongue. "Why came you here?" Though his language was unintelligible to her, Maria had the strong feeling he'd been expecting her. Amazed at the strength of the impression she'd received from the creature, she shook her head forcefully.

"You're not a cat," she said in a puzzled tone, "though you are rather catlike." It was his turn to shake his head. She stood for a moment looking into his luminous green eyes, then gestured to the ground, implying that they should sit down. He nodded and joined her as she lowered herself to sit cross-legged, a position he could never have managed. Then she held out her hand palm up, obviously waiting for him to place his hand in hers. When he did, she smiled and he could feel the warmth of her thoughts flow into him, though he couldn't feel her hand. There was a touching familiarity in that contact, and he felt a rumbling purr from deep in his throat.

"Now we can talk," she said, and he understood. "I came here seeking knowledge, but somehow I've lost my small companion. He sometimes walks with me on the dream plane, but this time he wandered off too far and I can't find him. I'm afraid to leave him here for fear we may not be able to return to the waking world separately. Can you help me find him?"

"If he is as you are, Dream-walker," Cat replied, "I cannot track him by scent, for he is a shadow in our world. But I will help you to seek him if I can. It would be an evil thing for an unhappy alien spirit to remain here for long; such things upset the balance."

"Thank you," she replied. "My name is Maria Santee. Do you have a name?" He experienced an instant of recognition for the name, but the whole concept of names had always seemed strange to him. Why should you need a word to recognize a person, when scent and touch and thought were so much more distinctive? But by the gravity with which she offered her own, and because he knew from his reading that this was a human custom which signified a matter of courtesy and trust he said, "I am Cat, the Keeper of the Old Knowledge for my people." This told her what he was, if not who. It was again her turn to look puzzled.

"In our world," she replied thoughtfully, "a cat is a small creature of limited intelligence and primitive drives."

"As once we were," he agreed, "but then Dr. Robertson changed us so we would be able to survive after the dead-time."

"The dead time?" she asked with a sense of cold dread.

"Yes," he replied, "after the world died."

"How did you survive, then?"

"We slept for many, many years in special chambers that kept us safe until the machines in the cave knew the world had changed enough to support life again. But that was long ago, and many generations have passed since we woke from our cold dreams."

"Cryogenics ... forced evolution ..." she mused. "I've heard of Dr. Robertson's work. She's developed a new method of altering the genetic coding that combines gene splicing with artificially implanted memory codes akin to what we call instinct, which augment or stimulate the increase of intelligence in the new species. As I recall, there was some talk of using human genomes; but the government has so far refused to allow that," she said, recalling a telecast she'd watched on the institute monitors just that past week. The Genetics Lab was in the same complex as the Cryogenics compound and the Parapsychology facility. "Do you know how or why you were altered?" she asked, her interest almost palpable.

"We were genetically engineered to simulate the evolution of a species. Originally this was just an experiment to see what could be achieved by subtly altering the DNA coding. Cats were chosen because we reproduced efficiently and had a relatively short life cycle." It seemed to her that he was rattling this off mostly by rote while she'd hoped he might be able to give her a detailed explanation of how this miracle had been accomplished. Still, any information had value.

"In the final days, Dr. Robertson became convinced that the world leaders had lost control of the military, and that the stockpiles of doomsday weapons would be let loose on the world; and she made the decision to alter us further. Conspiring with Dr. Nelson, one of the leading cryogenic researchers of his day, she formulated a plan by which at least one intelligent species might survive to start anew." Maria nodded. That fit what she knew of Nelson; he was just the sort of crazy renegade to throw in with such a scheme.

"Go on," she said, as he paused to watch her with wide anxious eyes.

"Our newly evolved forms were adapted to live in the world that the computers predicted would emerge out of the desolation of the war. When Dr. Robertson's work was completed, we were sealed in special chambers hidden deep within a cavern where we would be safe from the original upheaval and the radiation that would follow. There we waited, our minds wandering the cold, vast regions of the ghost-world, what you call the dream plane, until conditions were right for our rebirth."

"How would the machines know when to release you?" she asked.

"They were set to monitor the surface world to determine when radiation levels were safe. Then, periodically, probes were sent out to analyze soil samples and atmospheric gases for signs of life, breathable air and viable growth. We were provided with a supply of food stuffs, and genetically altered seeds and animal embryos with which to restock the biosphere. These, of course, would be useless unless certain environmental standards were met."

"Your creator took quite a gamble. What did she base her calculations on? Surely not just the computer projections." The concern in Maria's expression belied the calmness of her words.

"The Cat-mothers sing the memory of another woman, a dream-walker, who brought the vision of our creation to the creator. It is said that knowledge of our world was translated also from her vision." Cat looked pointedly at the woman whose name was Maria Santee. "They say she was held by a shadow to our world."

"Shadow ..." the woman murmured, "Of course, Shadow." Her eyes crinkled as she laughed, then sobered. "And we wasted six months and three lives.... Quickly," she said suddenly, "my time grows short. Does anything remain of these chambers?" He nodded. "Then take me there now."

Sensing the urgency of her need, Cat leapt immediately to his feet and drew her to the cavern's entrance. At last someone had need of the knowledge he'd so patiently guarded. For the first time since his mentor had gone, he triggered the mechanism in the presence of another. Without pausing to gaze about in wonder, as the few younglings who still bothered to come always did, Maria went to each of the machines and stood staring at the printouts they'd spilled forth.

Every few minutes she asked a question about one or another of the sheets or had him turn one over while she looked at a previous section. When she'd finished with that, she had him help her with the logbooks and journals. With the attitude of a trained observer she scanned quickly down the pages as he turned them, sometimes asking him to stop while she read the same thing over and over again as if she strove to burn each line she read into her memory. Finally, she went from machine to machine absorbing the details of each.

After what seemed an eternity but was really only about an hour, she turned suddenly to Cat. She clasped his hands with her phantom touch and said fervently, "Thank you, my friend. I'm glad that I lived to see your world and know that something will survive." Then she turned and fled the cavern, her form growing dimmer as it slipped through the solid rock of the wall.

Distantly, Cat heard purring and a senseless mewing sound like an unschooled kitten might make. He heard the woman who called herself Maria cry, "Shadow, thank goodness! We must hurry." An unearthly chill swept through him as he sat, silently contemplating all that had transpired. At last he understood how he had participated in closing the circle of fate—just as he, the last Guardian of the Old Knowledge, had been meant to do all along. That was what the old-one had come back to ensure. Well, as he had with everything else he'd done in his life, Cat had discharged this final duty with care and diligence. He sighed as he looked sadly around the room for the last time, knowing that his long vigil was ended. The younglings were right, now; there was no more use in the old knowledge. Unfortunately, there was also no further use for him.

It had never occurred to him that he would become obsolete. Perhaps he should go off and wait to die, as the old warriors did; but he had no wish to die so young. He would consult with his mate; she would help him decide what was best. Maybe they would go off together and see what lay beyond the narrow confines of the Big Lake territory. His eyes brightened at the thought. There was no reason to confine curiosity to the reading of books.

After a while he rose and, seeing that everything was as it should be, he started back to the caves of his people. There would be a new song-memory for the Cat-mothers to sing tonight, and a new life for him tomorrow.

SNAKE EYES

by Ann Miller and Karen Rigley

Fire! Searing heat. Smoke stinging eyes and hurting lungs. Flames crackling, popping, snapping pain....

Lori woke with a start. She sat up in bed, expecting to find the apartment on fire. Nothing but darkness and the scent of lilac wafting through the window greeted her. A dream?

It had felt so real! She could swear she'd been trapped in a burning room. A tremor raced down her arms. She'd never experienced such a nightmare before. She could taste the smoke on her lips and her throat ached as if parched.

Is this how Uncle Bert and Aunt Evelyn felt those last moments? Her stomach knotting at the thought, Lori kicked off the sheet and climbed out of bed, sniffing the air as she prowled toward her bedroom door. She placed her palm against the wood. Cool. She cautiously opened it. A soft glow from the bathroom nightlight illuminated the hallway. Safe, calm, she could see nothing wrong. Yet, she trembled from the terror of the fire.

Inside the bathroom, she splashed her face with cold water and tried to shake off the dream, all the while assuring herself it was indeed a nightmare. What else could it be? She'd not even been home when the house burned.

Though positive she wouldn't sleep another wink, Lori returned to bed and lay down, staring out the window at the star-studded night sky. Deep sadness welled up, filling her eyes and clogging her throat. That raging inferno robbed her of her home and the only parents she'd ever known in one savage stroke, leaving only their son, her cousin Ray—not much comfort. They'd not been close; neither in years nor relationship.

Now Lori wished for the warmth and caring she had shared with her aunt and uncle. She watched the stars.

Strange ... they began swimming about the sky, swirling and swooping ... twin vortices of stars whirling and forming ... EYES! Odd, compelling eyes with slitted snake pupils staring ... now other stars rushed nearer to form a head ... a snake's head? No, a ... a cat's head coming closer descending upon her quickly to swallow her up into the brightness. ...

Again she jerked awake. "Silver!" she cried, staring into those very snake eyes, now gazing back at her from feline form. The cat's heavy softness pressed upon her chest as he kneaded her crossed arms gently. She freed one hand to stroke the silver-gray head.

"I still have you, don't I," she said. "You mean more to me than my human cousin." Silver purred. She knew of the cat's deep devotion to her aunt and uncle, and realized he must be grieving, too. "Poor Silver, nobody thinks of a cat's sadness, do they?" He gave a little trilling meow as if acknowledging her sympathy.

Lori looked at the glowing numerals of her bedside clock; only five-thirty, but she knew sleep had deserted her. Two weird dreams in one night!

"Off, Silver. Let me up." She lifted the big cat over onto the bed. He clutched her with his paws, keeping his sharp claws sheathed, and tried to maintain eye contact. She stared into those sea-green eyes, almost colorless in the darkness, sparkling with starlight. ...

A tiny chill chased goose bumps across her shoulders. She gave the cat a hug and a pet and escaped from his grasp. Swinging her legs off the bed, she rose and padded to the bathroom with Silver twining between her ankles. He continued following her into the kitchen as she poured water into the coffee brewer. While the brown liquid trickled into the pot, Lori offered Silver cat treats and a saucer of milk for breakfast. She poured a mug of coffee and sat down at the table, mulling over her to-do list for the day. So much to sort and settle concerning the business.

Would Cousin Ray have sense enough to keep it going? Lori couldn't help but have her doubts. Only Uncle Bert's sharp supervision had kept Ray on the job. Ray tended to prefer recreation, trading on his family's social position. Lori knew of the tension he caused by his attitude and her aunt and uncle's disappointment in Ray's unwillingness to accept responsibility.

Lori realized Ray's irresponsibility had inspired Uncle Bert's decision to consider the offer tendered by Worldwide Home 'n Hearth to buy Morrison's Hardware. Ray's reaction to the proposed sale surprised Lori. She had expected him to jump on the money, but instead he balked, claiming he wanted to preserve the family business. Why, she wondered, when he'd never cared about it before?

"Do you want to go down into the store with me?" she asked Silver, opening the door to the stairwell. In answer, he zipped down the steep steps ahead of her, his tail curled over his back. She smiled to herself as she followed him. She'd never known a cat to carry its tail that way. Silver had always seemed a unique creature. Aunt Evelyn had brought him home thirteen years ago, a bedraggled little kitten needing love, food, and medical attention. He'd received all three and had thrived, pouring out affection and loyalty to his adoptive family. Except for Ray. There was no love lost between those two. Lori even suspected Ray might mistreat Silver, given the chance. Privately she believed "cat haters" were insecure, their egos unable to withstand a cat's inborn majesty.

His Majesty Silver perched upon the counter, awaiting the first customer. "You should be on the payroll," she told him, unlocking the front door and flipping the Closed sign to Open. Lori had moved into the apartment above the store after the fire, bringing Silver along. How he'd escaped the fire she didn't know, but she was grateful. Silver at thirteen was half her age. They'd been friends for a long time. Always enjoying the best care and most nourishing food, he didn't appear to be an elderly cat. He'd received some singed fur from the fire, no serious injury. The vet had pronounced him remarkably fit at the post-fire exam. Lori read of cats attaining ages into their twenties. Watching the gleaming pewter beast reclining beside the cash register, she hoped fervently Silver would be one of those felines.

"Miss Morrison?"

Lori looked up from the daily report into a craggy but kindly face. "Yes. May I help you?"

Flashing a badge, the man replied, "I'm Detective

George Myer of the Kingston Police Department. Do you know James White?"

"Yes, he's been doing the store audit for my aunt and uncle. They hoped to sell the business." She glanced at the wall clock. "In fact, I was expecting him over an hour ago. Why do you ask?"

"Ah ... unfortunately Mr. White was involved in a hit-and-run accident last night as he left his office."

"How terrible! Was he hurt?"

"I'm sorry to have to tell you he was killed, Miss Morrison."

Her hand flew to her throat. "My goodness. Oh, what a shock." She swallowed, attempting to corral her buzzing emotions. "Please forgive me, Detective. But this coming so soon after my uncle and aunt. . . ."

"Yes, ma'am, I understand."

Silver leapt onto the desk and butted his head against Lori's chin. She automatically stroked the cat. "Another death," she murmured, sighing. "You don't know who did it?"

"Not yet, but we're investigating. I saw in his appointment book that he had a meeting scheduled with you."

"Yes, and I didn't realize he was late. I'm getting some paperwork ready for him and ..." Her voice trailed off as she stared at the report. Now what? Would the audit firm send someone else to finish the job? She felt so confused. Silver arched against her stroking hand and purred, as if offering comfort. She fought the urge to bury her face in his soft fur and cry. Tears hovered very near the surface these days.

Lori tried to give coherent answers to Detective Myer's routine questions and evidently satisfied him as he closed his notebook and pocketed it.

"Thank you, Miss Morrison. If we have any further questions, we'll get back to you."

"Detective, will you please keep me posted?"

"Of course."

She let him find his own way out, too stunned to rise. Death all around. "Thank God you weren't killed in the fire, too," she whispered fiercely against Silver's neck.

A hit-and-run. Poor James. A perfect example of an auditor with his slight build, receding hairline, and horn rimmed glasses. But she'd come to appreciate his dry wit and had grown to like him as much as Ray disliked him. Her cousin's constant railing against James made Lori defensive about the auditor. She'd snapped at Ray more than once when he'd made snide remarks about James. Part of his resistance to the sale, perhaps? He certainly didn't want the audit, required by Worldwide.

The books. James had the books. In fact, the books were the reason for their planned meeting. "There are some things we must go over," James had said on the phone. "I'm sorry to rush this, but I think it's important."

Lori recalled his tone of voice as well as his words: grim. And yes, it was a bit of a rush. The fire; the double funeral; Lori, left with only the clothes she wore, shopping for bare necessities; this was actually the first day the store had been open since the fire.

And where was Ray? Not on the job. Not helping out, that's for sure, Lori thought bitterly. Since Ray had always kept the books, why had James wanted to speak to Lori about the audit? Especially since Ray had never let her near the books before, almost as if she were too dim-witted to understand bookkeeping. Which infuriated her. Ray considered himself bookkeeper and PR expert, hanging out at the country club, gladhanding "potential customers." Their customers came in for fair pricing, quality merchandise, and excellent service. Not because of Ray's socializing.

Pushing Silver aside, Lori attempted to concentrate on her unfinished work. Just because James got killed didn't mean the audit would grind to a halt. Lori wondered, now that Uncle Bert and Aunt Evelyn were dead, if Ray's opinion of the sale would change. After all, without them, who would actually run the company? Mr. Wonderful himself? Ha. Run it into the ground, if anything.

Later, while washing her supper dishes, Lori heard clinks and thuds in the closed store below. She ignored a flash of apprehension. "What in the world . . ." she muttered, wiping her hands and heading for the door to the stairwell. Silver darted past her to zoom down ahead, disappearing around the corner at the foot of the stairs. Lori snapped on the light and peered toward the office. A man's form stepped into the light.

"Ray! What are you doing?" She moved toward him. Silver stalked Ray, snarling and hissing.

"Shut up, you stupid cat," Ray snapped, rummaging through a file drawer. Silver hissed a retort. A large animal, he could appear quite threatening. "You'd better get this dumb cat away from me," Ray said, throwing Lori a glare. "If he bites or scratches me, he's dead meat."

She bristled at Ray's threat. "Silver, what's the matter with you? Usually you ignore Ray. Sweetie, come here. Stop that." Silver obeyed Lori's summons, but positioned himself between the two humans, still growling in low tones.

Lori felt like growling herself. She'd hoped Ray might be more subdued by the shock of losing both his parents, but it seemed to have the opposite effect, making him even more obnoxious.

"Ray, what *are* you looking for?"

"Just some papers. Don't worry about it."

"Did you hear about James White?"

For an instant, Ray ceased fumbling in the drawer. "What about him?"

"James was killed last night by a hit-and-run driver." She stepped closer trying to see what he wanted out of the files.

Ray flipped through more folders. "Is that so? Who did it?"

"They don't know yet. They're investigating." She scrutinized the stack of papers he'd piled on the desk. Assorted invoices, from what she could tell. He swept them up and stuffed them into his briefcase. "Are you pulling those invoices for the audit?"

He gave her a level stare. "The audit is canceled."

"Why? Because of the accident? You know they'll send someone to replace James."

"There's no need for an audit!" Ray's voice rose with each word.

"But Worldwide won't buy Morrison's without an audit, Ray. You know that."

"What's it to you? Listen, little cousin. With the folks dead, Morrison's Hardware belongs to *me*. It's not your concern. In fact, I no longer require your services. I'll be glad to write out your final paycheck tomorrow, and you'd better find another place to live."

Stunned, Lori stared at Ray's back as he strode through the store and out the front door, slamming it behind him. He'd fired her! And kicked her out of the apartment as well. Stifling sobs, she fled upstairs, slamming her own door. A scratching noise reminded her someone else wanted in. She opened the door and scooped Silver into her arms and carried him to the sofa. She sat down, still crying and the concerned cat licked at her streaming tears. "Oh, Silver, you're such a dear. We'll find a new home and I know I can get another job. I . . . I *know* Uncle Bert and Aunt Evelyn would never have wanted this to happen." But Ray was right—what could Lori do about it? Unfair or not, he called the shots.

Smoke rising into the night sky blending with stars swirling and mixing mist and starfire forming eyes . . . snake eyes staring rushing down closer so huge engulfing. . . .

"Oh!" Lori gasped and opened her own eyes only to meet Silver's mesmerizing gaze like the night before.

"Puuurrrrow," Silver trilled. He placed a paw gently on Lori's cheek and patted her, almost as if he wanted her to close her eyes again. Ridiculous. Why would he . . . ?

She blinked and turned her head to keep his paw away from her eye. Claws sheathed, he obviously had no intention of hurting her. Oh, well, okay. She closed her eyes.

The cat settled on her chest, purring. What a relaxing, soothing sound. She felt herself drifting.

Eyes again, shaped by smoke and stars, slitted snake pupils like Silver's. Yes, Snake Eyes! Uncle Bert's pet name for Silver. This time Lori allowed the eyes to complete their purpose, to merge with her, to become her eyes. . . .

Uncle Bert sat at his desk in the study, frowning down at something. Aunt Evelyn came to look over his shoulder at his summons. They acted disturbed and Lori strained vainly to understand what they were saying. Ray's legs passed by as he strode across the room to face his parents. Their voices clashed, blurring most of the words, but Lori caught a few phrases.

Uncle Bert's voice raised in anger: ". . . altered invoices . . . false entries . . . phony receipts . . ."

Ray shouting: ". . . you old fool . . ."

Aunt Evelyn's shocked expression, resting her hand on Uncle Bert's shoulder as she spoke: "... betray your family ..."

Lori wished she could see what Uncle Bert had on the desk, but she was looking upward. Why was she on the floor? Then she realized she watched from Silver's point of view and the idea stunned her into sudden wakefulness.

The cat still rested on her chest, gazing into her face with his sea-green snake eyes. Lori stroked him, gathering her wits, almost afraid to admit what she'd witnessed—and how. "This calls for a cup of hot herb tea," she told him, and headed for the kitchen.

Sitting at the table, Lori sipped her steaming fragrant tea and watched Silver finish off leftover bits of his supper. He certainly didn't behave like a cat who had just conveyed startling information in an equally startling manner to a human being. Had she dreamed all that? Somehow, though common sense demanded that answer, Lori was convinced she'd watched actual events with his eyes.

Now she understood Ray's strong objections to an audit. He'd stolen from the business and Uncle Bert must have uncovered it. Lori decided to pay Detective Myer a visit first thing in the morning. If Ray had been juggling the books, the police should be informed.

Daybreak cast a different light on the revelations of the night. Honestly confused, Lori doubted her own ability to separate reality from fantasy. She needed to examine the bookkeeping to determine the truth.

As she walked up to the dispatch desk in the police station, she hoped she didn't look as uncomfortable as she felt. "Excuse me," she said to the dispatcher. Before he could respond, the phone rang; he held up a finger and answered the call. The jarring background noise of the station bombarded her. She waited. The dispatcher continued his conversation, scribbling notes on a pad.

"Miss Morrison?"

Startled at the sound of her name, Lori turned and looked up into the face of Detective Myer.

"May I be of assistance?" he asked.

"I came to see you."

"Come into my office. We can hear ourselves think in

there." Detective Myer touched her elbow to guide her down a hallway and through a door, which he closed behind them.

"I hate to be a nuisance, but I need to ask a favor," Lori said, taking the seat he indicated. He sat down across his battle-scarred desk from her.

"Ask away."

"James White, the auditor, had our company ledger. I need it back."

He nodded. "I'll see what I can do." Giving her a hard stare, he added, "Any particular reason? Is there a problem?"

"I'm not sure. That's why I need the ledger."

"Miss Morrison, investigation is the job of the police. Why don't you tell me any suspicions you may have and let me check things out?"

Lori clasped and unclasped her hands. "I don't know if I can." What could she say? How could she explain? Her cat showed her in a dream that her cousin had tampered with the books?

Leaning forward, Detective Myer rested his elbows on the desk and propped his chin in one hand. "Does this have anything to do with your cousin, Ray Morrison?"

Her blush gave the answer.

"I'll see about getting that ledger for you."

"Thank you, Detective." Lori stood quickly, looped her purse strap over her shoulder and marched out of the station, dodging an officer escorting a handcuffed prisoner.

The bright sunshine and fresh breeze offered a welcome relief from the dank staleness of the police station. Pleased she'd walked the few blocks instead of driving, she waited for the light to change, then started across the intersection. Her visit to the station replayed itself in her mind.

"Watch out!"

Jarred out of her reverie by the warning, Lori glanced around as a car hurtled at her. She leapt frantically toward the curb. Pain stabbed as she landed on her hands and knees on the sidewalk.

"Are you hurt, ma'am?"

Hands assisted Lori to her feet. "I think I'm all right. Did you see who almost hit me?"

Her rescuer frowned. "It was a white Taurus, but I didn't see the driver."

By the time she reached the store, her scrapes and bruises throbbed. When she entered the back door, she noticed with dismay the store was closed. If Ray was too lazy to run it himself, why in heaven did he fire her? And why did he resist selling it? Questions chased around in her head until it pounded in tandem with her injuries.

As she reached the top of the stairs she heard her phone ringing and fumbled her key in the lock, trying to get inside before the caller gave up. Breathlessly she snatched up the receiver.

"Hello?"

"Miss Morrison? Detective Myer here."

"Yes, sir?"

"I tried to track down your ledger, but the audit firm understood Mr. White had returned it."

For a moment Lori didn't know what to say.

"Miss Morrison, is something wrong?"

"No . . . yes. I was nearly run down crossing an intersection on my way home today."

"Ironic. That's how Mr. White met his fate. Did you see who it was?"

"The car came at me too fast."

"Any witnesses?"

"Yes, the man who helped me up said it was a white Taurus." Suddenly weak-kneed, Lori sat down on the sofa. Silver jumped into her lap.

"Did you get the witness' name?"

"No, I didn't think to ask."

"You'd better come down in the morning and file a report. Meanwhile, make sure your doors and windows are securely locked. And get some rest. You've had a shock."

Sore and exhausted, Lori ate an early supper and turned in before nightfall. She took a magazine to bed with her for a bit of light reading, but fell asleep within the first few pages.

When the stars began whirling to form the eyes, it didn't surprise her. The dream swept her up, resuming from where it had left off the night before with Ray standing across the desk from his parents, exchanging angry words with them. Again, she found it difficult to catch more than occasional words, but their voices escalated into furious shouts. Suddenly, Ray grabbed at whatever Uncle Bert had on his desk.

The ledger! Ray tried to yank it away, but Uncle Bert hung on, resisting. Aunt Evelyn attempted to help her husband retain possession, but Ray was too strong and pulled it away. Uncle Bert lunged to recapture it and Ray swung the heavy book, slamming the corner of it into Uncle Bert's temple. The force of the blow knocked the older man into his wife and they fell like dominoes. Aunt Evelyn's head hit the edge of a side table with an audible crack and they crumpled into a heap, lying still. Very still.

Lori moved close to her aunt and uncle, noting the purpling bruise on Uncle Bert's temple and his half-closed eyes. Her heart squeezed. Was he dead? No. Oh, no!

This time, yanked abruptly from her dream state, Lori knew she wasn't the one who had stopped it. Silver had vacated her chest to sit on the window sill.

"Silver? What's the matter, boy?" Lori sensed the cat's distress and reached to stroke him. "Sweetie, you must come back and show me the rest. I know it hurts to remember, because it hurts me to watch. But I must know the truth. The whole truth. Do you understand?"

Her own words echoed in her head and she almost laughed aloud. She was asking a cat to project a dream into her mind. Had she gone insane? What could she be thinking?

Then Silver moved back onto her chest and stared at her with those eerie green eyes and she stopped doubting. Crazy or not, it was happening. Lori closed her eyes and watched the stars whirl.

Again, she crouched beside her uncle and aunt. CRASH! That smell ... kerosene? Her head whipped around and she saw broken glass amidst a spreading puddle. The lantern. Ray's legs. He'd broken the lantern. A scratching noise attracted her attention upward to see flame leap from a match that Ray held in his hand. He flipped it and she watched it arc down into the kerosene which ignited with a WHOOSH! Fire raced across the floor and the curtains caught ... smoke, flame, choking blinding pain. . . .

Lori sat up with a gasp and clutched Silver tightly. Tears squeezed from her tightly closed eyes to stream down her face as she sobbed against the cat's silken fur.

Her cousin Ray had murdered his own parents. Never would she have thought he could do such a thing, yet she couldn't deny the vision Silver had shown her. And Lori knew she'd seen the truth as he'd witnessed it. How, she couldn't explain. Perhaps his desperation to see Ray punished for such an evil deed opened a channel in his mind. But how would she pass on this information? No sane person would believe such a wild tale; that her cat produced visions in her dreaming mind to catch the murderer of his loved ones.

"What am I going to do?" she moaned, rocking back and forth with Silver in her arms. "How can I make Detective Myer believe me? I've got to convince him. But how?"

"That's all I can remember about my near-miss, Detective Myer." Lori watched the police officer write down the last words before handing over the statement.

"If you'll read and sign here, please."

She complied with his request, her mind racing. She still couldn't think of a way to reveal her information.

"Thank you," he said, accepting the signed statement. "Miss Morrison, we received the autopsy reports on your uncle and aunt."

She licked suddenly dry lips. "And my uncle died from a blow to his temple."

Myer's silence almost crackled. Very evenly he asked, "How did you know that?"

"I ... can't explain." She dared a glance at him. His gaze met hers and held until she looked back down at her clasped hands.

"I know you were receiving a late shipment at the store during the time of the fire, because I checked it out myself."

Lori quickly met his level stare again. "You thought that I ... ?"

He shook his head, then said, "We also have the Fire Marshal's report. The fire was started by—"

"Kerosene," she supplied.

Myer snapped his pencil in half. "Miss Morrison, if you are withholding evidence, it can cause you serious trouble."

"I wish I did have evidence," Lori replied, frowning.

"When is the last time you saw your cousin?"

"Night before last, when he fired me."

"He *fired* you? Weren't you basically running the store along with your aunt and uncle?"

"Yes, sir."

"Who's running it now?"

"Nobody."

Detective Myer heaved a sigh. "I wish I'd been able to locate that ledger for you."

"My cousin has it."

"He does? Miss Morrison, I really wish you'd tell me how you know these things."

"I can't," she whispered. "I can't explain. Please believe me."

Myer stood and walked around the desk to escort her out. "I don't have much choice, do I?" he admitted ruefully, adding, "Please watch your step crossing streets today, okay?"

"Believe me, Detective, I intend to."

But no mystery cars charged at her, and Lori reached the closed store without incident. She felt so aimless; unconnected. No job to go to, weighed down by the knowledge she carried, alone.

Not quite, she amended when Silver greeted her with trills and ankle rubs. Lori reached down and stroked him, grateful for his company, and carried the paper she'd bought to the sofa. "Hmmm ... rentals," she murmured, opening to the classifieds. She noted several available apartments, then laid the paper aside, trying to work up the heart to query about them. She'd need a place that accepted pets. No way would she leave Silver behind.

The cat jumped up beside her and curled up on the discarded paper. Lori scratched him under his chin and he closed his eyes in pleasure. She wondered, would the dreaming stop now that Silver had accomplished his purpose? Or would their unique communication continue? And—was it unique? Could there be others sharing mental links with their cats?

"Maybe I should start a support group."

"Purrrrrrowww," agreed Silver, stretching and recurling on the paper.

The long day ended without any further word from Detective Myer. How disappointing. Lori had hoped something would come of her meeting with the detective that morning. But what could she expect, unable to offer any proof or evidence to back up her accusations? Unable, even, to explain how she knew what she did. Should she try seeking proof on her own? Perhaps attempt to reclaim the ledger herself?

Lying down on her bed, Lori snapped off the bedside lamp. Silver stretched out beside her without climbing onto her chest tonight. She petted him and heard his rhythmic purr. "I wish you'd show me the answer," she said, but he simply continued to purr.

Lori's eyes snapped open in the darkness. No cat lay on her chest, no stars whirled in the sky, yet something had wakened her. She listened.

Silver leapt across her and trotted to the bedroom door, his tail curled over his back, and stared at the doorknob. Lori rose and padded to the door and turned the knob, allowing the cat through. She followed, moving as quietly as the feline.

There! Another sound—the creaking of that second step on the stairs. A chill prickled Lori's neck. Who would be on her staircase at this time of night? Her heart pounding, she made her way to the front door.

Pressing her ear against the door, Lori listened but heard no more creaks. But as she reached for the knob, it turned ever so slightly, as if someone were testing the lock.

Her heart banged furiously inside her hollow chest. Silver flattened his ears and crouched but didn't make a sound. What should she do? Scream? Who would hear her, alone in the apartment above an empty store?

Rap-rap-rap.

Lori nearly jumped over the sofa when the knock sounded on the door. "Who . . . who's there?" she called.

"Ray. Let me in. I want to talk to you."

"It's after midnight. Come back tomorrow." She shook with fright, waiting to see what he'd do. Then she heard his key in the lock.

"It can't wait," he said as the door swung open.

Lori retreated a step. "You have no right to barge in here." Her voice emerged a hoarse croak and she cleared her throat. "Leave right now."

He ignored her demand. "What did you tell the police?"

"Tell ... the police? What do you mean?"

"Don't play dumb. They're sniffing around, and I want to know why." He took a menacing step toward her and Silver growled a warning. Ray didn't even waste a glance at the protective feline.

Lori tried to inch away from her cousin, but he grabbed her wrist. "Stop it! You're hurting me." She pried at his strong fingers without success. Fear shivered through her body. Aware of what he'd done to his parents, how could she expect mercy?

"I know what you did, Ray," she said desperately. "And so do the police. You won't get away with it."

Instead of scaring him off, her threat seemed to inflame him. He gave her wrist a twist, sending a sharp pain coursing up her arm, and pulled her toward the doorway.

"It was an accident. You think I meant to kill them? Dad should've backed off! But no, he had to start raving at me, making with the big honesty act!"

Much to Lori's horror, Ray sounded like a lunatic. How could she reason with a madman? "What about James White? Can you call his death an accident?"

"That meddling auditor deserved it!" Ray yanked Lori through the door onto the landing. "He started all the trouble, blabbing to Dad about my loans."

"Loans?" Lori cried, clutching the doorjamb with her free hand. "You *stole* from the business, Ray! It's called embezzlement!"

Ray grabbed at her hand and tore it away from the doorjamb as he thrust his face inches from hers. Hate twisted his features. "No. That money belonged to me. You can't steal what's already yours. I had to take what was mine while I could, before Dad gave it away to *you*."

"Me? Ray, what are you talking about?"

"Dad told me he intended to leave half ownership of the business to you."

"Really?" She continued desperately, hoping to stall, hoping to think of a way to stop him from killing her. "So you thought that justified embezzling money?"

"Definitely. They always loved you best. I was their *son*, but they loved you the most. Sweet little daughter of Dad's younger brother, all alone—the baby girl my folks never had. Well, you can die with them. And everything will be mine, as it should!"

"Ray, no! You can have the business—"

"You bet I can." He tried to fling Lori off the landing but she resisted, her fear giving her strength. She struggled against him, but he was winning, his superior size and muscles overpowering her.

Lori screamed and fought, but felt herself dragged closer and closer to the steep stairs, felt her head and shoulders slammed against the wall, felt one foot slip off the landing, and knew she'd lost.

"Rrrrrrrooooowwwww. . . ."

Ray reeled away from her, a spitting, clawing, biting Silver attached to his face. Lori fell onto the landing as Ray pitched backward and tumbled down the stairs to land in a heap and lie still.

The cat jumped clear and began circling Ray's prone form, on guard. Lori stumbled down the stairs just as Detective Myer burst in the back door, accompanied by two uniformed officers. Silver leapt up into Lori's arms.

"Are you all right, Miss Morrison?" Detective Myer asked.

"Thanks to Silver, I'll be fine."

"I thought you'd need help, but obviously I was mistaken."

"Meow," Silver agreed.

"Is Ray dead?" Lori asked, watching the officers examine her cousin.

"No, ma'am," replied one officer, then added to his companion, "call an ambulance."

"Tell me, Detective. How did you know to come?" Lori asked, turning back to Myer.

"Actually, I was looking for your cousin—who you thoughtfully supplied for me. He's under arrest. I couldn't ignore your suspicions."

"You mean you found evidence?"

Detective Myer glanced down at his officers attending to Ray. "I traced that white Taurus. Your cousin rented it in the next town when he left his own car at a body shop to have the front fender repaired. Fortunately, we located the car before the hit-and-run evidence was destroyed."

Her hand flew to her throat. "He *did* run down James."

"That was enough to get me a search warrant. We discovered kerosene-splattered shoes and the company ledger in your cousin's house. The lab found traces of blood and hair on the corner of the ledger—a match to your uncle's."

Color drained from Lori's face and she began to tremble.

Detective Myer reached out a steadying hand. "Let me take you upstairs. This has been quite a shock."

"Thank you," Lori whispered, then much to her surprise, the detective lifted Silver away from her. She expected a hiss of protest. Instead, Silver snuggled contentedly in Detective Myer's arms. At the top of the stairs, he handed her back her cat.

"Remarkable animal," he said, scratching Silver under the chin. Silver purred, welcoming the attention as his due. "Fascinating eyes, almost like a snake." Myer redirected his gaze to Lori. "Please. Tell me how you knew what your cousin did."

Lori glanced down at Silver who half-closed his eyes at her, as if granting permission. She looked back up at the detective with a smile.

"Detective Myer, won't you come in? I have a rather amazing tale to share with you."

ONE TOO MANY CATS
by Sasha Miller

Ferdon the magician paced back and forth in the common room of the cottage, frowning. Ordinarily just the sight of his wife, Edanne, would have made him smile. She was tiny and slender, with a heart-shaped face, and her blue-green eyes tilted at the corners. Now she presented a charming picture as she sat curled in Ferdon's chair attempting to thread her needle by bringing the needle to the thread rather than the other away around. This improbable feat accomplished, Edanne began, with remarkable clumsiness, to darn the elbow of one of Ferdon's shirts.

Her lack of sewing skill, however, was not the source of Ferdon's displeasure with his bride. Edanne's shortcomings in certain domestic skills were easily overlooked; if he had wanted neater mends on the shirt elbows he was forever wearing through as he applied himself to his studies, he could always hire it done. Dala had been one whose needle had been for hire.

He looked at the ginger-colored cat lying limp and disconsolate by the fire. Its eyes and nose ran, making the fur on its muzzle soggy and matted, and as he watched, the cat went into one of its sneezing fits. *"Snit! Snit, snit!"* The sapphire and emerald beads on its earrings jangled. *"Snit!"*

"We have to do something about Dala," he said.

Edanne bit off her thread and looked up at him with innocent eyes. "You work spells to help the sneezing. What else should be done?"

"You know why. We've been over it again and again." He began to pace once more, marking his points on his fingers. "One. The spells are temporary at best. And they don't last as long as they once did. Two. It was wrong of you to turn Dala into a cat."

199

"Why? Switching places with her was the only way I could become a woman. Don't you love me better?"

"That's not the question, and you know it. Oh, I'll admit I thought I loved Dala at one time—"

Edanne bit off another length of thread with her sharp white teeth and began trying to thread her needle again. "She would have had me out of the house on the toe of her slipper if you had been unlucky enough to marry her. She told me as much the day she came to tell you good-bye."

"But by then she wasn't any threat to you. She was going to marry Allesando."

"So she said. The baron's son indeed! I had no way of knowing that. Not for certain. She could have been lying."

"Nobody in the village has seen Allesando since. He's gone into seclusion." Dala sneezed again. Ferdon picked her up and wiped her nose and eyes with the sleeve of his robe. "Couldn't you have found some other way of becoming human? You knew cats had this effect on her."

Edanne smiled. "Don't you like me better as a woman than as a cat?"

"Of course I do!" Ferdon's head was beginning to throb, the way it always did during one of these discussions, and he had forgotten any of the points he had wanted to make past the first two. "But Dala is no fit Companion. She is no help to me at all. How do you think it looks, a mage of my standing trying to work magic, and his Companion keeps sneezing all over him?"

"Then why don't you just change her back again?" Edanne said without guile. "Remove her earrings?"

Ferdon's headache vanished. This was the first time she had ever asked this question, and until now he had not been permitted by the laws of magic to ask her directly. "I can't do it without your assistance, my dear. The earrings can't be removed."

Edanne's forehead puckered. "Well, I did it. I thought Dala could help you."

"You could have helped me with your own transformation, if I had understood you wanted it, but Dala is obviously too ill to undergo the ordeal. Also, you were involved in the original spell-making. Therefore, you must assist me now."

"Oh." Edanne nodded slowly. "I think I begin to see. No wonder you've brought the subject up so often."

"I could have done it easily, if only I still had a certain book."

"Did it have a purple leather cover? On the smallish side?"

"Yes."

"I have no idea what happened to it."

He kept his temper in check by an effort. Might as well be angry at a cat for preferring to chase birds rather than mice. "You burnt it, didn't you?" He knew that the smell of burning shoes and the flash of purple in the fire that evening when he had come into his cottage to discover Edanne waiting for him had been the book she had thrown into the fireplace—but he wanted to hear it from her.

"Oh, was that the book you meant?"

"Yes, it was. *Magick et Jewelles et Cattes.* I wish I had read it thoroughly instead of simply finding out about you and the earrings you wore when you came to me. Obviously, it had the spells listed to create a Companion, and also to release one. With it, I could have removed the earrings and transformed her by myself, and done it safely. By safely, I mean keeping you with me as you are now, while restoring Dala and releasing her from her misery. Now, because you are the only one who has done it at all and must remember how, I must have your help."

Edanne's smile was like the sun breaking through clouds. She tossed her mending aside and leapt up. Ferdon barely had time to set Dala on the table before Edanne had hurled herself into his arms. "I love you so much," she said, and kissed him.

"Then you'll help me with Dala willingly?"

"If you really want me to." She smiled again. "In a way it will be almost like the old days, won't it?"

He chuckled. "And I will make us porridge dusted with cinnamon when we're done."

"I do enjoy using a spoon and sitting at the table rather than crouching on it." Her laugh delighted him.

"Thank you, Edanne. I love you very much."

Never had Ferdon made his magical preparations more carefully. Nothing—nothing—must go wrong, not in the least degree. He couldn't risk losing Edanne now that he had found her. His conscience twinged; he hadn't exactly told Edanne the entire story—a trick he had picked up from her. There was still an element of danger that he might simply switch the two and return Dala's humanity to her at the expense of Edanne's becoming a cat once more. If only he had that wretched book she had burned, he could have proceeded confidently.

Furthermore, he dared not put off the experiment much longer. Dala, the woman who had sneezed helplessly when in the presence of a cat, now looked extremely ill. Ferdon had heard tales of what happened to a mage who had the bad judgment to let his Companion die on him, and he definitely didn't want to find out if the stories were true.

He surveyed the powders and herbs, the distillations of rose and amber, the maze marked with chalk, describing the intricate, inward-spiraling path he and Edanne must walk. His wand of *lignum vitae* lay ready; he could almost see it pulsating with power. Then he shook his head, a little amused at his own overactive imagination.

You are worried only because you've never attempted this kind of transformation, he told himself. Altering Dala's looks while healing her of the deforming skin disease that plagued her, had been relatively simple and straightforward. That he had not been able to magic her into the shattering beauty he had envisioned—and, to be honest, had desired for himself—was mere happenstance, a consequence of Ede's leaping from his arms at the last moment when she sensed the way he had changed the spell without telling her first.

No such accident this time. As a cat, Ede had had distinct magical powers of her own in addition to what she had absorbed from the earrings, else she could never have used the book and switched places with Dala. He knew Edanne as a woman had even greater powers and would eventually, under his tutelage, complement him fully in his work.

And also as a woman— He smiled reminiscently. As a woman, Edanne's powers had no bounds as far as he was concerned. He had long ago realized that his infatuation with Dala had sprung from two sources only. First, he had pitied her for her disfigured skin; second, he had been stirred to lust for her ripe and beautiful body. But, alas, she had proved ungrateful—a fact for which he was now very grateful indeed.

All this was trivial, however. Now he had to restore her to human form even if he lost a Companion in the process. Perhaps another would come to him. If not, he would be more than content with Edanne by his side.

Edanne found it hard to believe she had agreed to Ferdon's impractical scheme. Good enough for Dala to be trapped in a form she could not abide. Edanne considered it simple justice, all things considered—which meant things Ferdon did not or could not comprehend, having to do with jealousy both from a cat's and a woman's point of view. Yet she had now promised, committed herself to undoing all her lovely work.

"Perhaps," she told the stray cat she had begun to tame by feeding it at the cottage door, "my way of thinking is becoming affected by my having human form. What do you think?"

The cat, a dark brindle tom with a rakish black splotch over one eye, miaowed at her and went back to his dish of dinner scraps.

"Yes," Edanne said. "You agree with me." She sighed. "Patch. I think I'll name you Patch."

The whole mess had begun, she thought, when Ferdon had done that first transformation of Dala, the one where he had unexpectedly added the beauty construct. What if, she thought, I added just a bit of extra spelling this time, to do a really thorough retransformation. I could return her to her state when Ferdon first met her, ugly pimple-spotted skin and all. Edanne smiled. It might not be as personally satisfactory as consigning her rival to a life in a body she couldn't abide, for that was, she could now see, injurious to Ferdon. But it would, at least, be something.

All preparations complete, all spells thoroughly rehearsed, no more delaying the moment. Dala the cat lay on a cushion covered with a long, soft robe, in the spot where Dala the human had once sat awaiting the transformation that would release her from her skin diseases. One last time, Ferdon wiped Dala's eyes and nose, and one last time Dala went into a sneezing fit that put his ministrations to naught. Edanne had to admit the cat certainly looked far from well. Her ginger-colored fur was matted and unkempt, looking like she had slept in it for a week, and she could scarcely raise her head. She had stopped eating and drank only when Ferdon held the bowl under her nose.

"Come," Ferdon said to Edanne. They stood facing each other. He was wearing his magician's robe, painted with the symbols of his craft. He took his wand in his left hand and Edanne's hand in his right. She then completed the circle by placing her other hand on his, just touching the wand.

Then they began to walk the maze widdershins, circling each other as they circled the object of the spelling. Their walk became a stately dance as they entered into a world of their own. The subject lay nearly forgotten in the center of their deepening engrossment with the power, and with each other.

"*Magicum cest commensorium,*" Ferdon chanted in a high, nasal voice. Edanne sang the words half a syllable behind him, confirming and strengthening, drawing upon a closeness that was at one with them and with the foundations of the very universe. "*Salvatum et requisat per transforamus.*"

They completed the first circle, closing the object of the spell within the magic being worked. With this part complete came a shift into even deeper intimacy as, lost in each other's eyes, they began the second, affirming circuit. "*Finadus et fulvia lex magicorum.*"

Warmth flowed through Edanne, sensual and primitive. In her vision, Ferdon shifted, transformed, and blended into every tom with whom she might have mated when she was a cat, and then back again into the man who was her human mate. His grip on her hand tightened and it didn't occur to her until later to wonder what he was seeing. Lost in the ecstacy of him, of her, of them, they began the third and final circuit when the spell would be complete.

The power began to solidify and grow firm. Edanne's mind cleared a little. The critical moment was approaching when Ferdon would release the hand holding the wand, dust the creature in the center of the web with the necessary ingredients, and pronounce the spell complete. Her stomach cramped as her body began to protest the drain magic-making put on it.

"—*fabulum tinus pro humanum occurit*—"

"—*fabulum tinus pro humanum occurit*—"

"—*delibe, declare, veritum est!*"

"—*delibe, declare,* non pulchra, *veritum est!*"

An earring hit the floor with a metallic jangle, followed by the clatter of the second earring as it fell. A crack of thunder rolled through the room making jars and bottles rattle on the shelves, as a great gout of smoke erupted in the center of the circle. Ferdon and Edanne stopped, both a little dazed; he stared at her, disbelieving the phrase she had inserted into the spell. A brindle streak raced silently out of the chalk circle, headed for the door. Patch, Edanne thought. How did he get in here?

Dala, naked as the day she was born, sat up. "Thank heavens I am rid of these wretched earrings," she said hoarsely. She hastily examined her wrists and touched her face. "Oh, no! The itchy spots on my skin are back! And the wen!"

Edanne could not have been more pleased. Her addition to the spell had worked perfectly. Furthermore, it looked as if the skin diseases that had ravaged Dala had been progressing during the period when she had been both beautiful and a cat, now had returned with a vengeance. A veritable shower of flakes filled the air around her as Dala rubbed at the red patches in her hairline. "It's a pity to be sure," Edanne said, "but at least you're back in your own body again. Don't touch the earrings."

"A lot of good you did," Dala said. "Just look at me! I'm down to bones!"

And truthfully, her skin did hang loose on her. Edanne could have counted her ribs. Also her hair was unkempt and matted. "Have a little decency and put on the robe," she said.

"Why did you let this happen, Ferdon?" Dala said resentfully. She picked up the robe and slipped it over her head. "I thought you had more feeling for me than this."

"Let what happen?" Edanne said. "He changed you back to your human form." She smothered a laugh. "And you aren't even sneezing."

"Ferdon, answer me!"

The magician looked from one woman to the other, non-plussed. He opened his mouth, shut it, opened it again.

"Miaow?" he said uncertainly.

"Oh, yes, you do have to help me get Ferdon's voice back." Edanne could have shaken the other women in her anger.

"Not me. Get somebody else to play cat for you. I've had enough of you, and of earrings, and of magicians to last me the rest of my life!" Dala tossed her head haughtily. "You're lucky I don't pull all your hair out!"

Edanne stopped abruptly, considering. She wasn't getting anywhere with Dala. She smiled, and her voice became a purr. "But if you help me, together we can transform you again into the beautiful woman you once were."

Dala regarded Edanne suspiciously. "And what makes you think I would trust you? Or even that I could do anything to help *him*?" She indicated Ferdon who sat—or, more accurately, hunkered—at the table holding his empty porridge bowl and staring into it with an unfathomable expression on his face.

He looked up. "Miaow, miaow," he said.

"More? Would you like more?" Edanne jumped up from the table to get the pot. Even if he had been capable of doing it, Ferdon had been too upset to make their porridge as was his usual habit and she had had to; however, her cooking had always been much, much better than her mending.

"Miaow," he said gratefully. She smiled and dusted cinnamon across the top of the steaming porridge, then poured milk on it. Ferdon started to lap at it, but Edanne put his spoon into his hand.

"As I see it," Edanne said, "you have no choice but to help us sort out this dreadful mess."

"You're the one who got us into this mess in the first place, with your petty little revenge during that spell."

Edanne shrugged. "Well, that can't be helped. It's done and over with. I could say that your threat to me was what started it long before then, but what good would that do once we got through blaming each other? You'd still be an ugly, scratchy, pimpled blob and Ferdon would still be in the shape he's in, unable to speak properly."

"I do see your point," Dala said reluctantly.

"Now I wish I hadn't burnt the book. But it did make a very nice blaze."

"You thought I'd use it against you, didn't you? You destroyed it so I couldn't use it the way you did, and switch places again, didn't you?"

"Of course. I certainly would have, if I'd been in your slippers—uh, paws." Edanne regarded her own slender feet, shod in fashionable red slippers much smaller, she thought with satisfaction, than anything Dala could fit into. A silence descended on the two women as shadows lengthened outside. A bump and rattle on the windowpane reminded Edanne that her stray wanted to be fed and she got up to attend to that small and pleasant task. She broke bread into a bowl, filled it with milk, opened the window, and set the bowl on the ledge.

The corners of Dala's mouth turned down and she looked like she had bitten into something sour. "Well, if you're so smart, how would you propose we begin this transformation?"

Edanne's heart lurched and she realized just how much she had been depending on Dala's cooperation. One thing this last bit of spell-making had done was make her realize why Ferdon had edged around the topic of Dala's restoration so persistently. A mage whose spell backfired or went awry put himself—or herself—into great jeopardy. Furthermore, this danger spread. Given the right circumstances, it would literally become a matter of life and death for everyone involved, especially the person who had created the situation. She dared not rejoice openly, however. Dala and the small bit of power she might have absorbed from the magical earrings while she was a Companion were crucial to any success she might have in returning Ferdon to his original state. Furthermore, she knew she could never trust Dala with the knowledge that she held all their fates in her hands. "I must do some reading. I will be up late tonight. In the meantime, you will have to stay here. You won't want to go back to your cottage, even if it were still empty. And you certainly don't want to risk bumping into Allesando, not looking the way you do. Assuming that he is still interested in you."

"You mean actually continue to live here while you try

to learn enough magic to do the trick?" Dala said incredulously. "And where do you suggest I sleep? There's only one bed."

"You and I, distasteful as it seems, will have to share it." Edanne eyed Ferdon, who was now attempting to wash his face by licking his hand and rubbing it over his beard. "I suspect he will prefer to curl up close to the fireplace rather than the foot of the bed where you used to sleep. I'll make a pallet."

Dala tossed her head. "Hmpfh!" she said. "Curl up with him. I always hated having to sleep with you and Ferdon and now you aren't sharing a bed or anything else with me. So there." She yawned so widely her jaws cracked.

Edanne shrugged. "Please yourself, then. Go on and go to bed. You look like you could use the rest," she added a little spitefully. To her pleasure, a little color came into Dala's face as she flushed in anger. "Take a candle. I'm sure you know the way."

Edanne searched Ferdon's books late into the night for some clue or direction to use in restoring him without further complicating a situation which, she had to admit, was growing worse by the hour. Ferdon seemed to be slipping deeper and deeper into cathood. She had prepared the pallet on the floor, hoping he would go to sleep as had Dala whose snores drifted in from the little curtained alcove they used as a bedroom, but he seemed disinclined for any such thing. As she tried to read, he insisted on cuddling up close beside her and trying to climb onto her lap, knocking her book sideways and threatening to crush her under his weight. She moved to the settle beside the window. The light from the candle she placed on the window sill was not as good as that from the same candle on the table, but at least she could persuade Ferdon to snuggle beside her as long as she scratched him gently behind the ears.

At last, fatigue and sleepiness overcame her. "Come along," she told her husband. "Good Ferdon. Nice bed, beside the embers. Very warm."

Obediently, he followed her. He made three circles, snuggling into the pallet before settling down in the warmest spot, between her and the embers. "Miaow," he murmured. He fell asleep almost immediately. Edanne put her arm around him and moved close, allowing herself a few tears. What if, she thought, I can't do it and my poor, beloved Ferdon is left like this the rest of his life?

Then, from sheer exhaustion, she, too, fell asleep. With her worry about Ferdon, Dala's eventual fate in all this was the least thing on her mind.

Edanne, chatting with the village women, gave out word that Ferdon would be unavailable for magic-working or healing for at least ten days. With a little respite from the townspeople and Ferdon's busy practice, Edanne alternately read, fed and petted Ferdon, and tried to keep her unwelcome house guest from becoming openly rebellious and departing before Edanne could remedy the horrible situation she had gotten them all in. She had considerably more luck where Ferdon was concerned. By now, all he wanted to do was cling to her skirts and rub his face and beard against her. It had become all she could do to make him walk upright, and getting him to use a spoon when he ate was out of the question. Sometimes he tried to exercise nonexistent claws on the table leg or the furniture.

Furthermore, now Ferdon was showing signs of wanting to fight with Patch whenever the brindle tom presented himself at the door or window to be fed and Edanne had to manage very carefully to avoid letting the two meet. Patch took no offense at Ferdon's bizarre behavior. He concentrated on Edanne, rubbing against her and opening his mouth silently as if insisting on something Edanne could not understand, though he did not try to come inside. Perhaps he still remembered the thunderous blast at the conclusion of the magic spell, and was wary of a repetition.

Dala, however, chose not to lift a finger to help, not with Ferdon nor any of the household chores, nor with any of the magical preparations. With so much to contend with, Edanne's temper began to grow short.

"Like it or not," she told Dala at the end of three days, "you are going to have to help me and quit acting like some great lady here to be waited on. You may be that, some day, if you can marry Allesando, if he has waited for you, and if he hasn't found somebody else in the meantime. Nobody knows."

That brought Dala up short. "I never thought of that,"

she said. "I might lose him. Very well, what do you want me to do?"

Suddenly reluctant to let Dala start taking care of Ferdon, Edanne pointed to the broom. "You can sweep the floor, for a start. And tidy up the place. Make up the bed. Put the books back on the shelf when I am finished with them."

"Scullery work," Dala said scornfully. But she did take the broom and begin to sweep.

With Dala not being an additional burden, Edanne's research went faster. Finally, in a huge tome entitled *General Magick For Ye Advanced Practitioner,* she thought she found what she was looking for. Several spells, in fact. She chose one at random.

"I need some lobelia, and some lime flowers," she told Dala. "Lime flowers don't grow around here, but I think I can substitute pennyroyal with no harm."

"You only *think* it will work?" Dala said dubiously.

"We still have plenty of rose and amber distillations," Edanne said. "And the powders. Those are standard ingredients. Of course it will work. The herbs must be fresh, though, and I never paid any attention to which ones Ferdon preferred." She picked up a basket and put it over her arm. "You'll have to look after things for an hour or so while I go searching for the herbs." She paused in the doorway and fixed her onetime rival with a steady gaze. "Don't do anything foolish while I am gone."

Dala sniffed and tossed her head. "You don't have to worry. Your precious Ferdon is becoming so catlike he's beginning to make me sneeze."

Comforted only a little by the thought, Edanne made her way quickly through the village to the little woods where Ferdon, in happier days, had gone looking for herbs and the occasional bit of mold or whatever else he needed for his spell-making. Edanne was quite familiar with the area for when she had been a cat she had frequently come here to hunt field mice and squirrels. When she reached the woods, Patch materialized out of nowhere and began following her.

"I'm glad for the company," she told him. He had become quite tame by now, and liked to brush against her skirt much the way Ferdon did these days. She reached down and let the cat trickle out from under her fingers, the way cats did when they were only halfway agreeable to being touched. His fur was surprisingly soft and well-groomed, no doubt a result of regular meals. With his company, Edanne's search for the lobelia and pennyroyal went more pleasantly than if she had been alone. Patch found a patch of catnip and began nibbling at it. "I used to do the same thing, when I was a cat," she said with a chuckle. "Very well, you might be right. I'll take some back with me."

Patch followed her back to the cottage, and for the first time since the day of the explosion, came through the door with her. Dala, on her way outside with a pail of dirty wash-water, immediately began to sneeze.

"Get that wretched creature away from me!" she cried, and flung the contents of the pail at the cat.

"No need for that," Edanne said angrily. The cat, drenched, disappeared down the path, a dark blur. "That was cruel. You've scared him off. He wasn't doing you any harm."

"A lot of harm," Dala said, blowing her nose. "It gets worse and worse. *Snit!*" As a quirky after-effect of Dala's latest transformation, she still sneezed like a cat. She blew her nose again. "Ferdon is definitely making me sneeze now. He's begun trying to chase mice. *Snit!*"

"Well, whatever, I've got what we need. In an hour, if we're lucky, Ferdon will be back to normal, you'll have your looks again, and you can go on your way."

"I assure you—*snit!*—you won't be any happier to be rid of me than I am of you. *Snit!*"

"Well, now what? You told me everything would be all right," Dala said.

"We're partway there." With one hand, Edanne spooned food into her mouth while with the other she turned pages in *General Magick For Ye Advanced Practitioner*. "The wen is gone from your temple and you aren't as ugly as you used to be."

"But now I have a great red mark all across my face and my skin is still blotchy and itches worse than ever! And Ferdon is unchanged. *Snit!*"

What could have gone wrong? She had prepared the

herbs and powders, and had donned Ferdon's magical robe. The garment was so large that it swallowed her, and she had had to roll the sleeves up and gird it high at the waist. Then, hoping that she would not trip over the hem and fall, she had taken Ferdon's wand and walked widdershins around the two of them while she recited the spell, verbatim, straight from the book. A most satisfactory bang and poof of smoke had resulted—but only partial success, and the addition of the red mark that looked as if somebody had thrown red wine in Dala's face. "Oh, I see. I didn't read far enough in the book. Lobelia sometimes has unwelcome side effects. Perhaps if I use helmetflower in the mixture. No—here it is! Hyssop. That's what we need."

"I certainly hope it grows around here. Or that you can buy some."

"It's rare. But I think I know where it can be found."

Edanne still had a couple of hours of daylight. She quickly retraced her steps to the woods and searched until she found a few sprigs of a plant that looked like the spidery drawing in the book. The brindle cat did not appear, but she hadn't really expected him to. Perhaps he would never come around again. Fond as she was becoming of him, it would be, she thought, a good enough exchange if she could be quit of Dala for the rest of her life.

"Very well, you managed to clear up the blemishes, but my skin still has the blotch on it," Dala said nastily. "And Ferdon is even worse than before. *Snit!*"

"I don't think Ferdon's condition was even affected by the spell." Edanne looked at the former magician worriedly. His physical appearance was definitely altering. His ears were more pointed than they had been and the pupils of his eyes were definitely becoming elongated. His hair was growing unnaturally fast. It now bushed out like a mane and she could feel whiskers not at all like his usually silky beard jutting out from his cheeks. He had, in fact, begun to look rather like a lion. His greatest pleasure now was in lying majestically by the fireside, and being waited on.

At least he was no longer trying to climb into her lap every time she sat down; now he appeared to be too dignified for such things though he still liked very much to be scratched behind the ears. And, lionlike though he was now, the only sound he could make, other than a clumsy purr, was "miaow."

Altogether, she thought, a wretched situation.

"I see no reason to give you another chance. You've had two tries, and no change!" Dala looked at herself in the mirror, frowning. "My features are nice enough, but that red blotch is a disgrace! Well—*snit!*—I'm leaving. Perhaps I can cover the mark with face paint. Allesando will surely know a mage who can finish what you've only started."

"No, you mustn't! Please, please, just one more try. And if it fails, then you may go. I'll even concoct some good face paint for you. I know how to do that. Free."

Dala peered again into the mirror and pecked at the stain on her cheek. "Hmmm," she said reluctantly. "Paint does cost coin and I haven't any. Very well, once more, but only once. My good nature will take only so much."

"Everything I have and everything I know will go into this last effort, I promise you."

In her heart, Edanne knew that she was overmatched, out of her depth. I should give up, she thought, and let that dreadful, ungrateful woman stay exactly the way she is, which is more than she deserves. I have grown to like being a human, but if I fail at restoring my beloved Ferdon, I know enough by now to turn him fully cat, and a proper one at that, not this bizarre thing he is becoming. Furthermore, I will turn myself into a cat once more and, together, we will go out into the world and fare as we may.

She sat down at the table where Ferdon had always sat to study and opened *General Magick For Ye Advanced Practitioner*. "There must be something missing, something that the books do not tell me. Dala, go into the workroom and bring me the red one with the brass hinges—*Spells For All Occasions*—if you please. Perhaps if I compare the two. . . ."

Something thumped against the windowpane. She turned to look. It was the brindle tom. "Patch!" she exclaimed. She got up quickly to find something to feed him while Dala was occupied. She glanced at Ferdon, but for the moment at least he didn't seem inclined to attack the smaller animal.

She went out onto the stoop and set the bowl down. The cat began eating gratefully and she stroked him. He looked up, opened his mouth silently, and went back to the food.

"I can't understand you at all now," she said with regret. "But perhaps when Ferdon is a cat and I am a cat, we can all be together—" She stopped, transfixed. Her whole mind seemed to light up at once. Of course! she thought. Why didn't I think of it before? It wasn't entirely my fault, after all, that things went wrong, and Patch is the missing element!

"Oh, how stupid I have been," she told the tom. "We had the answer between us all along but I was too worried—or too human—to understand."

Patch stood up, digging his claws into her skirt, miaowing silently.

"I think you know what must be done and this may even have been what you wanted all along, and why you were in the room that day. Is that what you've been trying to tell me all this time? Please understand, but I must ask you, do you agree to it?"

The cat rubbed against her. She stroked him; he vibrated, but even his purr had been muted. She picked him up and went back into the cottage.

"Dala," she said. "I have a surprise for you."

"No."

"You must."

"*Snit*! I won't! Not with that miserable cat around, or if I have to get very close to Ferdon. I don't like the way he looks or the way he acts."

Edanne had no patience left for any niceties. To get Ferdon to stay where she wanted him, she had had to rap him smartly across the head with his own staff, and now he lay stunned but conscious, his eyes a little crossed, inside the magic circle. She had no idea how long it would take him to recover. "If you don't cooperate," she said in a gritty tone, "I will turn you back into a cat forever—the ugliest, most unattractive cat in the world—and you know I can do it, too!"

"But—*snit*!—you don't understand!"

"I understand completely. And the sooner you do what you must, the sooner you'll be gone to the baron's son as you wanted." Edanne, holding the brindle tom in her arms, played her last card with all the persuasiveness she was capable of. "I have news of him. Allesando is still unwed."

Dala hesitated, obviously wavering before this new temptation in the face of her growing discomfort in the presence of both Ferdon and the tom. "Well," she said reluctantly, "if you'll be quick about it—"

"You've been the one delaying matters. Now, get into that circle, and take this cat!" Edanne hastily put the tom into Dala's arms.

"What? No! You didn't tell me I would have to *touch* the—*snit!*—beast! He'll bite me! He remembers I threw dirty water on him!"

"No, he won't. And here." Edanne pressed the earrings into the other woman's hand. "Hold these." She fairly leapt out of the circle and began dancing widdershins around Ferdon, the brindle tom, and Dala who looked too astonished even to sneeze. If she could complete the first circle rapidly enough, Dala would be unable to move.

The power built within her, tingling through the palms of her hands where she touched the wand, whirling her without conscious volition through the steps of the dance. She chanted the spell as if the words had risen from her heart rather than come from the pages of any book, and her voice grew until it filled the room. *"Trinea cum felis et oralis silencium! Paquesat in spiritus et magicum solanis! Pulque, pulque, magicum delibe, cureaum declare, veritum est!"*

The shocking explosion and gout of smoke brought her back to herself. She blinked and coughed. Dala, thrown clear of the magic circle, sprawled half conscious on the floor. The brindle tom leapt out of her arms, his earrings jangling. Ferdon sat up, looking very confused.

"Edanne?" he said. "Why am I in here and not outside the circle where I belong?"

"Oh, Ferdon, beloved, are you all right?" Edanne rushed into the circle and knelt beside him, checking him over hurriedly. His beard needed trimming and his hair looked a little unkempt, but otherwise he looked entirely normal, except for appearing a little dazed. "I'm so relieved! Do you remember anything of what happened after we finished the spell?"

He frowned, thinking. "Perhaps. I don't know. Everything is all mixed up inside my head. How did you come to be wearing my robe? And who's this?" The brindle tom had jumped into Ferdon's lap and now stood, paws on his chest, nuzzling him.

Edanne laughed for the first time in many days. "I think he's your new Companion. His name is Patch."

"What happened?" Dala said groggily. "Am I still ugly?" She sat up and groped for the mirror. "It's gone! The red stain is gone!" Despite her disheveled state, she now looked almost as beautiful as she had after Ferdon had done her first transformation. "It's incredible! And I'm not even sneezing!"

"It was a little something I threw into the spell," Edanne said, still checking Ferdon for signs of after-effects. "Please close the door on your way out."

"You don't need to tell me twice." Dala scrambled to her feet and rushed toward the door. "Allesando has waited long enough, and so have I."

"Edanne, I'm hungry," Ferdon said. "Ravenous. I'll make the porridge. Dala, you're human again! Uh-good-bye." The outside door slammed and the magician turned to look quizzically at his wife. "We did quite a nice job even if my robe did end up on you." He grimaced. "My back hurts, as if I had been sleeping on the floor. And why is my hair so long and my beard uncombed?" Ferdon got up stiffly, bringing Edanne with him. He blinked; his eyes cleared and he looked around as if aware for the first time of his surroundings. "I do believe you added something to my spell again, didn't you? That's getting to be a habit, and one you should endeavor to break. My, but my head is stuffy, as if I had a backlog of memory I can't quite get at yet. And now that I think about it, there may be quite a lot you have to tell me about what's been going on."

"Oh, gladly," Edanne said, limp with relief. She hugged Ferdon. "Gladly. In short, you've been, um, away for a while and I had to work hard to make Dala help bring you back. And now you even have a new Companion! I'm so happy everything turned out all right even if I did, well, mislead Dala just the tiniest bit, there at the end."

"What have you done now?"

"I told her Allesando was still unwed—which he is—but

I didn't tell her I had found out the baron had betrothed him to Count Ragis' daughter." She looked at him innocently. "I forgot."

"Oh, Edanne!"

The cat weaved in and out between the two of them, his purr like soft, rolling thunder. He opened his mouth once, then twice, in silence. Edanne looked down at him anxiously. "I do hope I got that part right—"

"Miaow," the cat said, his voice rusty but at last audible, and very definitely pleased. "Miaow!"

NOBLE WARRIOR
MEETS WITH A GHOST

by Andre Norton

Such a noise! Even ten temples' worth of rattle swinging, horn blowing priests at the heights of celebration could not drown out—this! And the smells! Thragun Neklop lifted a fastidious lip enough to show a very sharp fang. This was like the Ninth Hell itself and no proper place for the well conducted, feline or even human. He felt cross-eyed from watching through the narrow slit in his bamboo riding case, yet he dared not let down his guard.

The roar of a dragon sweeping on its helpless prey made him almost cower, but he was Noble Warrior, Princess' own guard. Dragon or no dragon, he faced danger directly and with both blue eyes wide open. The dragon crawled along one side of this infernal place and its side scales opened so that those it had previously devoured were issuing forth apparently unharmed. Would the wonders of this barbarian territory never cease?

Now another crowd was sweeping into those dragon scale doors. And Emmy, his own Princess Emmy, was hurrying along toward this unknown fate. Noble Warrior gave tongue in no uncertain yowl. He saw Emmy's head turn in his direction, but then her father swung her up and into the dragon and—

Noble Warrior's traveling cage swung aloft. He had been picked up. And the scent of this newcomer was unpleasantly familiar though he could not see more than a looming shadow. Emmy—he must be transported to join Emmy. Only that did not happen. The carrying cage rocked as its bearer picked up speed. Not toward the dragon but away from it. They burst out of the noise and confusion of the station into the open. But not the open Noble Warrior knew. There was the smell of horses, that was familiar, but there were other smells, nearly as bad as some in the poor villages at home. And the noise continued.

Noble Warrior threw himself against the front of the cage. He tried to slip one brown paw into the crack about the door, to free himself. But he did not have a chance. The cage was whirled up into the air and came down with a slam which brought another yowl out of him. The cage rocked with the floor under it and Noble Warrior was sure he had been loaded into one of those wagons such as Emmy often traveled in, sometimes taking Noble Warrior, who knew his place and sat statue still by her side while she pointed out various points of interest.

There was still that familiar scent. He could only think of the stable yard at home as the carrier rocked from a kick. Noble Warrior crouched belly to the floor to consider his present plight. He did not believe in the least that Emmy had abandoned him to this fate—whatever it might be. But Emmy was fast in the dragon and he was left to do battle on his own.

Alerting all his senses he tested as well as he could what might lie beyond the walls of the carrier. He could smell horse very strong. And there was also the smell of un-washed human—a human who drank the fire spirit—that groom the Captain had ordered off his land! There were other smells also. And all the while, the noise ebbed, roared, and ebbed.

The wagon came to a halt and there was a beam of light. Once more, Noble Warrior's carrier was swung out into the open and he caught a fleeting glimpse of a soot-stained brick wall and the iron pickets of a fence. Then he was again in drab shadow as the carrier thumped to the floor.

" 'Ere y'be, guvener. Right one an' all."

"So."

Noble Warrior's head swung around. He could not see through the weaving of the bamboo, but the fur along his back ridged and his ears flattened to his skull. But he made no sound—no guardian warned before attack, that was not the way.

Only there was evil here—just as he had sensed it at other times and in other places. Khon? Demon dweller in the shadows? Or more?

He had no time to speculate. Once more his carrier was swept up and off, to be placed on a flat surface again. Now it was surrounded by smells which made him sneeze and shake his head. There came a fumbling with the catch and the doorway to his temporary prison swung open. Noble Warrior made no effort to leave his conveyance. Make sure, instinct warned. Who knew who or what awaited him.

"Here, puss—puss—"

A large hand appeared in his range of sight. The skin was discolored in places almost as if it had been burnt, and on the forefinger was a large ring, the setting of which was the red of a half awakened coal.

Noble Warrior hissed a warning as that ill-omened hand approached. He readied his own paw for a good raking slash.

The hand remained where it was for a long moment and then a second joined it. In the hand was a round ball. There was a sudden squeeze and from the ball issued a puff which caught Noble Warrior straight in the face. He coughed, uttered the beginning of a howl, and subsided to the cushion beneath him.

The hand with the ring reached in to catch him by the scruff of the neck and dragged him out to dangle helplessly in the air while the owner of the hand surveyed his captive. Helpless Noble Warrior was—he could not even summon a growl.

"Soooooo—" The large head opposite him nodded. "Indeed—even as Jasper said—"

The hand loosened its grip and Noble Warrior fell, landing on a table top not far from his carrier. He tried to command his body, to leap for that refuge. But he was as helpless as if he were entangled in a bird hunter's net.

"We shall be friends—"

Noble Warrior managed the weak beginning of a snarl. What he saw was dark shadowed. It was even as the Great Old Ones of his own kind said, evil doers were always dark shadowed. This one resembled nothing so much as one of the carven Khons set up in warning.

His shoulders were hunched and his head, which looked too large for his body, might not sprout the fangs of a Khon to be sure, but his teeth were yellow and he showed a nasty snaggle of them as he grinned. Pallid, grayish skin was half concealed about a retreating chin by a straggle of fuzzy beard. But the spreading dome of his head was bare save for more fuzz over large ears which showed distinct points. He wore a loose coat or jacket which might have once been white but was now begrimed and stained into a twilight gray. His eyes had retreated into dark caverns under an untidy thatching of brow, but they held a bright glint which Noble Warrior caught. Maybe not a Khon—but certainly one who had willingly chosen the Dark Path.

"We shall be friends—you shall see—" The great head nodded. "Until we are, there shall be precautions taken."

Again the hand swooped and the helpless cat dangled in the air as the man shuffled across the dark room and pushed his captive into a cage, snapping the door behind him with a click, and turning his back as if he had fairly settled the matter.

Noble Warrior lay where he had fallen. There was a stench in this cage, and with it came the dregs of far off fear and pain. He snarled and tried to move. Whatever spell the Khon master had put upon him seemed to be lessening. Now he pulled himself up and sat as one of the Old Blood should.

The light of the room was dim. There were several windows, but they were barred and set very high on the wall, so covered with dust and the webs of long dead spiders that they might have been securely curtained. Over the table where his carrier still stood, there hung a lamp and there were candles posted here and there—a whole line of them on an old desk at one side where there was a pile of age-eaten books. His captor had settled down in a sway-backed chair next to that desk and had one of the books open now, impatiently switching candlesticks around for a better reading light.

There were a number of cabinets lined up under the windows at one wall, the doors of several hung open to show rows of bottles and jars of strange things Noble Warrior could not guess the use for. At the darker end of the room was a single door. That was flanked by two tables which bore—cages! Cages such as the one in which he found himself.

There were other captives—his cat sight was not defeated by the gloom. In one were rats—but such rats—their fur was white or else unwholesomely mottled in color and they scuttled about aimlessly. In the next—

Noble Warrior stiffened. There was no mistaking the scent, overpowered as it might be by the smells of this place, but there was a cat. Not one of his own regal breed, of course, but still another cat. Though its fur was matted and it seemed so lost in despair that it made no effort to cleanse itself, he could see now that it was a female, and had fur unusually long and black.

She was half curled against the bars of her prison, her eyes closed, her position crying out hopelessness and fear.

There came a buzzing sound and the man by the desk shook his head impatiently. "Time—never any time. Devil take Henry—" Leaving his book open, he got rustily to his feet and shuffled to the far door.

As he approached the cages flanking the door, the other cat's head came up a little. Noble Warrior saw its mouth open but without sound. The man brushed by it, paying no attention, while the rats scrambled in a wild dance around their prison.

When the door closed behind their jailor, Noble Warrior raised his voice:

"I am Thragun Neklop of the Royal Guard. Who are you and where is this place? What does this evil one want of us?"

The black cat raised its head and opened golden eyes.

"This is a place of pain, and hunger, and we are forgotten. I was—" the black cat shook its head slowly, "I cannot remember. What I am—what you will be—is one to suffer, suffer as he wills it. And will it he will!"

"I do not understand."

"Oh, you will, my fine would-be fighter, you will—as have the others before you. And probably not to any productive purpose."

Shadow detached itself from shadow, leapt to the same table as supported Noble Warrior's cage, to become substance. Another cat—the largest he had ever seen—this one also black, its ears ragged from ancient battles, its eyes bearing strange red sparks within their greenness.

The newcomer took a couple of strutting steps and then settled down, sitting upright, its tail end wrapped composedly over its forepaws. It looked Noble Warrior over, and the open contempt in that survey brought a snarl to the prisoner's lips, a flattening of ears in warning.

"You are a strange one," the black cat observed. "Yes, I can see why old Marcus was ready to pay a full guinea for you. Supposed to come from foreign parts if I heard their talk right. Maybe this time he will be able to do it—I've heard tell that in foreign parts they have other learning."

"Do what?" demanded Noble Warrior.

"Make a familiar out of you. Old Marcus, he's cracked in the noggin as Henry says. This place," with a slight sweep of his head, the cat indicated what lay about them, "is an old hidy-hole where those before Marcus thought to speak with the Devil and gather black power. Some of them—" the black cat paused, "some of them in the past had the Old Learning—but always on the dark side. There was Sir Justin Clayman—yes, and that Parson turned wizard—Master Loomis. They did things such as would make old Marcus' eyes pop right out of his skull. He tries, but he's far from learning even the first of the lessons. That's why he's trying other ways now, why he wants a familiar. He heard tell of the Princess first—" The cat inclined his head toward the captive on the other side of the room.

"She's a foreigner, too—comes 'cross seas from the Far East. But she's no magic maker and he can't turn her into one. So when he heard tell of another cat as seemed to bring luck to people—well, he made up his mind to gather you in and see if he would fare any better with his plans."

"What about you?" Noble Warrior had followed this garbled account as best he could, translating it into what he knew of old. One who would work with Khons needed an animal as some kind of a helper. Yes, he had heard of the priests of Kali and the serpents they were said to send to gather the souls of those who opposed them.

"Now wouldn't he just like that." The black cat opened his mouth in an unmistakable yawn. "Oh, I could be what he wants right enough. But I've served my time as the saying goes. Sir Justin, he was a right pleasant one to work with. Parson Loomis now, I'll not say the same for that one. No, old Marcus can't get his bonds on me—seeing as how I'm living in another time these days."

Noble Warrior's eyes narrowed. There had been so many

strange, dark, and unpleasant emanations in this place that only now he realized that other-space chill.

"You are dead," he said harshly as the fur along his spine quivered.

The black cat's mouth stretched now in a grin. "Just figured it out, have you, new boy? Only you may call it dead—I find my present state most satisfactory. You'd better be worrying about your own. The Princess there," he nodded again to the other prisoner, "she hasn't long to go now. He's decided she's not worth the trouble of feeding her."

Noble Warrior looked at that other captive. She had raised her head a fraction and was eyeing the stranger cat almost pleadingly.

"This herder of Khons is not going to get me to serve him!" Noble Warrior emphasized that with a deep throated growl.

"Keep on believing it, youngster. You'll change your mind quick enough. Not that Marcus can do it, you understand—make you his slave. But it'll be a rare fight and Simpson here will have plenty to watch while it's in the doing."

Noble Warrior edged closer to the door of the cage. He had neat, slender paws and he knew how to use them. The opening of cupboards and doors was no mystery—though the latch on the carrier had been out of his reach. Now he could wriggle past one bar and lay a paw to the fastening here, but in spite of his prying it would not give.

The ghost cat watched him. "Good try," he commented. "Only it is not going to work. You will have to think of some other way—and there isn't any."

Noble Warrior settled back once more. He was thinking again over all that had happened since he had arrived in this dire place.

"That thing—the one the Khon Master used—the one which puffed at me—" He was thinking aloud more than addressing Simpson.

"Got it on the first try, haven't you? Yes, a puff of that and you're as limp as a dead rat. He'll use it, too."

In all his life Thragun Neklop had never asked for help, but he realized that perhaps such a surrender of Warrior pride might serve him best now.

"If the Khon Master did not have that—"

For a long moment Simpson stared back. His eyes changed; deep in their centers that spark of red grew and began to glow.

"You want help, is that it?"

Noble Warrior met those flaming eyes squarely. This visitor from the shades had not helped that other cat prisoner. Would he be moved any quicker to give aid to him?

"She is no fighter." Somehow Noble Warrior was not surprised that this other read his thought. "She could not have defended herself as such a fine young fellow as you might do. So, Marcus has done little save twitter over books he cannot understand and brew stinks enough to take one's breath away."

"Not like those others," Noble Warrior inserted slyly, "the ones who knew your value."

Simpson nodded. "True, very true. I think—" He arose and stretched luxuriously, "that it is time old Marcus be shown his proper place in one world or another."

He was gone although Thragun Neklop, blinking twice, did not see him leap away. He extended his claws and rasped them across the splintered flooring of the cage.

Properly sharp, yes. If he could only get a chance to use them. Then he looked once more to the Princess. She was huddled in upon herself like a round black mat. If he got out—if he could fight free—what of her?

Then the door beside her cage scraped open and Marcus shuffled back in, a lamp in one hand and a small basket in the other. He set both on the table and, muttering to himself in a voice too low for Noble Warrior to hear, set about assembling a number of other things to join the light and basket he had brought with him.

Once more Noble Warrior blinked. Simpson was in plain sight, sitting on the edge of that table now watching Marcus' actions, disdain to be read in every tilt of whisker. It was plain to Noble Warrior that the old man was completely unaware of the big feline almost within touching distance of the bowls and boxes and small bottles Marcus brought from other shelves and set ready to hand.

At length, having combined a pinch of that, a drop of this from one container or another, the man nodded almost briskly and swept all the clutter away from the major portion of the table top. He then proceeded to draw on the cleared space with thick crayon markings and curlicues in red. In the end he surveyed critically a star between the points of which were scrawled convoluted shapings which made Noble Warrior spit in rage. This was truly demon dealing.

Having surveyed his handiwork with apparent approval, Marcus reached for something Noble Warrior had seen before—that noxious puffer. But Simpson's paw touched that strange weapon first, sending it rolling from the table.

With an exclamation the old man went down on his knees to retrieve what Simpson had rolled under the table. Noble Warrior could not really understand why this would-be demon commander was not aware of the ghost cat.

Beyond Marcus' groping fingers Simpson made a pounce and brought both forefeet down on the rounded end of the weapon. Noble Warrior could not see any puff of dust at this distance, but Simpson withdrew instantly as Marcus' hand closed upon the bulb. With a grunt of satisfaction he got creakingly to his feet, and weapon in hand, came toward Noble Warrior's prison. Steel muscles moved under the shields of fine fur. The training of kittenhood days was very much a part of him now. One human hand fumbled at the latching of the cage and the other advanced with the puffer.

Noble Warrior saw the fingers squeeze on it, but this time there was no dust to clog his nostrils and turn him into a limp fur string. As the cage door swung wide enough, with a battle cry, he leapt straight at that great round head, claws raking deep and true.

Marcus screeched in turn and stumbled back, striving to tear the cat's body from him. There was a rake across his eyes and then Noble Warrior dropped to the floor. The man blundered blindly along the table, sweeping off the contents to shatter on the floor.

Noble Warrior was across the room in two bounds and had gained the table where the other cage was standing. The latch, which had been placed outside the reach of the captive, was easy enough to get at now. He caught it in his teeth, gave a twist, and the door opened.

"Out!" he yowled at the Princess.

She squeezed by him, moving so slowly he wanted to hurry her along with a nip on the quarters.

"Neatly done," Simpson stood on the floor below. "Come along now. You've given old dog face something to think about—marked him good, you did. But we'd better be out of here before he gets some of those scattered wits back into his head."

With Simpson in the lead, the Princess pattering along behind, and Noble Warrior playing rear guard, they threaded through a hall upstairs and were shown a broken window in a nasty smelling, cupboardlike hole.

For the first time Noble Warrior had to think of what would come next. There was no Emmy to hand—she had been swallowed by the dragon—and her father, the Captain, was also already far away. He was alone—no, the Princess was with him, and in a strange country he did not understand at all.

"Simpson—" he began uncertainly.

"You're on your own now, fighter. Now the Princess—" In this strange light of day they stood in a mean little strip of sour, bare earth. "There's a place for her. There's a little girl down the street and across the square who will welcome her. But that's no place for you. I don't know what they teach kittens in those foreign parts of yours, beside how to be good fighters. But you should have that which will take you home even if you have to make it on your four feet. Look inside yourself, youngster, and find it."

Thragun Neklop looked. And he found. He knew the way—he need only go in that direction and keep on until he got there. Why, that was no problem at all.

"Simpson?"

The cat ghost was fast fading only to a shadow of a shadow.

"Get going, youngster. You've given me a good day. Old Marcus won't be trying to make himself a wizard—at least not for some time—not insulting the shades of Sir Justin and Parson Loomis with his messes. Seems like he met with his match and that one was one of us—very fitting. Good journey to you, my young friend, may the mice be many and the road a straight one. Now I'm to see this young lady to her proper place in life. As a good familiar ought."

The Princess hesitated and then wobbled to Noble Warrior and touched noses, before wavering along behind a fast disappearing shred of darkness. Thragun Neklop drew a deep breath and started to seek his own way.

CONNECTICAT

by Raul Reyes and
Elisabeth Waters

It had been a difficult death. The illness contracted in the humid lowlands had been bad enough. But the young man's dissolute life had left its mark on his character as well, and as he died the Lama found it hard to keep the parts of his being together. Each one threatened to leave separately as the corresponding sense died in the body. It took all of the Lama's patient counsel to keep the young man's consciousness together.

Finally the consciousness was free of the body, but the Lama remained, coaching the young man's spirit as it traveled through that dark realm on the other side of death. It was too much to hope that he might be reborn as a healthy son of a wealthy family, or even as a younger son dedicated by his family to a wealthy lamasery, with sufficient endowment to pursue a life of contemplation. But at least he might be kept from the life of a poor beggar, a criminal, or, worse yet, an animal.

There were demons on the path. The Lama explained these were illusions. So also were the clear streams and soft, grassy resting places by the path. The young man's spirit must pass all of these on his path to rebirth.

More serious were the distractions of the flesh. The young man had been all too prone to them in life, and the plump young maidens beckoning to him from cushioned grottos, pots of beer and wine by their sides, were almost too much for his shade. The Lama explained that they were traps for the unwary soul and the grottos were undesirable wombs. So far, the disembodied spirit had listened to his teaching and passed those illusions.

The path to rebirth was difficult and the spirit was tiring

rapidly. The Lama intoned a chant to give him strength. It flowed to the young man's spirit and revived his energy. The Lama allowed himself a moment of rest; the chant had taken some of his strength. Too late he realized his mistake.

The young man's soul, revitalized by the chant, became aware of a bower under some rhododendrons. A saucy young girl with sleek dark hair and sly cat eyes beckoned to him from a pile of cushioned rugs. A jar of sweet wine waited next to her. The Lama shouted a warning, but it was too late. The young man sank to her side and was lost.

Christina sat in her car at the New Canaan train station, waiting for the train from New York and her mother's dinner guest. In the passenger seat Tashi, her Burmese tom cat, protested vociferously the delay in their return home and his release from his carrier. Christina was just as disgusted with the situation, but not quite as vocal.

"It isn't my fault, Tashi," she protested. "I made the appointment with the vet three months ago, and I certainly had no way of knowing that mother would pick tonight to invite some Tibetan Lama she met in New York out here for dinner—or that his arrival would be timed so that we'd have to come here straight from the vet."

Tashi was definitely unimpressed by this argument. His suggestion, however, was not helpful.

"I can't tell my mother where to go; after all, my parents do live next door to us." She twisted to meet the cat's eyes. He stared back. "And while I'm sure that respect for one's parents is a totally foreign concept to you, it does mean something to me—even if my respect doesn't extend to marrying and providing them with grandchildren right now." She sighed. "I wish I weren't an only child; if I had brothers or sisters, *they* could provide grandchildren. I'm perfectly happy living with you, and I don't need some man cluttering up my house and my life!"

Both of them suddenly cocked their heads to listen to the sound of the warning bells at the railroad crossing two blocks before the station. "Oh, good," Christina said. "At least the train's on time. I'll be back in a couple of minutes—at this time of day there won't be many people." The next train, she knew, would be a multicar express straight from Grand Central Station, instead of the two-car "turkey killer" that connected with the main line at Stamford during non-commute hours. If she were meeting that train, she'd be lucky to get her car into the parking lot.

Finding her mother's guest was easy, even though he was dressed in a conventional suit rather than whatever type of robe a Lama traditionally wore. Only five people got off the train, three of them were women, and the other man was black. Besides, he was the only one with a shaved head.

Christina was opening her mouth to greet the man when he forestalled her.

"You must be Miss Lang," he said, smiling and extending his hand. "Your mother said you'd be meeting me."

"Yes, I am," Christina replied, shaking hands with him. His handshake was warm and firm, and felt oddly as if some sort of electrical current ran through his body. "I hope you don't mind cats," she said nervously. "Tashi and I are on the way home from the vet. He's in a carrier, so he won't shed on your clothes, but he's not a happy cat at the moment."

"Tashi?" the Lama raised his eyebrows. "That's an unusual name for a cat. Why was he named that?"

Christina shrugged, "I don't know. The breeder called him something different, but when I bought him—well, it just seemed like that should be his name. Why? Does it mean something in Tibetan?"

"There is a holy man called the Tashi Lama."

"Like the Dalai Lama?"

"More or less. The Tashi Lama outranks the Dalai Lama spiritually, but the Dalai Lama outranks him politically."

"Oh." Christina opened the passenger door of the car and reached for the carrier. "I'll put him in the back seat, so he'll be out of your way." She knew her mother would have a fit if she made a guest ride with the cat in his lap.

"That is not necessary," he replied. Before Christina realized his intent he had opened the carrier and cradled Tashi in one arm while he tossed the empty carrier in the back seat and slipped into the car. Christina closed the door quickly before Tashi decided to get out and explore downtown New Canaan, and went to get into the driver's seat.

She half-expected Tashi to have made a good start on the job of clawing the Lama to ribbons, but to her amaze-

ment the two of them sat there staring into each others'
eyes as if they were communicating.

She fastened her seat belt, looked to be sure that her
passenger had fastened his, started the engine, and pulled
out of the parking lot. She drove in silence for several minutes before saying, "We'll stop at my house to drop off
Tashi, if that's all right with you. My parents' house is next
door, but if we go to my house first, we can get the cat
hair off your suit."

"You share your life with a cat and you worry about a
little cat hair?" the Lama asked in amusement.

"Not usually," Christina replied. "Most of my sweaters
match Tashi's fur, so I usually pass a casual inspection."
She sighed. "Unfortunately, at least as far as my appearance is concerned, my mother's inspections are far from
casual." She smiled reassuringly at him. "But you're probably safe enough: you're a guest."

He chuckled briefly, continuing to stroke Tashi, who sat
quietly in his arms. "How old is Tashi?" he inquired.

"Three years old next month," Christina replied.

The Lama nodded slowly, apparently pleased with her
answer for some unknown reason of his own. Christina
gave a mental shrug and concentrated her attention on the
sharp curves of the road.

To Christina's horror, her spinster status became a topic
of discussion at the dinner table. In addition to Christina,
her parents and the Lama, there were two other couples
who were friends of the Langs. Since they came to Mrs.
Lang's parties frequently, Christina thought they must
surely be tired of hearing her mother bemoan her daughter's unwed state. But no one Mrs. Lang invited to her
house would ever be rude enough to say so. Either that,
or after a few of the drinks her father served before dinner
and the wine with dinner, they didn't notice that they had
heard this conversation many times before.

Mrs. Lang began with semi-polite inquiries into the family of her guest, who turned out to be the type of Lama
forbidden to marry and thus had family consisting of his
parents (father deceased), his brother (another celibate
Lama), and his sister (married, four children).

"At least your mother has the consolation of grandchildren," she murmured. "Her father and I do so hope that Christina will find a nice young man and settle down soon." She looked at her daughter and sighed. "She could be such a pretty girl if she'd just make a bit of an effort."

"You mean spend an hour each morning on makeup, an afternoon a week at the hairdresser's, and one day each month buying new clothes," Christina said lightly. "I know that I could look prettier than I do, but I have no reason to put in that kind of time and energy. My clothes are decent and appropriate, and since I spend most of my time in a library with my nose in a book, makeup would be a complete waste of time. Besides, it makes my skin break out."

"But you'll never get a husband that way!" her mother protested. She turned to the Lama. "Do you have this problem in your country?"

He shook his head. "Not in the manner that you do. My sister married the man my parents chose for her; there a girl is expected to obey her parents."

Christina decided to change the subject before he could suggest that her parents choose a husband for her. "What do you think of my mother's garden?" she asked, indicating the variety of plants surrounding the terrace where they were eating. "Do you have any of the same plants in Tibet?"

"We have rhododendrons," he replied. "I was admiring them earlier, Mrs. Lang; they are truly beautiful."

Mrs. Lang smiled complacently. "Yes, they do quite nicely here—although I did have a bit of trouble when Christina first got that cat of hers."

"Really?" the Lama sounded fascinated.

"It was dreadful," Mrs. Lang assured him. "Every time he got out—which fortunately wasn't too often; Christina is a conscientious girl and is generally meticulous about keeping him indoors—he would come over here and burrow in under the rhododendrons. It wasn't good for them at all."

"It's Tashi's favorite flower," Christina explained. "Finally we got a bush for my yard and Father extended the fence around my patio to enclose it, so now Tashi has his very own rhododendron and doesn't bother Mother's."

"A sensible solution," the Lama remarked, and the subject of conversation changed to landscaping.

Alone in his hotel room later that night, the Lama prepared for bed, turned out the lights, sat comfortably on the floor in lotus position, and cast his mind toward his brother's monastery in Tibet. The contact came quickly.

"Have you found him yet, brother?" the Tashi Lama inquired.

"Yes, elder brother, I have found our erring nephew. It was as you said: once I arrived in New York I was led to him."

"I sensed that he was there. Is he one of their 'street people'? Surely he would be rather young for that, unless he was born to—tell me he was not reborn in the womb of a drug addict."

"No, it is not that bad. He is in excellent physical condition. But still, this may prove more difficult than we had anticipated."

"Brother, all I asked was that you find him and instruct him, so that he may improve his way of life, and, if possible, that you bring him home. What is the difficulty?"

"Perhaps I should tell you how I found him. As we arranged, I gave a talk at the Open Center, which was reasonably well attended. One of the ladies in the audience, a Mrs. Lang, came up to me afterward and invited me to her home in Connecticut for dinner the following night. I felt that I should accept her invitation, and so I did, taking the train to New Canaan the next afternoon. Mrs. Lang's daughter Christina picked me up at the station. She was on her way home from the vet with her cat: a Burmese male called Tashi."

Several seconds of silence preceded the Tashi Lama's reply. "You are quite sure that it is not merely a coincidence of names?"

"I held him, and I looked into his eyes. He will be three years old next month, and he has such a passion for rhododendrons that they have provided him his very own plant, so that he will leave Mrs. Lang's alone. I have no doubt that he is our nephew."

"A cat." The Tashi Lama sighed. "Well, that does make the job harder, but it can still be done. Will the girl give him to you? Then you could bring him home, and we could do the transformation here."

"I have not asked her to give me her cat, nor do I feel it would be right so to do. I believe that he owes a debt, either to her or to her parents."

"What sort of debt?"

"A debt of family. Christina is twenty-five, an only child, unmarried, and so bound to Tashi that she refuses to look elsewhere for companionship or love."

"And, like our sister, I suppose her parents want grandchildren."

"They do; they devoted half of the dinner hour to the subject. As for our sister, I imagine she has quite a few grandchildren by now. I gather that Tashi does quite well in stud fees."

"Stud fees?" The Tashi Lama considered the implications of that statement and made his decision. "I refuse to tell our sister that she has grandchildren who are cats."

"Nor our mother. I do not think the knowledge would gladden either of their hearts."

"Would this Christina marry him and bear children if he were to be transformed? And would she make him a proper wife?"

"I believe that she would—and I fear she would be a better wife than he a husband. I intend to see her tomorrow, and I shall sound her out on the subject."

"Keep me informed of your progress. Advise me when you are ready to do the transformation. Rest well, younger brother."

"May your path be bright this day, elder brother."

The Lama opened his eyes, rose smoothly from the floor, and went to bed.

He awoke around nine the next morning, ate breakfast, and then made his way to the New York Public Library. It was not difficult to find Christina. She was in the genealogy section, going through the index of death records for the various boroughs of New York City. He sat down opposite her at the long table, his talent for stillness rendering him invisible to her, the other patrons, and the library staff. He spent several hours observing her while she did her research.

He had been correct to suspect that she had passion and determination; here, in the work she did, it was visible. To his eyes she glowed slightly every time she found something she had been searching for, another link in the chain she was tracing. She worked continuously for hours, apparently oblivious to such bodily concerns as lunch. When she finally gathered her notes together and returned the books she had been using, it was late afternoon.

He followed her as she left the library, coming up to her just as she walked out the front door. "Good afternoon, Miss Lang."

Christina started. "Oh, good afternoon, Gomchen." She had been told yesterday that 'Gomchen' was the proper form of address, although it was a title, not a name. Apparently Tibetans did not use names socially. "I didn't see you; were you in the library?"

"Yes. I saw you there. Did you have a profitable day?"

"Very much so. I've found five new people on this branch of the family." She laughed. "Some days I can't seem to find anything and I'd swear that some of my ancestors were the products of spontaneous generation."

He chuckled at the joke, then said, "It seems strange to me that you spend so much effort tracing a lineage that ends with you. Do you not wish to marry and have children to extend the line forward?"

Christina looked sad. "Yes, actually I do. I like children, and I wish I had some of my own. But for that, you need a husband—and, as the saying goes, 'the more I see of men, the more I like my cat.' It's too bad I can't marry him."

"Actually, that can be arranged."

Christina stared at him. "I was joking."

"Your marriage would make your parents very happy," he said persuasively.

"They certainly talked about it enough at dinner last night, didn't they? But I don't think they're so desperate that they would welcome a cat as a son-in-law."

"But if Tashi were human . . ."

"Tashi is not human."

"He can be."

She looked at him out of the corner of her eyes. "You're not used to the heat here—or maybe the pollution is getting to you."

"The heat does not bother me," he said calmly, "but a drink would be pleasant. My hotel puts on an excellent tea this time of day. Please do me the honor of joining me."

Christina considered running for Grand Central, but it was much too hot. Besides what could happen to her in a hotel dining room?

She was never sure afterward how he had managed it, but by the time Namtso Gomchen escorted her to the station, several hours later, she had agreed to marry her cat, as soon as he could be transformed to human. "After all," she pointed out, "we will need blood tests for the marriage license, and the clerk at the Town Hall is bound to notice if one of them comes from a vet."

Namtso Gomchen took the train to New Canaan Saturday morning to perform the transformation. As before, Christina drove him home from the station. He exited from the car in one fluid movement, his eyes scanning the woods behind her house with delight. It was so lush and verdant, so unlike his homeland. His briefcase, containing his monk's robe and a few other items he had not described to Christina, was in his right fist. He closed the car door behind him and waited for her to lead him in.

Tashi came out to meet them, or rather her. For some reason he affected to ignore Namtso Gomchen. The learned Lama returned the compliment.

"Is there somewhere I can change?" he asked. He had learned that Westerners had unusual ideas about clothing. It was considered appropriate for a young lady to appear in public in less cloth than it took to make a scarf if she was bathing at the beach, but if he disrobed within her home it was a serious breach of etiquette unless he did so in a room set aside for that purpose. She tilted her head toward a door.

"The bathroom is over there," she replied. He nodded his thanks and entered it. In a few moments he reappeared, barefoot, clad in a brilliant saffron robe, with a rosary-necklace around his neck. The "beads" were made of bone disks. Christina recalled what little she had heard of Tibet and decided against asking what the bone had come from.

"Will you brew me some tea?" he asked, handing her a

small package of the black Chinese tea he preferred. "I will need it for the ceremony." She nodded and went into the kitchen. Strictly speaking, it was not part of the ritual, but he needed some fortification prior to the ceremony. While she was busy, he scooped Tashi up in one motion that caught the feline by surprise and cradled it in the crook of his arm.

"Well, my unrepentant nephew," he whispered in Tibetan. "I hope you have enjoyed your life of cream and 'Meow Mix.'" The brand name came out oddly in the stream of Tibetan. "But now you must return to your proper life, and your proper duties. It should not be too onerous. She is attractive, has a good home, and her family is wealthy. Your main duties will be on the pillows, to provide her family with heirs. 'Right up your alley.'" It sounded odd in Tibetan.

The cheerful whistle of the teapot called him to the kitchen and he took Tashi in with him, his briefcase in his other hand. Christina smiled at him in greeting. He smiled back, making sure the door had swung shut before releasing Tashi. "Thank you," he said. "Tea is good in the morning. Would you like some of this?" he asked.

She smiled and shook her head. "I'll stick to Earl Gray," she replied.

He shrugged and added salt to his cup, then took a small jar out of his briefcase. Salt was readily available, but yaks, and yak butter, were scarce in New York and Connecticut. Christina kept her eyes on her own cup, and pretended not to notice that he was stirring butter into his tea.

"What do you need me to do for the ritual?" she asked.

"Just leave the room and wait outside. I must concentrate so that my brother may come here."

"The Tashi Lama will come here?" she asked.

He nodded.

Christina tried to think of an intelligent reply to this. Unable to come up with one, she took another sip of her tea, then stared down into the cup. When she looked up, Namtso Gomchen was setting up a pair of beaten brass lamps, filled with yak butter, on the counter top.

"We must move the table and chairs out of the room," he said. She set about helping him, glad of something to do. In moments the kitchen was stripped of all movable furniture, leaving a fair expanse of ceramic tile floor. He set the lamps on the tiles and settled down before them, placing a strangely docile Tashi between them. "Thank you," he said. "That will be all." It was a dismissal.

Outside, she sat in a chair and twisted her cup between her hands, staring down into it, as if she could divine the future in the swirling liquid. The scent of the butter lamps, mixed with incense, wafted under the door, along with the sound of clapping and low, sonorous chanting. Twice there were sharp explosive words that made her hair stand on end. Suddenly she remembered something.

"The smoke detector!" she gasped. She set the tea aside and raced into the kitchen. It had not yet gotten high enough to set off the alarm, but the lamps cast a lurid glow over a smoky, scented cloud.

Christina reached for the switch which would disable the smoke detector, but the sight of Namtso Gomchen stopped her in mid-motion. He was stiff in the lotus position, pale, and hardly breathing. Tashi sat immobile before him, staring up at his face. Slowly, a sigh escaped the Lama's lips, longer than any sigh had a right to be, and suddenly the Lama began to straighten up.

With a shock Christina realized he was growing. In moments he sat a full two inches taller, his shoulders were wider, and his hands were no longer the soft hands of a monk, but long and strong. Namtso Gomchen was no longer in her kitchen. In his place was a tall, lean, strongly built man, his skin tight over his skull, his face long and hard-featured, with eyes as black and hard as obsidian.

So this is what he meant when he said that the Tashi Lama would come here, Christina thought. Stunned, she sank slowly to the floor, her breath coming back in painful gulps.

The Lama did not seem to notice her presence. He continued to chant, only this time his voice was wild and haunted, and the language no longer sounded Tibetan. She recalled stories Namtso Gomchen had told at the dinner party. Stories of the Bon, the original people of Tibet, whose blood ran in the Khampa, the warrior/brigands of later Tibet, and of their religion, also called Bon. Tales of black magic and sorcery, not eradicated by Buddhism, but incorporated into the Tibetan version. She sat very still, not daring to move or speak.

Suddenly the Lama clapped his hands, the sound a thunderbolt in her head, and kept his hands together for a long time. Slowly he spread them apart, and fire grew between them, elongated, and reached out to Tashi, bathing him in flames.

Christina gasped and pressed a fist to her mouth. Tashi writhed in agony, and began to grow, changing in outline and shedding hair. A distant part of her mind noted that he shed hair constantly anyway. A long moan of pain escaped from between his lips as he became more manlike, and he fell on his side, his face, a human face, contorted with the pain of his transformation.

Another handclap to split her head with the sound of it, and the fire vanished. The Lama sagged forward in exhaustion, shrinking back into the form and appearance of Namtso Gomchen. Christina found herself breathing again, propped against the wall, and became aware of two distinct sounds: the smoke alarm, and the telephone.

She dragged herself to her feet, hit the switch to silence the smoke alarm, then picked up the phone. "Hello?" she said. "Yes, Daddy, that was my smoke alarm. No, everything's okay, you don't have to come over.... No, I'm fine, really. I was just cleaning the oven and it had a bit more grease than I realized. It's under control.... No, I haven't forgotten about dinner; I'll be over at six-thirty tonight. Good-bye, Daddy."

She turned to the Lama. "You won't need the oven for anything for the next few hours, will you?"

He looked surprised at the odd question. "No. Why?"

"Good." Christina set the oven dials to self-clean, engaged the locking mechanism, and started the cycle. "Daddy isn't dashing over here right now, but I bet he'll drop in some time this afternoon, and I'd better have a just-cleaned oven." She sighed. "I try not to lie to my parents; it makes life much easier when all I have to remember is the truth."

She looked at Tashi and added, "And when the truth won't serve, we'd better have a very convincing story." She went to sit next to him. He was still lying on his side, motionless and silent. She pillowed his head in her lap, put out a hand and gently stroked his hair, which was dark, short and curly. "Tashi, are you all right?"

Tashi gave her a pained glance and closed his eyes.

She turned to Namtso Gomchen in alarm. "What's wrong? Can't he talk?"

"He can talk," the lama replied calmly. "The transformation is a bit of a shock, however, and it may take him a while to adjust."

Christina looked stricken. "What if he doesn't want to go through with this?"

"He has gone through this," Namtso Gomchen pointed out. "He is human again now."

Christina swallowed. "But what if he doesn't want to marry me?" Tashi's head twisted to butt up against her hand, as he always had when he wanted her to pet him. Automatically her hand stroked his hair.

"I do," he said. His voice was a soft purr. "I want to marry you and have children with you."

Christina blushed, and then suddenly realized what her mother would consider an appropriate wedding ceremony. Staging the opera "Aida," triumphal procession and all, would be simpler, quicker, and require fewer people. "I think we had better elope," she said firmly. "First we get married, then we tell my parents. They'll throw a gigantic party; but if we're already married, they can't insist on a big fancy wedding."

Tashi looked curious. "What are your wedding customs like?"

Christina shuddered, imagining her mother's version of same. "You don't want to know."

"But surely you do not intend to marry without your parents present!" It was the first time Christina had seen the Lama look shocked.

"If we get married in my church," she pointed out, "they read out the banns—it's a sort of announcement—for at least three weeks beforehand. And the church requires that the bride and groom have premarital counseling with a priest, who will, at the very least, ask us how we met, why we want to get married, and all sorts of questions about our future plans—to say nothing of our current religious beliefs and what we intend to teach our children. He's also bound to ask where Tashi lives, what he does for a living, and what his home parish is."

"I see your point," the Lama said.

"And we need another name for him," Christina went on. "I can't very well say that my husband is named after my cat—particularly when I can't produce the cat."

"He can take your surname when you marry," Namtso Gomchen said, "as a compliment to your family." He smiled suddenly. "As for a first name, it seems to me that 'Tom' would be appropriate."

"Thomas Lang." Christina nodded. "Sounds all right to me—is it okay with you, Tashi?"

He smiled up at her. "Just call me Tom."

The Lama stood up briskly and picked up his briefcase. "Very well, Tom. I brought clothing for you. You will accompany me back to the city."

Christina and Tashi started to protest together, but the Lama overruled them. "You do not want Mr. Lang to find you here before the wedding. Christina, come to my hotel Monday morning. I shall arrange to have the blood tests done and find someone to marry the two of you as soon as possible." He pulled his nephew to his feet and headed for the bathroom. "Do not worry, Christina; you will not have to be alone for long."

It was less than a week, but Christina had never realized how lonely she could feel. By the next Friday, she was so glad to have Tashi home again that introducing him to her parents and telling them that she had eloped seemed a small price to pay.

Of course, the first question her mother asked was "Are you pregnant?"

"Not yet," Christina replied serenely, "but we plan to have children very soon." She realized that she had a death-grip on Tashi's hand and tried to loosen it a bit, but he simply squeezed her hand and smiled at her.

"And what do you do, Tom?" Mr. Lang asked.

This was one of the first questions covered in Tashi's coaching ("fifty all-purpose questions for cocktail parties" was how Christina had described it). "I am a student of philosophy, sir. And I believe that you are acquainted with my uncle, Namtso Gomchen."

By the end of the evening the Langs were enthusiastic about their new son-in-law, and Mrs. Lang was happily planning parties to introduce him to everyone she knew.

Christina suspected that she was starting to plan a baby shower as well.

Two months, one gigantic wedding reception, and twenty-three dinner parties later, Christina woke up one morning feeling truly dreadful. Tashi was draped all over her as usual. *In some ways,* Christina thought *I don't think he's ever going to get over being a cat. And now he takes up even more of the bed.* She started to sit up, but lay back down quickly—moving made her feel sick to her stomach.

Tashi had half-wakened when she moved, and now he absentmindedly began to nuzzle her breast. Christina yelped and pushed him violently away. "Don't do that! It hurts!"

Tashi, who had not been expecting the shove, fell out of bed and landed hard on the floor. He sat up, groaning. "When I was a cat, I would have landed on my feet if you had done that," he complained. He looked at her. "What's wrong with you? You look as sick as I feel. What does your father put in those drinks he serves anyway?"

"About three ounces of alcohol per drink," Christina replied matter-of-factly. "How many did you have last night?"

"I can't count that high. Remember, I am only a simple cat."

"Tashi, that's not funny. Besides, if you drank like that in cat form, you'd die of alcohol poisoning."

"If I were a cat, I wouldn't be putting that garbage in my body. If I were a cat, I wouldn't have to go to your parents' stupid parties."

"My mother's stupid parties," Christina corrected him. "My father hates them as much as you do—why do you think he makes the drinks so strong?"

She tried to move and felt sick again. "Hand me the phone, will you?"

She dialed, still lying flat on her back. "Mother, do you know any good cures for morning sickness? I think I'll throw up if I try to get out of bed."

"That's wonderful, dear!" Her mother was obviously thrilled. "How far along are you? When is the baby due?"

"Mother, I'm not even sure I'm pregnant yet. I just feel very sick. Is there anything that can be done about it?"

"Saltines," her mother said promptly. "Keep a pack of them next to your bed and eat a few before you try to move in the morning. Have Tom get you some now." Christina relayed the instruction and he nodded and headed for the kitchen. Her mother was still babbling on. "Be sure to go see Dr. Shaw today, and let me know your due date as soon as you figure it out. Oh, this is going to be such fun!"

Maybe for you *it is,* Christina thought as she hung up the phone. *It doesn't feel too great to me right now.*

To her mother's delight, Christina was indeed pregnant. Namtso Gomchen, who stopped by every couple of months to check on his nephew's spiritual progress (or lack of same) was delighted as well. It was he who told Christina that she carried twins.

"They will be human, won't they?" Christina asked uncertainly.

"Yes, of course," the Lama replied. "Why shouldn't they be?"

Christina led the way to the den. Tashi was sprawled along the couch, staring intently at the television. The Lama watched fish swimming about on the screen for several minutes. "What program is this?" he inquired.

"It's a video made for cats," Christina replied a bit grimly. "The breeder I got Tashi from gave it to him last Christmas. He liked it then, and now—well, he spends hours watching it every day. Most of his waking hours, in fact." She took a deep breath and finished in a rush. "Uncle, I think the transformation is failing."

"What?"

"I think he's turning back into a cat. Maybe his humanity went to the babies—I don't know. But ever since I've been pregnant, he's been more and more catlike. He refuses to go anywhere, even next door to my parents' parties. He lies around all day, napping and watching this video, but sometimes I wake up at night and hear him pacing about the house." She looked uneasily at the Lama. "I've tried to be a good wife to him, truly I have. I don't think I'm doing anything to cause this," she gestured at Tashi, who was still staring raptly at the screen and ignoring them, "but I just don't know! Uncle, what shall I do?"

Namtso Gomchen sighed. "It's not your fault. I told my

brother at the start that I feared you would make a better wife than our nephew would a husband."

"He's still very nice, for a cat," Christina said earnestly. "But when he looks like a human, people expect more of him. My parents are having fits; Mother is mortally offended that we're not coming to her parties—but he *won't* and I feel sick so much of the time. . . ."

"I could take him back to Tibet with me," the lama said, frowning at his nephew. "Perhaps in a monastery his concentration on higher thoughts would improve."

"How do we know he's not concentrating on higher thoughts now? He can do that as well as a cat in Connecticut as he can as a man in a monastery in Tibet." Christina pointed out. "And I don't want him to go back to Tibet. I love him; he's all I have left of Tashi!"

"You will have your children soon," Namtso Gomchen reminded her. "You won't be alone."

Tashi's head swung with preternatural suddenness to face them. He even gave the impression of twitching his ears. He jumped over the back of the couch and stalked gracefully across the room to stand beside Christina. "Don't badger her, Uncle," he said firmly. "I am not going back to Tibet. I am staying with Christina."

"And the children?" his uncle challenged. "What kind of a father are you going to be?"

Tashi smiled sardonically. "As good as any other cat." He looked thoughtful for a moment, then continued, "I've been a cat, and I've been a human. It's better to be a cat; it's a much more contemplative existence. Humans alternate between rushing around making themselves too busy to think, and drinking themselves into a stupor so that they won't *have* to think."

He glared at the Lama in open challenge. "Keep me in a human body as long as you can, Uncle, but you can't make me into that kind of human. No matter what form I wear, I *am* a cat."

"Do you expect Christina to raise your children alone?" the Lama protested.

"I'll be here," Tashi replied. "Unlike her father, who spent her entire childhood working in New York, and came home each night in such a bad mood that she used to hide from him."

"Is this true, Christina?" the Lama asked.

"Well, he didn't *mean* to be so cross all the time," Christina said hastily. "But you've done the commute, even if it's only been a few times and not during rush hour. Daddy would get up every morning, spend an hour on a crowded train, half an hour on an even more crowded subway, work a full day, then spend half an hour on the subway and another hour on the train. Then he'd get home and Mother would tell him everything that had gone wrong with *her* day, and ..."

"And they'd have a couple of drinks apiece to calm down, and if Christina was lucky, they'd simply ignore her," Tashi finished the explanation. "If she wasn't lucky, they'd hit her. Cats make much better parents than that!"

Christina was still trying to defend her parents. "They didn't beat me or anything like that," she told the Lama, who was looking grave. "They never spanked me when I didn't know why they were doing it."

"Because you were there." Tashi did not sound as forgiving. "I've seen too damn much of your parents since we got married—and I hope you never plan to ask them to baby-sit."

Christina dropped into the nearest chair and burst into tears. "He's right," she sobbed to Namtso Gomchen, who was staring at his nephew in shock. "He *has* seen too much of my parents—he's picking up Daddy's vocabulary."

"Merciful Buddha!" The Lama looked from his weeping niece to his nephew, who had curled up on the arm of her chair and was patting her cheek with his fingertips.

"And my mother complains all the time that he's lazy— and I want my cat back!" Christina wailed.

Tashi faced his uncle squarely. "Perhaps it was not an accident that I was reborn as a cat, Uncle. Change me back. Please."

"Christina?" the Lama asked.

Christina mopped her face with her sleeve. "Change him back. He's right. Cathood is a more contemplative existence. And he's a very good cat."

"And your parents?"

"We'll tell them he went back to Tibet with you for a visit, and in a month or two you can write and tell us of his untimely accidental death." Christina shrugged. "As long as no one questions her grandchildren's legitimacy, my mother will be happy. And as long as Mother's happy, Daddy's happy."

"How will you explain Tashi's reappearance as a cat?"

"Nobody knows he's been gone. In a few months I'll get a card from the vet, reminding me to bring him in for shots and then I'd have to explain his absence, but right now, as far as anyone knows, Tashi's been here all along." She faced the Lama. "He *has* been here all along. Please, change him back." She rested a hand on her abdomen. "I have my children; my parents will have their grandchildren. He's done what he agreed to do."

Namtso Gomchen sighed. "Very well." He picked up his briefcase. "Go set up the kitchen—and this time, please turn off the smoke detector before we start."

"Absolutely." Christina smiled radiantly.

The twins were born at St. Joseph's Hospital a few months (one baby shower, six dinner parties) later. Christina named them Christopher and Katherine, and called them Kit and Cat. Tashi seemed to approve.

THE CAT-QUEST OF MU MAO THE MAGNIFICENT

by Elizabeth Ann Scarborough

Within the sacred land of Shambala, barricaded not only by rings of snow mountains but by the powers of faith and magic from the destruction of the outside world, lived Mu Mao the Magnificent. After everything had ended, when the outside world was a shambles of death, starvation, and radiation, Shambala was the last safe haven for the living, and the only place where the souls of the dead could find living bodies into which they might be born.

In a secret compound within another hidden valley in the remotest part of Tibet, an evil magician had gathered from the corners of the earth a select group of people (and one cat) with the idea of forming his own small kingdom. To gain power, he bottled the wandering spirits of multitudes of the dead, imprisoning them for his own use. Lover of freedom, seeker of wisdom, Mu Mao the Magnificent, sole surviving descendant of the original cat and her mating with a snow lion, had always hated those bottles.

Then one day to the compound came the bodhisattva, Chime Cincinnati, who had abandoned the safety of Shambala to seek those still trapped outside its boundaries. She was quite bright enough to grasp the obvious, of course, and lead the living to Shambala, but had it not been for Mu Mao's help she would never have been able to complete her mission. Furthermore, only Mu Mao the Magnificent had the courage to liberate the bottled spirits. Because of Mu Mao, these trapped spirits were able to join the living and cross the magical barrier into Shambala, where they instantly achieved rebirth.

Thus, among those who had been liberated by him, among those who had seen and remembered the liberation,

Mu Mao was venerated. Since Mu Mao was a highly evolved being, having spent many of his former lives as a holy person of one persuasion or the other, he had the wisdom to accept graciously this veneration in the spirit it was offered. He did not demand worship, as his ancestors once had in Egypt. Was it not the responsibility of each being to seek and find his or her own path, after all?

No, Mu Mao did not care for honor (at least no more than was his due). He certainly did not care for power. But he did feel, in view of his position as the Cat-Companion of Shambala, possibly the last of his kind on earth, that his nature should have been considered by those who made the barrier to Shambala so difficult to cross.

For he found, after so many adventures trying to get In to Shambala, that he now wanted to go Out.

Such was the way of his species.

Or at least, that's how his racial memory recalled the nature of his particular kind. The larger felines, the snow lions, never went in and therefore had no need to go out. Mu Mao alone was the repository of the instincts, desires, and perogatives of the cat-companion. No one else seemed to remember.

Mu Mao remembered much, not only of this lifetime but of his previous ones, the lives in which he had been a monk, a priest, an official for the Chinese in Tibet, even then, seeking, always seeking wisdom and enlightenment. Until at last, in this life, he had been elevated to the highest possible life form and had become Cat.

He had thought that in this form, once he came to Shambala, he could live out the remaining days of this life in meditation, purring his mantras, practicing his graceful postures, and dwelling on inner truths. All of this he would do, of course, when he wasn't busy making sure that some of the lower life forms were not doomed to remain in their present, rodent or avian bodies long but with his help would be released and sent on to other incarnations, to learn other lessons, while he used their cast-off bodies for sustenance.

So he had thought and so he had done. Life was good in Shambala.

Except for one thing. A certain—urge, a natural life process that, as a monk, he had succeeded in quelling to a large extent anyway. As a cat, he found the urge more compelling. Since this was his first life as a cat and he was singular among his own kind, he sought out the next best thing, the snow lions who roamed the mountains surrounding Shambala. He sought out, in particular, the youngest daughter of the nearest clan of snow lions, feeling that, as someone closer to his size than her relations, she would have more insight into his difficulty than others. And slyly, to himself, he admitted that he felt, most strongly, that if she could be convinced, she might help him with his problem in other, more material ways, as well.

"Greetings, O Alabaster Lioness," he said when he had sniffed out her lair, having lain in wait until her mother and her siblings were elsewhere. So many other predators, all larger than himself, made him somewhat apprehensive. Perhaps they would not realize that he, unlike the smaller creatures upon which *he* fed, was not a lower life form but rather a more sophisticated and streamlined version of their own.

"Oh, it's you, Mu Mao, last of the little fat housecats," she said.

"Your wisdom is all I had hoped for, O she whose fur is as soft as the touch of the sun's last rays on the sacred mountain. You've come right to the heart of the problem."

"You speak in riddles, catling," she said with a warning growl lurking behind her purr. "What problem? Other than the one you're going to have when my kin return and see the tasty morsel I seem to have caught."

"It is you who are the tasty morsel, most captivating of catkind, but it is true that I am caught."

Her ears flicked, rotating slightly backward. "Not yet," she said, biting off the words. "But you will be if you linger. My kin will kill you like a mouse."

"I beg your pardon?" Mu Mao said, sitting back on his haunches, his tail now flicking quickly. "Princess of Lionesses you may be, but please do not make the mistake of treating me without honor, for I am of good lineage, and on my mother's of a line so honored that my mother's companion brought her above all others to survive with her the fall of the world. Now, as you say, I am the last of her line."

"Which will soon be extinct," the snow lion's youngest

daughter said with impatience, but now he heard in her voice that it was not anger or scorn that caused her to say so, but true warning.

"Unless I find a mate," he said urgently, for he was not a wise being for nothing and understood that her warning was a valid one. "Lioness, I am asking you to be my bride."

The snow lion kitten jumped backward. "Who? Me?"

He purred persuasively. "You're young and feline and very lovely."

"No, I'm lovely, feline, and *very* young. I'm not of an age to bear kittens yet. And I shouldn't even suggest it to my sisters or my mother, if I were you. They would gobble you in two bites."

"True," he said. "Besides, they are very large. You are the only one the right size in all of Shambala."

"Then there *is* no one in Shambala, little fat cat," she said. "I'm very sorry for you, but you must understand that even if I were to breed with you, our kittens would be mostly snow lion and probably my mother would kill you to feed them and that would do you no good."

"No," he conceded. "I suppose not."

He could have pressed his suit a little longer, but in the distance he heard the snow lion's hunting cry and knew her family would be returning soon.

He bounded down the mountain, sliding on his belly and rump where the snow and ice would have sucked his paws down too deeply for him to move. Below lay the bustling city of Shambala, with all of its houses and businesses spread around the smaller mountain sheltering in the shadow of the horned mountain Karakal. At the foot of this smaller mountain lay the blue-green jewel of the sacred lake. Surrounding this lake was the rhododendron jungle.

Sitting in the jungle beside a stream was Chime Cincinnati herself, his guide to Shambala and one of his favorite humans. He bumped his head against her hand and she picked him up and held him in her lap, stroking his ears with her small brown hand. "What troubles you, little master?" she asked. She was a woman, it was true, and now, after many journeys beyond the borders of Shambala, she was an old woman, but like Mu Mao she also had lived many incarnations and thus understood him, where many other humans did not.

"Out," he said. "Chime, I would go out."

"Why?" she asked, not sounding surprised, merely curious.

"I have—a need. And as I am the last Cat in the world, the world has need of me."

"Oh, Mu Mao, Shambala has need of you, too," she said, burying her wrinkled face in his ruff. "And the world since its ending has grown very cruel. Surely the last cat in the world is a treasure worthy of preservation."

"Preservation is for dead things," he said. "I am not dead—yet. But when I am dead, I hope to live again. Having by virtue of my collected good karma in former lives finally evolved into my highest form, that which you see before you, I have no wish to be reborn into a lesser form. Cat I am and Cat I would be again except, there is a slight logistical problem . . ."

"If you are the only one, then there will be no kittens for you to be born into in a new life as a cat?"

He purred. "You are a very *good* human being, Chime. So quick and clever. Perhaps if I succeed, you, too, may be privileged to be a cat in your next life."

"Perhaps," she said softly and he thought, to one so old, perhaps it was not polite to mention the next life.

He continued quickly. "You see, I am thinking, suppose I am *not* the only cat left in the world. Suppose I am merely the only cat left in Shambala."

"That is surely possible," she admitted. "Why, in one or two countries, war never touched much of the population though famine, plague, and natural disasters destroyed almost as much. Still, if one cat remained, perhaps more did as well."

"My thinking exactly. And even if only one survived, if she is female, and I can find her, my species is not lost."

"Maybe," Chime said slowly and with a note in her voice that Mu Mao didn't care for.

"What do you mean maybe?"

"Mu Mao, you were full grown when you came here and by the power of Shambala have lived a healthy life among us for more than fifty years by outside reckoning. But perhaps you are forgetting that if you go beyond the magical barriers of Shambala and into the world where time proceeds normally, within a few days you will age to a very old cat indeed. Then I doubt you could find your mistress in time to still be alive when you meet her, much less get her with kittens."

He lifted his hind foot and scratched his jaw thoughtfully. "Hmm. Yes, of course, I did *know* that." And so he probably did, in a former life.

Chime obligingly scratched under his chin for him, as if she thought he had the reincarnation of one of the Chinese high party members infesting his fur. He purred his thanks. "You are one of the few who goes out and comes back in to Shambala, Chime Cincinnati," he said. "You have, of course, seen no other cats or you would have mentioned it?"

"I would have," she said. "And I would, of course, offer any cat I met refuge in Shambala, but I have met none. And now that I am by outside reckoning over seventy years old, I am growing too old to travel more widely in search of one. Still, perhaps, if you are patient . . ."

"Hmmm," he said. "Cats are very patient, it seems to me, but I do not feel patient at this particular time. Really, I think I *must* go Out. Now."

"I know the feeling," she admitted. "I, too, had a terrible urge to leave Shambala my first time out, and because the others feared for me, I had to sneak out through a forgotten subterranean passage."

Mu Mao cocked an eye at her. "That sounds promising. Does it still exist?"

"It does. It involves a great deal of swimming, however."

Mu Mao spat disgustedly. "That won't do."

"The only other way is over the mountains. And I am afraid that is a very long way for you to go alone. The snow is deep and you would sink. Even if you didn't sink, it would hinder you in hunting and you would starve."

"But I have to go *owwt*," he said. "Naoww."

"I wonder why now," she mused. "When you have lived among us so long without this need. Perhaps it is because you are now, like me, very old, and it is time to consider your future incarnations. Very well, little friend, we will make one last journey."

The people of Shambala were alarmed to see Chime Cincinnati go, for they knew she might not return. However, although many of them had loved him and fed and petted him, even slept with him, by the time Chime and Mu Mao set off, the people of Shambala were well content to see him leave. For his need and his impatience grew with every moment, and he constantly insisted at all hours of the day and night to everyone he met, "Oaowwt. Naoww. Oaowwt. Naoww." Until, had he not been a venerated hero and the last known living cat, someone would surely have risked dreadful karma and drowned him in the sacred lake just so the peace of Shambala would no longer be disturbed by his demanding cries.

As was her custom, Chime Cincinnati made the long trek from the city through the mountains to the barrier alone. Normally, she carried very little with her, but in this case, she carried a supply of food for Mu Mao. He rode on her shoulders and warmed her ears, keeping warm himself by snuggling between her hair and the hood of her parka.

"It does not look like a *lot* of food," he observed, settling himself down as she started up over the first mountain pass.

"It will not be a very long trip to the border," she said. "Not when I am walking *lung gom* style." She referred to the secret discipline that enabled the advanced practitioner to walk very long distances in a very short time. Mu Mao had never himself remained in one body or devoted enough time to one practice long enough to develop the skill, but in old-time Tibet, it used to be characteristic of the most advanced rinpoches or teachers that they were able to cover vast amounts of terrain in this fashion. Their feet, it was said, often did not touch the ground over which they crossed.

He couldn't tell if Chime's feet touched the ground or not. He was on her shoulders and he meant to stay there. But as soon as they were out of sight of the last houses, she began breathing in a certain fashion and walking up and down the mountain paths as if they were no more challenging than the path from her home to the communal latrine.

One white snow-mountain looked much like another one to him, and even his sense of smell was dulled by the snow-cleansed, high thin air. Between the boredom of the surroundings and his hostess' swaying gait, coupled with the reassurance that he would soon be, as he wished to be, outside the barrier, he dozed through much of the journey, waking only long enough to accept a handful of crumbly momo with meat mixed into it and to lap melted snow.

Some time later—he had no idea how long—he was awakened by a tickle under his chin. "Rise and shine, venerable puss-face," Chime said. "We are now crossing the outer boundary."

He yawned and stretched and cocked one eye sleepily but it still looked like more mountains to him. He said so.

Chime took two more steps and he noticed that now her breath came with more difficulty and her step faltered. Her voice was raspy as she said, "No, the plains lie below, in that direction." He stood up on her shoulders and peered around into her face.

"Are you growing old already, woman?"

"No—not yet. It takes three days for the time to catch up with you. But walking *lung gom* has its cost and these days, it exacts its payment sooner with every trek."

She started to sit down on the path, but her foot, now feeling the effects of the long, fast walk, slipped out from under her and she sat down heavily. Mu Mao jumped from her shoulders onto the path, so that she would not be burdened by his weight. He was preparing to leap back onto her lap to speak to her when from the mountain above them came a terrible rumbling and skittering and all of a sudden, with a great roar, a rain of rock and snow plummeted toward them.

Mu Mao flew down the path away from the landslide, but Chime had no strength left to do more than raise her arms above her head as the snow covered her completely.

After a moment, the slide stopped. It hadn't been bad as such things went, and the mound of snow that covered Chime now blocked the broad path entirely. At least she had not been carried off down the mountain. If only the rocks had not killed her!

"Chime!" he cried. "Chime Cincinnati!" Without waiting for the response he feared would not come he began digging, scooping with front paws, and when his pads were caked with snow and ice, turning around to kick with his back feet.

He was so frantic he dug until his feet were all bleeding but he hated to stop long enough to remove the ice from his pads and free his claws.

"Chimee—oowt!" he called to her.

And finally, after what seemed like forever, when he had dug a hole no bigger around than his own head through the mound, which kept filling partially back up as soon as he'd dug it out, he heard an answering groan and a gasp.

He snaked a paw into the hole and touched something. It wasn't very warm, but it seemed alive.

"Ptttew," it said in a gaspy voice. "Take your paw out of my mouth, cat."

He wriggled into the hole, purring happily.

"I'll—breathe—better if you don't block the air," she said.

"Oh, certainly. Excuse me," he said, sitting back down on the path to clean himself more thoroughly and finding at that point that he, too, was very tired. "Can yeww get yaout?" he mewed more plaintively than he realized. He was far too exhausted to dig another hole in the mound, and it would have taken him weeks to dig all of the snow free from her. Yet he had to free her. She had all the food!

"I'll—try—I just need to get my—my breath—with—correct breathing—I can—can do *tumo* practice."

"Ah," he said, a bit more hopeful. With *tumo,* another secret sacred practice, she could warm herself from the inside out and melt the snow besides. She had done it back in the ice caves and it was most impressive. He had spent hours in the sunlight, thinking that if he collected enough solar rays in his fur, he could perfect this practice, but that didn't seem to be how it worked.

After waiting for some time, however, for the snows to melt and her form to be freed, and seeing no visible results, he called, "Chime?"

When she didn't answer, he became alarmed and dabbed his paw back into the rapidly freezing hole again. "Chime!" he cried.

"Mu ... Mao," her voice whispered. "Too ... weak ... from ... walk."

Frantically, he began digging again, enlarging the hole. As much snow landed on his back as it did on the ground and he was in danger of being buried himself, but he persevered.

At last he had uncovered her head and face, but she was pale and icy looking. "Mu Mao—Kalagiya," she said.

He had heard that word before, the secret word of summoning which brought aid to any Shambala being in distress.

"Kalagiya," she gasped. "Kala . . ."

He yowled it, as loudly as he could cry, his voice ringing through the valley and echoing off the sides of the mountains. Maybe snow lions or other wild animals would come and try to eat him. Let them! If they were Shambala animals, they would know of Chime Cincinnati and they would help him dig for her.

He finally had to stop when the vibrations of his voice began causing other avalanches, small, but nevertheless threatening to bury himself as well as Chime again. He jumped down from the top of the snow mound and curled himself about her head to warm her. Fresh new crystals of snow began to settle softly, one at a time, atop the crusts snarled in his fur.

The last thing he was aware of was trying to fit himself tightly against her hair, remembering his mother and her warm milk, as his torn and bleeding claws tried to knead and the ghost of a purr rumbled and stopped for lack of strength.

Then his whiskers picked up movement and he looked up through the blinding snow into a furred white face that frightened a hiss out of him. Two long clawed hands reached down past him and shoveled the snow away from Chime, then scooped her up, limp as the tail of a dead mouse, into its fur-fringed arms.

Mu Mao couldn't even hiss, he was so tired, but at any rate, the thing didn't seem to see him.

He tried to leap up and hang onto Chime, so as not to be left behind, but his claws were broken and his legs weak with exhaustion. All he succeeded in doing was tangling his paws in the tie to her pack, causing himself to get dragged several feet before the big white hairy thing—yeti—he remembered—yeti—causing the yeti to kick out blindly, as he himself might kick at a flea.

He fell onto the path, sprawling exhausted, as the yeti disappeared into the snow with Chime.

He knew, however, that he could not remain there or he would perish. He followed along the path as far as he could go. It led back into the mountains, and he trotted wearily, following until all of a sudden he found himself facing what appeared to be a blank wall.

His appetite saved him, for his nose detected a smell marginally richer and more tantalizing than the mere scent of snow—bits of meat momo lying nearest the wall, buried beneath just a few flakes of snow. He gobbled them as he found them, but when he tried to eat the last piece it seemed to be caught. He pawed at it and to his surprise and satisfaction, more than the momo came loose. An intricately balanced doorway, camouflaged to appear to be part of the mountainside, swung inward with very little additional scratching and pushing. A trail of momo bits and other items he recognized as coming from Chime's pack let him know that this was where the yeti had brought her. Aha!

Stealthily, keeping his tail to the wall but his nose on the momo bits, he stalked down the passageway, following the trail until it gave out.

What now? He was wondering, just as his ears swiveled to pick up the sound of Chime's much-weakened voice. "Thank you, Vajra, but ... I think ... I'm too weak ... to ... go ... further."

A rumbling, which must have been the yeti speaking, answered her, his tone too low for Mu Mao to hear, even if he could have understood it, which he doubted. Not that Chime Cincinnati was any better at languages than he was, it was simply that she apparently had previous acquaintance with this creature, as Mu Mao had not, and therefore had the advantage of more opportunity to practice.

"Your ... secret ... is safe ... with me," she replied to the yeti. "But how fortunate ... for me ... that these caves are ... part ... of Shm ..." Here her voice faltered and failed. Gingerly, Mu Mao peeked around the corner of the wall, to where his friend lay on a pallet of dirt the yeti had scraped hastily together. She quieted and seemed to rest, then suddenly twitched and called out, "Mu Mao!" but her weakness once more overcame her before she could elaborate.

In a moment, the yeti straightened and turned from her, heading down what appeared to be a side passage. Was he abandoning her? Some friend! Mu Mao crept close and insinuated himself beneath her arm, purring reassurance. Her arm moved and her hand feebly brushed his fur.

The yeti was undoubtedly going for help and Mu Mao hoped he knew *lung gom* walking if he meant to seek all the way to Shambala City for assistance. Poor Chime was in a bad way; who could tell what injuries she had suffered from the avalanche, her body temperature varied wildly from burning to freezing. No wonder she couldn't do *tumo!* At least, if this passage was part of Shambala, her age—and his—would not advance while they were here.

He thought he would need to wait with her a long time until the yeti returned, but within a very short time the ground vibrated with the footsteps of the beast. It seemed never to have left the tunnel, but someone was now with it, and not another yeti.

"Oh, dear. Oh, dear," an ancient voice cried as the owner almost stumbled over Chime. Wizened hands, impossibly old, groped Chime's face and Mu Mao managed to scoot free and back to his hiding place before she felt his fur—for he could tell from her groping that either she could not see in the dark or else was very blind. "How sad. It's little Chime and she is *very* ill. You were quite right to fetch me, Vajra. Give me my bag and I will examine her for wounds. You must fetch help in the city. Go quickly!"

Mu Mao fully expected the creature to go back outside, but when the yeti walked back toward the tunnel again, he followed it. Back there, he saw that there were many tunnels. From the central core of this passage, tunnels branched off like the spokes of a wheel. Vajra selected yet another spoke near the one he had previously taken, and disappeared down it.

Mu Mao sat back on his haunches and licked his chest, considering. Vajra had played the hero by going for help for Chime Cincinnati. So that role was taken. No need to duplicate effort. She also had a nurse who, if blind, at least possessed opposable thumbs, which were handy in medical situations, if not quite so handy as a nice soothing raspy tongue.

Therefore, Mu Mao concluded, Chime would *want* him to continue the mission for which they had both risked their current lives. However, there was no need to be hasty about it. If this tunnel system was a branch of Shambala, and his time outside of Shambala was limited, perhaps he ought to explore a branch or two and see where it took him. The thought of this excited him. It could be anything out there—why, there could be a whole city of other cats—not as wise or experienced as himself, of course, but cats, nevertheless. Since Mu Mao had no wish to return to the city, he chose the corridor in the opposite direction to the one the yeti had taken, and trotted down it.

And realized very quickly that if he didn't keep his wits about him he could become quite hopelessly lost.

This tunnel had many side branches as well, many twists and many turns. Guessing the right one was not going to be easy.

He padded carefully up to the first tunnel and peered down it. He had the cat's standard night vision, of course, but as he sat, wondering which way to go, visions of the journey he had just made replayed themselves against the canvas of the dark tunnel. He saw Chime Cincinnati walking *lung gom* and trying to use the *tumo* practice to free herself from the snow. The fact that she was too weakened to do so had nothing to do with it—she had tried. Her practice was not used just within the safe confines of Shambala. She used it to help her—and others—in her adventures.

Except for the adventure of helping her and the lost souls attain Shambala, Mu Mao had had a fairly restricted life, going from one secret valley to another larger, more magical and far more secret valley and in these two places he had spent most of his life. This new venturing forth was so thrilling and so frightening at once it made him tremble to the tip of his tail.

Recalling farther back, he thought on how, though he had never as a man learned *lung gom* or *tumo,* he had developed his sight beyond even what a cat—well, even what *he* as a cat, had developed in this life. He had been using only his bodily eyes. He now had to use his intuitive knowing, his Buddha eye. Turning around, he pointed his tail down first one turning, then the other, his corporeal eyes closed, feeling the vibrations of the various places. The middle passage felt—right.

He took this passage, began walking down it. In time, he noticed that unlike previous passages, this one was littered

with various objects—bones, both of men and animals, stat
uary, symbols placed in the walls, rotting tapestries, and
moldy furs. Was this tunnel, then, the outreach of some
abandoned monastery?

As he was wondering, he heard it, a soft, plaintive sound,
the one sound he had been hoping to hear. He heard it
only once, and then he heard a gong, echoing far far off,
as far off as Shambala now was.

He hastened his pace as much as he could with his sore
paws and exhausted muscles. Soon, however, he met with
increasing obstacles. The roof of the cave had collapsed in
some places, presumably during the destruction of the
world, though avalanches and road work or mining blasts
by the Chinese occupation forces had been known to do
much the same thing. He should know. In his very last life
he had worked with the occupation forces, even though his
true aim was to help the Tibetan people. Still, he understood the damage the invasion had done to Tibet's wilder-
ness, its animals, and its ancient treasures.

Scrambling over and around debris, he found his way on
tortured paws. Periodically, surrounded by rubble, he felt
he was hopelessly lost again, but he would turn around and
use his intuitive eye to tell him that he was on the right
track, so his confidence never wavered.

For all of the scrambling and climbing that he did, the
passage was still far shorter than he had any right to expect
it to be. Soon he found himself at another impasse, a solid
wall of rubbish, but recalling his experience with the wall
in the side of the mountain, he poked his paw under it.
That failing, he climbed up as various items slithered beneath his paws and clattered to the cave floor. He thought
he heard a hiss beyond the wall. And then he was at the
top, digging with all his might, though he sometimes slid
halfway back to the floor and he thought his paws were
worn to the shoulders.

Finally, Mu Mao opened a window and looked through.
There sat an ancient man, still as a stone, and Mu Mao
knew that the old man had died sitting that way, facing a
statue of the eight-armed Tara, patron saint of Tibet. The
statue had once been covered with gilt, but was now
molded black. Crouched at the feet of the man, nudging

the carcass of a lizard toward him, was Mu Mao's intended, his incipient true love, the second to last cat in the world.

For scrawny though she was, dusty though she was, untended though her fur was, she was a cat and she was, to his keen nose, undeniably female.

At the moment he spotted her, she looked up at him, ears laid back, and hissed.

"Peace, beloved," he said. "Never fear, love will strengthen me and despite my weariness from my previous heroisms, I will tunnel my way through to you."

"You'd better *not*," she hissed. "Or I will claw your eyes out. *My* territory. *My* lama. *My* lizard. Go away."

Right then he knew that this was a cat in need of instruction, one who had yet to learn the path to enlightenment of sharing and compassion toward all. "So they are, so they are," he conceded. "And I wouldn't dream of depriving you of them. Or even asking you to allow me to join you. Fortunately for me, my home is rather more comfortable than this, with silken cushions and fragrant trees, all the birds and mice and lizards I care to liberate, and many people, most of them extremely learned, to tend my wants. Your lizard, on the other hand, looks rather emaciated and—er—perhaps somewhat the worse for wear? And I hate to be the one to break it to you but your lama seems to have passed on to Nirvana."

"I *know* that," she yowled, her grief suddenly breaking through her hostility. She continued to yowl in such a way he feared for an avalanche, twining herself about her lama and crying most piteously. While she was distracted with mourning, he tunneled—if not to actually brave her claws, at least to make a way for her to escape with him should he be able to talk her into it from the safety of this position. "I came with him to this cave when I was but a kitten, and ventured outside only to hunt for—in the beginning for me, but after the night-of-blinding-light-and-loud noises ..."

"That was the destruction of the world," he informed her kindly.

"After that, I had to hunt for him as well. He had been in his middle years when I came to him, strong and *very* wise. But after that night, he was blind and stumbled around for days beyond the cave until I could coax him back in here. By then he was old, and I am old, and he has left me aloowwn. At least I no longer have to hunt beyond the cave. All of the prey decided my lair was safer than the world beyond the cave, so the hunting has been good up until recently. Now even that is fading and I— and I—"

"Well," he said, cautiously inserting his head, shoulders and forepaws through the tunnel he had made, so he could look down into the cave from his exalted position. "I can certainly see why you wouldn't want to share all of this splendor with another cat, even one as lonely for his own kind as you must be. Even one who has never known the joy of love, the delight of twitching his tail for little baby kittens to chase, however well-endowed he is with fine food, many friends, and warm places to lie."

"Kittens!" she wailed. "I have gone into heat many many times and no one has heard my cries, though my beloved lama said they disturbed his meditation and were enough to bring every tomcat in Lhasa. We are too remote here."

"Then come with me," he said. "I, too, long for a family."

"And leave my lama?" she said.

"What are you, a dog?" he asked with a break in his saintly patience. "Your lama no longer needs you but *I* do, our kittens do, my many friends in Shambala do—many of the young have never seen a kitten and they are not like the young of the outside world, beloved. They are kind, the children of Shambala. All kind and curious as kittens themselves. The mice are fat and the birds sing their thanks to you for delivering them from their current life form even as you catch and eat them."

"If it's such a good life," she asked. "What are you doing here?"

"Looking for you," he said.

"Good answer," she replied, beginning to climb the rubble. But when her face was even with his, she asked in a steely tone, "But how do I know you won't just lure me away from my home, get me with these kittens you say you want, and leave me, not in that lovely place you say, but in desolation, where I have no one and do not know the hunting grounds?"

Mu Mao groomed his whiskers with his paw, "I admit I'm somewhat the worse for wear, my dear, but if you look closely, you will see that I am well-fed and my fur is glossy. As for the rest ..."

"Mu Mao!" a voice echoed faintly through the corridor behind him. "I will not go without Mu Mao!"

Mu Mao hastily backed out of the tunnel, gave his mightiest yowl in response, and peered back in at the cat who was now peering through the other end at him. "That is my good friend, the wise guide to Shambala, the bodhisattva Chime Cincinnati, who made this trip especially so that I might locate you." He let her think about it.

"Me?" the other cat said. "A bodhisattva guided you to *me*?"

"That is true. So that you would return with us to Shambala and make to myself and our barren land the gift of your offffspring."

"Mu Mao!" the call came again and this time he knew it was the boy Fred, another special friend of his. So, somehow, that yeti *had* gone all the way back to the city and returned with help. These caves were truly wonderful shortcuts. He had heard of underground networks throughout Tibet, thought to be very secret, but now it seemed the yeti knew of them all along.

"Your name is Mu Mao?" she asked, and he could tell she was becoming charmed.

"The Magnificent, as I am often called," he admitted modestly.

"My lama called me Black Jade," she said, licking her shoulder to call his attention to her dusty black coat—he had already noticed her luminous green eyes.

"I soon shall call you Ama-Mao," he said. "Come quickly now, we must return to Shambala with my friend Chime, who has been injured."

And Black Jade came with him willingly. Though many times she was startled by the new and wonderful things she saw, always she was calmed by the presence of the magnificent cat by her side. They returned to Shambala, where Chime Cincinnati soon healed, and in time, which in Shambala does not count, Black Jade gave birth to a fine litter of kittens, two black and two spotted, and one orange, with tufted ears like the snow lion. They were the wonder of Shambala, and their little bodies inhabited with the spirits of only the wisest, best and noblest of beings. That litter was shortly followed by others, until cats in Shambala were soon as common as birds or yaks.

And at that point, leaving Black Jade once more big with kittens while the previous litter still suckled, Mu Mao once more sought out Chime Cincinnati.

"What is it now, Mu Mao?" she asked affectionately, scratching his head between his ears.

"Chime, does it not seem to you that a creature of my wisdom and talent is wasted here, where there are so many other cats?" He didn't say younger cats, nor softer of fur, nor more beautiful, but someone less self-assured might have done.

"But isn't that what you want? To be surrounded by your own kind?"

"When the poor ruined world is bereft of cats, to waste myself where people take my kind for granted? No, Chime. I would go, I must go *OUT*."

THE CAT, THE WIZARDS, AND THE BEDPOST

by Mary H. Schaub

The morning air was cool and tinged with aromatic leaf scent. Flax said the season was autumn, and therefore one should expect a rain of leaves.

"A dry rain, one might say," he added. "Not at all like the spring downpour that accompanied your arrival, Drop."

Having been a boy for only those few months, Drop was still discovering both advantages and disadvantages to being human. He had come to the wizard's cottage as an injured cat, but upon waking the next morning on Flax's desk, Drop had mistakenly eaten an enticing lozenge that had fallen from a nearby bottle. Immediately, Raindrop, the rescued cat had been transformed into Drop, the bewildered human boy, for Master Otwill's Keep-Shape Spell insured that the swallower would assume his second intended form after his birth shape. Flax was vexed to find no reversal instructions attached to Otwill's bottle, and since Otwill was unavailable for consultation, Drop remained a boy. He learned how to speak, how to deal with his peculiarly altered body, and subsequently how to be of assistance to the old wizard. Once his broken paw/hand had healed, Drop had tried to master writing, but despite his best efforts, his fingers failed to cooperate.

"Never mind," Flax had said. "Very few cats of my acquaintance correspond. You read quite well, which is most useful when my hands are occupied and I need to refer to some scroll or other."

This morning, Drop had listened with great care to Flax's description of an array of desired mushrooms. In his own previous cat experience, Drop had once been driven by hunger to devour some wild mushrooms, with resoundingly uncomfortable digestive results. Under Flax's supervision, he had gathered a large basket of edible mushrooms, as well as a smaller basket of medicinal fungi and herbs. Flax was spreading their harvest on a cloth in the side yard when a sharp-eyed hawk abruptly swooped down to perch on the back of the chair that Drop had brought outside for the wizard.

To Drop's surprise, the hawk peered at Flax and cried out hoarsely, "Find Flax! Find Flax!"

The old wizard blinked, then remarked as if he often entertained talking birds, "You have found him. I am Flax."

Ruffling his feathers, the hawk bobbed his head, but said no more.

"You look oddly familiar," mused Flax. "I've seen that patch of copper crest feathers before ... I have it! You're Otwill's hawk. He asked my opinion on your eye irritation some years ago. I suggested Utmar's ointment, of course— very efficacious. Trust Otwill to send a message by a hawk instead of a common pigeon. If I may unlace your leg capsule, we shall see what has prompted Otwill's dispatch."

The hawk quietly allowed the wizard to extract a tightly rolled parchment strip from the soft leather tube laced to its leg.

Drop studied Flax's face. Interpreting human reactions was a complicated skill that he practiced at every opportunity. Due to the isolation of Flax's cottage, Drop's chief subject for observation was the wizard himself, and now his face quickly reflected several strong emotions. His frost-white eyebrows rose first in evident surprise, then his lips tightened and he frowned. When he looked up from the parchment, his usually bright blue eyes were dark with concern.

"Drop," he announced, "this is news of the gravest kind. I never thought to hear that Otwill, of all people ... but listen for yourself. The message, by the way, is not from Otwill, but from his apprentice, Koron. 'Master Flax, I pray you, rescue my imprisoned master, Otwill! At his life's risk, to avoid discovery, he has concealed himself within a bed-post in the very castle of the enemy. A great Druzanian sorceror may soon arrive, and will surely discern his pres-

ence. Come at once to Zachor. Haste, I implore you—
haste!' " Flax lowered the parchment and sighed. "The
poor lad is frantic, and doubtless for good reason. We must
travel to Zachor immediately."

"Far?" asked Drop, whose idea of a long journey was
still mentally defined by the geographic range of an active
cat's body.

Flax was absently scooping the mushrooms back into
their baskets, his thoughts clearly elsewhere. "What? Oh,
you mean how far is Zachor. Let me see—I was there once
as a younger man. It must be four days' journey from here
by horse, or possibly five. Speaking of horses, let me give
you a note for Farmer Hopworth, for we must borrow his
cart horse. And where did I store that carriage? Was it in
the cowshed . . . or the root cellar? You can give Hopworth
our excess edible mushrooms, except for a few for our
lunch. Come along—there's a great deal to be done before
we can leave. There's Ghost and Cyril to be provided for.
Dear me, I do dislike unexpected crises! Perhaps I should
have become a wool merchant, as my parents intended."
Still muttering to himself, Flax strode into the cottage,
closely followed by Drop.

Some time later, Drop returned from his errand, gingerly
leading a very large cart horse. In his former cat's body,
Drop would have had no anxiety at all about evading the
horse's enormous hooves; in his erratically clumsy human
form, however, he felt oversized and less agile. Until he
learned the horse's temperament and reach, Drop planned
to remain wary.

Tethering the horse near the door, Drop entered the cottage to find Flax busily packing. In his characteristically
haphazard fashion, the wizard was striding from one room
to another, scattering clothing, scrolls, and assorted utensils
as he passed.

"Ah, Drop—back so soon?" Flax exclaimed, glancing out
a front window and nodding approvingly at the cart horse.
"Good Farmer Hopworth! I shall make a special effort to
encourage his barley crop this year. Assist me now, if you
will, with Cyril. We shall require that wicker hamper from
the back guest room, and some old bedding to make him
comfortable for the trip."

"With us?" asked Drop dubiously. He was not yet entirely at ease in the same room with the great snake; his cat nature kept warning him to avoid the reptile. To be fair, he conceded that Cyril had so far given him no cause for alarm. In fact, together with Flax's albino owl Ghost, Cyril had played a major role in thwarting the evil intentions of Skarn the sorceror. Recalling Flax's introductions to his two fellow cottage dwellers, Drop had alerted Cyril to the danger by tapping the snake's head, so that Cyril most helpfully bit Skarn on the leg just as Ghost, alerted by Drop's cry, swooped down and buffeted Skarn about the face. These vital distractions occurred at the height of the magical duel between Flax and Skarn, who had come to steal a potion from the wizard. Before Skarn could pronounce his threatened Death Spell over a temporarily disabled Flax, Drop seized the opportunity and popped one of Otwill's shape-changing lozenges into the sorceror's gaping mouth. Skarn was at once transformed into a warty, mouse-scented demon, which the recovered Flax promptly dispersed.

"I've thought of the perfect place to send Cyril," Flax said. "A colleague of mine has recently retired to a villa in the south where the warm weather would suit Cyril admirably. We can leave him on our way with a merchant I know who trades to the south. If you will line the hamper's interior with the bedding, I'll lift Cyril inside ... hum ... part of Cyril ... there! All of Cyril. Now, secure the lid, please; not too tight. Splendid—that settles one of our stalwart companions. As for Ghost ..."

Flax reached up and coaxed the drowsing white owl down from a high shelf to perch on his arm. The wizard walked slowly, talking to the owl all the way outdoors to what Flax fondly called his garden shed. "We must go away for a while, Ghost, to try to aid my old friend Master Otwill. I know that you can fend for yourself quite well, but I shall feel more at ease if you have a dry refuge for roosting. If I open this loft shutter and wedge it firmly, you can come and go as you please. What do you think?"

The owl's pink eyes opened wide as it stalked across the soft dried hay scattered on the loft's floor. Twisting its head nearly all the way around for a survey of the dim space, Ghost made straight for a half bale of hay, hopped atop it, and settled back to sleep with a satisfied flutter of feathers.

Flax bustled back down the rough ladder to the ground, reciting to himself lists of items to be packed or put away. "By the way," he interrupted himself, as they started back toward the cottage, "I found my old carriage right where I'd left it, in the cowshed. I'm too stiff in the joints nowadays to ride a horse, and I'm not at all sure that you would care for riding, having been used to conveying yourself as a cat on your own four legs. Better we employ the carriage. It is a trifle antiquated, but still basically sound. I've pulled it out in the backyard where we can clean it more easily. It's amazing how much dust accumulates on stored objects."

As they rounded a corner of the cottage, Drop simply stopped and stared. While a kitten, he had seen carriages in what humans called "a city." The cobweb-festooned object to which Flax pointed with such evident pride struck Drop as a curious reflection of Flax's cottage: eccentric in proportion, devoid of fancy ornamentation, but beneath the dust, webs, and dry leaves, both were serviceable. Drop fetched more rags while Flax dislodged an abandoned bird's nest lodged between the spokes of one wheel.

"I have sent Otwill's hawk back to Koron," Flax said, as he scrubbed mildew from the leather seating. "I felt the lad needed encouragement." He paused for so long that Drop looked up from his own cleaning.

"We have to ask ourselves a troubling question," Flax resumed. "Was this message actually sent by a friend of Otwill's? I do not like to postulate double meanings and deceptions, but I must say, Drop, that our brief acquaintance with Skarn has inclined me to be exceedingly cautious when anything Druzanian is mentioned. Better to err on the safe side." Flax flourished his rag for emphasis, then sneezed from the resulting dust.

"How?" asked Drop, always a cat/boy of few, but relevant words.

"How to be safe? One can't ever be entirely secure," Flax replied, "but it seemed prudent to me to employ some artifice in my reply. I suggested a meeting place in Zachor known to Otwill from my previous visit with him there, and said I should use a certain name which Otwill should likely have imparted to his true apprentice. We shall see when we get there how successful my obscurity has been. If the message falls into enemy hands, it should be of scant use. I do despise ambushes—so unsettling to the digestion."

Once the carriage was moderately presentable, Flax and Drop had to clean themselves before snatching a hasty lunch. The packing process afterward was delayed only briefly while Flax considered what, if any, magical paraphernalia he should take on the trip. He finally decided to rely on Otwill's own store of materials, for, he told Drop as they harnessed the horse, "I have no way to know what I may need, and if I carry useless things, they will occupy space and weigh us down. I shall drive to begin with," Flax added, settling into the driver's seat. "I'm sure you can learn the skill as we go, but we must set off at our best speed while the weather is fair. Did Farmer Hopworth confide to you the name of this horse?"

Drop thought back over his extremely terse conversation with the farmer. "Horse," he said, at last.

Flax sighed. "I feared as much." He raised his voice and declared firmly, "Horse! I name you 'Bay,' and impress upon you the urgency of our errand. Proceed!"

Bay flicked his ears, and set off at a quick pace for a horse more used to pulling farm carts than carriages.

Over the succeeding days, Drop came to appreciate Bay's stolid reliability. Bay wasn't fast, but he was steady, and Drop quickly learned the knack of signaling with the reins. Flax didn't believe in the use of prods or whips, preferring to talk to any animals in his service. Drop doubted that the wizard needed to employ any magical persuasion, suspecting that Flax's kindness elicited most of the behavior he desired. Throughout his time at Flax's cottage, Drop had noticed that his skin tingled and his hair tended to rise whenever magic was being used. He had no such reactions during this trip.

In the second town along their way, they unloaded Cyril's hamper to be sent on south by the trader.

Late on the fourth day, they entered the narrow streets of Zachor. Flax directed Drop to a sprawling inn whose weathered sign displayed a spiky, segmented wedge painted a vivid green.

"Just as I remember it," said Flax. "The Sign of the Dragon's Wing. Drive into the inner courtyard, if you will. They provided ample stabling room there on my last visit."

As Drop halted the carriage, a stout woman wearing a long apron hurried out of the main building to greet them.

Before she came within earshot, Flax murmured, "For the sake of our disguise, we seem in luck. This is not the same woman who saw me here years ago." He climbed out of the carriage, and nodded briskly to the woman. "Proper care for our equipage, if you please. I am Martan, and I shall require two rooms for an as yet undetermined period."

For so large a woman, her voice was surprisingly high-pitched. "You be most welcome to the 'Wing,' sir," she twittered. "I be innkeeper's wife. There's a young man been asking for you, sir. I took the liberty of showing him to our upstairs parlor in case you came today. He's asked every day this week."

"I trust he gave his name?" Flax inquired.

"Only said he was fair keen seeking after furniture, sir—beds, most particular."

"Then we follow the same trade," said Flax, withdrawing his valise from the carriage. "I travel great distances, madam, to procure fine furniture for the outfitting of castles. I shall speak to this man as soon as we have been shown our rooms. Come along, Gray."

Drop followed respectfully behind, carrying their two carpetbags. He had wondered what name he might be given. As a cat, his unusual white-tipped gray fur had initially inspired Flax to name him "Raindrop," but upon his shape change to human form, Drop had lost all his fur (plus his glorious tail), except for the gray thatch on his head. "Gray" was thus a reasonable name, and scarcely to be linked with Drop, the faraway wizard's lad.

Once indoors, they were intercepted in the upstairs hall by a haggard young man whose downcast face brightened at the sight of them. "Can it be?" he implored. "Are you Master Martan?"

"I am he," Flax declared. "I assume that you must be the sender of that interesting message concerning castle furnishings?"

The young man seized Flax's hand. "I am that very Koron," he exclaimed. "Pray let us find a quiet place to talk."

The innkeeper's wife beamed at the prospect of prosperous business being transacted in her establishment. "Leave your baggage, sir," she insisted, "for your servant and I can take it to your rooms. Yonder is the parlor—quiet as an empty wine cask, with no one to trouble you."

Flax bowed his approval, but corrected her on one point. "Gray is my apprentice, and thus accompanies me at all times to continue learning the fine art of bargaining."

As soon as the heavy parlor door closed behind them, Koron sank wearily onto a bench. "Oh, Master ..." he began to say, but Flax raised a warning hand.

"Given the delicate nature of our business," Flax said, "let us not yet mention names in case we might by chance be overheard."

Koron blanched, but nodded jerkily, and took a moment to revise his tale into safer obscurity. "I must tell you," he resumed, "that I have been apprentice to my current master for only one year. Before that, I had studied several years with a ... an old gentleman near this city who is learned on the subject. My current master kindly took me to learn his style of ... trade."

"Just as I have young Gray, here," said Flax. "Do go on."

"Recently, my master discovered an unsettling arrangement was being planned by some extremely unsavory ... competitors. He felt obliged to investigate the matter himself, and actually entered the place he understood to be the focus of the ... pending conspiracy. While there, he realized he was about to be found, and since the people have been known to resort to violence if thwarted, he ... concealed himself."

"Dear old ... fellow," exclaimed Flax. "How like him! Popped inside a cupboard, did he? Or was it a wardrobe?"

Koron looked relieved to be spared further invention. "Something of that sort," he agreed.

"And I fancy he became stuck within, considering his unusual girth," Flax suggested. "What a trying predicament. I take it he hasn't yet recovered from the experience?"

Koron shook his head decisively. "No, sir, he is, in fact ... still indisposed." Reaching within his tunic, he extracted a small shell-like medallion suspended from a fine chain.

Flax's eyebrows rose. Although Drop had no idea what

significance the pendant had, the wizard evidently recognized it. "No doubt he discussed with you something of his estimates on the ... worth of the disputed furniture he had observed?" Flax inquired.

Koron tucked the silver pendant back out of sight, his fingers shaking in agitation. "That's the difficult part, sir. He ... made a sort of list, but it was ... rained upon, and I can't make it out at all. With his condition being what it is, he cannot tell us. ..."

"Quite lost his voice, eh?" Flax interrupted. "Probably caught an ague, poor fellow, from that rain you mentioned. Let us not dally further—the sooner we see him, the better. Perhaps he may feel able to sit out in the sun with us in his favorite garden near the river."

Koron jumped to his feet. "I know where you mean," he said. "If we hurry, there might still be time before sunset."

Pausing only to locate their assigned rooms, Flax bustled the party back onto the street and strode rapidly away from the inn. Two detours though twisting alleyways led them to a vacant, overgrown area where Flax plumped himself down on an overturned discarded tub.

"We may now be more specific," the wizard stated grimly. "Where exactly is Otwill?"

Koron clenched his fists in frustration. "Within the very heart of the enemy's stronghold, sir. He forbade me to go with him, but he bespoke me by his mind-touch medallion so that I might know how his search progressed. Oh, sir, we are opposed by great force of evil—Walgur himself is due to come!"

Flax pondered the name. "I claim no knowledge of this Walgur, but I can believe any ill of a Druzanian, which I gather he is."

"Of most frightful sorcerous repute, sir," Koron exclaimed. "His minion in residence here is Trund, who poses as caretaker of the castle. It was his sudden approach that forced Master Otwill to essay his desperate action."

"At least Otwill was able to convey to you his strategem," said Flax thoughtfully. "Could he provide any directions to the room in question?"

"His sending at that time was somewhat constrained," Koron replied. "Just as he thought 'bedpost,' the message trailed off, and I could not reestablish contact."

"I'm not at all surprised," mused Flax. "When one becomes solid wood, one's freedom of expression is necessarily affected. Still, he did manage to tell us 'bedpost,' so we are spared having to examine all the wretched furnishings. By the way, I have not properly introduced you to Drop, my assistant, currently traveling under the name 'Gray.' Before he accidentally ate one of your master's Keep-Shape Spell lozenges, he was a cat."

Koron's eyes widened. "I was told about a certain misfortunate result of that spell, but it concerned a toad. I had not heard of a cat into a boy."

"The example came to mind," Flax explained, "because I was thinking if Drop had been a dog, he might still be able to scent Otwill's presence for us, but I don't believe cats track people by scent in the same fashion, so that notion is likely unproductive."

"This nose not as good as before," Drop inserted apologetically.

Koron's face showed confusion, then genuine distress. "You talk of scent, and dogs and cats—surely you can discern my master by your magic. I thought . . . I hoped. . . ."

Flax hastened to reassure the anxious apprentice. "Do forgive me, young man! Of course I can identify Otwill's hiding place—in the dark, with my eyes shut, for that matter. No, what was troubling me was the likelihood that any display of magic would be detected by our opponents. This Trund you mentioned . . . is he also a Druzanian sorceror?"

Koron seemed partially mollified. "Otwill assumed that Trund was Walgur's assistant. Trund was sent here to occupy the castle until his master's arrival. Sir, I am so fearful for Master Otwill's safety. I would have consulted my former master, Gilmont, but he is more of a scholar than a mage, and away just now on a visit to an ailing relative."

"I think we may assume that Master Otwill's maneuver has so far protected him," said Flax. "Had he been forcefully restored to his body, you should have been alerted by your medallion; likewise if he had been injured or killed. Tell me, what is the nature of Otwill's suspicion concerning Walgur and Trund?"

"Master Otwill did not want me to be endangered," said Koron in a husky voice. Drop judged him to be near tears, a peculiar human state that often accompanied extreme emotions. "I begged him to let me enter the castle with him, but he said I must wait outside in case he was entrapped and would require additional help."

"Very wise," said Flax. "But what was he seeking within the castle?"

"He had received a report that ancient manuscripts had been found and taken to Druzan, suggesting that a few rare sites could upon occasion offer access into ... other worlds." Koron paused, abashed. "I could not understand exactly what that meant, but Master Otwill said that evil forces could be loosed upon us if such a portal were carelessly conjured."

"And he deduced that a portal of that sort was located inside Walgur's castle," Flax declared. "Just like Otwill to charge in by himself. He should have sent for assisting mages ... but I'm sure he felt he could not wait."

"No, sir, he was most emphatic," Koron said. "He judged that the positions of the moon and other bodies were drawing to a juncture at which time this portal could be conjured, and he said that he must verify its situation before Walgur took possession of the place and blocked all access."

"If Walgur has not yet come," reasoned Flax, "Perhaps we may still have time to slip in, rescue Master Otwill, and thwart Walgur's plans. I feel most strongly that the least hint of magic could ruin our prospects. Are any tradesfolk allowed into the castle?"

Koron blinked at the abrupt question. "Yes, although few are required. Trund keeps no bodyservants. There's a stable lad or two, and three city folk work in the kitchen to provide for Trund, but they all leave each day at sunset and return at dawn."

Flax burrowed in his belt scrip, extracting a fold of parchment, a pen, and a traveler's inkpot. He muttered to himself as he wrote a brief message, then scanned the result. "I am requesting an audience with Trund as soon as he may allow it, on the grounds of my busy schedule as a traveling castle outfitter. Now for a token to pique his interest. . . ." Flax searched through his many pockets until he triumphantly produced a tooled silver bookmark. "We shall have the innkeeper's wife dispatch this note at once. Perhaps we may receive a reply by morning. Trund could well be bored waiting for his master in a virtually empty castle; a furniture buyer of generous means could be a welcome distraction. Drop, let us hasten back to the inn, whilst Koron seeks rest at his own lodgings. Try not to fret, young man! Our plan has the virtue of simplicity, plus a certain guile. It may be the enemy is completely unaware that Otwill is concealed in their midst."

In this hypothesis, however, Flax was mistaken. Even as they spoke, Trund was communicating with his master, staring into a cloudy crystal set in a network of dark metal filigree. The exchange was soundless, but Trund cringed beneath the impact of Walgur's transmitted scorn.

"You have not yet located the intruder? Have you learned naught from me?" The current of menace always latent under the surface of Walgur's thoughts buffeted Trund with chilling force.

"But Master, I have pronounced all of the seeking spells you have provided." Trund's frantic response moderated as he offered his sole item of good news. "With great diligence, I have set your infallible detection and binding spells, and there has been no sign of magic since that first strange residue I reported to you."

If Trund had expected to be congratulated for his actions, he was miserably disappointed. Walgur's retort burned like a lash against raw flesh. "Lackwit! The damage, whatever it was, had already been done. The only local mage likely to be aware of our prize has to be Otwill. He is a fool, but a subtle one. He may be hidden near you, even now."

Trund started violently. "But . . . what if I find him, Master? I might not be able to defend the prize."

"Calm yourself. I have a puissant spell to disarm all but the mightiest of wizards. Proceed at once to the upper tower room—the one with no windows. Once this spell is pronounced within a chamber, none can break free from the space so sealed. No magic intended to aid in escape can be mustered against these wards. I shall set the spell in your mind to be delivered the once, then it shall be forgotten by you entirely."

Trund pressed his sweating forehead against the crystal. "I hang upon my master's will."

"That you do, most assuredly," Walgur's thought agreed grimly. "Attend!"

Drop awoke early the next morning, as was his habit. Although he'd been shown to a bed in the small adjoining room, he had preferred sleeping on the floor near Flax's grander bed. Not having to bother getting dressed since he hadn't previously undressed, Drop shook out and folded the blankets and riding cloak he'd wrapped himself in to counter the floor drafts. Flax was still snoring gently under a soft down coverlet when the innkeeper's wife tapped at the door to deliver a pot of hot tea and the desired reply from Trund.

Flax, instantly awake, thanked the woman, and gracefully dismissed her from the room so he could read Trund's message in private. "Success!" he exclaimed to Drop. "We are to present ourselves at the castle at the third hour of the morning. If you will see to Bay and our carriage, I shall order our breakfast."

The castle was the largest building that Drop had ever seen, a massive stone-walled assemblage of watch towers and dormer-pierced pitched roofs anchored by a central keep. The castle crouched on a rise of ground bare of trees or useful clinging vines for unobtrusive means of entry. Drop drove beneath a heavily fanged portcullis, surrendered Bay and the carriage to a scruffy stableboy, and followed quietly behind Flax into a vast entrance hall.

They were immediately met at the foot of a wide expanse of stone stairs by a stocky man robed in rust-colored velvet. His close-cropped brown hair was trimmed to a point on his forehead. The chain of office draped across his shoulders was made of a dull, dark metal, with the squared links sharpened to clawlike spikes at their corners.

Drop took an instant dislike to the man. The closer they drew to Trund, the more furiously his nose itched. It wasn't, Drop thought, as if Trund reeked of pepper as Skarn had, but Walgur's assistant was accompanied by a vague aura rather like moldy cheese. His features were undistinguished except for his eyes, which were a muddy brown reminding Drop of two puddles of stagnant water.

Flax proclaimed himself as Martan, buyer of fine furniture, and carelessly jostled his belt purse, producing a most promising jingle of coins. Trund's eyes widened appreciatively at the sound, then he yawned suddenly, excusing himself as having been very late abed the previous night.

"I understand from the innkeeper's wife," said Flax solicitously, "that as caretaker for an absent master, you are solely responsible for this entire castle. It must be an enormous burden, but I'm sure that you manage most capably."

Trund grunted. "What is it you seek to buy, Master Martan?"

"Any spare large pieces you do not need—wardrobes, beds, tables," Flax replied. "I, too, have an absent master in the form of a client who requires a castle of almost this size and grandeur to be fully furnished upon his return."

"Come, then," said Trund, starting up the stairs. "There are many rooms here that are seldom used."

Drop trudged behind them from room to cavernous room. Flax exclaimed enthusiastically over a number of pieces, and suggested prices which Trund appeared to find tempting. Among the items was a large, ornately carved bed with substantial posts extending upward to support a fringed canopy. Flax declared it to be of perfect dimensions to fit his client's primary guest chamber, especially since there was a huge wooden chest of matching design to accompany it. Trund declined to be drawn into idle chatter, hurrying Flax up one set of stairs and down another, until they returned to the entrance hall. Drop's feet ached. He still found shoes to be unnaturally confining, and longed for his own four unshod cat feet.

"Can you then arrange for my prompt removal of these—let me see ..." Flax paused to count. "Seventeen items? I shall, of course, pay you ... let us say, half now, and half upon the removal."

Trund, in turn, hesitated, one hand extended to accept the considerable sum being proffered. With obvious reluctance, he withdrew his hand. "My master is journeying hither from afar," Trund said. "I expect his arrival late upon the morrow. It would be best to be assured of his complete approval in this matter ... and the size and weight of the goods will require the hiring of many carts."

"I quite understand," Flax declared, seizing Trund's hand and pressing a small purse of coins into it. "Let us part now, each to set in order our separate arrangements. I must marshal sufficient carts, and you must prepare for your master's reception. May I call again to confer with him in two days' time?"

Trund pocketed the purse, and showed yellowed teeth in a satisfied smile. "I look forward to that meeting," he said.

Flax's face was grave as they drove back toward the inn. "I dislike being pressed," he complained to Drop, "but we must rescue Otwill this very night, before Walgur arrives."

"Remove the whole bed?" asked Drop plaintively, recalling the endless stairs.

Flax laughed aloud. "I certainly hope not! Otwill is contained in the left footpost, and if we can detach it— *quietly*—we can be away and restore him to his body in safer surroundings. I noted in the inn's stables a most useful flat-ended metal bar. We shall ask to borrow it for prying open a water-soaked chest. And we must confer with Koron. He'll want to come with us, of course ... but I think his most valuable position will be as our outside watchman."

Low clouds obligingly obscured any celestial illumination of the castle grounds as the rescue party made their stealthy approach late that night. As Flax had predicted, Koron had at first demanded to accompany them into the castle, but he was finally persuaded by Flax's argument that an outside guard was vital to their success.

"Consider how well this tactic worked for Otwill before," Flax had pointed out. "Otwill still has his medallion, and should we be forced to unspell him within the castle, he can warn you instantly or transmit instructions. Besides, you have the horses to keep ready."

Flax had been obliged to admit that Bay and the antiquated carriage were not the most rapid means for retreat, so Koron had hired four nimbler steeds which he could bring closer as needed. Drop reconnoitered silently, returning with the welcome news that a window in the kitchen quarters had been left unlatched, and he could easily climb in and admit Flax through a side door.

It was only a short while later that the two of them stood regaining their breath at the foot of the canopied bed concealing Otwill. Flax extracted from his belt the metal pry bar and pushed it gingerly into the joint securing the left footpost to the footboard. His initial pressure on the bar resulted in an alarmingly loud creaking sound.

"Bother!" he whispered to Drop. "The joiner has employed entirely too effective a glue. If we persist, we may

well attract unwelcome attention. Perhaps the side board's
joint is less well secured ... no, I fear not. I do not sense
the presence of any active magic in this room, or nearby;
the feel of it comes from more distant quarters. I see no
other alternative, Drop. I must restore Otwill here, and
then we must *run*."

Three things then happened with remarkable dispatch.
As Flax pronounced several quiet words, Drop's skin tingled fiercely and his hair rose on his neck; the bedpost
glowed a startling blue, disgorging an elderly, somewhat
disheveled man who sat down with a thump on the floor;
and worst of the three events by far, Drop simultaneously
felt his body paralyzed, as it had been once before when
Skarn had employed an immobilizing spell. Both Flax and
Otwill were similarly affected, frozen in slightly off-bal-
ance positions.

Soon after, at the open door, a flaring torch appeared,
flourished by Trund, who seemed initially startled then
deeply gratified by the bountiful catch in his trap.

"Caught you!" Trund crowed. "Master Walgur will be
pleased." He poked the hapless Otwill, who tumbled over
on his side, unable to prevent the fall. "So this was our
original intruder—Otwill." Trund spat the name. "Thought
you were clever, did you? Master Walgur will find out how
you concealed yourself. I placed his binding spell myself,
so that the instant any magic was invoked, the participants
would be bound. And now to settle you in special quarters
to await my master. You will admire the containment spell
cast there—no magic that could assist escape can function,
not even something subtle like jiggling the stone blocks to
loosen the mortar. I shall take one of you at a time, I think
... you first, old fool."

To Drop's distress, Trund shoved Flax over from his
standing position onto a narrow rug, which he then folded
back across the wizard so he could haul him roughly across
the floor. Otwill went next, then it was Drop's turn. Trund
chuckled as his unwilling burden bumped crosswise up the
stairs. This, Drop thought to himself, has to be worse than
bouncing about on a horse; I shall be bruised all over.

Not for Drop's sake, but due to his own physical strain,
Trund relented after the second flight of stairs, throwing
Drop over his shoulder for the rest of the trip. Long

stretches of dark corridors reeled past, more endless, narrow stairs—Drop tried to focus his battered thoughts. They must be climbing up into one of the towers. Trund lurched through a metal-bound door into a shadowed room, dumped Drop callously on a very hard floor, and slammed the door behind him. Above the metallic rattle of a key in the lock, Drop heard Trund's repellant chuckle, then that, too, receded and he was left in cramped silence. Although drastically diminished from his cat's night vision, Drop's ability to see in the dark was better than most humans. He quickly made out a nearby leg belonging to Flax, and unable to move to see beyond that, he could hear labored breathing, presumably from Otwill.

Just as he had recovered faster than a normal human from Skarn's binding spell, Drop again recovered movement first. After rubbing his aching limbs to check for broken bones, he hurried to examine Flax, aiding the old wizard to coax his stiff back into a sitting position. A muffled groan signaled Otwill's return to self-control.

Massaging his fingers, Flax at once apologized to his companions. "I deeply regret this outcome, but I saw no other way to free you, Otwill. I must say, Walgur's binding spell was masterfully formulated. There was absolutely no warning indication of its presence until my release spell freed you, and entrapped us."

Otwill extended a somewhat shaky hand to steady himself. "Think nothing of it, my dear friend. I should have done the same in your place. Do you suppose, from what that scoundrel said, we might be allowed to conjure a small light?" A pale spark erupted from Otwill's finger, and grew to a respectable light source, making movement safer and examination of their cell possible.

"Well done!" said Flax. "Could you signal ... a certain person with your talisman? He is waiting to hear from us."

Otwill cocked his head to one side, fishing within his robe for his own pendant. Flax and Drop waited expectantly, but Otwill's face mirrored his lack of success.

"No," he reported. "The hampering spell on this chamber evidently will not allow any calls for help as well as purely physical efforts to escape."

Flax critically surveyed the bare cell, walled and floored with smooth stone. "Singularly unattractive abode, isn't it?

No windows, no furniture, not even a wall hanging. Hmm ... I do see a pair of narrow slits above the door, presumably for ventilation, but none of us is of a size to fit through them. By the way, Otwill, this is Drop, my assistant. He was a cat when he came to my cottage during the Spring rains, but he accidentally ate one of your Keep-Shape Spell lozenges, and turned into a lad."

"How do, young man?" said Otwill warmly. "So much more congenial, cat to lad, than my own sad experience with that spell. My human apprentice who tried it turned into a toad." Otwill's amiable mood sharpened into active cogitation. "*Cat,* you say? Flax, I may have a solution to our problem, but not one that you may welcome."

"Nonsense," Flax declared. "Any solution is preferable to waiting helplessly here for Walgur's triumphant arrival, which his minion told us was to be late on the morrow."

Otwill nodded. "The more reason for haste, then. Suppose ... if Drop were restored to his original cat form, might he not pass through one of those ventilation slits and seek ... our mutual friend?"

Drop could see that Flax was perturbed. After a moment's consideration, the wizard turned to him and said, "You must be the one to decide, Drop. We cannot ask you to do this against your will. Do not answer lightly, for if Master Otwill has in mind the spell I suspect, once it is invoked, its actions may not be again undone. You must understand that if you agree, you will be a cat again for the rest of your life."

Against my will? thought Drop. From the instant he had heard the words "restored to his original cat form," Drop's body had tensed into total alertness, as if an unwary mouse had poked its head out of a sheltered nook. To be *himself* again! To possess his night sight, his cat's nose, his tail, his matchless sense of balance, his rightness of being as he was born to be. . . .

"Yes, please," Drop said firmly. "I would like to return to my real self."

"Brave lad!" said Otwill, and Flax clapped him on the shoulder.

A daunting thought struck Drop. "But could such a spell work in this room?" he asked.

Flax looked at Otwill, who shrugged. "If I recall aright,

the stricture is against any magical effort to escape," Otwill observed. "I conjured our light without interference. Changing the shape of this lad is scarcely an overt effort to escape, strictly speaking."

Flax gazed at Drop. "If you are *sure*," he said, "then we can but try the spell."

In wordless answer, Drop knelt before Otwill. Otwill shut his eyes for a moment, then pronounced some unintelligible sounds. At first, Drop feared that Walgur's escape-prevention spell was again prevailing; then suddenly his human body began to shrink. His field of view lowered to his old familiar range, and yes! His great clumsy human feet reduced to their proper neat, clawed size. He shook himself free of his confining former clothes and stretched himself luxuriantly. To have a tail again, and whiskers—to *be* a cat!

Flax drew closer to Otwill and whispered, "Could you possibly set a message in your talisman . . . a message that Drop could carry to our friend so that he would know that the cat is actually Drop, and he must follow him to our aid?"

"Just so. A splendid idea." Otwill pulled his neck chain off over his head and concentrated on the pedant. Drop came forward so that the chain could be secured around his neck.

Flax, being taller than Otwill, lifted the cat up as far as he could, and by reaching with his front claws extended, Drop just barely attained enough foothold to pull himself up to the ventilation slit. With a wriggle, he was through to the other side. By setting his claws in the rough wood of the door, he climbed far enough down for a safe leap to the outside corridor's floor. Now to find the quickest way to Koron.

Drop raced down the hall, descended a twisting flight of stairs, and started through another corridor. His attention was so firmly fixed on his goal that he didn't sense until too late the cross current from a side passageway. He had just registered the stir of air against his fur when a much greater force was applied to him: a human hand closed cruelly on the nape of his neck. Instinctively, Drop first froze, then relaxed, as all cats do, the behavior pattern ingrained in them from kittenhood when their mothers carry them so.

The master of this grip, however, was Trund, and his intentions for transport were not those of a protective mother cat. "First wizards break in, and now cats run loose," he muttered. "What other vermin next?" Tramping irritably on the rush-strewn paving, Trund strode out onto a small balcony open to the still-dark sky. "We have a quick remedy for vermin here, cat," Trund exclaimed, and before Drop could take a breath, he felt himself pitched violently out into space.

Instinct again ordered his reactions. Like any cat dropped from a height, Drop first straightened his back, then sought to level his head. His night vision revealed a courtyard rushing up from below. When he landed on the gravel surface, his legs were fully extended and his muscles loose. The considerable impact did strike the breath from his lungs for an instant, but he soon recovered. As he examined his surroundings, Drop reflected that while being thrown from a balcony had not been his favored means of descent, it *was* undeniably the fastest way to reach Koron at ground level.

The sound and scent of horses drew him quickly to Koron's hiding place behind the hedgerow nearest to the castle. For a few moments, Drop was frustrated in not being able to attract Koron's attention. Human speech, he realized, did have certain advantages in that regard. He *had* to deliver Otwill's vital message in the talisman. Drop finally chose the direct approach. He leapt into Koron's arms and rubbed the pendant firmly against the apprentice's wrist.

Koron naturally bent to examine the dangling metal object and recognized it at once. "Master Otwill!" he blurted. Squatting to place Drop on the ground, Koron swiftly unfastened the chain from the cat's neck and held the talisman in his palm.

Drop watched with interest as Koron's face consecutively registered relief, dismay, and grim determination. "Drop," Koron said, "I hope that I may show bravery such as yours. Master Otwill tells me you have given up your human form to secure his escape. He has described their spell-blocked cell, and suggests a means I may use from outside the door to free our masters. You must guide me there at once. These horses will be safe here tethered to the shrubs. Lead on—I follow." Koron slipped Otwill's medallion over his head to join his own pendant, leaving his hands free for any climbing or fighting that might be necessary.

Drop thought it wise not to attempt their second entry at the same place, in case Trund might have set a trap there. On his way out of the castle, Drop had noted a tradesman's gate in a remote back wall. Its interior latch was closed, but the gap between gate and wall provided ample space for a sturdy knife blade to be inserted to lift the bar. Koron dealt quietly with the gate, leaving it unobtrusively ajar for their hoped-for return passage. Otwill had evidently impressed upon Koron the necessity for complete stealth. Drop led the way cautiously, using all his cat senses to provide advance warning of any sign of Trund. The cat and the apprentice sifted through the shadowed passageways almost without stirring any dust. Drop deliberately sought a different route to the tower stairs, desiring no further encounters, if possible, with Trund.

They reached the cell door without incident. In the semi-darkness, Koron pressed his hands against the lock mechanism. Trund, regretfully, had not left the key in or near the lock. Koron whispered to Drop, "Master Otwill has suggested that a basic unlocking spell applied from this outside corridor should be beyond the strictures of the containment spell holding within the chamber. If it works, we must then run for the horses by the most direct way."

Drop moved to one side. In his cat form, all his fur tended to rise during magical pronouncements. Koron's simple spell only stirred Drop's fur, but it had a more gratifying effect on the lock. As Koron eased the door open, rays of Otwill's conjured light spilled into the corridor. In seconds, Flax and Otwill joined their rescuers. Otwill hastened to reduce his light source to the merest glow near their feet so they wouldn't fall down unexpected staircases.

Drop had already started toward the quickest escape route, but to his surprise, Otwill tugged at Koron's sleeve and murmured, "This way—we must hurry!" As Otwill darted off down a branching passageway unfamiliar to Drop, the apprehensive party tiptoed after Otwill's dim shape. He led them to an anteroom outside another tower room, and paused to catch his breath. "Not fit for this sort of midnight exertion at my age," he grumbled.

"Master," pleaded Koron, "let us away! I have horses waiting. . . ."

Otwill patted Koron's shoulder. "Most efficient of you, but we have an urgent task here that must be accomplished first. Let us protect ourselves from unfriendly interruption. Flax, if you would pronounce Brand's magic-aversion spell? I shall deal with this door."

Drop's fur rose as the two wizards chanted. Otwill swung open the door into a sparsely furnished tower room whose outer wall was pierced by two slit windows suitable for firing defensive arrows at besiegers.

"This *has* to be the room," Otwill declared, pacing impatiently to and fro, as if he expected at any instant to bump into some invisible barrier.

Flax quartered the space behind him. "A portal, you said? Can it be detected before it opens?"

Otwill sighed. "That is the difficulty. We know so little of such rare manifestations. My studies suggest that this castle occupies a particular space which under certain celestial influences can provide access to other . . ."

"Spaces," finished Flax. "We had best occupy ourselves in locating the access point. Koron and Drop can stand guard for us."

Koron nervously scanned the room for a better potential weapon than his belt knife, settling at last on a narrow but sturdy chair. Drop slipped out into the corridor to listen and smell for intruders. He was well justified in this precaution, for Trund was even then drawing near. Unfortunately for the friends, Trund's approach could not be easily sensed, for he was stalking through a passageway concealed in the castle walls.

Trund was highly agitated. As soon as he had locked the captive wizards away, he had sped to contact Walgur, but all his repeated efforts to reach his master had failed. Walgur was not concurrently attuned to the crystal, and no amount of cursing or importuning succeeded in summoning the sorceror. When Koron had opened the tower door, freeing Flax and Otwill, Trund was lashed by Walgur's warning spell. He made one last frantic, useless attempt to call the sorceror before plunging into the secret passageways. Finding his captives gone, Trund roared with frustration, then focused his attention on locating the escapees.

The warning spell again jangled Trund's nerves: he was momentarily stricken to realize that the enemy had identified the very room from which they *must* be excluded at all costs. If only Master Walgur were here, Trund thought desperately ... but he was not, and Trund was his sole agent at hand capable of defending Walgur's prize. He cudgeled his memory for useful spells. A plague of scorpions might be effective, or blasts of dragonfire. Resolved to protect his master's property, Trund fairly sprinted along the secret passageway, slowing only when there was scarcely room to creep forward. He emerged surreptitiously behind a tapestry in the very corridor outside the anteroom.

From the corner of his eye, Drop caught an unnatural stirring of fabric. Boots protruded slightly beneath the wall hanging—Trund! Instantly, Drop raced inside to warn Koron, who paled, but braced himself resolutely beside the door, out of view to any entrant, his chair balanced for offensive action.

Trund stepped gingerly across the threshold, then halted, raising his arms. Sighting Flax and Otwill busily moving about within the tower room, Trund bellowed a vile spell. Simultaneously, Koron took a step forward and broke his chair over Trund's head. Dazed, Trund sank to the floor, as Flax and Otwill rushed to the tower doorway. Koron lifted a broken chair arm and clouted the groaning Trund, who was struggling to rise; this time, Trund fell back senseless.

Otwill's face registered shock. "Flax, did you hear what spell he was invoking?" he demanded. "Flaming slime *and* scorpions!"

"Fortunate that we had anticipated some such attack," said Flax genially. "As for you, young man," he added to Koron, "I commend your swift action. Let this be a lasting lesson to you—a wizard must *always* be on guard for unexpected assaults, both magical and nonmagical."

Koron hastened to share the praise. "Drop alerted me that someone was coming."

Flax stroked Drop's head. "Come within, both of you, and see what Otwill and I have discovered."

Drop's skin prickled and his fur rose when he entered the tower room. He quickly moved well to one side to keep a prudent distance away from the most prominent feature now dominating the space. Near the center of the room, about a foot above the stone floor, hovered an oblong opening rather like a great tear in a curtain, except in this case, the pierced fabric was the very air itself.

Koron gasped when Flax casually stepped through the hole and vanished from their sight. Drop stared at the eerie gap, which shimmered in the light Otwill had conjured to illuminate the room. This magic portal, Drop thought, looked like a panel of white satin whose shifting texture suggested a moving surface. Although one couldn't see into what lay beyond the boundary's opening, sound penetrated freely, for they could hear Flax's voice clearly.

"I believe your conjecture is valid, Otwill," Flax called. "This portal is not evil in itself, but what lies on this side of it might be used for evil purposes."

Otwill followed Flax, disappearing through the opening as if he had dived into a pool of milk. "Then you agree with me, Master Flax, that we must prevent Walgur from gaining access to this portal?"

"By all means!" Flax concurred.

Drop looked at Koron, who was apparently torn between a desire to join his master and a strong reluctance to take the necessary final step after him.

Again, an unnatural peripheral movement alerted Drop. Trund had recovered consciousness, and was creeping silently toward Koron, whose back was turned to the tower door. From Trund's point of view, the sole visible human occupant of the room was Otwill's apprentice, and Trund planned to dispatch him with a dagger stroke since the two scurvy, happily absent wizards had blocked any magical assault.

Hoping to warn Koron, Drop hissed loudly, and leapt at Trund, but Trund was simultaneously lunging forward, and the cat's claws merely scraped Trund's boot tops in passing. Startled by the noise and movement, Koron half turned in time to parry Trund's dagger thrust. Recovering his balance, Drop surveyed the struggling pair as they lurched back and forth. Choosing his opportunity, Drop inserted himself at Trund's feet just as Trund was leaning far forward. With a despairing cry, Trund tripped over Drop and fell through the portal, carrying Koron entangled with him.

Drop heard a flurry of muffled blows from the other side,

then Otwill's voice exclaimed, "Now that we've bound him with your outer robe, Flax, we must keep this Trund fellow with us on this side of the portal to prevent him from warning Walgur."

"Oh, spare me, masters!" Trund wailed. "I beseech you! Walgur has forced me to slave for him against my will. I would gladly serve you."

"Would you, indeed?" remarked Flax dryly. "We shall have to consider such a proposal." His voice took on a more scholarly note. "Otwill, have you noticed? The portal opening seems to have contracted."

"I'm not surprised," Otwill replied. "The conjunction of the moon and other factors shift constantly over time. Unless we exert a counterforce, the portal will probably close by itself."

"But then it could potentially be reopened," Flax pointed out.

Drop could now see that the size of the opening was visibly shrinking. The wizards' voices from the other side were also becoming thinner and more tenuous.

"Better for us to be on this side of the portal, and Walgur on the other side, don't you agree?" Flax suggested. "If we pronounce a sealing spell here, this portal will be permanently inaccessible to Walgur."

"But we couldn't get out, either," objected Koron.

"We're wizards, lad. No doubt there are other portals to be discerned in this peculiar place. We must hasten while we can work our spell in peace." Flax's voice was now only a mere thread of sound. "Farewell, Drop! We may not meet again for some time," he called, "but . . ."

Otwill's fading voice overrode Flax's with a parting exhortation. "Drop—go to Gilmont! Gilm . . ."

Any further words were lost as the remaining small shimmering area rippled, and quite abruptly, the opening in the air was gone as if it had never been.

Drop's fur slowly settled back in place, aided by a few swipes by his paw. He knew that the portal was by now magically sealed from the other side, never to reopen in this castle. Walgur would not be able to reach that strange other space as he had planned. Still, Walgur was probably well on his way here to attempt the transit, so it was not prudent to linger overlong. Drop doubted that the sorcerer would be at all favorably impressed by the information he would retrieve from his warding spells, nor would he be pleased by Trund's disappearance.

Pale, pre-dawn light was penetrating through the castle windows as Drop made his way warily to the outer world. He recalled Koron's saying that the hired staff came to work about dawn—another reason for haste. He blessed Koron for leaving their exit gate ajar, since his paws could not have worked the heavy latch mechanism. Happily, cats' paws were quite sufficient to scratch loose the horses' reins, which Koron had merely looped over the hedge bush branches. Freed, the hired horses ambled singlemindedly back toward their home stables, and would probably arrive in time, Drop thought, for a hearty breakfast.

Drop himself also required provisions, but he had no worry about his ability to feed himself in a city populated by more rats and mice than people. Still, winter was coming. Koron had briefly mentioned his former master, Gilmont, whose house was near the city; Koron had neglected to say exactly where Gilmont lived. As a noted scholar, though, Gilmont must frequently seek scrolls and books, so Drop could listen for his name in likely places. Besides, Otwill had virtually ordered Drop to find Gilmont. It was therefore reasonable to assume that if and when Otwill and Flax managed to return from the space beyond the portal, they would expect to meet Drop at Gilmont's house.

Drop's strategy of finding clues to Gilmont by listening around the shops and barrows of booksellers proved to be inspired. Scarcely a week later, Drop overheard a tradesman tell a stallholder at a corner market that old Gilmont had just returned to the city, and he had a shipment of books to be sent to his house. Drop nimbly jumped aboard the wagon, and was delivered directly to Gilmont's door.

Gilmont was a more sedentary scholar than Flax, chiefly due to his girth. His country house was all that an active cat could desire—it had several warm hearths, and padded window seats where a cat could doze in the sun, and besides a champion cook (whose savory fare was responsible for Gilmont's stoutness), the grounds abounded with meadow mice to vary Drop's indoor diet of fish and cream.

Gilmont had been somewhat surprised to find a blue-eyed gray cat among his boxes of books, but he was delighted to acquire so keen a mouser.

Drop felt that he was perfectly situated to await the return of Otwill and Flax. Meantime, he could keep up his old human skills while perching on the back of Gilmont's chair.

"I could swear," observed Gilmont, as he unrolled an ornate scroll, "that cat is reading every word over my shoulder."

Of course, said Drop, but all the old scholar heard was a contented purr.

TO SKEIN A CAT

by Lawrence Schimel

Almost like surgeons in a prep room endlessly putting on and taking off their gloves, the kittens sat on the bench of the loom and played with their mittens. They could not tire of watching the sudden transformation, when the anonymous digits of mitten and paw became fingers. They would curl their human hands into a fist, or flex each finger singly, before tearing the mittens off to try them on again, watching more closely for that moment the change took place.

The hands were massive on their slim kitten limbs, though the kittens would, in time, grow into them. The skin hung tight like a glove over each invisible hand, the extra flesh dangling limply past the wrist like a tattered hem. Curious, they tried to peek beneath the skin, to see that magical hand underneath, but each time they tried found only their furred paw and the mitten slid off. They might have marveled less if it were their own skin that was lifted off, the peeling back a layer of paw which revealed the fingers underneath, unfurling like petals from a single bud. Whenever the mittens were removed they expected a slight distortion—an afterimage of the hand, perhaps—but the only fuzziness they found was their own fur.

Lachesis smiled as she watched the kittens play. They were wholly absorbed by their mittens, completely uninterested in the tapestry mere inches away, that vital tapestry she wove.

Even after agreeing to Clotho's begging for a kitten, Lachesis had been plagued with doubts. Atropos had been against the plan from the outset, arguing that "a cat will get in the weaving" and "you can't keep a cat from thread." It had been, in part, these insistances which swayed Lachesis, for Atropos said them with the assurance of having the last word. The arguments had also too closely matched Lachesis' first instinct to Clotho's plea: to declare, "absolutely not."

But the company, Lachesis realized, would be welcome: motion and life about the house, a warm body curled against her on the bench as she worked, soothing with a gentle purr. The others were hardly there, Clotho always outside playing, spinning, Atropos lost in memory, conversing with old friends now long dead.

"No good will come of this," Atropos had said. "Mark my words." After which, she said no more against the matter. Even when Clotho and Lachesis came home from the pound with three kittens instead of the proposed one, Atropos did not comment, though the tight set of her lip and the reserved, steely gray of her eyes were ample evidence she thought the affair an exercise in folly.

Lachesis and Clotho had been torn with indecision, each preferring a different cat. They convinced themselves that a single kitten would be lonely, and therefore chose more than one. Three was the logical number—one for each, despite Atropos' adamance against the idea.

Clotho picked a white Abyssinian, fussing over it tremendously, hardly willing to put the kitten down. She deliberated on a number of names, wanting especially to call him Cloud because he was soft and fluffy. In the end, she settled on Cotton. Upon being introduced to him, Atropos' one remark was, "It will shed everywhere."

Lachesis chose a frisky calico. "I will name you Mischief," she told her kitten, "for there is mischief in all creativity. But I will call you Chief so that you learn to tame your spark, to harness it. Your personalities will war with each other as the colors on your back do: order and law with magic and wild mirth." At their introduction, Chief did not stay long enough for Atropos to make a comment, but bounded from Lachesis' arms to sniff and explore the house.

For the third, Clotho and Lachesis had decided upon a gray kitten, small enough to fit into a single cupped palm of Clotho's delicate young hands and smooth as a pussy willow blossom. All Atropos would say when they presented him to her was, "grim," which Lachesis and Clotho assumed was what she wanted the cat to be named. And so he was called, though the name did not seem to suit him, for he was lively and playful, even long after he out-grew kittenhood.

Despite her own delight in having the new kittens, Atropos' comments had continued to nag Lachesis, though the old woman no longer voiced them. But seeing them now—their obvious pleasure with the mittens she had made them, the possibilities open to them with the transforma-tion—Lachesis could not help but feel assured those doubts were groundless. She tried, therefore, to ignore the relent-less clacking as Atropos tipped forward and back in her rocker, mute, concentrating instead on Clotho's gentle laughter and the kittens' own pleasures.

Soon, of course, the kittens discovered the usefulness of thumbs:

They could carve turkeys they took from the refrigerator.

Gates and doors no longer posed an obstacle. Likewise drawers and tins of sardines or tuna.

Garbage lids could be quietly removed, the cans them-selves slowly lowered to the ground, and the neighbors never the wiser that Grim was browsing.

Dogs could be discouraged by well-aimed objects: flow-erpots, hard rocks, whatever lay nearby. Or, playing on their highly distractable canine natures, the kittens threw sticks or balls, giving themselves time enough to execute a dignified escape, or, as a most desperate measure, scale a tree.

The kittens could not, alas, walk with the mittens on. Their fingers were not strong enough to support their weights, and, when they tried walking with the hands rolled into fists, they bruised their knuckles and could not use the hands from pain. So they pulled the mittens off when they moved between place, and wondered at the odd sensations of walking on four limbs. Often they looked like a trio of mother cats on parade, with their newborn kittens dangling by the napes of their necks, for they carried the mittens in their mouths, waiting only for the moment they could stop and put them on once more.

The mittens were not without their purposes, mere toys; the kittens were required to help with the weaving.

"By requiring them to work with the wool," Lachesis had often explained to Atropos, "they will satisfy their kittenish instincts for string in a useful and productive manner. Furthermore, as they will be under my supervision, I can insure that no harm is done to the tapestry."

The reassurances were mostly for Lachesis' own benefit, for Atropos continued to remain silent on the matter. The only reason Lachesis was at all nervous, was because things seemed to go *too* smoothly. They were, after all, kittens, she thought.

But nothing happened. Grim and Chief would spend hours on either side of the loom, tossing the shuttlecock between them as Lachesis worked the foot pedals. Cotton lounged on the bench, too dignified and prim for such playful sport. Often, his purrs and cuddles against her side were rewarded by gentle strokes of Lachesis' now-free hands.

A cat is a big change in a person's life. The change is directly proportional: three cats spread over three women is easily enough havoc for nine lifetimes.

"We should have gotten a Manx!" Atropos cried out, whenever Grim's tail got caught beneath her rocker. She would lift her great iron shears above her head and threaten the kittens: *snip, snap.*

It was only natural the kittens should be attracted to Atropos; she was a challenge. Atropos also liked to sit in the sun all day, until she was called upon to cut the threads for the next day's weaving when evening fell.

"You must agree," Lachesis demanded of Atropos, "that they have their merits. The extra pair of hands around the house."

Grudgingly, Atropos mumbled her agreement.

Though Lachesis was quite pleased with the results of her fabrications, and the extra help around the house, she was concerned that the hands were making the kittens too human. Hands are a big change in a cat's life; their human thumbs, it seemed, made them think with human logic.

In the kitchen, for instance, while Clotho was still too young to take much interest in the preparation of their meals, and Atropos disinterested in such matters because her diet was heavily restricted, the cats never tired of playing with food. Lachesis could leave them at work—Grim chopping wild asparagus for soup, Chief kneading dough with even pressure—and spend an idle moment staring out the window at Clotho in the back yard.

Have I done more harm than good with the mittens I wove, Lachesis wondered. They've become so independent that Clotho has lost interest in playing with them, though Cotton remains always ready to be fussed over.

Perhaps I worry too much. Clotho is simply busy with work, Lachesis thought. The child was always spinning.

Lachesis smiled as she watched Clotho spread her arms wide and spin the maple seeds down from their trees.

The kittens were, however, still kittens, and Lachesis' musings were curtailed by a hiss from Cotton. Turning from the window she found them engaged in a foodfight: a barrage of the hard, leftover bottoms of asparagus stalks flying through the air. Once discovered, Chief tossed up a handful of flour, creating a smokescreen white as their victim to cover their escape.

"They act like such children, sometimes," Lachesis would tell Cotton as she tried to soothe his injured pride, pulling sticky clumps of dough from his long fur and scratching beneath his chin. It was because of Cotton's vanity, his disdain of work, that they ganged up on him. Though Lachesis often wished he would reform—both for the work he might accomplish, and so there might be domestic peace—she enjoyed having someone to spoil, a youngest child. She fed Cotton chicken livers as she finished the preparations Grim and Chief had abandoned.

Life settled back into its routines. There was always the work to be done: for Clotho the thread to spin, Lachesis the fabric to weave, and Atropos the lives to cut short. Though the work was always the same, it had its daily sense of achievement to carry them through. The kittens likewise helped keep things from becoming monotonous: a vole left upon the doorstep, their playful tussles upon the rug, even their simple presence: familiar and comfortable as if they had always been part of that household, and yet so surprising in their freshness, the way the world looked new to them no matter how often they looked upon it.

The kittens remained curious about their mittens, and the magic hands that sprang from them. Bored one day, when Lachesis and the others were out, they sat together in a corner and tried to puzzle out the workings once more. They tried to peek beneath each others' mittens, but without success. They decided to turn a mitten inside out.

Chief took her hands off, and shifted her weight back and forth between her paws as Grim began to turn the left mitten inside out. He inverted the mitten slowly, tentatively pulling back the woolen fabric. His nervous prudence might have been more noble had the mitten exploded when its magic was reversed. But after he had revealed the moonwhite lining and the mitten was completely inside out, it simply disappeared.

Chief yowled as she stared at the empty spot her mitten had once occupied. She dove for her other mitten, shoving her paw deep into its warm depths. Nothing happened. Without its mate to complete the pair it was a normal mitten.

Cotton's tail swished in agitation as he tried to shush Chief. He was nervous at being found in their guilty company.

Grim gave Chief his left mitten to try on, to see if having a pair might not revive hers. Chief thrust her left paw into it, and watched as the familiar transformation took place, endowing her with a human hand. But only one. Her own mitten lay lifeless still, a simple piece of fabric.

Chief and Grim stared at each other's single hands, desperately trying to think of a way out of this dilemma. How could Chief live without her hands? Cotton folded his hands under him and sat on them, guarding them by keeping them hidden from sight.

Chief gave Grim his hand back. Grim flexed them both, twiddled his thumbs for a moment, then slipped the right off. The magic seemed to be on the inside of the mittens, since their power dissipated when they were turned inside out; placing a still-magical mitten *over* Chief's now-mundane one might revive it.

Gingerly, Chief slipped her own mitten on, irrationally hoping they had made a mistake, that her magical hand would appear as it used to before their experiment. When it did not, she tried to stifle the disappointment, pushing it deep down inside of her, past her stomach into the tip of her tail, which swished back and forth. Not daring to hope this time, she tried Grim's mitten on atop her own. Nothing happened.

Grim felt a tingling in the fingers of his left hand, and suddenly they went numb. He reached out to take his right mitten back, but his human hand slipped off and fell to the floor, a normal mitten, leaving his naked paw outstretched.

Both Grim and Chief turned to Cotton, who hissed and bolted away, running on the tops of his knuckles since he didn't dare to take the mittens off.

Grim and Chief chased after him. He was their last hope. Sometime, before Lachesis or the others came home, Cotton had to weave them both a new set of mittens.

Their human hands had unlocked the mystery of doors for the kittens, the secrets that lived on the other side. But doors were once again Grim and Chief's bane; Cotton had closed the bedroom door behind him. Desperate, Chief and Grim had tried to weave the mittens on their own, but again the door proved their ruin, the slamming door that signaled Lachesis and the others were home. The noise startled them, and Atropos' huge iron shears fell from their paws, slicing through the tapestry to clatter against the floor.

Lachesis came running at the sound, followed almost immediately by Clotho. Even Atropos hurried in, although it might have been simply for the pleasure of saying "I told you so."

The kittens were too frightened to run as the women ran up to them and saw the hole in the tapestry. "Atlantis!" Lachesis cried. "I had such hopes for you!"

"I knew it was a bad idea to get a cat," Atropos said, slowly lowering herself against the bench to retrieve her shears from beneath the loom.

"Why?" Lachesis yelled at the cats, "why did you have to sink all my plans."

"Look," Clotho said softly. "They've lost their mittens."

Lachesis looked down at the mittenless kittens and said, "We, especially, should never have tempted fate by trying to change their nature. We made them too human by giving them hands. And of course we couldn't see what would happen; the tapestry is cut here. And the fault lies right in front of our noses, with ourselves."

Grim and Chief relaxed slightly when they realized Lachesis was no longer yelling at them, but they still felt nervously guilty sitting there on the bench of the loom.

"We?" Atropos asked, at the same time as Clotho wondered, "But where's Cotton?"

Hearing his name, Cotton opened the door to the bedroom and hurried into Clotho's arms.

"These were too much of a good thing," Lachesis sighed, as she pulled Cotton's mittens off. He didn't protest. Cotton would miss them least of all, Lachesis thought, especially since this means he'll need to be coddled more.

Life settled back into a routine, of course.

There was always the work to be done, the spinning, the weaving, the cutting of the threads.

Some nights the kittens' paws twitch, as if they still had hands: Chief carves turkeys in her sleep, while Grim slowly lowers the neighbor's trash can to the ground.

Though Chief still likes to be independent and do things for herself, she has learned to let herself be coddled and fed, and Grim now takes great satisfaction in the clatter of trash cans falling to the ground. Grim has, in fact, become enamoured with noise in general, and, with the help of a few local toms, caterwauls atop the fences all night.

The women have grown used to them being ordinary cats. Clotho has begun to help in the kitchen, and the kittens sit on the counter and demand to be fed scraps. They still love to play with string, but won't go near the loom, not even Cotton. Lachesis is too busy to stroke his fur, now, but he waits for her, each night, while the other cats are out wandering.

Even Atropos has come to appreciate them. When she rocks over Grim's tail she still says they should have gotten a Manx. But, sometimes, when no one else is looking, she'll reach down and scratch behind his ears, or even put her iron shears on the floor and let him sit in the sun on her lap, so long as he doesn't purr too loudly.

ASKING MR. BIGELOW
by Susan Shwartz

They'll think you're crazy. It was the same tape that always played in her head. Lisa had spent a lifetime cringing when she heard those words from parents or friends, never daring to ask them to stop. She dodged a suit, a street person, and a stroller that seemed determined to pass right through where she was standing and headed down into the station.

As she fished her sunglasses out of her purse and thrust them on with shaking hands, she nearly jabbed herself in the eye. You were allowed to wince if you poked yourself in the eye, weren't you? You were even allowed to cry.

People cried all the time on the subway. Discreetly, like secretaries who'd just gotten laid off so their bosses could have bigger bonuses. Noisily, like toddlers who had the good sense to hate the E train. Unabashedly, like the teenagers who'd just broken up. Or wildly, like the crazies who could turn hysteria into a great way to get a seat at rush hour.

No one noticed. Not the poke in the eye, not the red sunglasses she had bought to make herself look more cheerful, and certainly not Lisa herself.

You'd think someone would ask "what's wrong?" She even had her answer all ready. "I've got the mother of all migraines," she'd say. Brave, perky, guaranteed to win a smile. If Dana at work said that, people would be pulling Advil and Excedrin out of their purses, practically dragging her to the nurse, and sending her home in a taxi. (Last time Lisa was sick, with a bad back, they had heaped her desk with everyone else's least-favorite projects. "Who's your backup?" the cockiest of the secretaries had asked. "My back's fine," she had replied, touched that someone had bothered. "That isn't what I asked. You weren't here, and I needed those memos." Seething, Lisa had apologized and fetched the memos.)

No one asked. No one ever asked. And she was proud of herself: she didn't actually cry.

You don't want people to think you're weird, the usual self-help tape in her head came on. No, she didn't. She was armored against it, not just in the sunglasses, but in concealment that, over the years, had become solitary confinement. And she had avoided it so successfully that people barely thought of her at all. Especially not for promotions at work. Her fingers caressed the yellow envelope of the card she held—a picture of a black and white cat holding a salmon skeleton, with the message inside: *Better luck next time.* It wasn't losing the promotion and the raise; it was the unexpected kindness that made her glad that the red sunglasses were so big.

The younger woman who got the job—no one said she was weird. Or scared her for making a dumb mistake. Or assumed that of course she'd be in the office the day after Thanksgiving just the way she always had. Or that she wouldn't mind covering while all the people the next level up went to lunch with the new Senior Vice President. Dana would go now, too. Of course.

Also, of course, Dana had gotten cards congratulating her; hard to believe that there were that many dancing-cat cards in the world. *You don't want them to think you're a sore loser.* So Lisa had stopped by the party Dana's friends had thrown, made herself smile, sip the sweet cheap champagne, and even eat a bite of chocolate mousse cake. She had even meant congratulations. You couldn't help but like Dana, especially when she smiled.

But still ... but still, Lisa kept waiting for it to be her turn. She worked hard and got good performance reviews. She tried hard. She had always tried hard and never taken a cent from anyone. And she'd succeeded after a fashion. *Nice life, for a rough draft.*

You try too *hard,* she had always been told. People could go crazy between not trying and trying too hard, yet that was the place she'd lived her whole life.

"*Ask* for the job as executive assistant," a coworker had urged her. She liked mothering Lisa, worrying over her and giving her advice and didn't even get mad at the "yes buts" that were all Lisa could muster in the way of reply

"It's not like a secretary—more an assistant manager. You're qualified. And it's still posted. You could get it. But you have to ask."

The post called for someone to be right-hand man—or woman—to the new senior VP, who was so new that no one knew his name. Or her name, though Lisa was betting on it being a "him." Lisa's stomach clenched. Her usual way of dealing with senior management was to duck her head and ask someone else to bring in whatever material had been asked for. If she got this job—assuming it didn't go to someone with more flair—she would have to work directly with vice presidents, and maybe worse. Besides, she would have to *ask,* risk being turned down, risk being scolded for thinking of herself, risk—worst of all—being laughed at. *You actually think we'd give anything that good to* you?

Real people didn't ask. *Real* people didn't have to. She could still hear other people, lucky, entitled people saying "It just happened!" and laughing over the good fortune that meant opportunities simply dropped into her lap. *That's not really the way it is, you know,* the tapes in her head told her. But those messages clashed with all the other ones that *nice people wait to be asked.*

Was a raise worth all that worry? Maybe not a raise, but a career, a life. Yet what if she failed?

Damned if you do, damned if you don't. And if not damned, stalled. Paralyzed, unable to move, let alone to climb. As indeed she was.

Lisa fixed her eyes on the Purina Cat Chow poster with its pampered ginger cat across the subway car from her and wished that this could have been one of the cars with the broken lights. Even if those weren't safe. No one noticed her. It stood to reason, a mugger wouldn't either.

The E train lurched out of World Trade. The Purina Cat Chow poster cat seemed to be dancing . . . chow chow chow . . . in and out of focus, a cha-cha in exact rhythm with the pounding in her temples. Her stomach ached. Her hands were cold, but the rest of her was sweating. Good thing she had the bench to herself. She hadn't even lied about the "mother of all migraines," but it was coming true.

By Canal Street, she could practically hear the cat on the poster. "Purina Cat Chow ... chow chow chowwww," it chanted at her.

By Spring Street, she knew for sure that the mousse cake and champagne had been a *bad* idea. But if she'd turned them down, she'd have been a bad sport. She swallowed hard, wanting to cough, but knowing better. Damn air-conditioner seemed to have stopped working.

"Purina Cat Chow ... chow chow chow ..." mewed the poster cat. *When had it gone from being a red cat to a big, fat black and white like the cat on her card?* The train pulled into the West Fourth Street Station and jolted sickeningly to a stop. More commuters erupted into the car.

Chow chow chowwwww! The idea of food, let alone cat food—! Just as the doors were sliding shut, Lisa thrust past three briefcases and a baby carriage and onto the overheated platform. Her eyes were squeezing shut, and she avoided the bad exit, the one that smelled like a catbox, in favor of the one by the bank. With any luck, she could get a cab, one with air-conditioning. If things got really bad, she'd make it take her straight to an Emergency Ward. *With all the druggies. They'll think you're crazy.* Damned tapes—every reprimand she'd ever had (and she'd had plenty, despite a rather timid life) seemed to replay in her mind, scolding her at every step—she wished she could turn them off.

They had all meant well, from her parents and older sister, to her roommates to coworkers. Everyone saw her as a source for all their secondhand advice. *It's because we care. Would you rather be left all alone? What would happen to you then?*

I'd manage. Don't care, she had retorted once. The aftershocks had gone on for years. And she had had to eat her words.

They felt as if they were coming back up on her.

The broken concrete stairs tripped her up three-quarters of the way up. Something darted by her feet—was it a street cat? She teetered backward with a despairing cry, imagining every bump down to the concrete and, probably, broken bones and lying there while muggers stole her purse and her wristwatch. A rough hand caught her arm and pulled her up.

"Thanks," she muttered.

When she saw who had caught her, she managed—but only just—not to recoil. One of the panhandlers who worked this staircase, the one with the ski jacket and the dreadlocks. But he had crumpled the stained coffee cup he used for donations in his haste to rescue her, and he steadied her on her feet as carefully as if he were sane, and she were well, and they were normal people together.

She fumbled with her wallet. She might not have gotten the promotion, but she could give him a buck. Maybe five. Let somebody be happy.

He took the money on his palm, admiring the crisp bill. "Lady, you in bad shape. You better go ask Mr. Bigelow." It came out as "axe." She wondered if he really meant her to turn axe-murderer, but he pointed to a sign. *(Illegible Old English Initials) Bigelow, Chemist Since 1838.*

Dwayne Reed or Rite-Aid aren't good enough for you? A real drugstore with antique jars of colored water in the windows. It would be as pricey as Caswell-Massey. But it would have aspirin. It would have tissues. It would even have a pharmacist, maybe the second or third Mr. Bigelow to run the place, and he might help her.

"Thanks," she said again. "I'll ask him."

And tried not to weave like a drunk as she walked past the hot dog stand on the corner, the noisy electronics store, and what looked like an S&M version of Frederick's of Hollywood, and into the drugstore—no, it was classier than that. Into the chemist's.

It smelled of expensive violet soaps and cool, clean air, with a hint of antiseptic: a high, clean room with glossy, weathered paneling and glassed shelves built in to protect the perfumes, the costume jewelry, and the fancy velvet bows. She might have liked to hold one, even buy it, but *You can just imagine the markup on that junk,* the usual censors told her.

The pharmacist's counter was at the back of the store. She hoped there wouldn't be a long line of people waiting for their prescriptions, people tapping their feet and clicking their tongues at her as she blurted out what she needed. He'd probably say, "I'm not your doctor, lady."

Here were the over-the-counter remedies. She'd save everyone the trouble. She bent down, squinting to read the labels, bracing herself against a heavy cardboard box some fool had left in the aisle. . . .

And just what do you think you're doing? Like the "don't-be-weird, don't-be-crazy" scripts in her usual tapes, the voice filled her mind.

Lisa saved herself from sprawling in the aisle, crowded with natural sponges, $9.00 for the small size, by a twist that sent pain shooting through her temples.

I've lost it this time, Lisa thought. If she had lost her mind, she wouldn't have to worry about promotions. Everybody knew crazy people lost their jobs, their friends, their homes, and they wound up . . . *maybe I can get handouts from people by telling them 'Ask Mr. Bigelow.' Maybe I should ask him where the Thorazine is. Now.*

"Sorry," she muttered and started to lever herself up.

Owwwww, that was a bad one. Sorry to hurt you when you're hurting already.

None of her voices had ever bothered to apologize to her before, not in all her life. A cold nose nudged at her knee, and Lisa nearly leapt for the ceiling.

Easy, kitling. She had the sense of a kind of purring amusement.

She looked at the carton she had been ready to shove aside. On its lid was taped an index card: THIS BOX AND ITS CONTENTS ARE THE PROPERTY OF MR. BIGELOW, with an arrow pointing downward. Someone had cut open the carton and fitted it with a square of carpet and a towel, a comfortable bed for the large, fat, black and white cat who stared at her, then yawned.

"You're Mr. Bigelow?" she whispered.

You were maybe expecting Bustopher Jones? Again, the purry amusement.

"Well, you look like him," she retorted, chuckling a little herself at the black and white, portly clubcat from *Cats*. She had loved Eliot's poems. And even though she'd been out of work at the time, she'd managed to see the musical— standing room at a matinee at the Winter Garden on Broadway, wishing she had had the nerve to move down into an empty seat; wishing especially that she were the lucky woman in the front row whom the lithe, sinister Rum-TumTugger pulled onstage for a wild dance in the first act.

I am Mr. Bigelow. At your service. You might scratch my left ear. . . .

Lisa obeyed before she thought. The cat leaned into her fingers.

"I was told to ask Mr. Bigelow . . ."

The big cat raised his head with supreme assurance. Lisa had never been what *she* would have called "cat people." If the truth be known, she envied cats more than she liked them: their sleek, bored looks; their ability to do any damned thing they wanted with complete confidence; the way people were charmed by anything they did. For example, here she was, talking to a cat. Did anyone at all think that was strange?

The big cat heaved himself to his paws and rubbed against Lisa's legs. She rubbed his back, then scratched his ears again. *Gentle hands,* the cat approved. *Your eyes don't look good. Your nose looks warm. If you were a kit, I would show you which plants are the right ones to eat when you don't feel well. All these humans and their hairballs.* . . . The cat's mental voice seemed to sigh like an exasperated physician. *What you need, though* . . .

He nudged Lisa down the aisle.

"You've made a friend," said one of the salesclerks. One or two of the customers smiled at the cat with its latest human in tow. Some of the smile went to Lisa, too, and she dared to smile back. No one thought it was weird to be following the cat.

Not those things, he growled in her mind when she looked at the shelves of pills in sealed bottles. *Those are for foolish humans. This should help you.*

Lisa bought and paid for a tiny round vial, brave in red paper, gold foil, and Chinese lettering, with "Tiger Balm" stamped across the top.

Then Mr. Bigelow herded Lisa toward a chair in a secluded corner of the store, across from an ancient clock.

Down, ordered the cat. She sat and, at the autocrat's next mental order, she opened the tiger balm. She sniffed, sneezed at the aromatic, even pungent scent, then rubbed it on her temples. Heat filled her sinuses, and the headache dissipated, as if some vein had been tapped in a volcano and the magma drained.

Better, eh? Mr. Bigelow jumped on her lap, sniffed at her, nose to nose, said "huuuuu" aloud, then yawned.

"Much better," said Lisa through a yawn at least as wide. With her headache going, all she wanted to do was sleep. But the cat lay on her lap, it would be rude to dislodge it . . . *him,* corrected the voice in her mind.

She yawned again and shut her eyes. The Muzak from the loudspeakers, the absence of pain, and the purring warmth in her lap reassured her. For once, she was glad that no one ever seemed to notice her. She would rest here for just a minute where it was quiet and sweet-smelling and with the comfort of a living creature who didn't see her presence as a reason to make demands.

She let her clutch on her tote bag drop and stroked Mr. Bigelow's soft fur with both hands. The big cat started to purr. Sound and vibrations passed into her until her hands went slack on his warm back, and the room darkened about her.

Lisa's eyelids snapped open, and her stomach chilled. *Oh. My. God.* Across from her the big clock, lit by one or two orange lights, showed 10:30 p.m. She'd been right that no one would notice her. They'd gone and closed the store around her.

She'd be late for work. Then a second, and more frightening thought struck her. Bigelow's Pharmacy had to have burglar alarms. Burglar alarms were keyed to an electric eye—probably one of the little lights that picked out details of door or glass case or shelf. Sooner or later, she was going to have to get up and move. She couldn't cower in this chair all night. The alarms would go off; the cops would come. That's *one* way of getting out of here, she thought wryly.

Promotion? She'd be lucky to keep her job if the pharmacy prosecuted for trespassing.

Let's have that again, miss. You say you fell asleep in that chair with a big cat purring on your lap. Right.

Now she'd have been glad to lose three promotions, if that would have meant her standing outside the pharmacy. What was she going to do?

Ask Mr. Bigelow. The tape inside her mind replayed to show her what a fool she had been.

Then she opened her eyes. What did she have to lose?

"Okay, what now, cat?" Even her whisper was absurdly loud in the empty store.

Mr. Bigelow rose on all fours. Standing on her lap, he stretched and yawned. *We have had a good nap,* he announced. *So we will be right. Or almost right. Hmmmmm.* The purr sounded so thoughtful that she almost laughed.

Wait here.

The cat jumped off her lap and padded off into the shadows, which promptly magnified themselves and began to dance in a way that reminded Lisa of the horror film she had seen as a result of "you pick the movie; I really don't care." *Next time, I am* going *to care,* she told herself.

One by one, white and orange lights at knee height flicked off. Did Bigelow know how to turn off alarms? Some cats, she knew, could open doors, flush toilets, and raid cabinets: why not this one?

A cold nose brushed her knee and she nearly jumped ceiling-high again.

Follow me, said the cat. She could have sworn he sounded amused.

He led her behind the foremost glass case, the one with all the elaborate headbands and bows stored in it.

You must look right.

Lisa stuck her hands in her pockets. Her suit was serviceable and of good quality, and that was about all you could say about it. Still, she hadn't charged it; it had years of wear in it; and if she touched anything in that case—even if she could get it unlocked, they'd probably find her fingerprints. What a spoiled cat this spoiled cat was if he thought he could turn her into as big a thief as he probably was. She just bet they had to lock up the catfood and anything else edible around here.

Mr. Bigelow made a *humph*ing noise, as if aggravated by her thoughts.

He nudged with his nose, and a cardboard box slid out from beneath the counter. A shimmer of metallic thread and rhinestones met her eyes.

They were going to throw it out, said the cat. *You take it. Wear it.*

Fine, Lisa thought. *I've got a cat as a wardrobe consultant. Well, it worked in* Puss in Boots.

Rhinestones and glitter were never her thing; they made her too conspicuous and weren't worth the money. Still, she found herself putting the bright headband in her hair, like a punk tiara.

Come on! Bigelow urged her. He rubbed against her legs, then darted toward the door leading downstairs to the storage basement. Reluctantly, Lisa followed. This was New York. God only knew what kind of rats . . .

You have *to be kidding to think I would permit rats. This is my home,* Bigelow told her. *Come* on. *Unless you need the . . .* discreetly, he let his mental voice trail away.

It was tempting to find out a cat's view of human litterboxes. But Bigelow's urgency was contagious. Stifling her fear, Lisa followed the cat downstairs, past case after case of diapers and perfumes and canes and goodness knows what all else. Past supplies to a side door, Bigelow led her, and out the door into the darkness.

Come on, he said. *What are you afraid of* this *time?*

"I'm not afraid *of* anything," Lisa said. Strangely enough, it was true for a change. "I'm afraid *for* you. You're too small to be walking around alone late at night."

Bigelow fuffed and arched his back.

"And much too cute," she tried flattery as a ploy. "*Anyone* seeing you would want to take you home; and you'd never see your store again. But I have an idea."

She held out her arms. Mr. Bigelow swarmed up into them, to perch heavily on her shoulder. People were always walking around Greenwich Village "wearing" cats and, in the process, getting lots of attention. *Making themselves conspicuous. You wouldn't want to do that,* the tapes admonished her. But making herself conspicuous, even making herself ridiculous, was better than risking a cat's life, Lisa reasoned as the fifth person in one block approached and rubbed Mr. Bigelow's ears. He took it with the grace of a corpulent prince whose loyal subjects approach at his levee to kiss his hand. Some of the smiles rubbed off on her, too.

Head east, would you? asked the cat. Was she imagining it, or was he reluctant to break away from his "public"?

"We have to go now," she told people who wanted just one last ear-rub from the cat. "I think he's getting nervous." He hid his head demurely against Lisa, and she almost choked.

Past Second. Past First Avenue. Into Alphabetland where the wild things—and wilder clubs—are and onto Saint Mark's Place.

"Bigelow," Lisa murmured, the cat's whiskers brushing her cheek, "if we get any farther east, we could be in big trouble."

Over there. You'll know it when you see it.

Lisa found herself staring at a sign, splashed with graffiti. "Bigelow, that's a rehab center."

Don't you remember the Electric Circus?

"Ohhh." The summer she was 18, she had come to New York. It had been the greatest adventure of her life. She had seen *2001*—maybe not stoned, but she had seen it and gotten through the light show without falling asleep. She had gotten her ears pierced, and they hadn't gotten infected. She had helped drink her first bottle of wine (she had never let anyone throw out the straw-covered Bardolino bottle, which still held silk flowers). And, carefully togged out in her cousin's least-freaky gear, she had gone to the Electric Circus.

I wanted to have fun. The years fell away, and she saw the careful, cautiously pretty girl she had been. Oh, granted, she danced. She raised her hands above her head; she closed her eyes; she whooped with the music (half a beat behind everyone else to make sure it was all right). As the strobes flashed on and off, she watched herself in the mirrors. Amazing: she looked like everyone else. She, too, looked like magic—but she knew the truth: it was a magic she saw, but somehow couldn't quite break through to share. She closed her eyes, threw herself into the music and the lights and the comforting press of bodies, and almost—a man with long hair tied back with a ribbon reached out for her hand, to pull her further into the crowd *... and maybe after the show, we'd wander in Washington Square ...* but she was afraid, and hung back for an instant.

And then the house lights came up. The sleek young man disappeared, the music died, and the moment was gone.

She moaned with everyone else, then left the Circus and hung up her borrowed beads and satins. The next day, she had left New York, not to return for years. And her pierced ears had turned infected. *That'll teach you to let your damn fool cousin lead you around by the ears.*

And that was the closest she had ever come to breaking through to touch the magic she sensed all about her.

She had failed to reach it at the Circus, but, even so, she had mourned just a little when the Circus had closed. Whether she could share it or not, there was too little wonder in the world.

What do you call this? demanded Mr. Bigelow. *Nothing good is ever lost. Around back, here. Follow your ears.*

Follow her nose was more like it. She'd bet there were a lot of street cats around here. She tightened her arms around Mr. Bigelow. Maybe he talked to her, mind to mind; but he was still a cat and he might decide to fight or give chase. Claws pricked at her. *Okay, so I'm stupid,* she retorted silently. *I'm sneaking around a building in Alphabetland. You just bet I'm stupid.*

Feral cats rubbed against her ankles, meowing a welcome—not to her, but to Bigelow. *Bigelow, it's dark here. Those cats may have Fe-Luke, feline leukemia. And there may be muggers.*

I've had my shots. Trust the guides, said the cat.

The street cats steered her toward a low door, marked with garish paint. "I'm not going in there," Lisa muttered. But three of the cats reared up and pushed with their forepaws against the door. It gaped open, and other cats pushed at her legs, urging her forward as if she faced an opened refrigerator, crammed full of cream and chopped meat and tuna, and all for them, if she'd only get it down from the shelves.

The image in her mind was so strong when she ventured through the door that she expected to feel cold and hear a refrigerator hum.

Instead, LIGHTS, MUSIC, ACTION! just the way an old-time director might shout before the cameras rolled struck her. She stepped back, but only for a moment. The cats urged her forward, the door shut behind her, and she was inside.

"Ohhhhh." She forgot her fear and touched wonder. Her memories came alive. And the old heartache of loss and failure dissipated.

It *was* the old Electric Circus, complete with bands and

records screaming, strobes catching the crowded dancers in infinite freezeframes, and mirrored balls flashing on the high ceiling. The projection screens on the walls glowed with bright life, just as they had when Lisa was 18. She remembered being dazzled by the rainbow colors and caparisons of merry-go-round horses, dancing up and down on the screens in rhythm with the dancers on the floor. Now, instead of horses, she saw cats, leaping and writhing and pouncing on the screens overhead. Cats of all colors, shapes, and sizes—though black and white cats like Bigelow predominated.

Unafraid of the dancers, the cats who had brought her inside darted into the crowd. An instant later, Lisa saw them on the overhead screens, too.

Bigelow gave a happy little meow. *We're here. I told you so. Nothing good is ever lost.*

"You want down, boy?" Lisa said. She plucked him off her shoulder and held him, despite his girth and dignity, in front of her face. In his glowing eyes, she saw her own, kindling with an astonished surmise.

"Bigelow, have you brought me to the Jellicle Ball?" Beneath the calls and drums and songs of the band whose old T-shirts read Cats Laughing came the rollicking electronics of Eliot's poems, set to Andrew Lloyd Webber's music. " 'Jellicle cats come out tonight.' "

The Jellicle moon *had* been shining overhead. And Bigelow had brought her to the Jellicle Ball. She had seen *Cats* in the Winter Garden. Here, there wasn't a recreation of an alley, with giant replicas of discarded boots, milk cartons, or spare tires. Here, she had found the old Electric Circus, before psychedelics and the world had turned dark, and she had lost . . . she had lost something, she knew; and she had lost it here.

Nothing good is ever lost, said Mr. Bigelow.

So, here she was at the Jellicle Ball. Turn, swing around, raise your arms, sing with the chorus, stamp, commanded the music; and she did. Astonishing that she could. And even more so that she could enjoy it.

At the end of the Ball, sometimes, someone was selected to go to the Heavyside Lair and be reborn. *I could use a miracle,* she told herself, as she told herself every day.

You two-legs worry too much. You are warm, you are fed, you do not hurt. Dance!

Bigelow leapt from her arms like a kitten, and she saw his image, capering on the screens, touching noses with a hundred other cats, who greeted him with ceremonious feline respect before tumbling in a playful heap.

A hand caught her hand and drew her into the mass of human dancers. Guitars, electric keyboards, and voices swelled and twanged. For now, this was her miracle. So Lisa danced. She saw bodies moving and freezing as the lights flashed on and off—fast, graceful, strong, and free. Her own motions, mirrored on screens and in the dancers' eyes, were as sure and as happy. And when the set ended and the band paused, throwing back their long hair, wiping their foreheads, and saluting the humans dancing on the floor, the cats dancing in an inner ring at the center, she cheered and clapped, hands above her head.

Lights rose about her. Faces grinned into her own. The girl she had been, who mimicked the dancers rather than become one with them, had been afraid. Eyes would have closed against her, and people would have drawn back. But this Lisa, despite her grown woman's knowledge of muggers and AIDS and a thousand other fears *plus* the warning tapes of a lifetime's fears and reprimands, laughed and danced and hugged the people around her. Like a wraith in an empty house, the girl she had been flickered briefly in her mind, then vanished into the colors and the shouts.

My night, she thought exultantly.

Bigelow's image grinned down at her from the projection screens.

Cats and humans danced. Lisa remembered the story line from the musical; at the end of the Ball, someone would be chosen at the Ball to ascend to the Heavyside Lair and be reborn into a new, Jellicle life.

Maybe me? I could do with a future. A future that was young, free of tapes, and free of fears. Where she could ask for what she needed, where she could dream, where she could dance without feeling foolish. Ever again.

Maybe, said the cats' enigmatic, moonlight eyes.

Maybe, blared the music.

Yes, flashed the strobes. *No,* flashed the strobes. *Maybe.* Lisa peeled off her crumpled jacket and threw it onto a chair. She abandoned her shoulder bag. She kicked off her shoes. A young man with long hair and a gypsy vest drew her further into the room. At the center of the dance floor, fenced off by glass, was a sunken area where the cats danced, safe from humans' clumsy feet, and where they paid respect to a huge, white-muzzled cat. *Old Deuteronomy?* Lisa thought. She pushed closer to meet the cat, to show him ... *am I actually going to ask a* cat *for a second chance?*

She was not eighteen anymore. She had earned the right to not think, to not listen to the tapes. She had earned her magic.

The cat looked up and met her eyes.

Ask.

Lisa felt herself kindling into wonder. Had it been that simple, all her life?

She laughed, pointed to the big cat, shouted something to her partner, and pressed against the partition separating human from cats. He laughed back and gestured.

Go ahead.

There was a door in the partition. She had only to push it open, go down there, and ask the big cat for what she wanted: rebirth, a new life, freedom.

"Hey!" Lisa yelped in pain as claws raked down her leg.

Mr. Bigelow leapt back, tail held protectively high against the stamping feet of the dancers.

Tears of shock and disappointment filled Lisa's eyes. She had trusted Bigelow. He had led her here. Why, at the moment when she was about to try ... ? *never mind, if you had been* meant *to have it,* the tapes told her ... even he betrayed her.

Look over there! came the cat's voice in her head.

Lisa looked. Her purse and jacket lay on a table, not on the chair where she had stashed them. A young girl was sitting on the chair watching the dancers. From time to time, she put out her hands, as if dancing in place, rapt with delight at the sight of the dancing cats.

A boy emerged from the crowd and asked her to dance. She shook her head.

Me as a girl? Lisa asked Bigelow in her mind. But she had learned her lessons, and now she was dancing.

She turned back to the glass partition. She had learned.
So would this girl.

Bigelow stood between her and the doorway. His back
arched, and he glared at her.

Why did you bring me here? It seemed so unfair.

Unfair? asked the black and white cat. *Look!*

Lisa edged in for a closer look, her dance partner with
her. She owed Bigelow that much, at least. One good look,
and then she would ask Old Deuteronomy for a second
chance.

The boy had persisted, holding out his hand to the girl
who sat, as if guarding Lisa's jacket and bag. He took her
hand where it rested on the table and tugged.

The girl shook her head. Splotches of color, feverish in
the off/on of the strobes appeared on her face. Her eyes
glistened with—that was *anger*, Lisa realized. She pushed
away from table, from the dancers—and almost fell. Her
chair wobbled and started to overturn.

In an instant, Lisa and her partner had leapt forward,
were steadying her, righting the chair.

The girl glared at them and drew the checkered table-
cloth across her lap, hiding her legs, the left so much
shorter than the right. Then she grasped Lisa's jacket and
covered her face with it.

She doesn't dance because she can't.

Lisa waited for the tapes to begin. She could just imagine
what they'd reproach her with this time: selfishness would
be the least of it. But the tapes were silent. So was the
entire room.

She backed away, allowing the girl what scraps of privacy
she could. It was all she could give her.

Oh, it is, is it? asked Bigelow.

In a moment, the music would begin. She might even
make it to see Old Deuteronomy at the center of the dance
floor and ask for her new life, and they would all dance
again.

Not all of us, Lisa thought.

All she had to do was ask. Ask, and she'd have it all:
youth, fearlessness, a chance to live her life over without
the fear and the tapes. And that girl would still be sitting
there in the midst of wonder, weeping into a borrowed
jacket.

What sort of second chance was it at *that* price?

Ask Mr. Bigelow. Just ask. She had never been a person to ask. But she would now.

She walked across the floor to the glass partition, opened the waist-high gate, and stepped down toward the biggest and oldest of the cats in their sunken dancing ground. She knelt and held out her hand to him, and he sniffed it—imperial permission rather than Bigelow's mere princely graciousness.

Then she pointed—straight at the girl who had set down her jacket and was trying frantically to smooth her face into some semblance of party manners.

Bigelow purred and rubbed against Lisa's legs. Old Deuteronomy leaned forward and touched noses with her, as if she had been promoted to feline status. Then he rose, stalked over to the girl, and rubbed, first against her straight right leg, then against the withered left one and its black leather brace.

All you have to do is ask.

Lisa squeezed her eyes until red and black lights flashed inside her eyelashes. With all her heart, she concentrated on asking: *let the girl dance. Let* her *be reborn.*

The strobes flashed. When the lights came on again, the chair was empty, except for Lisa's jacket, slightly tear-stained. The leather brace lay unstrapped by its side.

Old Deuteronomy was back in his place, and all around him, the cats were dancing. Lisa looked around for Mr. Bigelow. He wasn't next to her, and she wouldn't have had him there, to be stepped on. There he was, on the screens, clasped in the arms of a young woman whose face shone as she danced, shone as if she had been reborn.

Lisa's smile of joy hurt, and she wiped tears from her eyes as she raised her hands on the upbeats, dancing, still dancing.

Lisa glanced back at the leather brace. The second chance she had longed for with all her heart—she had asked for it to be given to someone else whose need—and whose heartbreak—were greater. So her chance was gone, her rebirth was gone, and, judging from the way Mr. Bigelow clung to his new friend, so was Mr. Bigelow.

Look what you threw away, the tapes reproached her.

Look what I got, she answered. *Now shut up. I'm dancing.*

Her feet had never felt so light or so much attuned to the music. She *was* the music and the lights. And, seeing herself in her partner's eyes, she knew she was the magic, too.

And then the house lights flashed on.

The crowd of dancers groaned. Shielding her eyes from the glare, Lisa hugged her partner, then released him. He was magic, too, and if she never saw him again, it did not matter. It wasn't as if the Circus were real. She knew a Rehab center occupied this building here and now. And in another way, it was the most real place she had ever been. Bless it; bless them all.

Nothing good is ever lost, the big cat had said. It wasn't. It was inside her now.

Retrieving her jacket, Lisa stumbled past the discarded leg brace—so that much was *true* change, she thought with satisfaction and a total lack of surprise. She looked around for Mr. Bigelow, but the cat was gone, probably riding home in triumph on the healed girl's shoulder. She smiled at the thought and waited for the tapes to tell her what a sap she'd been.

Silence, except for a line of a ballad. *And I awoke and found me on the cold hillside.* The silver and rhinestone band Bigelow had made her wear tumbled from her sweaty hair. *What? I thought fairy treasure disappeared at dawn.* Maybe things were different in New York than Under the Hill. She tucked the bauble away in her bag, to be treasured forever. And maybe she'd wear it again—next time she went dancing.

A street beggar, his hair in dreadlocks, ambled past, not even asking for a handout. "Are you lost, miss?" a man asked, standing at a distance so she wouldn't be startled.

She surprised both of them with a wide smile. "I was," she said. "But not any more."

She had had her night of magic, and she would always have it—and the memory of the joy on the girl's face as she realized that she would not be trapped forever in a body tied to a clumsy brace. They were both free—and she had freed them.

She smiled at a pair of entwined students, and when a

yellow cab prowled by, she hailed it and went home. Maybe later this week, she'd stop by the drugstore with a tin of catfood for Mr. Bigelow, but now she was tired, she had dreaming to do, tomorrow was work—and there was something she needed to ask for.

In the morning, she dressed with care, sailing past even the senior receptionist (whom everyone whispered reported people's comings and goings to management) with her head up and her smile sparkling. She waved at Dana, already ensconced in her new office, and Dana waved back. Maybe a friend, if what Lisa had in mind worked out. . . .

"Lisa! Where were you last night?" Her coworker's hands and voice reached out to ensnare her, attracting the attention of half the room. "I tried to reach you." Then, in a carefully pitched whisper, "I was worried. How *are* you?"

Lisa studied the woman. Yes, there was actually concern there under the theatricality.

"I went dancing," Lisa said. And managed not to laugh at the woman's stunned face. *A promotion lost and she went* dancing? Easy to see the sort of tapes running through *her* mind. She heard whispers from the secretaries who had gathered to see how she had gotten through the night. Admiring whispers. *Did you hear that? Lost out on a job, and she went* dancing. *I'd be home crying my eyes out, and she went partying without a care in the world.*

The respect hit her blood like brandy.

Ignoring requests that sounded like demands for details, Lisa went to her workstation, printed out her resume, fished her performance reviews out of her files, and went back to her friend's desk. "Do you have the specs on that executive assistant job?" she asked.

The woman flushed.

After all that nagging, she hadn't even bothered with the job description. She must have been very sure that Lisa would back out.

"Well," said Lisa, "I guess I'll have to ask personnel about that. Or maybe ask the new VP what he has in mind. Do you know where he sits?"

Stupid question; he had to have a corner office, and only one of them was vacant. "By the way," Lisa said as she headed down the hall, "do you know his name?"

The answer made her laugh. She was laughing when she knocked on the door with its shining brass nameplate, M. BIGELOW, and when she was asked to enter.

A tall man, no longer young, was rising from behind his desk. His polite "business" mask changed into a genuine smile.

"I heard you laughing. Nice to know that someone here has a sense of humor. What can I do for you?" he asked.

"I'm here," said Lisa, "to ask what I can do for you. I'd like to apply for that position as your assistant."

He spread out his hands in a gesture of frustration. "They have these headhunters out beating the jungle for an assistant for me, but ..."

"Headhunters are expensive," Lisa cut in as smoothly as if she had rehearsed it. "So I thought I'd ask. After all, if you don't ask ..."

"... you don't get. Sit down, please," said Mr. Bigelow. Would he be pleased by her resume? Did he like her? Just as important, did he seem to be the sort of person she could work with?

Maybe she wouldn't get the job. It was a risk she took.

Maybe she wouldn't get a *lot* of what she asked for. But she had to ask. Somewhere in the city, there was a woman who could walk and dance because Lisa had cared to, dared to ask.

Do you really think you're ready for this kind of responsibility? What if he thinks you're out of line for asking? came the voices in her head.

I thought I'd shut you up at the Electric Circus. Now go away! she told them. You didn't ask the tapes, apparently: you told. There was a lot she'd have to learn. But, for the rest of her life—all she had to do was ask about it.

Now that she had turned off the tapes, her mind was quiet of any thoughts but her own. Still, she distinctly thought she heard a big cat purr with satisfaction as the man across the desk turned back to her with a smile.

Ask Mr. Bigelow indeed!